The
Woman
at the Light

Enjoy this rare look at early Key West!

Joanna Brady

THE
WOMAN
AT THE LIGHT

Joanna Brady

THE WOMAN AT THE LIGHT. Copyright 2011, 2016 by Joanna Brady Schmida. All rights reserved.

First printing by St. Martin's Press, New York, N.Y. 2012. Printed in the United States of America.

For information, address West 26th Street Press, 21 West 26th St., New York, N.Y. 10010,
Email: DigitalRights@WritersHouse.com

1.   Women lighthouse keepers – Fiction.
2.   Fugitive slaves – Fiction
3.   Key West (Fla) – History – 19th century - Fiction

For Walter, Terry, and Kevin
with much love

Man is born free, but everywhere he is in chains.

—Jean-Jacques Rousseau, *The Social Contract*

Prejudice is the reason of fools.

—Voltaire

The Woman at the Light

PROLOGUE

Key West

April 6, 1883

It is my day to honor the dead.

As Charles brings the victoria to a halt outside the Key West cemetery, I feel a certain pride—it almost borders on vanity—when I reject his arm and step down, making my way through the main entrance without his assistance. Yet, he follows me closely, carrying my floral tributes in his strong brown hands; once inside, he lays them carefully near my family's markers.

"You sure you don't want me to stay, now?"

I wave away his suggestion. "No, no. I'll be fine." It is the same conversation we have every week. "Go on ahead and see to your errands. Come back for me in an hour."

"Yes, ma'am. You just take your time. I'll be waiting for you right outside the entrance, over there. On Margaret Street." He draws out this street name slowly.

I suppress a smile. We have performed this charade every Friday morning for . . . how long? I can no longer keep track. As my years advance with alarming determination, Charles worries that my state of mind is deteriorating in lockstep with my withering body. We both know that instead of tending to errands, he will be watching my progress protectively from the carriage. Then he'll wheel up to the entrance when he sees that my visit is over.

He leaves, and I survey the field of angels and crosses. Fresh graves remind me that life, and especially death, go on with relentless ferocity. And those stone angels spread out before me . . . are they breeding when not under our watchful eye? There appear to be more of them this week. Many of the new markers are tiny, reserved for our babies, those poor little ones with no resources to fight the fever.

I exult in the delicious solitude of this peaceful sanctuary. Domingo, the caretaker, who usually nods with a cheery "G'mornin', Miss Emily!" has left to work in a cigar factory, so no one is around to distract me early on this spring day. Only those hiding under stones remain: Their silence speaks volumes of island stories yet untold.

My two husbands have been slumbering here these many years. I tend their graves dutifully, placing flowers as I softly intone spiritual murmurings for their souls, perfunctory words I manage to summon from the well of my pantheistic heart.

I lay the traditional generic wreaths before my spouses' markers. But for my only sister, Dorothy, I have brought freshly cut fiery red gingers and heliconias in a blazing orange color. She was always fond of them. Another bouquet is placed before Gran's vault, which I fashioned from her favorite purple cattleya orchids. Crotchety old Gran, who, I can admit, is far more cherished by me now than ever she was in life.

My duties performed, I move on eagerly to the remote grave at the farthest corner of the cemetery, the real reason for my weekly visit. For this sacred plot have I reserved the wildest, most fragrant flowers and the lyrical hymns of my own authorship.

It is just after daybreak on this Key West morning, already sultry, and I kneel before the grave under the canopy of a mahogany tree whose sheltering arms reach out to offer shade. A cooling breeze occasionally stirs the air; the throaty ripple of mourning doves stabs the silence. And the pungent dampness from recent rains on the leaf-scented ground assaults my aging knees. I place my flowers and whisper softly as I arrange their showy blooms. Against the bleakness of the darkening gray stones, their vivid color brings the air to life, like joyful wedding confetti scattered on church steps.

The day grows increasingly hot, with the sun scorching the early mist, and my hair curls into damp tendrils around my neck as my clothing begins to cling to my skin. Feeling light-headed, I sit on the coral stone bench beside the grave—the grave of the one man I truly loved.

I think back on all that has happened these past fifty-four years. Condemned to have lived on, alone and wiser, I recall the bitter and the sweet, the grief and the rapture—for in my life, the one cannot be chronicled without the other.

PART ONE

New Orleans and
Wreckers' Cay
1829–1840

ONE

Wreckers' Cay

May 13, 1839

It was fully three years after we first arrived on Wreckers' Cay—almost to the day—that my husband vanished one May afternoon. I had just completed the children's school lessons when it occurred to me that Martin was late coming home. He had sailed off earlier from the dock, smiling and waving lazily at our only son, Timothy, who was pouting at being left behind—that last wave a gesture forever etched in the chambers of my mind.

It was a remarkably ordinary day in the Florida Keys. The sea was calm, a teal blue-green so clear, it revealed the shadows of plants and darting marine life in its shallow waters. The steady wind was no more than a light tropical breeze, cooling our skin from the blistering sun. Martin was an experienced sailor, and catching our supper in the late afternoon was something he often did before igniting the lamps of the lighthouse tower just before sunset.

Located twenty-three miles from Key West, our desolate outpost at Wreckers' Cay was a solitary place. We were the sole inhabitants of that tiny speck of land, tending the lighthouse with monotonous regularity. It was demanding work, and we had arrived there under duress. Yet we had soon grown accustomed to this island, a beautiful place to raise our young family.

But that day, minutes stretched into long, worrisome hours as my children and I waited and watched for him well into the night. Initially, I was angry. Had he just lost track of time? It meant that in addition to looking after the children and preparing dinner, I would now be responsible for lighting the lamps.

It was only later that my anger dissipated, and a nagging anxiety slowly began to take hold. As I kissed the children good night and the sun plunged below the horizon, a growing fear was quietly gnawing at my heart.

I slept little that night—Martin still had not returned. And the next morning, when our watchdog, Brandy, announced the arrival of our old friend Captain George Lee on his supply tender, the *Outlander,* my heart sank: Lee's boat had Martin's empty fishing skiff in tow.

The captain and his mate, Alfie Dillon, usually came on the fifteenth and at the end of each month, stopping on their way to and from Havana; they brought our food, mail, newspapers, and provisions from Key West. I was much relieved to see that they were slightly ahead of schedule on this occasion.

Just offshore, the captain called out to me: "Ahoy, Miss Emily!"

Alfie leaped from their boat to our dock. He said, "Tell Martin we found his fishin' boat about a mile out to the west. Must have come loose and drifted out."

I felt the blood drain from my face. Mutely, I shook my head as I watched Alfie secure their boat.

"Martin went fishing yesterday afternoon," I finally said, "but he hasn't returned."

Their smiles faded. As men who spent much of their time

at sea, fishing and salvaging vessels run aground, they were quick to intuit trouble.

"No storms about." Alfie muttered, "No sign of Mr. Lowry anywheres we could see. Jes' his boat. Must've hit an unmarked shoal."

"But nobody knows the reef better than Martin. He would never have gone aground," I protested.

The sky was blue and cloudless. We had not even had a rain shower for a couple of weeks. Silently, they looked out over the water, protecting their sun-crinkled eyes with weathered hands. They seemed to expect Martin to appear, as I had last night, a living mirage in the hazy heat of the early afternoon. The sun was high in the sky now, and it was hotter and even more humid than the previous day. Slicing through our silence, cicadas shrieked in the low-growing shrubs behind the house, and a chorus of bees hummed as they hovered near Martin's mango trees, grazing over the burgeoning fruit.

Finally, the captain grumbled quietly, "We're always tellin' 'em at the department that the reef out here is poorly marked. They never pay us no mind. It'd cost them money to put in a few more lighthouses. And you know how close Superintendent Pendleton is with a dollar."

He was silent for a moment. "Had to be somethin' out there," he said finally. "We'll go back out a ways and see if we kin find anything."

After quenching the lights in the tower after dawn, Timothy and I had already gone out together in our larger boat, the *Pharos,* while Martha looked after little Hannah, but our search had yielded nothing. The captain and his mate, with their better-equipped boat, might have better results. For the next few hours, as my children and I waited anxiously, they sailed out about a mile or two, circling the island a few times, dragging their nets in what proved to be a futile search. Finally, the two sailors returned, grim-faced and shaking their heads.

"Nothin' out there," Lee said gravely. He took my hand gently in his sunbaked, calloused one as I fought to hold back tears. The children were close by, so he quietly added, "Our condolences, Miss Emily."

Alfie removed his cap and mumbled something similar.

I nodded numbly, scarcely able to answer.

Lee said, "Here now, we won't give up, though. No ma'am. We'll look around again in the mornin'. We'd have stayed out longer, but we wanted to git in before sunset; can't see much after that."

"Thank you," I said, my voice barely above a whisper.

Optimist that I was, at the back of my mind the thought that they had not found Martin gave me a shred of hope. It meant he could still be alive.

Captain Lee and Alfie unloaded my provisions, with Timothy and Martha helping to carry food items from the dock to the cookhouse. Miscellaneous supplies and bulk foods, the men hauled to our storage building. Thinking to cheer me, my two Good Samaritans continued a patter of genial conversation.

"We got some coconut sweets in Havana for the young 'uns," murmured Alfie quietly, out of earshot of the children. "No coffee this time, but we found some chocolate for you, and some tobacco for—" He realized his gaffe and stopped himself.

Some building materials Martin had requested were also part of their delivery. We needed fencing to keep our three goats from invading the vegetable patch—the garden, when fresh water flowed freely, was an invaluable source of food.

"Maybe next time we're here—that is, if Martin ain't back— we could put up the fence for you," ventured Lee.

But I did not want to even entertain the thought that Martin might not return to build the fence.

"Could you please take the lamp fuel over to the oil house?" I asked. Alfie set to moving it there immediately as I went through the motions of preparing a meal for us all. My two eldest, Martha, almost nine, and Timothy, about to turn eight, were old enough to share my anxiety, yet still young enough to be optimistic and cheerful about their father's speedy return. While acting as though nothing was wrong, I prepared dinner; I could not bring myself yet to tell them my worst fears.

Normally, the captain and his mate did not linger, but this time they offered to remain overnight. "We'll stay over and help with the lights," Lee said. "And have another look on the reef in the morning."

Over the years, Martin and I had grown accustomed to the light. We'd learned to sleep lightly enough to be aware of its caressing beam as it glimmered through our bedroom window. A blazing flame in our lighthouse lamp meant life and safety for vessels at sea. I was so used to the beacon after three years on Wreckers' Cay that when the light went out that night under the captain's watch, the dark cried out to me immediately. I awoke in terror, lit my lantern, and raced up the stairs of the lighthouse.

There I found a sleepy Captain Lee fussing with the wicks, confused and startled by my ghostly apparition. I had to direct his labors and instruct him anew on the proper way to trim the wicks and relight the lamps to keep them burning. Remembering how long it had taken Martin and me to learn the intricacies of working in the tower, I could easily forgive the captain's ineptitude at the light.

I showed him again how to log in the oil consumption for accounting to the Department of the Treasury, and to note weather conditions as the ships passed, lanterns twinkling, on their way through the channel. The coral reef on which our island was located extended about six miles out to sea, and sailing vessels making their way through channels beyond it were now numerous. The busy straits handled most traffic to and from the United States and the Caribbean Sea, as well as ships from the states on the Gulf of Mexico heading north up the East Coast.

When we had managed to relight the lamps, I said, "Come down with me to the cookhouse and I'll make us some tea."

"Why thank ye kindly, Miss Emily. I'd not say no to that."

I stole a glance at him in the lamplight. He looked so much older and more tired than in those early days when I'd first met him and Martin in my native New Orleans, ten years ago. I noticed he was growing quite bald on top, and his remaining ginger hair was streaked with gray.

Captain Lee had been a widower for about a year. His wife had left the captain her family home on Eaton Street in Key West, a fine inheritance. Yet grief had undoubtedly taken its toll on his once-handsome features, for though he was still tall and firmly built, his wrinkles had deepened, carving crevices in his weather-beaten skin.

"Martin was a fine man," the captain said to me now as he stirred sugar into his tea. His native Massachusetts accent was still a bit harsh to my southern ear. Not yet convinced that we should be talking about my husband in the past, I said nothing.

"He was one of my best crewmen on the wrecks. Not a lazy bone in the man's body."

"No. He's a very hard worker," I agreed, switching to the present tense.

"He done wonders with this place out here," he said, glancing through the window of the cookhouse. "All them trees. Hard to believe how one man could've planted 'em all."

"Yes," I said, nodding. The bleak, unfinished look of Wreckers' Cay, scarred and barren from a hurricane when Martin and I had first arrived, flashed through my mind. Martin had indeed done much here, just as he had at the lovely home in Key West we had been forced to leave behind.

I saw Lee's eyes rest on Martin's bottle of rum on a pantry shelf.

"Would you care for a drop, Captain George?" I asked.

He brightened. "Well, now, if you're twistin' my arm . . ."

I poured him a generous shot and placed the bottle in front of him. He downed his drink, then reached for the bottle to pour himself at least a tot. Wiping his mouth on his sleeve, he said, "You'll probably miss this house now that you'll be goin' back to Key West."

"I've no immediate plans to return."

He looked up, surprised. "You're not thinkin' of stayin'?"

"We don't know for sure that Martin is dead."

"But if he is, how would you manage out here?"

It was the question I'd been asking myself all day.

I stood up and cleared our cups from the table. "I'm very tired, Captain George. You'll forgive me if I take leave of you. The lights are fine now that we've trimmed the wicks. Pray, go back to your boat and get some sleep. Don't waken Alfie. If there are any more problems, I'm sure I can deal with them."

He nodded and bade me a good night. As I swept past him, heading toward the house, I saw him reaching again for the rum.

Preparing the men's breakfast the next morning a thought struck me. If Martin's body were to wash up on the beach, what would I do?

I waited till the children were out of earshot. "Do you suppose I could ask you one more thing? Could you dig a grave for me?"

They stared at me, surprised at my sangfroid.

"There won't be much left of Mr. Lowry, not after the sharks and barracudas . . ." began Alfie. He paused, then selected a shovel from Martin's implements. "You'll want to bury 'im right away, I'm sayin' . . . so the children won't see. . . ."

I saw Captain Lee elbow Alfie in the ribs. "Beg your pardon for speakin' plainly, ma'am."

The theory that continued to visit my thoughts was that a mako or tiger shark might have attacked Martin's boat—perhaps lured by his baitfish. If Martin had reached into the water to retrieve something he'd dropped, he could have easily been wrenched into the sea. But I tried to push such thoughts from my mind.

I served the men a hearty breakfast with fresh eggs Martha and little Hannah had gathered at the chicken coop, some Cuban pork Martin had previously smoked, a large bowl of grits, and biscuits fresh from the oven.

Then, quietly, without alerting the children to what they were doing, they dug the grave not far from the beach, where a body was most likely to wash up from the south.

TWO

Wreckers' Cay

May 1839

"Y ou really should think about returnin' to Key West," Lee said as he stepped onto the *Outlander* and rolled down his sleeves. His face was red from the sun, and his clothes were drenched with sweat from digging. "If you need help with packin' up, I'll bring your sister and one of her servants next time."

I frowned. It was as though he had not heard me the night before. He removed his cap and wiped the sweat from his pate before he spoke again. "I'll let Mr. Pendleton know what's happened, so he can start lookin' for a new light keeper. May take a month or two, if you can manage till then."

Pendleton was the eighth auditor of the U.S. Treasury Department and superintendent of lighthouses for the whole country. Lighting up a Cuban cigar, Captain Lee looked at me expectantly.

"Martin may be missing, Captain George, but we do not know that he has indeed perished. I will have many decisions to make eventually, but as I told you last night, I've no intention of leaving for Key West—at least not at the moment."

"I'm concerned, Miss Emily," he muttered. "It's not the best place for a woman, out here alone. This is the most remote lighthouse in the Florida Territory—perhaps in the whole country." He took a deep puff on his cigar. "You should reconsider."

"Perhaps. But for now at least, I want to remain." I managed a slight smile. "You forget that I've been tending the light here with Martin for three years. I'm not without experience."

"Ain't a question of experience. It's havin' th'energy and time to do it all. And out here on your own? Ain't much to do, for a well-born lady like y'self."

The company of others was an issue. My sister, Dorothy, tried to come to the island as often as she could, and continually implored me to return to Key West in her letters. But I was not about to admit how much I missed Dorothy and her family—and even my cantankerous Gran. Or how lonely I was sometimes when Martin and I were here together. So I just smiled, "I'll carry on as long as I'm able."

We were silent for a moment. Alfie watched us from the stern of the *Outlander,* looking back and forth between me and the captain.

Lee was nodding, but his expression was dubious.

"Besides," I added, "I shall need the money more now than ever before. This position at Wreckers' Cay was supposed to be compensation for the loss of our property."

Lee nodded again. Money was something he could understand. "Yes, ma'am. That's so."

Finally, he sighed with resignation.

"I'll make out a report when I get back to Key West. Pendleton will be out sooner rather than later. He'll want to make sure you're doin' right by the light. Should warn you, though: The Treasury Department people don't even like to see young families in isolated places like this. A woman by herself . . ." He shook his head. "I'd be mighty surprised if they'd go along with that."

Then, smiling, he leaned over and said good-bye to little Hannah, who, clutching a small stuffed rag doll, was chattering in her own kind of baby talk, which only the family understood. An ear infection had left her unable to hear, and when strangers addressed her, as the captain now did, she would laugh and hide behind my skirts.

Lee's parting words were no more reassuring: "Good thing Martin taught you how to use a gun. There's been news of more Indian massacres on settlers up the Keys. Then there was the light keeper's assistant that got killed off by some Seminoles up at the Cape Florida lighthouse recently." He lowered his voice. "I'd hate to tell you what they did to that woman in the attack on the settlement at Indian Key." He then turned his back to me and fussed with the sails. "Good luck to you, Miss Emily. We'll see you in two weeks."

"Godspeed," I managed to say as they prepared to shove off.

While serving in the army during the War of 1812, Martin had accumulated a collection of pistols, muskets, and rifles, keeping them in the locked cupboard of our bedroom. Every week, he made a ritual of cleaning them, and he would set up targets to teach me the rudiments of shooting. Personally, I hated the guns. I loathed their noise, the hardness of the metal, the smell of the gunpowder, and the way a rifle could jump out of my hand and hit me in the cheek as I fired it.

Because Martin was adamant about teaching me, I had persisted in my shooting practice. But when I discovered he was planning to teach our son, Timothy, I was horrified. "He's still only a young child!" I had protested.

"If ever you and I are unable to defend ourselves, we may need to have Timothy use these weapons," Martin said.

Initially, our son had no interest in even holding a gun; the noise frightened him. But he was always trying to please Martin.

Gamely, he listened to his father's instructions, and though he practiced only with reluctance, Timothy eventually learned to handle our firearms with a modicum of dexterity.

At the time, I could not picture an unlikely or ridiculous situation like the one Martin had described, but now, as Captain Lee and Alfie pulled away from the dock, I remembered his words. And for the first time since my husband's disappearance, another possible theory occurred to me: Could Martin have met with a war party in canoes? I shuddered, unable even to contemplate what horrors might have befallen my husband if that were the case.

For many long days and nights after Martin vanished, I walked the beach at Wreckers' Cay, shielding my eyes from the sun as I trained them out to sea. In the late afternoon, when the tide was low, I took the children to the sandbars to swim and play on the shallow ridges of firm sand carved by the waves. These were happy times for them and good moments to scoop up a fish that strayed from its school, or to seize scurrying stone crabs or crayfish for our supper. It was always the best part of the day, when breezes were cool and soothing and the sun's relentless blaze began to abate before it dipped into the sea.

Timothy and Martha understood that our playtime was yet another search for their father, and together we scanned the beach and the horizon, examining anything that washed ashore, no matter how trivial, as Hannah played in the sand.

"We'll find him, Mama," Martha assured me every evening, taking my hand in hers.

"Yes," I replied vaguely, finding solace in her touch. I refused to let myself cry in front of the children. With a hug, I assured her: "He'll be home soon. I'm sure of it."

Timothy offered his own explanations as the days continued. "I think he just got lost and floated to a nearby island.

He's probably living on local animals and fish, and fruit. Father knows how to take care of himself."

I would smile, ruffle his hair, and agree with him—though as each day passed, I knew such possibilities were the false hopes of a child. On one occasion, Timothy frowned and said, "If you'd only let me go out on the skiff—or on the *Pharos*—I'm sure I could find him. I could explore some of the little cays nearby."

"Absolutely not, Timothy," I said firmly. Secretly, I felt proud of my son's ambition, but the thought of him going out to sea alone was beyond consideration. In truth, I had thought of trying it myself, but with my husband now missing, if anything happened to me, it would be disastrous for my family.

"If Captain Lee and Mr. Dillon couldn't find him, and if the rescue crew from the Lighthouse Services was unable to, how could we? Besides, darlin' "—I knelt down to give him a hug—"I need you here."

This was true. Since Martin's disappearance, I was desperate for the children's help; the responsibility of guiding ships through channels, warning them away from the treacherous coral rock, was daunting. Even before Martin's disappearance, it had become something of a family affair, and in his continued absence, I needed my children close by—now more than ever.

Yet the actual lighting of the lamps was a task only I could perform. Each evening just before sunset, as the tide began its long slow roll toward the shore, its waves gently blanketing the sandbars, I headed for the tower. Against the shrill calls of seabirds plunging hungrily into the water for fish, I watched the sun reaching downward toward the horizon.

I made my way up the circular wooden staircase to the lantern room of the tower and, breathless, finally entered the cocoon of glass perched at the top like a glowing jewel. The glass enclosure was warm from the heat of the day, but I welcomed the soaring vista it offered. High above the island, it was perfect for viewing the luxuriant foliage on the one side and the glittering waters on the other.

"Martin, where are you?" I whispered. His familiar words— "Don't worry, I'll be home in plenty of time for the light"— resonated still. But now I heard only the low roar of the tide. As I prepared to light the lamps, my eyes continued to sweep across the shallow water surrounding the island, always searching for a lone figure in a fishing skiff.

When I lit the lamps, their soft glow immediately filled the little room, spilling brightly out to the ships at sea. I often remained at the south windows of the lantern room for a time, watching the afterglow of pink and golden clouds after the sun dipped below the horizon.

And always when I emerged from the door of the tower, little Hannah, my two-and-a-half-year-old, would be standing there waiting in her little white nightgown, looking like an angel in a nativity scene. She was happy to see me, but she still expected to see Martin. This had normally been her time with her daddy, not me. I would scoop her up in my arms and kiss her soft skin, nuzzling my face into her neck, which smelled of soap from her bath, and bury my cheek into her soft, damp curls. I could not make up for Martin's absence, but she would still lift her face for the little kissing game they had played together, and I gamely tried to do it properly—one kiss to the right cheek, one on the left, and then we rubbed noses Eskimo-style.

She would giggle then, and seem happy as I took her hand. We'd stroll back to the house for supper with Martha and Timothy. And as I did, I realized that I was becoming both father and mother to my children.

And to the new baby I was beginning to suspect I was carrying.

THREE

New Orleans

June 1829

E mily *chérie*, do come here, please. I'd like you to meet some of my husband's clients from the chandlery." A gentle hand was touching my arm. It was my hostess, Madame de Saumur. And with these words, my life was changed forever.

It was a warm, humid summer evening in New Orleans. I was eighteen years old, attending a glittering reception in the French Quarter to honor a visiting government official from France, the usual New Orleans socialites in attendance. Bored to distraction, I wondered when my younger sister, Dorothy, and I could politely slip away with our chaperone, Eurydice.

To my surprise, Madame de Saumur was flanked by two scruffy-looking men dressed in shabby homespun clothes. Their greasy, unkempt hair was too long; their rough, weathered hands were calloused, their fingernails grimy. Even madame's slaves, circulating with trays of food in their carefully pressed livery and immaculate white gloves, were a startling contrast to the two rustics by her side.

"*Chérie,*" she implored me in French, still smiling for the men's sake. "Please chat for a while with these people, will you?

Jean-Philippe invited them. I don't know what he was thinking. They are here from Key West, a little settlement in the Florida Territory. Your English is perfect—so much better than mine. Do take them off my hands."

Switching back to her heavily accented English, she introduced the elder of the two as Captain George Lee, and his companion, a Bahamian carpenter and fisherman, as Martin Lowry.

"Imagine, they've come all the way from a little island south of the mainland of Florida. Gentlemen, this is Emily Dinsmore, one of New Orleans's most beautiful young debutantes. Her grandparents are among my dearest friends." Looking at Martin, she added, "Her father was one of your countrymen— from the Bahamas. Isn't that correct, Emily?"

Having been raised to be unfailingly polite, I nodded mutely. Before I could say anything, she flashed her inimitable smile and fluttered away like a hummingbird.

Oblivious to the amused looks and murmurs from other guests, Captain Lee let his attention wander around the ballroom, taking in its prodigious art and elegant furnishings. The younger man, Martin, however, looked only at me. No doubt in an effort to avoid staring rudely at my ample bosom, he fixed his gaze instead on my eyes.

"It's an honor to meet you, Miss Dinsmore," he said, bowing courteously. A confident smile revealed perfect white teeth, which contrasted sharply with the deep color of his face.

I don't know why he intrigued me, but I found myself responding to his pleasantries, despite his rustic appearance. At first, I was taken aback by his voice, for he spoke in the same accent as my late father, who'd been raised in Harbour Island. Martin Lowry's disheveled hair wreathed an unmistakably handsome face, and though his appearance was ragged, he spoke like a gentleman. I quickly realized he was better educated than an average fisherman or carpenter of that time.

He asked about my parents, and I told him about my father, a lawyer with wrecking interests who had settled in New Orleans, and of my French mother, who died giving birth to my sister, Dorothy. "Your speech," I said shyly, "is very like that of my father."

"I would like to meet him. It's possible that we know many of the same people."

"I'm afraid that won't be possible. He drowned while traveling aboard a ship bound for New York City some years ago. It was wrecked on a shoal during a storm."

He lowered his eyes respectfully. "I'm sorry. Did it happen on the Gulf Coast? I know many a storm finds you here."

"No. A hurricane off Cape Hatteras."

Captain Lee, who had been inattentive until that point, nodded knowingly. "Aye, Hatteras is a demon place for ships," he said, seeming eager now to join our conversation.

Stealing a discreet glance at Martin Lowry, I reckoned him to be older than I by about fifteen years. He was also at least a head taller. His hair was tawny-colored, streaked by the sun; his eyes, like mine, were an intense blue; and I noted a sprinkling of freckles under his deeply tanned skin, which lent him an ingenuous charm.

The captain looked to be in his late thirties. Like Martin, he was tall and sinewy, with rough features. Creases had etched his sun-charred skin, particularly around his green eyes, and his hair was beginning to thin. His accent was deeply northeastern. "Quite a place they have here," the captain marveled as he took in the enormous Baccarat chandeliers with their flickering candles. "Quite a place."

"Yes," I agreed. "The owners have very refined tastes." Our host, Jean-Philippe de Saumur, was a wealthy third-generation Frenchman who had made his fortune importing fine furnishings.

"What is it that brings you to New Orleans?" I asked Lee.

"I've come to buy rigging to outfit some boats we'll be usin' as supply tenders for lighthouses in the Florida Territory. My mate Martin here came along to help."

"Have you many lighthouses around Key West?"

The men smiled. "Not many," Martin said. "There are only three for the whole area right now, but we expect more will be built in the next year or so. When the United States acquired the Florida Territory, they opened a naval depot in Key West. Marine traffic is growing by the day, so ships traveling our waters will be sorely in need of them."

"Oh? Are there so many dangers to passing vessels in your part of Florida?" I asked.

"Aye, there most certainly are." The captain grinned. I confess his expression took me slightly aback, since we were discussing potential disasters. "We've rid ourselves of the pirates, but there are shallow waters throughout the Florida Keys. And with our coral reef, wrecks are a common occurrence."

To pass the time, the men and I chatted further about life in New Orleans since the Louisiana Purchase, and about Key West's future as a new American territory. Barely twenty-five years had passed since the United States had acquired Louisiana, and Americans were becoming firmly entrenched in France's former holding. Yet, the crème of New Orleans's elite—people like my grandparents and our host, Jean-Philippe de Saumur— had been born in the old Louisiana and were firmly of French heritage.

"Well," the captain laughed, "that's all changing. Once we Americans get hold of a territory, we tend to make our mark."

Martin must have noticed my annoyance, for he tactfully changed the subject. "You mentioned a sister. Is she here this evening?"

"Yes," I replied, relieved by his question. I pointed her out. "She's the girl with the blond curls in the blue dress, over by the piano."

Dorothy—unlike me—was very outgoing. Now she was engaged in flirtatious conversation with a young man from a wealthy New Orleans family.

"Ah"—Martin nodded—"the young lady who has been singing this evening."

"Yes," I said. "And she has always been the beauty of the family. She's just fourteen! We are all very proud of her."

But Martin seemed unimpressed with this—his gaze had already returned to my face.

Monsieur de Saumur finally arrived to extricate me. Bidding the Key Westers a good evening, I stepped out for some fresh air on the spacious jasmine-scented terrace. It was easy to dismiss the loud captain from my mind, but the memory of his handsome mate lingered still.

"You're wrong, you know," said a voice behind me.

I wheeled around, recognizing the Bahamian lilt. Smiling, he said, "Your sister isn't the family beauty. You are, by far."

I felt a blush of heat fill my cheeks; I lowered my eyes. "You flatter me."

"Hardly," said Martin. "I suspect you know how beautiful you are."

I smiled but said nothing. Without Captain Lee to control the conversation, Martin proved himself much more inclined to talk. Although he worked as a fisherman and was not much interested in books, I soon learned he had attended an Anglican school in the Bahamas, which accounted for his precise speech. And I found myself looking past his appearance and listening with amusement to tales of his life in the Bahamas and Key West.

When I look back now, I see our meeting on that terrace as a moment suspended in time, a pivotal moment of my young life. Had I left then, the road would have taken a completely different turn. But, of course, I did not leave. I stayed, and smiled encouragement at Martin. What can I say? In one evening, he had captured my heart, when none of the prominent young men of New Orleans had been able to. Perhaps it was his age, which in my eyes lent him greater maturity, or his good looks and easy smile, but I fell hopelessly in love. When he called upon me at home the next day, I agreed to join him for a walk, and by the time he returned me home later that afternoon, he was calling me "my dearest Emily."

Following a courtship of just a few weeks—closely supervised by Eurydice, and frowned upon by my family, Martin proposed marriage. We were just returning from a walk in the French Quarter when, noting that Eurydice had stopped to chat for a moment with a slave of her acquaintance, Martin boldly lifted my chin and kissed me lightly on the lips.

"Emily, I can't bear the idea of going back to Key West without you. Would you come with me? As my wife?"

My heart surged with joy. "Yes," I replied happily. "Oh yes!"

No one really approved of my choice. Eurydice made it known that she thought it foolish. And Dorothy was clearly displeased. "Sugar," she drawled—for we always spoke English between us—"I find him just as cute as a bug. But he's so poor! And I shall just die if you leave me and go off to live in Key West, over in Florida. It's so far."

My grandparents were appalled. "You're being a very foolish girl," Grandmère said. "He is déclassé, has no manners, and no money. What's more, he is a Protestant! You've nothing in common with such a man."

My grandfather's reaction was all the more fierce, for he fell into the greatest show of his fury: utter silence. Grandpère would even rise from his chair and leave the room when Martin came to call. Even Gran—my father's mother, Hester Dinsmore—who was then still living in Harbour Island, expressed bitter disappointment when she heard I intended to marry a man with no social status, despite the fact that he was Bahamian, like her. In her letters, she heaped blame on my maternal grandparents for allowing me to entertain such an idea.

"An old Bahamian family, but definitely not of our class," she wrote to me of Martin. "And how on earth will the two of you manage? You'll be as poor as church mice!"

But all this negativity only strengthened my resolve. I was young and thought little of money. And Martin had come into my life at a moment when other human desires were stirring in my young body. In the end, unable to bear the miasma of tension prevailing in her household, my grandmother finally persuaded Grandpère to consent and even grant me a small dowry. The only stipulation was that I would have to wait until the autumn. They were hoping that a few months of waiting would change my mind.

After the announcement of our betrothal, Martin returned to Key West with Captain Lee, and I did not see him again until he returned to New Orleans that autumn to marry me.

"We'll have the rest of our lives together, dearest," he assured me as he ran his hands through my thick chestnut-colored hair one last time.

Then he kissed me tenderly, and was gone.

We married in St. Louis Cathedral that October, within just four months of meeting, the exchange of our vows taking place afterward in the sacristy. Our wedding date had been decided on by Martin, to coincide with the departure of a mercantile schooner sailing from New Orleans that very day. The appropriately named *Innocencia* was bound for England, carrying a load of cotton, and had scheduled a brief stop in the port of Key West. After a somewhat stilted leave-taking of my grandparents, and many tearful hugs and kisses exchanged with Dorothy, I boarded the ship that afternoon with my new husband, and we immediately set sail for Florida.

"I'll come often to visit you!" were Dorothy's last words to me. Little did either of us know then what Key West had in store for her.

The arduous voyage to Key West was rendered miserable by the rough October thunderstorms and the discovery that I was prone to seasickness on rough waters. Indeed, so ill was I, we did not consummate our marriage until well after we arrived in Key West.

FOUR

Wreckers' Cay

August 1839

The stress of Martin's disappearance and my sadness at his loss had affected my appetite, which caused me to lose weight and brought about other changes in my body. But there was no denying my morning sickness. By the month of August, I had accepted that another child would be arriving to bring joy to our family—and additional responsibility to what I was already shouldering.

It was proving a difficult pregnancy. By the third month, I was experiencing unusual physical problems, and I was close to exhaustion from tending the light.

Martin and I had never felt quite the same way about the lighthouse. He regarded tending it as a job, while I had always intuited its magic. The flame we created each evening spoke to faceless people beyond the reef, warning them of its dangers. And I loved the feeling of being high up in the tower, surveying my world from its vantage point. But now that I had to tend it, day in and day out, I came to understand Martin's attitude better.

The superintendent of lighthouses, Inspector Stephen

Pendleton, finally came to see if I was doing things correctly. "You surprise me, Mrs. Lowry. . . . Uh, for a woman, you appear to manage rather well."

"Thank you," I replied, bristling at his reference to my gender. There was no reason for him to act as if I were unique. There were other widows nearby who had become lighthouse keepers, like Barbara Mabrity in Key West, and Rebecca Flaherty at Sand Key. And I had read about women up north in the Great Lakes region and New York who were also in charge of lights.

"I didn't really expect that you'd be able to," he continued. "But after spending today here, I would have to say that everything appears to be in order. . . ." He was checking off items on a list. "Lamps . . . reflectors . . . the oil-storage house—yes, everything has been well tended. . . . Good log on fuel consumption, matching our records. . . . Even your home looks good"—here he gave me a condescending smile—"despite your having children."

Pendleton was a tall man in his early fifties, with a large mustache that turned up at the ends, and a belly that threatened to pop the buttons of his vest. And while I found his manner businesslike, he wore a kindly expression.

"Would you care for some tea?" I asked him when his inspection was done.

"I would be delighted!"

I poured him tea on the veranda, served with freshly baked scones and some of my mango jam. Chewing appreciatively, he regarded me with a combination of suspicion and growing admiration. "How long have you been doing this on your own now?"

"Since my husband disappeared in May."

"Three months. You've managed well."

"I've worked alongside my husband ever since we lost our land in Key West and moved here."

He nodded thoughtfully. "Yes, yes, of course. That was an unfortunate thing, taking your land. Quite regrettable." Possibly, officials in Key West did feel some guilt at the way we had been treated. As he seemed sympathetic, I pressed my advantage.

"Until my husband has been found, there is no reason to make any radical changes in my life or that of my family. I trust you're satisfied that we can keep the light in good running order. We're still confident that my husband will be returning."

He nodded slowly. "I must confess I came out here to tell you I would be replacing you." I held my breath until I saw that under his mustache a smile was taking shape on his thin lips. "But I admit I have been most impressed today."

I exhaled with relief.

He looked down for a moment, choosing his next words with care. "Mrs. Lowry, has it ever occurred to you"—he fumbled for words to express his question with tact—"that your husband might have . . . well . . . just left, gone off . . . or might have decided to end his life? Perhaps he was troubled. The isolation here . . . it wouldn't be the first time someone lost his sanity tending a light. It has occurred to some of us at the Lighthouse Services . . ."

I felt my face flush with indignation that such a notion might be circulating in Key West.

"No," I asserted firmly. "My husband and I were devoted to each other. And Mr. Lowry was a wonderful father. I believe that he is still alive, having survived a mishap or some kind of attack. If he were dead, his remains would most certainly have washed up by now. No, my husband is alive; I'm certain of it."

I began to clear the tea things from the table to indicate that our social time together was over. In truth, his words had stung me, echoing a faint suspicion that had festered in the depths of my own mind from the beginning.

Sensing my agitation, he stood up. "Yes, of course. But you

must admit that his disappearance was—is—rather mysterious."

This required no comment from me, so I remained silent. Gathering his things together, he prepared to leave, and I walked him down to his boat.

"You're a strong woman," he said in an unctuous tone as he took my arm. "If you think you can manage without your husband, then we'll try it this way and see. Since you're already here and seem to be managing, I would have no objection to having you continue." He smiled benignly and tightened the hold on my arm. When he finally released it, I felt his hand at my lower back, and it began to slide down over my buttocks.

"I will require a new contract with your department," I said, moving away. "As you can see, I have the same family responsibilities and work tending the light as my husband did, and without an assistant, which he had. I will expect the same salary of seven hundred dollars a year that my husband earned."

His mouth opened to speak, but no words came out. And his eyes widened with genuine shock. "My dear lady!" he said when he regained his composure. "Women cannot be paid the same as men!"

I had expected him to say that, so I said nothing. At least my demand had ended his groping as he contemplated what I'd asked. In the end, we negotiated a compromise. He would pay me six hundred dollars annually to do the work of two people, with a promise of more in a year if I performed well. He would send out the new contract with Captain Lee on the next tender.

Had I not been pregnant and in a weak bargaining position, I might have pressed on. My condition was a secret I could not keep forever, but I wanted to hide it from him until he was convinced that I could manage. Fortunately, my height could carry and conceal added weight. Corsets and shawls helped when the supply tender was expected, but as I usually wore neither of these on the island, I was vulnerable to surprise visits.

Truthfully, I had no idea how I would tend the light and look after everything else once I was in labor and during the time immediately following my delivery. My fervent, if fading, hope was that Martin would soon return and life would be the same as it had been before.

Cautioning me about Indian attacks as Captain Lee had, Pendleton untied his boat and left, while I hurried back to the children and the evening's chores ahead of me.

The night following Pendleton's visit, a heavy gale ravaged Wreckers' Cay. This in itself was not unusual for the summer season, when storms frequently brewed in the Caribbean. Still, the winds that night had been strong enough to suck the very breath from me. While my children slept soundly through the storm, I was mostly awake and alert to the lamps. Drafts swept eerily through the tower, their whispers rising to shrieks as they extinguished the lamps in ghostly puffs of smoke. More than once during that night, I had to leave the house in pelting rain and run up the stairs to trim the wicks, clean soot from the lenses, and rekindle the light.

The heat and anxiety were a difficult combination during the long hours of darkness. When I tried to nap, I was jolted awake by a curious clanging sound that stirred bad memories through my veil of muffled dreams. I was also awakened by the barking and howls of our dog, Brandy, who was terrified of the crashing thunder.

Outside, the wind was blowing savagely, creating its own high-pitched hissing. It whistled through palm fronds, bending trees with a frenzy against the roof of the house. A loose shutter I had forgotten to close beat reproachfully somewhere at the back of the house. "I can't think of everything!" I wailed miserably into the storm. "Why isn't Martin here to help with battening down the house? To look after us when it's stormy?"

And further, I thought, I needed him in our bed, to hold me tightly and assure me that all would be well.

The next day, I rose at dawn to a blessed calm. I collected small branches that had snapped off our mahogany tree and tried to tidy up the minor damage to our outbuildings. Mercifully, no large sheared boughs had landed on our rooftops.

A bad case of morning sickness made me too ill to eat. Numbly, I assigned chores to Martha and Timothy. Brandy seemed more interested in staying outside, and I kept hearing her bark and whine over by the storage house.

Though feeling ill, I began my early-morning tasks at the light, climbing the tower staircase to begin extinguishing the fifteen wicks. The lantern room was hot from the flaming lamps and the heat from the rising sun. I was already warm from the exertion of the climb, and by the time I began turning down wicks to quench the flames, my clothing was drenched and sticking to my skin.

Once the lamps had cooled enough to touch, I took off the glass chimneys and removed them from the candelabra. Wiping down the silvered fifteen-inch parabolic reflectors, I covered them with protective cotton covers. Next, I poured the whale oil from each lamp through a strainer into a clean copper oil can, disassembled and cleaned them, and trimmed the wicks. Finally, I put the lamps back together and mounted them again on the candelabra. After I polished the brass oil-reservoir chambers, I refilled them with the filtered oil, and the circular wicks were reset for the evening lighting. Mindlessly, I completed these tasks, wondering if I could realistically continue this routine every morning. My back ached as I swept up insects and small birds that had been attracted to the lights during the night and died in the heat from the lamps.

From the balcony of the tower, I could see vessels in the distant shipping lanes as I cleaned the windows to remove the heavy salt spray. For a fleeting moment, I envied those men aboard the ships. They were heading somewhere—anywhere. They were free in a way I could never be again. Going to places I would never see, to do things I would never experience.

Back at the house, Martha had taken charge of things.

"Timothy, after breakfast you should rake up outside for Mama," I heard her say as I came in. He had just lit the fire to boil water for coffee and grits. "Hannah, go check the coop for eggs. Then you can help me set the table. There's a good girl."

I smiled as I watched Martha sign and enunciate clearly to make Hannah understand. Our situation was making her efficient beyond her years. We had breakfast like any normal family, and it marked the first day I could remember in which none of the children asked about Martin.

Afterward, too tired to sleep, I strolled along the lower beach and scanned the shallow waters of the sea with Brandy, who whined restlessly. As always, my eyes swept the horizon; it was now second nature to me. But then as I looked down, I stopped in my tracks. Footprints! Barefoot prints in the sand, tracing from the sea into the low shrubbery.

Martin had returned. My prayers had been answered! But on closer examination, I realized the footsteps looked much larger than my husband's could have been. My joy was replaced with terror. Perhaps it was an Indian scout, sent ahead to spy on our supplies and the island's defenses. This prospect gripped me like a python, robbing me of breath.

I hurried back to the house, trying to act normal in front of the children, and quietly selected one of Martin's rifles from the locked cupboard. Thus armed, I toured all the outbuildings, except the locked storage shed—I saw no signs of a break-in there, and the keys were kept in my bedroom. With Brandy whining at my heels, I stalked the island in silence but found no one.

Finally, exhausted from the heat, I returned to the house, satisfied, at least, that our boats had not been stolen, and relieved that I'd had no cause to use the rifle. Later, as the tide rose, the footsteps washed away, but my fears remained. Someone had invaded our island and might indeed still be with us.

Over the next several days, I was jittery at every sound. And my suspicion about an intruder strengthened with each day. It occurred to me, for instance, that our stores of food were suddenly being used up at the same rate as when Martin was with us. My children were growing fast, I reassured myself, and eating more.

It was time I discussed my pregnancy with Martha and Timothy, for I had procrastinated long enough. After their studies one night, I settled Hannah into bed and summoned them to our front parlor. The room was sparsely appointed with household items barged over from our home in Key West. The furniture and rugs were becoming worn and seedy, with spots where Brandy had accidentally made her mark. But even in its genteel shabbiness, it was still our most official-looking room, where I could feel most comfortable sharing this news.

They quietly settled themselves onto the plush horsehair couches, resting their heads on the antimacassars.

"I want to tell you," I began, "that you are going to have another brother or sister."

They met this announcement with silence.

"You're probably surprised," I continued, "since your father is no longer—"

"Oh, we knew," Timothy said. "We've heard you being sick."

"And we hadn't seen your . . . hygienic cloths on the line for a few months," added Martha.

Then they both started to giggle. I, too, began to smile, but not without considerable embarrassment. Seeing my color rise, Martha came over and put her arms around my neck. "Don't worry, Mama," she said, kissing my cheek. "We'll manage. You can count on us."

I hugged her gently. I suspected that Martha knew she might even have to help with my delivery if Dorothy did not come over in time. And I had to ask myself if I wasn't placing too much on her young shoulders.

Before I could say anything more, she and Timothy looked nervously at each other, smiling. He nodded. She turned back to me. "Timothy and I have something we want to tell you, too. Something we've been keeping a secret."

I smiled. "Oh! What kind of secret?"

Martha nudged Timothy, urging him to speak. He was silent for a moment, taking the measure of my mood. "Well," he began, "we think we have some help for you. We have . . . well, we have a slave."

I sat up suddenly. "What on earth are you talking about?"

"He came ashore the night of the storm. He escaped from a slave ship bound for the Caribbean."

"A slave? Here on our island?" I realized I was shouting—something I rarely did with the children. "How—where is this slave?"

They cowered into the couch, and both pointed toward the storage shed.

"Promise you won't hurt him," entreated Martha. "He's very nice."

"You've been feeding him!" I exclaimed, suddenly making the connection about our missing food.

They nodded. "He said he could help you tend the light if you let him stay."

Immediately, I was on my feet and flying up the stairs. I removed a shotgun from the locked cupboard, seized the keys to the storage shed, and raced back down the stairs.

The children watched in silence.

"Take me to him this minute," I said.

"Don't shoot him," Timothy pleaded. "He's a nice man."

"Why didn't you tell me about this before?"

"We were afraid. . . . We thought you'd be angry," Martha said.

"We think we should keep him," said Timothy. "He could be a big help to you."

They led the way to the storage house. I gave Martha the key and she unlocked the door as I kept the firearm aimed ahead of me. The door opened, and I nearly gagged on the malodorous fumes inside.

He was huddled by a slop pail in the far corner of the room. Palmetto beetles were feasting on the pail's contents, and flies buzzed above it. As he stirred, I heard the clanking sound and realized that was the familiar sound I'd heard the night of the storm: the rattling of slaves in chains that I'd heard so often during my New Orleans childhood. His wrists and ankles were shackled. One of Martin's toolboxes was open next to him, with a file and various other cutting tools the children had been using to try to remove his chains. Small bugs crawled around him, and I suspected that his hair was full of lice and nits. I could only make out his features with difficulty, but I immediately discerned that he was not an African slave; rather, he was the hybrid result of generations in the South. His skin was a much lighter brown than the rich ebony color of newly landed slaves I'd seen in Louisiana. Even more telling were his eyes, which were a light hazel.

Seeing the chains, I could feel my muscles relax with relief and my breathing return to normal. While I still kept the shotgun on him, I let my hand loosen its grip. "You speak English, of course," I said to him, holding a handkerchief over my nose and mouth.

"Yes, ma'am," he replied. He was looking apprehensively at my firearm, yet I could read a certain defiance in his eyes. It was the look of someone who understood how to fight for survival.

"Well, then, you'll understand this," I said. "I don't know what my children told you, but you are not welcome on this island. When our supply tender returns, you will be on it, heading for Key West. Is that clear?"

He nodded slowly.

"Is that clear?" I repeated, my voice rising.

"Yes, ma'am," he replied hastily, his eyes following my gun.

"Until then, we will feed you and look to your basic needs," I said, trying to assert more control in my voice. "If you give us any trouble . . ." I paused here and raised the gun.

He stared back at me.

With that, I picked up the tools, turned, and left. Herding my children on ahead of me, I locked the door as I pondered just what his basic needs would be. He'd clearly been unable to wash for days. Shackled as he was, just getting to the slop pail must have been difficult. And while the children had been feeding him, he couldn't have been getting much sustenance.

"Mother, you are being so cruel," Martha said when we were outside. "It's not his fault he's here. He was on a ship that got into trouble during the storm."

I held out my hand to stop her. "Martha, there is something strange about this. He isn't an African; he's a slave born in the United States. What was he doing on a slave ship heading to the Caribbean?"

The children shrugged. It hadn't been legal to transport slaves from Africa since 1808. But even my young children knew that illegal slavers were still out there. Importing free labor from that continent was far too profitable to bring to an end. And in any case, the practice of slavery itself was still flourishing quite legally in the United States and in many islands in the Caribbean. It had to be an illegal slaver that he'd been on, one that had made a stopover at an American port on its way to the islands or to South America. With enough money, a rogue ship could always find a place to dock for supplies or repairs en route. Such a stopover would be an opportunity for an American slave owner to sell off a fractious slave.

"This is not a question of begging for a pet and promising to look after it," I said to Martha and Timothy, trying to speak more gently now. But they just looked ahead and didn't respond. I sighed wearily as we all trudged back to the house in silence.

FIVE

Wreckers' Cay

1839

I could never confess this to anyone, not even to my sister, Dorothy, but a few days after Martin disappeared, I was certain I felt his presence in my bed one night as I was drifting off to sleep. With a start, I felt him touch my shoulder.

It could only be a hallucination, I was sure. But every night, just as I settled into a twilight sleep, I felt that slight brush against my shoulder and I heard his voice: "Rest, Emily. You must take time to rest."

I would entreat him with questions: Where was he? How could he have left us? But all I heard was trite reassurance: "Everything will be fine, Emily. You're doing very well. Carry on."

Such positive—albeit otherworldly—messages were ironically somewhat out of character with the husband I remembered. Usually at some point in this ghostly conversation, I would reach for his hand and realize he was not there. Or often, I would be drifting off to sleep, imagining his arms were around me, only to be jolted awake in my empty bed, having doubts about my sanity. Was it the loneliness? The new pregnancy? The light outside my window, always drawing me awake at odd hours? I was obviously going mad.

Struggling now with a decision about the slave, I asked "Martin" what he thought.

"What harm, Emily? He might be a big help to you," he said.

"But he might be violent . . . or dangerous."

"No, Emily. I don't think you need worry. Take him on. It will be fine. You really need help."

And thus assured, I drifted off to sleep.

The next morning, by the time I could see the sun erupting like lava over the blazing horizon, I had pretty well made up my mind. There was no way I could keep the Negro imprisoned under such deplorable conditions for ten more days. He might well die. And I realized, too, that my anger with the children was unreasonable. The slave had made his own way to our island. What could they have done? All they were guilty of was showing him some human kindness, and hiding him from me.

I rose and prepared to start my responsibilities at the tower. Then a light tap on the bedroom door nearly sent me for my shotgun.

"It's me, Timothy."

I saw my son standing there, a younger version of Martin, more man than boy. Was he only about to turn eight? He seemed so serious. A great surge of affection flooded through me. I leaned forward and put my arms around him. I did not often hug my son now, as he would shy from affection, but this morning I was in better spirits and I realized what a fine, sweet human being he was becoming, and how much I loved my children. They were my world.

Timothy was surprised at this display of affection. "Mother . . . Martha and I . . . we . . ." He was hesitating, not sure what to say next.

"Hush, I know, I know. You both meant well, and I'm grateful that you were thinking of me," I said, running my hand through his sun-streaked hair. "I've been thinking . . . and I realize I was unreasonable yesterday. But you do understand that with your father gone, I must be very careful.

"Perhaps we could give the Negro a chance," I continued kindly. "We certainly have enough work for him to do. But we'll have to exercise caution. I still have many reservations about keeping him here."

Timothy brightened. "He said he'd be glad to help us with any kind of work."

"If he tends the light, I can't pay him anything."

"That's fine. He knows that," said Timothy cheerfully. "He's a slave. Money isn't important to him."

"What's more," I added, "we'll have to keep his existence a secret. Otherwise, he will be ferried immediately to Key West, where they will try to locate his owners or sell him. This is not a man with any legal right to be here, and we are breaking the law just by helping him."

Timothy nodded. "But what about Aunt Dorothy?"

I hadn't thought about Dorothy. She'd be coming in a few months to stay until my delivery. My sister and her husband, Tom, owned a black housemaid, a nanny, and a gardener.

"I don't know yet," I said. "We'll keep him a secret from her for the moment. After all, we don't even know if he's going to work out. If he's lazy or uncooperative, we may not want to keep him on."

Our first problem was to remove the slave's iron shackles—not an easy task. Timothy had tried to help him file the chains, but between them they had barely scratched the metal. He had considered a hatchet, but the Negro was understandably nervous about having Timothy swing the tool down in the direction of his feet and hands.

The fact that he was in chains surprised me, as I had always heard that once slaves were herded down to the slave deck of a ship they were shackled two by two with a bilbo. Why had they chosen to manacle this one with loose chains that permitted him to wander around?

Holding my breath as best I could in the stench, I entered the storage shed. Seeing that the shackles were similar to chains Martin used for securing our boats, I sent Martha upstairs to fetch the bunch of keys he'd kept in a drawer of his desk. Then we each took turns trying them. In the end, an oddly shaped key on the ring opened the locks like a charm. As the shackles fell away, I could see the raw wounds around his ankles and wrists. A deep sigh signaled his relief. Timothy helped him up, but he was so stiff, he could barely stand. And walking was next to impossible. Both children assisted him in taking steps around the outside of the shed until he was able to support himself.

We had to get him cleaned up, but I hesitated at the thought of letting him use our facilities. "I don't want him getting into our tub with all that filth," I told the children. "Get him into the sea to rinse off. Then he can bathe with soap in the wash-house."

Timothy and Martha led him to the shore, while I followed to supervise. When he removed his filthy shirt, I gasped when I saw the wounds on his back. Over long-healed seams of scar tissue was a set of fresh lashes, still festering. He gingerly made his way into the water; I heard him moan with pleasure as it washed over him, even as he winced with pain from the salt on his wounds. When he emerged from the water, still wobbling, his ragged, wet pants clung to his body. I could see his sex through a rent at the front, and I turned away.

I did not want my daughter viewing his exposure. "Martha," I called out, "you go on ahead. Start the water in the tub and light the fire to heat it. Fetch some soap upstairs, and towels for him to dry off."

Martha went off happily enough, pleased that I was at last showing their slave consideration, if not wholehearted kindness. Clearly, he would need clothing. While he bathed in the washhouse, I gathered together some of Martin's personal items. I found the toiletries and shaving equipment I had put away after my husband had been gone several weeks. Despite my apprehension at giving him a razor, I brought everything down, along with some clean rags and a salve for the infected wounds on his back.

A shirt, some underdrawers, light trousers, and a hat completed his new wardrobe. Shoes I did not bother with, for the slave had much larger feet than my husband.

He seemed to take forever bathing and shaving, and I was taken aback when he emerged. To my amazement, he had shaved not only his face but also his head, which was now a shining, clean dome, and I had to admit that he looked much improved. He remained shirtless, revealing a body that was young and well proportioned. I judged him to be about my age, if not slightly older. And though emaciated, he was still quite muscular for someone who had been confined for God knows how long.

"Here's the shirt you done give me," he said. "Wouldn't want to mess it up with my wounds."

"Turn around," I ordered.

He obeyed, but I could see he was suspicious. On some clean strips of cloth, I spread some medicinal balm with a table knife, then gently applied the strips to his back. He flinched, but when he turned back toward me, there was gratitude in his eyes.

"Put the shirt on. It can be washed." Again, he did as he was told. "The sun will heal up your wrists and ankles," I said, and he nodded in agreement.

I told him to sit down at the table while I busied myself making him breakfast. He fairly devoured the food I set down before him, and drank the tea in great gulps. The irony of me, the daughter of Louisiana slave owners, waiting on a slave, was not lost.

"You'll be helping us tend the light," I said curtly. "After breakfast, we'll go to the tower and I shall instruct you on what needs to be done. I have everything written down"—I paused, as the obvious occurred to me—"but, of course, you can't read."

He shook his head. "No, ma'am."

"I'll hope you have a good memory, then."

"I remember things pretty good."

After he had cleaned up in the storage shed, we climbed the tower together. He was gasping for breath when we reached the top, while I, though pregnant, barely felt my heartbeat race. He looked at me with surprise. "You be pretty good on them stairs."

"I've been doing this two or three times a day," I said. "Sometimes more, if the light has gone out during a windstorm at night; I've often had to rush over quickly."

"Lots'a stairs," he observed between labored breaths. Despite my misgivings about having him there, I had to smile.

When we reached the top, we stood facing each other in the small, hot glass enclosure—a pregnant white woman and a breathless runaway slave, eyeing each other in mutual suspicion.

SIX

Key West

October 1829

When my new husband and I first arrived in Key West, I had really very little idea of what to expect. And Martin had said little on the voyage over that would enlighten me—though in truth, I had been so seasick, it's unlikely I would have paid much attention.

It was midday when the *Innocencia* docked. The settlement was crowded, lively, and noisy, with people—mostly men—milling around in the port area. Vendors were hawking fish, turtle meat, birds' eggs, conch, crawfish, and crab. Negro women—freed slaves, I assumed—in colorful turbans and brightly flowered dresses called out to passersby in lilting accents to buy their freshly picked tropical fruit. Cubans were selling strong coffee and lottery tickets. There were buskers playing fiddles or drums, and jugglers tossing oranges in the air, all to cadge money from sailors.

Several ships stood in port, their tall masts swaying gently in the southeasterly breezes as their crews cleaned decks, worked on the complex webs of rigging, and wandered back and forth into the settlement. Chandleries, riggers' shops, food stores, and sailmakers' workshops were all filled with mates from the vessels, crowding in to buy supplies, fresh water, and necessary parts. Grog shops were doing a good business, too, as crew members flocked to them. And even though it was only midday, questionable-looking women strolled lazily near the ships.

There was much activity at the row of warehouses near the docks, where goods taken off vessels run aground were stored. There were pilots, sailors, and ships' captains, along with well-dressed men in fine suits and tall silk hats congregating around O'Hara's warehouse.

The agent's bell sounded loudly over a brouhaha of chatter in various accents and languages.

"Looks like an auction's about to start," Martin shouted as we made our way through the throng crowding the dock. I glanced at his animated face; he was clearly happy to be home.

"Who are all these people?" I asked weakly. Still feeling poorly from the sea voyage, I leaned awkwardly on his arm.

"Let's see . . . there're a couple of insurance agents I recognize, some underwriters, a few wreckers . . . some folks that have come to buy cargo, and the auctioneer and his assistants, of course. The rest are maritime lawyers representing shipowners and captains."

"Where do the buyers come from?"

"All over. Mostly Mobile, New Orleans, Charleston, even some from up New York City way. Key West, too. Our local people love auctions." He stopped and waved. "There's George and his wife. Remember Captain George Lee? You met him on that first night in New Orleans."

Martin found a mule driver with an ample wagon who would taxi us away from the dock. With great effort, he helped him load my many cases. Then Martin helped boost me up to a seat next to the driver, and he clambered onto the back of the wagon.

"I was expecting something more comfortable after such a long trip!" I exclaimed with dismay.

Martin simply laughed. "We don't have far to go."

We left, with the auctioneer's booming voice ringing in our ears.

"Take us to Mallory's . . . Coconut Grove," Martin called out to our driver.

I assumed that this, at least, would be a comfortable hotel, in keeping with the fact that it was, after all, our honeymoon. I settled back, anticipating a picturesque drive. But looking around me at the village that was to be my home, I took in the passing dusty landscape with growing distaste.

After New Orleans—then third-largest city in the United States—I was thoroughly disheartened at my first look at Key West, which counted only three hundred souls. What greeted me was a settlement of shabby wooden shacks weathered gray, with chickens and goats wandering from backyards onto the unpaved streets. Outdoor privies fouled the air. The roads, littered with malodorous garbage, were muddy and rutted. Sidewalks, when there were any, were wooden, and they offered no protection from mud splashes and feces stirred up by mules and horses.

Despite the steady trade winds, I found the climate hot and oppressive—especially bundled as I was in my petticoats, bonnet, pantalettes, and silk gloves. These were the latest style back home in New Orleans, but I could already feel how impractical they would be here in Key West.

The cart had not traveled but a block or two before it stopped.

"This is where we'll be staying," Martin said.

Frowning, I looked up. We were in front of a poorly maintained two-story frame building with cracked windows and a couple of shutters hanging off their hinges. A sign out front said ROOMS FOR RENT. ELLEN MALLORY, PROP.

"How long will we be staying here?" I asked, clutching Martin's arm as he helped me alight from the cart.

He shrugged. "I haven't decided yet, dearest. This'll do us for now."

"But . . . where did you live before?"

"Mostly, I camped out on fishing boats. When I was in town, I stayed here."

Inside, he introduced me to Mrs. Mallory, the kindly Irish Bahamian owner. "Come in, come in," she said, greeting me warmly as she took the measure of my clothing and apprehensive expression. "Welcome to Key West."

I looked around in vain for signs of slave help, but I saw only a young lad she called Stephen. It took some time for them to help Martin haul everything to our room. Once my large trunk was carried in, we could barely move. With a quick kiss and instructions for me to unpack, Martin left for the grog shops to gather with his friends and ask about securing work.

I looked around in disbelief. I'd been used to a civilized life at my grandparents' elegant town home, with its spacious courtyard, large, well-appointed rooms, and servants to take care of everything. Being set down abruptly with orders to unpack in a shabby boardinghouse with peeling wallpaper, stale odors, and huge cockroaches did not sit well with me.

By evening, Martin had not yet returned, and I realized that my menses had appeared. I went to bed but slept badly. Our room was on the ground floor, so I did not feel protected. To catch a breeze off the Gulf, I opened the windows, inadvertently inviting an invasion of mosquitoes. Having neglected to secure the netting, I was repeatedly awakened by insects buzzing and biting my exposed face and neck. Whenever I dozed off, I was shocked awake by the shrill call of roosters, or the noisy scraping of a lively fiddle in the street. Loud singing and laughter resounded from the grog shops; noisier still were the drunks passing by. Cigar smoke continually wafted through the windows. At one point, I heard someone urinate against the building, and I was subjected to the sizzling hiss of his stream, followed by a contented sigh.

The other residents of the house argued, cursed, and laughed loudly in the halls, stumbling into walls and doors in the dark as they staggered to their rooms.

That first night of my new life, I hardly slept at all.

Martin often signed on for overnight fishing trips, so the nocturnal horror of that first night in Key West was played out for several more evenings that week. By the time he arrived home, I was usually asleep, and he slept in the late mornings after I was up. Afternoons, he spent at the port looking for work.

In his absence, I took my meals with the widowed Mrs. Mallory, who continually urged me to eat. "You'll be looking like a wraith, Miss Emily. Try a little of this fine conch chowder."

"I . . . I can't get anything down."

"Ah, 'tis the homesickness that's got to you." She smiled sympathetically. "It'll get better when you get used to the place."

I wasn't sure I ever would. One night, after we'd been there about a week, the permanence of my situation descended on me like a falling brick. I started to panic, alone in our small room. So this, I thought to myself, is adventure! This was what I had thought I desired back in New Orleans? What a fool I had been!

Finally, Martin arrived early one night, smelling faintly of musky sweat, fish, and grog, and he slipped into bed beside me.

"No fishing tonight, dearest," he said tenderly, planting a tentative kiss on my cheek. "We're in for a bit of weather."

Then, moving closer, he kissed me delicately on the mouth. Despite his disheveled appearance and the smell of rum on his breath, I was grateful that at least I would not be alone that night.

The feelings for him I remembered from before our marriage were suddenly reawakened as we lay there side by side.

"So, are you over it, then, Emily? The female thing?" he asked softly as his mouth continued to seek mine.

"Yes, it's over," I whispered, moving closer to him.

"So you're up to it, then?"

"Yes," I said, catching my breath in anticipation.

In reply, he moved his hand down, lifted my nightgown while he kissed me a few times. Then he came over and gently separated my legs. I suddenly felt a sharp pain shoot through me as he swiftly drove his body inside me, moving urgently. As I muffled a cry, a drunk began to fumble with his key in our lock. When it failed to open the door, he pounded on our door with his fists. Martin hurriedly finished off. Then he shouted at the door, "You've got the wrong room!" as he rolled off of me. I looked up at him, somewhat confused. My first time making love—was that it?

Martin kissed my forehead quickly. "You'll get used to doing it after a while, dearest," he said, then yawned, gave me another kiss, turned over, and quickly fell asleep.

The drunk in the hallway cursed loudly and began to cough. I heard a dull metallic clang as he stumbled down the hall, hacking into a spittoon. I could hear a sailor singing a crude sea chantey in the distance as he strummed a banjo. A horse trotting by stirred up dust—a fine coral mist I could taste in my mouth—and with that, my misery was complete. Watching Martin sleep, I closed my eyes and released a silent flood of tears, which trickled down my cheeks.

SEVEN

Wreckers' Cay

August 1839

The slave's silence and proximity to me in the lantern room was unnerving. His normal breath was beginning to return, and finally I had to speak. "I hope you don't sleep too soundly. Our posting here calls for lighting the lamps every evening at sunset and to keep them burning brightly until sunrise. It's important to train yourself to be alert to the workings of the light."

"I'm a . . . light sleeper . . . ma'am," he assured me.

I launched into explanations. "On a clear night, our light can be seen for quite a distance out to sea. The reef extends for several miles. If a ship goes aground, it can mean disaster. The ship captains know from their charts that it's here, and they look for the light."

"You ever . . . git any wrecks?"

"Yes," I admitted. "A few accidents have occurred in the past three years, despite our diligence."

I showed him a chart of the area. "I know you can't read their names, but these are the Florida Keys, the tiny islands along here. Earlier charts referred to them as Islas de los

Mártires, or the Martyr Islands, for the suffering of those whose vessels perished. The whole area has coral reefs and shallow waters that can be extremely perilous. It's one of the graveyards of the Atlantic."

He looked at me and smiled bitterly. "Florida Keys? . . . I didn't even know," he said. "Nobody explains things to passengers that is shackled."

"No," I observed drily. "I don't suppose they discussed the route with you."

He looked around the lantern room. "Does this lamp move around?"

"No. It's fixed, like the light twenty-three miles east of here, in Key West."

He was listening carefully. Occasionally, he would nod.

I read over my notes. "To make sure the light can be seen, we must keep the lamps, reflectors, and lanterns very clean. They call light keepers 'wickies' because of our attention to the wicks. We have to trim them frequently, and evenly—usually around midnight. I shall come with you tonight and show you how.

"If the lights go out in the middle of the night, you have to rise from your cozy bed and head for the tower to get them blazing again, even in a storm. And do it quickly. There are ships passing all the time. We use whale oil here. It's very expensive, and the superintendent wants an accounting of how much we use, so this must be logged." I hesitated. "Do you know how to do sums?"

He shook his head.

"Well, then, that's something I'll see to myself."

"Yes, ma'am."

"Carbon has to be cleaned from the reflectors. Every few months, we have to polish the lens with alcohol we keep in that cupboard. Once a year, we give it a cleaning with a compound the superintendent provides. The fuel is kept down in the little oil-storage room.

"We keep this little cot up here for nights when it's stormy and the lights get blown out. When that happens, you can just spend the night here. I keep some blankets in this box over here. And we keep the tools we need up here separately. They're in that case under the workbench."

I wondered what he was thinking. Surely this heaven-sent help was too good to be true. I imagined he was already planning a dash for freedom, possibly stealing one of my boats to escape. But his expression betrayed nothing.

"To keep the light bright, we have to clean the steps, landings, floors, and windows of the tower often, so they're dust-free. The brass and copper fixtures on the apparatus in the lantern room and the window over the little balcony all need to be kept polished.

"That's important, as we never know when the inspectors from the Lighthouse Services will pay us a surprise visit just to check up on me. You will have to hide somewhere when they stop by."

He looked alarmed. "How often do they come?"

I shrugged. "Our dog will give us fair warning when they approach. You'll have time to hide."

"How long do they stay?"

"Not long. They do an inspection of all the lighthouses in Florida a couple of times a year." He absorbed this with a concerned frown. "All they care about is that the light stays lit, and that they don't have to pay me very much," I reassured him. "They have no idea you are here, so they won't be looking for you. And there are many places for you to hide on the island."

He looked dubious, and I could understand what he was feeling. A slave like him was worth money—though he probably wasn't aware of how much. He also knew that if he were found, the lighthouse inspectors would immediately take him to Key West.

"How long you bin doing this by y'self?"

"Since my husband left in May," I replied. "About three months."

This raised yet a new fear. "He comin' back?"

I was reluctant to reveal more about my situation just yet. "I'm not certain," I said vaguely. Then I continued. "As you can see, tending a lighthouse is very demanding."

"What time you turn off the lights?" he asked.

"It varies with the time of year. It's always at sunrise. After you turn them off, you must trim the wicks and get ready for the evening. I'll do it along with you for a few days. Small birds and insects frequently hit the lights out here, and they must be swept up every morning."

He nodded slowly.

I smiled. "I know it's a lot to learn at once, especially if you can't take notes. Can you repeat it all back to me?"

To my surprise, he did, and I had to admit to myself that in just a few minutes he had already picked up a better understanding of the light's workings than Captain Lee or Alfie.

He spoke with an accent I placed around Georgia, without the incomprehensible patois I'd been accustomed to hearing when slaves spoke among themselves. Yet, being a Negro slave, he was not educated. My guess was that he'd spent a lot of time as a handyman or house slave and had picked up a decent command of proper English.

"Good," I said when he'd finished speaking. "Very good."

"That be all for now?" he asked as he started for the stairs.

"Where are you going?"

"Downstairs, to sweep up the birds and insects. Then I thought I'd see if young Timothy and I could start puttin' up the fence around the garden and the playhouse. He told me that your palings had been delivered."

He was actually eager to get started. Secretly I was pleased, but I couldn't help feeling mistrustful. Was he just trying to curry favor?

"I bin shackled so long, ma'am," he explained, "I want to git moving again. Doing things. Git my body strong again."

"Ah." I nodded. Then I realized something curious. "Why were you in chains? My impression was that once down on the slave deck, slaves were always put in irons."

At first, he just lowered his gaze. When he looked back up, his eyes were angry. "Well, ma'am, I reckon I must have been getting real special treatment."

I stiffened. I could not let myself forget that here was a slave possibly so troublesome that he'd been sold off to an illegal slaver so his owner would be rid of him.

I changed the subject. "I don't know if Timothy and Martha told you, but we have no money to pay you anything."

"I have no use for money, ma'am."

"I can give you food and shelter; that is all."

"Yes, I understand," he said. "That's all I need now."

Now? Was this his way of telling me he would not be with us for long? I decided then to get as much work out of him as I could. Perhaps if he felt well treated, he might stay until after I had the baby.

He seemed to read my mind. "Martha and Timothy said you was in a bad way, with another chile coming."

I felt my color rise, but there was no denying my condition. I nodded. "Let's go down, and I'll show you the construction materials for the fence."

Our fencing around the animal pens, garden, and playhouse had blown away during a storm the previous season, and Martin had been waiting for materials to replace it. Captain Lee and Alfie had promised me they'd put the new fence up, but so far they had not done so. By dinnertime, my new assistant had made an excellent start. I watched him working with my son and was pleased to see that, unlike Martin, who preferred to perform such chores alone, he was making sure Timothy was helping.

I invited him to sit at the family table at midday, smiling as I thought of how horrified my sister and Gran would be to see a slave eating with us.

The playhouse seemed to be the best place to lodge him. Martin had constructed a small sleeping alcove with a single bed for Dorothy's rare visits. It was a tiny building with a high ceiling, and there were shelves that Martin installed to keep playthings in order.

Despite its diminutive size, the playhouse at least provided privacy for an adult guest. He was delighted with it, and it occurred to me that he'd probably never had his own quarters. I'd seen enough slave shacks in Louisiana to know how cramped and unsanitary they could be, with ten or so people in a room nowhere near as big or bright as our playhouse.

After several days, his hard work had, despite my original misgivings, impressed me, and I was beginning to relax more around him. I still did not trust him entirely—he was a runaway slave, after all—but my relief at having an extra pair of willing hands to help at the light made me feel much more kindly toward him.

"What do they call you?" I asked after dinner one day.

"They usually call me Hannibal."

Hannibal was a typical slave name. Owners had different ways of naming Negroes. For some, it was customary to give them monikers that could be given to pets; others named them after cities. Still others gave them names of exalted persons in antiquity, a practice that poked fun at the slave.

"You have no other name, then? Just Hannibal?"

"I have my African name, which my mother gave me. That would be Dembi; it means 'peace' in her dialect."

"That's actually a nice name," I said, smiling. "Peace. But I think since you're starting a new life here, we should give you a regular name." I thought of several possible names, mostly of politicians I had heard of. When I thought of the Virginia law-maker, John Tyler, I said. "Perhaps I should call you John, af-ter John Tyler of Virginia. Or John Dembi?"

He smiled at me for the first time, revealing his even white teeth. "John Tyler? Ain't he a slave owner?"

"Well, yes, but John is a fine name."

He paused. "Seems to me, ma'am, you're doing the same thing my master did."

"Not at all," I replied. But I felt the heat of a blush creeping around my neck. "I just thought you'd like to be rid of the name Hannibal."

He thought for a minute, and I could tell the idea of choos-ing his own name amused him.

"I kind o'like the name Andrew," he said.

"Andrew? Yes, that's a good name."

"How about . . . Andrew Dembi Tyler?"

"Perfect," I said, relieved, for I'd begun to find it awkward referring to him as "the Negro," "the slave," or nothing at all.

"The children will address you as Andrew"—I paused—"unless you would prefer Mr. Tyler."

"Mr. Tyler?" he repeated incredulously. He laughed out loud, and I was surprised to find myself laughing for the first time in many weeks. Even little Hannah, braiding the hair of her rag doll at my feet and understanding nothing of our con-versation, laughed with us.

Andrew reached down and picked her up. "Hey there, you laughin' at Mr. Tyler, missy?" he asked playfully. She rewarded him with a happy smile and reached up to kiss him, giving him a peck on the right cheek, then on the left. After that, she reached over to rub noses.

I felt my blood run cold. My laughter stopped. "Come, Hannah," I said, picking her up. "It's time for your bath."

EIGHT

Wreckers' Cay

September 1839

After the exhausting months of doing everything myself, having Andrew's help was like a vacation. Apart from having to cook his food, he was no trouble to have around. He cleaned his own quarters, did his own laundry, and when he completed one chore, he looked for another.

He tried not to intrude on our family time, staying in the background. Rising early, he made a special effort to help even with those chores I had assigned myself, and he was particularly adept at tending the vegetable garden. He found joy in weeding, planting, hoeing, or picking insects off plants. He rigged up a scarecrow with some of Martin's clothes and a hat to keep away plundering birds, like the hawks that swooped down to snatch baby chicks.

When he found free time, he wandered the island, looking for herbs. Our vegetation was different from that of Georgia, but he felt that some of our plants were of value medicinally, and he tied bunches of them to rafters in the playhouse to dry.

My children had all adjusted to Andrew's presence, and over time I learned to accept his interaction with them. Whereas

Martin had indulged in parental scolding, Andrew was more of a friend to them. Martha and Timothy often sat under the mahogany tree with him, chatting about his past life, and even asking him questions about slavery. Little Hannah adored Andrew unconditionally. Her pretty little face would light up at the sight of him. She had been the one who'd missed her father most, and it seemed she now accepted Andrew as his replacement. She had turned three several weeks after his arrival, and I realized her hearing problem was beginning to take its toll. She was still not speaking clearly, and I was coming to understand that the fever of her infancy had slowed her in other ways, delaying her walking and speech—everyday things my other children had achieved much earlier. These delays saddened me, but Andrew sensed her need for patience and attention. Often I found them together in the garden, where he would be showing her how to dig properly and pull up weeds. He never shouted, and always repeated instructions gently when needed. I noticed, too, that he was even beginning to learn a rudimentary kind of sign language with her.

On the day Captain George Lee and Alfie Dillon next came with our supplies, Andrew hid in the playhouse, and we took turns taking him food and water. The men unloaded our supplies and I served them tea.

"How'd ja get that fence up?" the captain inquired. He was studying our new enclosure, and I grew nervous because in doing so, he was approaching the playhouse.

"Timothy and I put it up," I said, lying. "Can I offer you some more tea?"

Lee was staring at the fence in silence. "A mighty fine job," he finally muttered, testing its sturdiness. He looked at me. "We were going to do that for you one of these days, Alfie and m'self."

"Thank you." I smiled brightly. "But as you can see, we are managing well."

He glanced up at the lighthouse tower, its clean glass sparkling, and nodded. He seemed disappointed. Or was that look one of . . . suspicion?

Hannah ran over to us and tugged at the captain's sleeve. She pointed with her other hand at the playhouse, chattering excitedly. Alarmed, I picked her up quickly and kissed her cheek to distract her.

"She's a mite retarded, ain't she?" he said, looking critically at my little angel. "She don't make no sense when she talks."

I bristled, annoyed at his rudeness. "She was just telling you about her new doll," I replied defensively. "She might be less articulate than most, but she is quite intelligent."

Captain Lee simply grunted. With nothing more to say, the pair left, leaving me the *Key West Enquirer,* a letter from my sister, Dorothy, and our supplies. We then hurried to the playhouse to let Andrew know they were gone. Leaving his hot, stuffy room, he headed for the ocean to cool off before supper.

While his old scarring remained, the recent wounds across Andrew's back had healed nicely. With good food and grueling physical work, he was filling out and developing muscle again. He had not as yet told me his story, and I had not probed.

It was his good cheer that made me aware of his excellent baritone. One afternoon, he began to sing while he worked, and as his work on the fence continued, he moved from gospel hymns to old African lullabies, which, I suspected, had been forbidden on the plantation.

When he burst into song, the children would stop and listen. And even though her hearing was impaired, Hannah would lead a cheer. Martin and I had always applauded our encouragement when Martha was at her piano, or when Timothy played his violin, and now Hannah would clap for Andrew, dancing back and forth on her chubby feet, laughing as he sang—as though he was singing just for her.

Soon after Andrew arrived, I sensed his presence one day as I taught the children at the worktable in the cookhouse. While Martha and Timothy were excellent readers, my attempts to teach Hannah her letters were not getting very far.

I turned around and saw that Andrew had stolen in quietly, hat in hand, listening intently while I explained a point of grammar to Martha.

"Yes? What is it Andrew?"

"I was wonderin' . . ." he began, fingering his hat.

"Yes?"

"I was wonderin' if you'd consider . . . teachin' me. I'd like to learn to read them books," he said, gesturing to the bookshelves. "And to form my letters . . . so's I kin write."

I stood up, startled. In all my years in Louisiana and Key West, I had never met adult slaves interested in becoming literate. But then, had I ever bothered to explore the subject with any of them?

"And I'd like to know how to do my sums," he persisted. "For the log and the oil and such."

I considered this. If he could look after the log, it would be one less thing I'd have to do. Still, I hesitated. "I'm not sure. I have much to do as it is. I'd have to design a separate program for you. Let me think about this," I said.

He nodded, put his hat on his head, and went back out to work.

Later that night, drifting off to sleep, I asked "Martin" what he thought.

"What harm, Emily?" he asked. "After all, the poor devil has been working hard. Why not give him some education?"

The troubling memory of the literate Nat Turner and his rebellion was still fresh in every southern mind. Teaching a slave to read and write was considered not only unsafe, it was unlawful. In Louisiana, the punishment was a year in prison if you were caught. But then, wasn't I already breaking the law by harboring a runaway slave? Grandpère's words echoed in my mind I repeated them now to Martin: "Best to keep 'em ignorant. Start teaching a Negro to read and such, and you'll have a worthless Negro. He'll be no help to you at all."

"Emily, forget all that. You're not paying him, so it's the least you can do to compensate him. Do it." I repeated them now to Martin.

I scoffed. In life, Martin had been every bit as skeptical of educating slaves as my grandfather. As I turned over to settle into sleep, it occurred to me that for the first time I was thinking about my husband in the past tense.

After breakfast, the next morning, I told Andrew I would school him. I produced some paper and pencils and spent an hour teaching him his alphabet. He listened intently, repeating everything. I showed him how to form the first few letters and how to spell out his name. I left him with simple homework, which he eagerly accepted, and in the days that followed he worked hard at his letters, quickly mastering the alphabet and forming small words, then larger ones. Soon he began to ask questions about history and geography, and though I had hesitated initially, his eagerness was just so refreshing, I found myself teaching him more than I'd planned. He loved maps most of all and was eager to read the names of places.

"Show me Africa," he would say. "Show me the different places and how you spell them. Europe . . . America . . . Georgia . . . the Caribbean Islands . . ."

Then one morning, he said, "Show me the slave routes."

I froze. "Perhaps," I said gently, "we should finish our lesson for today?"

He agreed. But a few days later, he again pressed me about the slave routes, and the discussion I dreaded became unavoidable.

At first, I tried to keep my answer vague: "I think they originated in European ports. And later, from some of the northern American states."

"And from there?"

"The traders would go to West Africa and trade manufactured goods there."

"In exchange for slaves."

"Well, yes," I admitted. "For people. A workforce."

"Then where?" He was looking steadily at me. "To America?"

"Yes. They put them on ships and sailed to America and the Caribbean to sell them, or to trade the African people for . . . things."

"What things?"

"Well, I don't know exactly," I said irritably, wanting to end this conversation. "Sugar, I suppose, and coffee, tobacco, rice. And cotton, of course. Lots of cotton. Indigo . . . Rum . . ."

"Where did rum come from?"

"I've always heard that it was invented by slaves working on a sugar plantation in Barbados. They boiled the dregs of the canes and turned that into molasses . . . and then . . . distilled it somehow."

He thought about this. "So, the slaves invented rum . . . and then the white people used their invention to trade it for more African slaves?"

He was relentless. I sighed. "Really, Andrew, I'm hardly an authority. . . ." I decided to change the subject. "You know, you must tell me your story sometime," I said, closing our geography book and clearing the worktable. "You've never told me how you happened to be on that slave ship with those Africans. Or why you were whipped."

He looked thoughtful. "I was a freed slave," he said finally. "I was grabbed while walking on a street near the port of Savannah. They clubbed me over the head, chained me, and sold me; when I woke up, I was on a slaver goin' to Cuba."

I looked at him in surprise. It was possible. I had heard of instances where a freed slave would be pressed in a grog shop and knocked unconscious, only to wake up shackled on a ship bound for a plantation somewhere in the Caribbean.

"You were free?"

"No. I *am* free," he replied, correcting me.

When he rose and headed off to his quarters in the playhouse, I was left feeling oddly stimulated by our discussion. Had he been freed? Most slaves who gained manumission had benevolent owners. The scars on his back told me this was not the case, for clearly, he had been badly used. I found myself wondering idly about his past. Had there been a particular woman in his life? Was he a father? He was certainly good with children. Had he been with many women? But then I forced such questions from my mind. Why on earth should I care to know such things? Andrew was an excellent worker. That was all that should concern me.

NINE

Key West

1829

The early days of my marriage were a huge disappointment. It was one thing to live in reduced circumstances; I had resigned myself to that. But as it turned out, I was not only poor; I was completely at the mercy of my husband: I was his property, just as Eurydice belonged to my grandparents. And I was stuck in Key West, impossibly far from my family and friends.

Weeks passed. I had no one to talk with except Mrs. Mallory, and she was always busy. Martin's overnight fishing trips had resumed, leaving me to quake with fear under the counterpane when other roomers rattled my doorknob. They knew my husband was often away, and did so not accidentally.

"Open the door," one would regularly call out on his nightly return from the grog shops. "Yer husband ain't around to know!"

"Let me in, darling. I've got something for ye," another would cajole. And then I would hear his lascivious chuckle as he made his way to his room. Sometimes it would take a loud scolding from Mrs. Mallory to keep them quiet. "Sure, they mean nothing by it," she assured me one morning after I complained.

"If ever you opened the door, they'd be tongue-tied. Pay them no mind, child. They're just out to tease you."

Still, the whole situation was more than I could bear. My only contact with the rest of the world I had left behind was the arrival of the *Isabelle,* a ship that brought mail to Key West twice a month via the post office in Charleston.

"I hate this place," I admitted one day. "I want to go home. I miss my family. And I miss New Orleans."

Martin ignored me, but I kept on: "There are no shops in this settlement. And the people are so crude! And there are no recitals or concerts . . . no theater."

"Here now," he said at first, "give it time, dearest. Key West will be an important port someday. Quality folks are moving in."

"But do we really want to live in this tiny, dreary place? Why don't we move to some town on the mainland of Florida?"

He looked at me as if I were a stupid child. "What town? There's St. Augustine, and some primitive Seminole Indian villages, and there's Key West. That's all! Do you want to live up with the Indians?" He broke into a laugh. "Yes, that would be interesting to see: you, fending off those Seminole braves with a parasol, dressed in your frilly petticoats and fine New Orleans gowns!"

I was about to vent my feelings further, but he gave me a stern look—I had never seen my husband glare in such a way before. "Anyway," he said, "this is the way it is. Get used to it and stop acting like a pampered little rich girl."

I felt like I'd been slapped. How little, I was starting to ask myself, did I know this man who'd so easily won my heart? In Key West, his ready smile and humor had virtually disappeared. In its place were now a firmly set jaw and a stubborn determination. It was to be the first of many such arguments.

I eventually learned to hide my unhappiness and tried to appear cheerful, at least during the hours Martin was home. My feelings for him had turned ambivalent, but I was desperate for his company. We'd sometimes take short walks together, carefully sidestepping horse manure, chickens, stray dogs, and feral cats. I tried to make these walks happy events, but inevitably I found something negative to comment upon before I could stop myself. When I learned the island had been bought a few years previously from a Spaniard named Juan Salas by American businessman John Simonton for about two thousand dollars, I remarked tartly, "I think he paid too much."

The Louisiana Purchase seemed like a good decision to me. I could even understand the Americans' interest in the Florida Territory. But acquiring these tiny islands south of Florida made no sense.

"Please, Emily." Martin sighed. "Leave off all this grumbling. It is becoming annoying."

I learned that before the Spaniards, the islands had been inhabited by Indians, most of whom had coalesced by then into one tribe, the Seminoles. There were pirates, too, although most had been driven back to the Caribbean.

Yet for all the talk about Indians and pirates, the major threat to marine traffic in the Florida Straits was one not of man's doing at all, but the natural configuration of coral rock surrounding the islands.

"They've been slow about building lighthouses this far south; ships are still running aground on the reefs," Martin told me once as we walked near the port.

"How terrible," I murmured.

He looked at me incredulously and laughed. "Terrible? Hardly. That's why we have such a thriving wrecking and salvaging industry here. We go out to help, and lay claim to the valuable goods aboard crippled ships. It's what puts food on our tables."

"But . . . isn't that a form of piracy?" I asked.

He looked annoyed. "Have you understood nothing of what

I've been telling you these past months? We don't take anything we're not entitled to. It all goes through the courts. We share the proceeds of the cargo sales, usually about twenty-five percent of the value of the goods. And believe me, with the risks we sometimes take, we deserve any spoils awarded to us!"

Although I was not about to challenge my husband's word on the moral probity of wreckers, I was relieved at least that the United States, with its navy, was in charge of the island. At least that seemed like a positive thing at the time.

We had been in Key West for several weeks when I received a letter from Gran, my paternal grandmother, Hester Dinsmore of Harbour Island. It was delivered to me by Martin's friend, Captain George Lee, just in from a Bahamian fishing trip.

"A fine lady, your grandmother," he said as he handed it to me. "Gave me tea. And told me she's moving down here."

"Gran is moving here?" I was sure he was joking. "To Key West?"

"Aye. She is that."

"How did you come to meet my grandmother?"

"A business venture," he said importantly. "Word came to me from a shipowner that a cultured lady in Harbour Island was looking for property in Key West. I went to see her about the piece of land my missus's father owns on Caroline Street. She's looking to buy it. That's when she gave me this letter for you."

How odd, I thought, for my father's mother to move to our settlement. Of those few settlers who had come, many were English subjects who'd lived in pre-Revolutionary America. Loyal to King George, most of them had moved to British-controlled territories like Canada and the Bahamas after the American patriots drove the British out.

Gran's parents had been among the British Loyalists living in Charleston before the war. Outspoken in their condemnation of America's breakaway from England, they felt constrained to leave the country under George Washington's fledgling Continental government. Unwilling to face the weather in Canada, they had chosen the Bahamas, where they raised my grandmother. There she met my grandfather Dinsmore, a British official in Harbour Island, and married him.

I remembered how sharp-tongued Gran could be. She had bitterly disapproved of my marriage, and had made her views known to me in no uncertain terms. But circumstances, it seemed, had chastened my grandmother's feistiness. She now had friends leaving the Bahamas. Accustomed to a warm subtropical climate, some were heading to Key West. With their departure from places like Green Turtle Cay, Spanish Wells, Marsh Harbour, and Harbour Island, the fear of being alone had become a powerful incentive for her to follow.

"I've decided to move to Key West," her letter read. "It seems like a good idea, with friends going over, and you living there and all." She had added, "Perhaps you and I can get to know each other a little better now."

Although this news did not please me initially, I was so lonely and homesick, any family member would at least be one more than I had now.

Gran lost no time. She arrived just a few weeks later. Martin and I helped her find a small house on Front Street, which she rented while a shipwright she had known in the Bahamas built her a splendid residence on the Caroline Street property she bought from Captain Lee's father-in-law.

Over the next few months, I did get to know my grandmother better. She introduced me to her elderly Bahamian friends, and because I was bored, I would join them for tea and card games. In those days, Martin was still very busy with his fishing and wrecking jobs, and we continued to live at Mrs. Mallory's.

My husband, I was to discover, was very good at working with his hands, a fact not lost on our landlady. "If you could

help me fix up the place, I'd give you your room for free," she
told him one day.

Martin considered this. "Very well . . . I'll do it," he said.

"That'd be wonderful," she replied. Together, they worked
out what repairs she required. In the following weeks, during the few hours I normally had spent with my husband
when he was not off fishing or salvaging, he was now off doing
repairs.

Martin also had considerable imagination, always thinking
about designing and building a house for us. At certain moments, his eyes would brighten and he would become very animated, sketching designs in the air for me.

"The cookhouse will go here . . . my workshop here . . . our
bedchamber on this side . . . and the children's bedchambers
and playroom over there . . . the privies here . . ."

The site where we would build the home consumed him,
and on the evenings he was home, he would take my arm and
escort me on walks to show me land he had scouted. We spoke
gently with each other during these times, and I was grateful
to see glimpses once more of the attentive handsome man I
had first met on that terrace in New Orleans.

Our quest for the perfect plot was restricted to a very small
neighborhood on the island. With the Gulf of Mexico on one
side, and the Atlantic Ocean on the other, the island was only
about two miles wide by four miles long. Most of it was unin-
habitable, with swampy mangroves thick with mosquitoes.
There were indented pockets in coral rock everywhere, with
rotting fish, flotsam, and sea grass trapped inside concave pools.

John Whitehead, the mayor of the settlement, hired his
brother William to plot the streets in the higher, northern
part of town, near the busy natural harbor on the Gulf. At
that time, Eaton Street backed onto a forested area where, using slave labor, the mayor ran a prosperous lumbering operation to the south, near the ocean.

With access to freshwater from numerous cisterns, elegant new homes like my grandmother's were being built, mostly along Front Street and on Whitehead. A business district was also taking shape there.

The heavily forested areas were of great concern for Key Westers, as hostilities with Seminole Indians were accelerating. The villagers felt vulnerable, fearing that the Indians would skim down from other Keys in their canoes, circle the island, slip inconspicuously onto the southern beaches, and plan attacks on the village.

A lagoon on the western part of the island meandered into the middle of the busy port downtown, becoming a dreadful insect-infested tidal pond. A footbridge over it extended to become the town's main street, a partly bricked road known as Duval Street. At high tide and during storms, the pond regularly flooded the downtown area.

Because the settlement was eager to grow, some of the plots of land, usually just big enough for a tiny house, were actually being given away to lure new workers to the area. These were not acceptable to Martin, who was willing to wait and pay money for a larger plot, for he wanted a good-size home and a garden.

"I've found us the perfect spot," he announced excitedly one day. "Pardon Greene is selling off a big plot just off Whitehead Street. It's the extension of Front Street next to the navy base, overlooking the water. Fourteen acres!"

I could hardly fathom such space. "But that's much too big for us!"

Martin looked delighted. "I have a plan—pineapples! A few years of good crops and we can easily earn our money back."

I considered this. "How much is it?"

He hesitated. "Just one thousand dollars. An incredible bargain."

"You jest! One thousand dollars? Why, that's half what you

said John Simonton paid for the whole island!" I was appalled, for although he involved me infrequently concerning our finances, I knew that we had not a fraction of that put by. "Even combining what remains of my dowry with your savings, we still cannot afford to purchase that land and build a home."

This put him in a despondent mood. Finally, I said half-heartedly, "I could write to my grandfather."

"By the time he'd get your letter and send us a check, it would be sold," he said glumly.

"Then I'll ask Gran if we can borrow it from her."

Gran readily agreed. And though usually too proud even to consider such a loan, this time Martin agreed to accept her help. He bought the land and immediately ordered materials to begin construction.

I was of two minds about our new property. The idea of getting out of the boardinghouse and having a real home was appealing, but the plot was more land than we needed or could practically care for. And in truth, I was still hoping we might move back to New Orleans someday. Putting down roots meant I'd be stuck in Key West forever.

Over time, I conceded that my husband had been correct in his assessment of the harbor's value. Shipping was becoming a big business in the port. Great numbers of vessels traveled weekly through the Gulf of Mexico and the Florida Straits, especially from nearby Havana; Key West rapidly began to prosper. Heavy traffic in the shipping lanes meant plenty of work for everyone in the settlement, servicing and supplying vessels. Martin was always busy fishing, wrecking, or working at the boatyard.

He divided the rest of his time between Mrs. Mallory's repairs and the cultivation of our own plot, on which he built a charming frame home—I was more than happy with the Greek Revival style he chose.

"Do you like this?" he asked me one day. "I'll whitewash it and decorate it with gingerbread trim. And add wraparound verandas."

He had it all decided already.

With all the unexpected challenges I faced early in my marriage, intimacy remained by far the biggest disappointment. Martin was always tired, usually happy just to flop into bed and sleep. Sex seemed like just a necessity, and it was over with quickly. I had notions of improving the state of things after our shaky start, but these were soon squelched. Fatigue made Martin cranky. And since the only time he was truly happy now was when he was building, he was continually off working. At home, he was difficult to live with, so we settled into a routine of devoting five or ten minutes a week to this unsavory act, performed in lifted nightclothes.

One evening in January, Martin returned to the boardinghouse in unusually high spirits. "The house is done!" he announced.

"It's ready?" I clasped my hands together with delight. "My own house!"

"You deserve it, dearest," he said affectionately as he took both my hands in his. "You've been very patient with me, and with living at the boardinghouse all this time. I reckon we can start to move some of our things over there in just a few days. And we must start attending auctions to find furnishings."

I leaned into him and kissed him. "This will be a wonderful year for us." In my mind, I was thinking about how I would decorate one of the rooms to accommodate a baby, for I had an announcement of my own. "I am in a family way, Martin."

He drew away and held me at arm's length, registering shock. Then he smiled broadly. "Are you serious? A baby?"

I nodded. "Yes, we must ready not one bedroom, but two."

"Why . . . why, that's indeed good news, Emily. Wonder-ful, in fact! Yes, this *will* be an exciting year."

The prospect of a child was yet another tie that would bind us to the growing village of Key West, so he joyfully welcomed this news. I, on the other hand, as thrilled as I was with our new house, felt a certain ambivalence, for I saw every child I might bear as a weighty anchor that would keep me from flee-ing my island prison.

Although Martin's pineapple crop grew vigorously, harvesting the fruit was excruciatingly hard work. When we married, my grandfather in New Orleans had offered me a slave named Caliban as part of my dowry. To my surprise, Martin wanted no part of having a Negro as part of our household—even as a slave—so we had declined the offer. Grandpère had shaken his head, and instead, he gifted us a set of encyclopedias, which were in their own way a help, providing information on the various cultivars of pineapples and how to care for them. But at harvesttime, when his prickly fruits required handling, Mar-tin rued his decision to reject Caliban. We could not afford to buy slaves of our own, and in any case, very few were available for sale in Key West. Instead, we made do with renting them by the day from Key West slave owners.

Thus, we settled into a life in the new village of Key West. I was sure we would remain in our lovely home forever and that the only changes ahead of us would be the children to come and the future of growing old together.

TEN

Wreckers' Cay

November 1839

My latest pregnancy, coupled with Andrew's arrival on the island, had turned me into a rather secretive person. The effort it took to disguise my condition and make sure Andrew took to hiding in time when outsiders approached our island was wearing on me. And it disturbed me that my children were having to learn to tell untruths, as well.

Of my pregnancy, I told only Dorothy, and swore her to secrecy. She had been appalled to learn of my condition—still thinking I was actually doing all the work at the light myself—and wrote to me that I should return to Key West at once:

You are quite mad, Emily. How on earth are you to continue with all your own responsibilities while nursing a new baby? Martha and Timothy are only children, after all. But of course I shall help you—I shall come this last time, but please consider winding up your affairs there and returning to Key West with me afterward. I will contact Mr. Pendleton to ask him about a replacement, if you wish. I cannot bear to think of you alone out there on that wretched island! Besides, your children need to be in a regular school, and to hear the word of God on Sundays.

The last paragraph raised my hackles. Although Dorothy and I had gone to the Ursuline convent on Chartres Street in New Orleans, our religious convictions had become very disparate. She had embraced her husband Tom Farrell's Anglican faith with great devotion, whereas the lack of a church in Key West—and the total absence of any organized rituals here at Wreckers' Cay—had radically altered my own fervor. Over time, I had moved to being a deist, or perhaps a pantheist; I wasn't sure what the difference was.

I now intuited God's divine presence everywhere, and with all my senses. From the moment I rose in the mornings, I saw it in the continuity of the bucolic life we enjoyed on the island. I could feel it sweep through me in the balmy humidity that met me at dawn, the freshness in the air before the sun rose to its apex at noon. I could see it every evening in the fiery sunsets that rimmed clouds with gold and purple in the twilight afterglow, and in the brilliant stars that stabbed the indigo sky.

God's touch was in the wings of colorful butterflies and in our bougainvillea. God's scent was in the jasmine and frangipani that we grew on the island. The word of God was not in in the oration of a preacher, but in the splashes of the pelicans and gulls diving, the calls of mockingbirds, the hums and chirps of insects and tree frogs, and the gentle winds rustling in palm fronds.

When I prayed—and since Martin's disappearance, I prayed often—it was to this benign spirit out there on the water.

Martin had done much to make life comfortable for us on Wreckers' Cay. In the few years we had been there, even though the lighthouse keeper's home was government property and we had no pride of ownership, he had nonetheless modified it to accommodate our family. He had enlarged our latrines, added a chicken coop, rabbit hutches, a smokehouse, and a small barn to house our little goats.

An oil-storage shed was needed next to the tower. Then he had constructed a washhouse, cleverly rerouting water from the existing cistern to the little building with a copper tube so we could heat it in tubs for laundry and bathing. He had built our storage house with pine siding, and even carved some lacy gingerbread for trim.

The island already abounded with native fruit trees like custard apple, sapodilla, mamey, and guava, the seeds of which had probably been delivered by droppings from birds many years before our arrival. Martin supplemented them with plantings of Key lime, mangoes, papayas, pineapples, breadfruit, carambola, and avocado in our garden. Bushes of Surinam cherry, carissa, and sea grape yielded other fruit I could preserve. We kept chickens, so we had plenty of eggs and, of course, poultry to eat.

There were rabbits, which the children adored, and yielded up for our sustenance only with difficulty and copious tears. The goats supplied fresh milk, and we had a big vegetable garden. I blessed Andrew's arrival, for he was adept at gardening, and showed great sensitivity in slaughtering the animals when it was time, removing them to the lagoon area, where the children would not hear the proceedings.

Fishing around our island had always yielded far more fish than we could use at any one time. Timothy showed Andrew how to smoke surplus meat and fish—a skill that Martin had taught him.

Martha would join them in diving for conch, the mainstay of Key West and Bahamian diets. They would catch crayfish and tasty pink-and-black stone crabs. Occasionally, the light keeper from Garden Key, in the Dry Tortugas, would stop off with a catch of deep-sea creatures like dolphin fish, cobia, mackerel, turtle, tuna, or even shark, sharing them with us in exchange for some of our garden produce. Andrew would happily clean the fish and cook them for us over an open fire outside.

Yet I still relied on our provisions from Key West for many basic foods. And as my stores of rice, grits, beans, sugar, and flour became depleted, I would find myself looking anxiously out toward the water, hoping for some sign of the worthy Captain Lee, who was my lifeline to Key West.

In the months after Martin's disappearance, before Andrew's arrival, I found myself anticipating the captain's arrival as never before. Besides parcels of clothing and books he delivered from my sister, Lee had begun to bring me small presents that he purchased at his own expense: a new utensil for the cookhouse and, one week, a new Bible. For the children, he brought small toys.

He would also bring music sheets for Martha and me to play on the piano, or for Timothy to learn on his violin. Often, he brought me cotton fabric remnants, which I sewed into clothing for the children. Lee had spread the word about Martin's disappearance and delivered many letters of cheer and sympathy from friends and family in Key West, New Orleans, and the Bahamas. I treasured these words of comfort, even as I thought them premature, since Martin had not yet been found, nor his death confirmed.

The captain also offered to bring a marker for Martin's grave, as yet unoccupied. But to me, this signaled a finality I was not yet ready to accept.

When Martin was still with us, he and the captain usually visited for a short time on the veranda, drinking Cuban rum. Sometimes their voices would drop to a low hush, followed by loud guffaws and an embarrassed smile from Martin as he looked to see if I had overheard.

After his disappearance, Captain Lee and Alfie started spending longer periods at Wreckers' Cay. Initially, I delighted in having them to dinner, just to have other adults to talk to. They always volunteered to take over the light on their visits, but on the basis of their initial performance, I did not relinquish this chore to them.

The delivery of provisions to lighthouse families kept the pair busy a couple of times a month. But they were still primarily fisherman who supplemented their income by salvaging at wreck sites. It was clear that wrecking, with its substantial profits, was their greatest love, and Lee was continually talking about it. "As Martin well knew, wreckin's a fine business," the captain often said to me, usually over dinner. "Mostly, we happen upon the wrecks when we're out fishing, then head for the reef to lay our claim—" Then he caught himself. "And . . . to help out where we can, o'course."

I'd heard all this before, but the captain delighted in repeating it, overlaying the procedure with color. "Often the spoils are such that we have to send for help in town. When they call out 'Wreck ashore!' the lot of them head for the water, and never mind the weather or what they're doin' at the time."

The scene he described was legendary. There were many tales of Key West judges abandoning the bench, or ministers leaving the pulpit in mid-sermon when the shouts came in like a clarion call. The rush to get to a lucrative wreck first was tantamount to a stampede.

As their visits continued in Martin's absence, I found myself more relaxed with Alfie Dillon, who, unlike the captain, did not continually urge me to leave Wreckers' Cay. When they were leaving, Captain Lee usually pressed my hand and repeated what he'd said that first time he brought Martin's skiff back to the island: "A lot of people would love to see you come back to Key West, Miss Emily."

My answer was ever the same: "And how would I live?"

"Miss Hester has that fine big house, with plenty a'room for a big family, and lots of help. Three or four darkies from South

Carolina, if I'm not mistaken. Can't keep 'em busy enough. Rents 'em out t'other folks who can't afford to buy Negroes th'selves."

During one such visit, his gaze was steady on my face. He added, "A fine-looking woman like y'self should have no trouble finding a gentleman who'd have her."

His suggestion was so tasteless that I laughed out loud. "I rather doubt that, Captain George. And are you forgetting that I'm still married?" It occurred to me then that his gifts were not just gratuitous. I made a mental note to steer future conversations in other, less personal directions. I withdrew my hand, which he seemed to press longer than was necessary. "Godspeed," I said. "I will pray for your safe trip back to Key West. I am most appreciative of all you've both done."

He waved away my gratitude. "Believe me, Miss Emily, it's my pleasure. Always good to see you, ma'am. And your charming family, of course."

With Andrew's arrival, however, all this conviviality was about to change.

ELEVEN

Key West

1829–1836

In the early days, Martin fretted continually about money. Most of his income came from crewing on fishing boats and sporadic salvaging at the wrecks, supplemented by extra earnings from repairing boats in port. Wrecks were occurring with growing frequency. The reef at the south of the island stretched seven miles out, and with only the Sand Key lighthouse to guide passing ships, the increase in marine traffic meant that many unwary vessels ran aground. Wrecking was poised to become a very big business, and it was a highly competitive one.

There were many tales of dishonorable sea captains bruited about. Stories circulated of lights placed strategically on ships moored on the reef to look like they were in a safe channel, luring unsuspecting vessels from the safety of their own course.

"That's utter nonsense," snapped Martin when I once mentioned this. We were visiting the home of our friends, the Watlingtons, and he turned to the other men at the table. "She doesn't know what she is on about. Every wrecking captain we know is honest and hardworking."

"Aye," added Captain George Lee indignantly. "You'll not find that practice hereabouts among any boat captains of our acquaintance."

Another sea captain, William Loxley, who had studied maritime law in Boston, agreed: "Anyone who'd resort to a Judas ship in the Keys would be subject to laws governing piracy, and severely dealt with. The rest of us would ostracize such a man; he'd never get to work around Key West after that."

"Aye," agreed our host, Francis Watlington. "And why would anyone do that? We put our own vessels in jeopardy when we go to the exact dangerous spots of those ships that run aground. And mark me, there's no insurance on wrecking vessels, either."

In spite of the fact that it sounded legal, there was something ghoulish to me in the act of hovering around, watching a distressed crew try to save a hapless ship. Yet I said nothing; in Key West, I usually found it wise to keep my opinions to myself.

"Who is in charge of such operations?" I asked Martin on our way home from the social.

"The wrecking master. He's the first sea captain to arrive on the scene. It's up to him to direct the operation. If anybody on board is hurt, his first duty is to get them ashore to be looked at by the doctor."

"And then?"

"He might also send for friends in Key West to help unload cargo from the boats."

"Do you aspire to be such a wrecking captain?"

He shook his head. "No. I don't own a ship. And even if I did, when would I have time to attend court sessions, with my many jobs? No. I'm content to be one of the help. As part of the crew, I'm well enough paid when Judge Webb adjudicates the cargo and awards us our percentage."

It's an ill wind, the saying goes, that doesn't blow someone some good. The growth of the wrecking industry stimulated Key West's economy, and the village flourished with many other businesses. Numerous warehouses were being built to store the booty from wrecks. Home-furnishing stores and pawnshops also started up. Dry-goods store owners like Alexander Patterson became auctioneers, doing a good business as buyers flocked in.

Wreckers took all manner of cargo from disabled vessels— from loads of ice or coal to livestock or expensive spices. It was no longer legal to transport slaves, but occasionally the wreckers could happen along such treasure as silver and valuable jewelry. And the local villagers, who had no other way to acquire such luxuries, quickly snapped up cargo like furniture, art, lace, silks, and fine European artifacts. In this way, Martin and I even managed to acquire a piano.

When my children arrived, Martha and then Timothy, we made the transition to an active family. My grandmother lavished attention on the babies, often vying with Ellen Mallory for the chance to look after them. I'd had very little contact with small children before my marriage, but when I held my first baby, Martha, an instinct I did not previously imagine I possessed welled up from deep inside me. As I placed her gently to my breast to nourish her, I knew in that moment, I would treasure and defend my precious child in the face of any odds.

Now, when I thought of Martin, he had become for me a provider. We still came together once or twice a week, but I had long stopped hoping for these encounters to bring any pleasure or romance; I merely started to view his body as the conduit that could fill my own with new life.

I sought out newcomers with babies or young children. At this juncture, Bahamian wreckers and a few professional men were beginning to trickle into town. A number of them brought their wives, as promises of sudden wealth from salvaging ventures were attracting residents from all over, including the Caribbean islands. Against a background of this diverse texture, Key West began to grow and truly thrive.

An important segment of Key West's early settlers were those affluent Americans from southern states and New England who'd been involved in the original purchase and subsequent partitioning of the island. These "quality folk," as Martin had called them, lived in stately new homes, waited on by slaves, and enjoyed Key West's weather.

It was a young attorney from this group who swept my sister, Dorothy, off her feet. We'd been in Key West for about three years when my sister came to visit us for a month after Timothy's birth. (Martha was by then an active toddler.) I had invited my sister to be Timothy's godmother, and was delighting in her visit after such a long time apart.

St. Paul's Church was not yet completed, so the christening took place in Gran's garden, performed by Martin's cousin, a priest from St. John's Anglican Church in Harbour Island. A few days later, we held a welcome reception for Dorothy and invited all our friends. Mayor John Whitehead brought along a distant cousin of his, Tom Farrell, who was visiting from New York City.

Dorothy set her cap for Whitehead's cousin as soon as she saw him. Pulling me aside in the cookhouse as I fussed with food and supervised Gran's servants, she asked, "Sugar, who is that handsome, charmin' man?" She took out her fan, adjusted her hair, and smiled. "Do introduce me to him."

I did so, and watched with amusement as Dorothy brought to bear the full power of her southern-belle charm. She was just eighteen, the age I was when I met Martin, and had blossomed into a real beauty, making the most of her blond curls, blue eyes, and creamy ivory skin.

At twenty-five, Tom Farrell was strikingly handsome, a tall man with dark hair and the pale skin we'd come to expect in northern visitors. His jawline was as firm as his handshake; he had deep blue eyes and a large mustache. And here in Key West, where rough, sun-scorched men cared nothing of their appearance, he stood out like a beacon.

"Isn't he just marvelous?" she whispered to me. "Who'd have thought I'd find such a perfect man here in this tiny little village instead of in New Orleans?"

I had to agree; an ambitious young lawyer, he was a great prospect, although, based on my own experience, I felt protective. I wanted to reach out, warn her to slow down, to tell her what might lie ahead if she rushed into love too quickly. But as the music and dancing in the garden continued well into the warm night, Dorothy monopolized Tom Farrell. Clearly, she was smitten, yet she so cleverly concealed her feelings that he never seemed to realize how much he had piqued her interest.

"Do you think your sister would allow me to call on her?" he asked me tentatively as he was leaving.

I pretended to give the question a few moments of consideration. "Yes," I finally said. "I think she might."

Their ensuing courtship was fascinating to watch. Away from the strict formality of New Orleans's French society, Dorothy could spend time freely with Tom, without a chaperone. They saw each other almost every night in our front parlor, or sat holding hands, swinging on our veranda as they sipped lemonade. And no one kept track of their whereabouts when they went for walks and attended parties.

I was happy for them, even though it made me painfully aware of how empty my own love life with Martin was. When I saw them laughing merrily together, so obviously in love and so responsive to each other's presence, I had to bite back my envy in favor of my sister's happiness. It was their shared laughter that I coveted most. Except for the weeks of our whirlwind courtship, Martin and I rarely laughed together; life had become a very serious affair. He valued hard work, stability, neatness, and diligence—all admirable traits, to be sure, but in the absence of any levity, his view of life often seemed very dour indeed.

In contrast, Tom was always ready with quips and stories and looked for the lighthearted side of everything. And despite his cosmopolitan charm, he found Key West's exotic frontier life fascinating. He began to wear lighter clothing, put his heavy boots away, and delighted in the feeling of the heat and humidity on his skin.

Then he surprised us one evening when he announced that he'd decided to stay in Key West. "I'm tired of living in a cold northern city, competing with so many other lawyers," he explained, smiling at Dorothy. Even so, I was still totally unprepared for Dorothy's announcement.

"We're getting married next week!" she told me one night after Tom brought her home.

"Married? You're not! Next week? But you've known him such a short time!"

"We're in love. There's no reason to wait. Gran is thrilled. I told her this afternoon."

"But what about Grandmère and Grandpère? Surely you'll want their blessing beforehand. And they'll want to give you a nice wedding in New Orleans."

"We might go to New Orleans for our honeymoon. I'll surprise them then. And anyway, I don't want a big wedding there. I want to be married here. We'll have it in Gran's garden, as you did for the christening. It will be lovely."

Secretly, I was deeply hurt that she had presented this most important decision in her life to me as a fait accompli, and even more hurt that she'd chosen to tell Gran first. But I did not wish to spoil her happiness, and so I put aside my own feelings—I had grown quite adept at doing so anyway—and hugged her tightly. "That's wonderful!" I said excitedly.

The wedding was every bit as lovely as Dorothy had promised. Despite her convent background, she eagerly accepted Tom's Anglican faith, and Martin's cousin officiated, postponing his return to the Bahamas. Gran arranged to have Martin and her handyman slave Cato build a little pergola for the occasion. She had taken to growing orchids imported from South America, and for the wedding she directed her servants to festoon the little structure with vanda and cattleya orchids in purple and white. My sister carried a large bouquet of beautiful gingers in a tropical range of red, orange, and yellow, threaded with stephanotis and hibiscus from neighbors' gardens, and all the guests lavished the happy couple with gifts of silver and art treasures, most, I suspected, acquired from vessels run aground.

There was no time for a proper honeymoon. Tom quickly found legal work representing shipowners involved in wrecks, and Dorothy and her new husband settled into a happy state of newlywed bliss. "I just love bedding my handsome husband," she would confide with a giggle. "It's so wonderful; I could do it every night!" Their trysts were also productive, as it turned out, for Dorothy immediately conceived my niece Maureen. During her confidences, I would simply smile and nod, happy for my sister, but regretting once again that such romance and enthusiasm had been denied to me as a bride.

Life was good, I reflected. Yes, there were worries about the Seminole Indian War. And captains still whispered their fears of piracy, but for our growing clan, these were not matters to dwell on. Since our land abutted the naval depot, we felt safe from such dangers as pirate or Indian raids.

Still, the war with the Seminoles was on everyone's mind,

and the government began to consider an expansion of naval land. Perhaps Martin and I should have read the warning signals, but in our innocence, we did not. Thus, our calamity hit us like a lightning bolt.

I was reading a story to Martha and Timothy, who were still toddlers, on the day it happened. My grandmother's housemaid, Hagar, was on loan to us, polishing silver while she, too, listened to the story. Martin came rushing in, looking ashen as he waved a white envelope in my face.

"Do you know what this is?" he thundered. His eyes were blazing with anger, his mouth contorted, spittle at the corners.

The children were frightened, hiding their faces in the shelter of my lap. So alarmed was Hagar at his outburst that she scurried into the playroom, where she could still hear everything.

"It's a letter from the U.S. government! They're extending the naval base," he sputtered.

I tried to calm his shouting. "Martin—are they confiscating our pineapple crop to feed the men?"

Martin rolled his eyes. "No, not our pineapples. They've expropriated our land! This new Commodore Archer," he spat out the name, "he's planning to extend the naval station onto our property."

I could feel the blood slowly drain from my face. "Good God," I finally said hoarsely. "Can he do this? Have we no recourse?"

Martin collapsed into a chair and buried his head in his hands. "Not even a bloody apology," he muttered bitterly. "Our property is now government land."

"With no compensation?" I was having trouble coming to grips with the full meaning of this catastrophe.

He looked up, glaring. "Aren't you listening to me, Emily? It's been confiscated. He's taking it with no more regret than if it were a pig or a chicken, or a pile of lumber." He shook the letter at me. " 'Expanding the navy to protect Key West from Indians and recurrences of piracy.' Ha! We get nothing!"

I was stunned. After all Martin's work and the money we'd invested in our home, we were about to lose everything.

"From what I've heard," I stammered, "the navy would be better off spending the money on more lighthouses, not expanding the base here."

"Indeed? Well, then, you tell the government that," he retorted, and stormed out of the house.

Were we to be ordered off our land like squatters?

Over the next few weeks, I alternated between panic and confusion. We did everything possible to turn the decision around. We tried to make appointments with Commodore Archer, but he was always too busy to meet us. Dorothy's husband filed petitions to Washington, but it soon became evident that the suit would not be looked at for a long time, perhaps not in our lifetime.

We were devastated. Our life savings were all invested in our home and, in fact, we still owed money to Gran. Martin fell into a fit of melancholy so profound, he was barely able to function.

"I'll kill him," he muttered several times. "The man has ruined us."

"Hush. Those are seditious remarks. If something ever does happen to him, you'll be blamed," I cautioned him.

He could only grumble in reply.

"We're young," I said weakly. "We can start over."

"And how are we going to do that?"

"If we could acquire another plot of land, we could move the house. People do that all the time. It's the land that he wants, not the house."

"Do you think I haven't thought of that? The house is too big to fit on a free plot of land, and we've no money to buy a larger one. We're in debt as it is. And do you think a house can be moved for nothing? It's an expensive undertaking. You can be sure Archer won't pay for it. He'll probably want to live in it himself. My house. The house I built with my bare hands!"

For indeed, by law, it *was* Martin's house, not mine.

After numerous petitions, Commodore Archer finally agreed to meet Martin. When he returned home, he looked no happier than when he had left earlier that day.

"They've offered me the post of lighthouse keeper at Wreckers' Cay," my husband said bitterly.

Recently, I had seen an article in the *Key West Enquirer* that shipowners' demands were finally making an impact on Washington. They were hiring lobbyists to plea for the construction of new lighthouses throughout the Keys and along the coast of the mainland. I knew plans were being accelerated but had not heard of one going up at the little island called Wreckers' Cay.

"It's not even built yet," he said. "He'll let us stay here until the lighthouse tower and the keeper's house are built. It could take a year or two. He actually had the cheek to try to convince me he was conferring an honor on me with such a splendid position."

"An honor?"

"It's an appointment that needs presidential approval." This was true—despite the low pay, tending a beacon was considered a respectable post, usually granted to war veterans or trusted friends of government officials. And finding responsible lighthouse keepers was difficult because tending lights was not nearly as profitable as salvaging; it was hard work, and often it could be a lonely life. Wreckers' Cay, with its shallow waters, was considered a particularly dangerous spot for ships, one where a light was sorely needed. But it was a terribly isolated island.

This olive branch was by no means a real compensation for the loss of our land and home. But in the end, Martin and I had to bend to the financial considerations. Quite simply, we needed a place to live.

Gran was upset when she heard we were moving to Wreckers' Cay. I stopped by her house with the children the day after we received Archer's letter. While Hagar amused Martha and Timothy, I took tea with Gran in the parlor. I was unprepared for her reaction when I told her the bad news. She brought her cup down into its saucer with a dramatic crashing gesture.

"What are you saying?" she demanded sharply. "You're leaving . . . barely after I've arrived? I came here to be near my family and friends! And to watch my great-grandchildren grow up. This will ruin everything."

I shrugged helplessly. I understood how she felt.

"Martin should have known, buying all that property over on the water," she continued. "Any fool could have seen it was the obvious place for the naval station to expand."

Her diatribe began to anger me, for instead of blaming the commodore, and offering me solace, she was finding fault with Martin.

"You didn't raise that point at the time," I retorted. "And if you are worried about your money, be assured that we will pay you back every penny we borrowed."

This merely fueled her ire. "Did I mention the money to you, ever?" she challenged, her rheumy blue eyes flashing. "I lent it to you because I wanted to help you. I never expected to get it back. In fact, I'd be happy to lend you more to keep you here."

"That's out of the question," I snapped. "We do not wish to remain in your debt forever." And with that, I got up and left with my children.

The truth was that I had finally begun to love Key West and our growing community here. The prospect of having to start over again at Wreckers' Cay made me so anxious, I starting waking up in the middle of the night in a sweat. I knew I would miss my sister and her family terribly, as well as our friends. And yes, even my difficult grandmother. But I dared not reveal my feelings to Martin—he was already living in a perpetual state of anger and depression about the move.

Finally, in January 1836, we were officially informed that all was ready at the island. We were expected to move out by May. I had just found out that I was again pregnant, so I had to struggle for composure when the eviction notice was delivered.

Dorothy organized a social for our friends and neighbors to bid us good-bye. "You're all set up over there," Captain George Lee told me brightly. He had recently secured a contract with the U.S. Treasury Department and collector of customs to captain the lighthouse supply boat, which would be our lifeline to civilization.

"How does it look?" I inquired anxiously.

He shrugged. "It still needs some work. You'll want to be puttin' on some whitewash and all. A few plants . . . a garden. Hang curtains and such. Things to make it homeylike."

I sighed. "I shall hate it, won't I?"

Seeing the tears welling in my eyes, he touched my hand and quickly reassured me. "Listen, Miss Emily, anything you need, you just tell me, y'hear? I'll be coming by twice a month on the *Outlander.* You just write me out a list o' things and I'll move heaven and earth to git 'em for you. Your Gran or Dorothy want to send letters or packages out, all's they have to do is let me know and I'll see that you git 'em."

I smiled my thanks, patting his arm. "I'm grateful to you for that," I whispered. "Very grateful."

With great reluctance, we packed up our worldly goods on a warm, sun-filled day in May and, with a fair trade wind at our backs, headed southwest toward Wreckers' Cay aboard a new government sloop, the *Pharos*. Behind us trailed Martin's wooden fishing skiff. Captain Lee and his mate, Alfie Dillon, promised to barge over larger items, including my piano, within the month.

As I expected, I grew ill during the trip, the more so because of my condition. But with two young children to care for this time, I forced myself to remain alert and nurturing, despite my inclination to take to my berth and bury my head beneath the coverlet.

TWELVE

Wreckers' Cay

May 1836

W e arrived in the late afternoon at low tide, with clear, shallow waters gleaming a brilliant turquoise in the sunlight. My first look at the island was a shock. Part of the jungle growth had been cut down for the new construction, and that area was bare and unsightly. Elsewhere, uprooted trees and broken limbs told the tale of a bad tropical storm the previous season. I stared at the harsh, inhospitable land, trying to visualize how a garden could be coaxed from the patches of coral sand that glittered before us. The rest of the island was still thick with wild mangrove, hiding only God knew how many species of vipers and biting, stinging insects.

From the dock, the Wreckers' Cay lighthouse soared into the sky, a dramatic, elegant structure, which arrested my gaze and beckoned us to enter and explore it. I could only imagine the beauty that would emanate from its glorious rays as it illuminated the darkest nights.

"We're home!" I announced cheerfully to Martha and Timothy, putting my arms around them for reassurance. They peered out from the boat, apprehensive for only a moment, for the lure of the lighthouse held them in awe, as well. And being children, they were eager to escape the confines of the boat and get their bearings on the island.

The big two-story house, the dock, and the cistern for the keeper looked raw and new; they needed finishing touches to complete them and make them truly home. Knowing how good Martin was with his hands, I could see its potential. I glanced at him when we docked, noting how, despite his ongoing melancholy, his eyes were already appraising what needed to be done, and assessing which materials and tools he would require.

Looking out to the straits, we could see the ships Martin had been hired to protect, with light traffic moving steadily in both directions.

"Get used to looking at them," he said sourly. "That's all we're going to see from now on."

Clearly, it was going to take some time to get this latest humor turned around, but if only for Martha and Timothy, I was determined to be positive: "The view must be lovely from the top of the tower."

"Bloody tower," he muttered. "That's going to be a fine muddle to maintain and repair."

I sighed. In fact, I had meant what I said. I thought the tower was beautiful, and I was eager to see the sweeping vistas from the top.

The children were quick to discover the island's two beautiful beaches. One was a long stretch of golden sand on the south side, facing the straits; the other was a protected little beach on a lagoon, hugging the northeastern shore. Timothy and Martha stripped down to their drawers and waded into the sea, soaking in the cool crystal water.

"I found some conchs!" Timothy called out proudly as he waved his catches in the air. "We can have them for supper."

In Key West, we had acquired a taste for the meaty white mollusks burrowed inside the glistening iridescent pink shells.

"There are so many fish!" shouted Martha. I looked to the pristine water and saw a school of yellowtail snappers. At the very least, I knew we would never lack for food here.

The children loved the smallness of the island and exploring the jungle growth. Within a few days, they had declared the place their own, staking out hiding places and inventing games. Initially, Martin and I had to caution them, for we worried about insects and snakes. And I worried about sharks, barracuda, jellyfish, and stingrays lurking in the water. But we soon learned that the island's environment was a remarkably friendly one. There were far fewer insects on the island than we'd anticipated, perhaps because there were no pools of stagnant water. Or it might have been because of the steady trade winds constantly sweeping across it from the southeast.

The next few weeks flew by as we settled in. Martin constructed a tree house for the children in an ancient mahogany by the cookhouse. Later, he added the playhouse. Slowly, Martin emerged from his lethargy and put the hardships of Key West behind him. Over the next three years, we managed to make a decent life for our family on Wreckers' Cay. Without the distractions of wrecking and overnight fishing trips, and with no more fraternizing at grog shops, he immersed himself in constructing our new outbuildings, and tackled the tending of the light. Occasionally, though, I looked into his eyes and saw a yearning for his old life: the excitement of landing huge fish from the middle of the ocean, the discovery of a lode of valuable cargo aboard a crippled ship, and the bustle at the port of Key West. I knew he missed it all.

I eventually came to understand his moods—I could even predict them. Happily, his Calvinistic tendencies were dissipating and he was becoming gentler and more caring, especially with the children. To my delight, he was spending more time doing things with them, and it was clear that they adored him. He was still not always patient with them, however; he even seemed a bit stern sometimes, to my mind. I would hear him shout, "Timothy, that's no way to bait a Fish! I've told you a hundred times." Or "Martha, go help your mother and stop messing about. You're wasting your time with all that drawing. And you're wasting paper." Later, even little Hannah did not escape his flare-ups: "Hannah, I told you to pick up those toys! Don't pretend you didn't understand!"

But overall, he was greatly improved over the husband and father he had been. Our isolation also led to a new closeness between us. I like to think he was rediscovering a part of himself that had been worn down with hard work and worries about money. Perhaps, too, he was looking to recover some of what had sparked our love in New Orleans. He would often take my hand in his and smile affectionately at me, or reach over and touch my hair. If he were working at his desk, I would sometimes put my arms around him and he would turn for a kiss. We started making love more often, and he began to ask me questions in the bedroom, trying to satisfy me, and would hold me in his arms afterward.

Hannah was born in December of the first year we arrived. Dorothy came out to assist at her birth, and when I met her at the dock, we bounded into each other's arms and held hands as I led her up to our home, showing her our garden and the tower, while she marveled at my large belly. "How big you are," she said, laughing.

As she looked around, she marveled at what had been accomplished in such a short time. "And how beautiful everything is here. My children would love this island! I must go up the tower at once. I've always wanted to climb a lighthouse. I can't wait to see the views of the water from up there."

The lighthouse had a seductive effect on people.

عـلــی

Yet, despite the changes in our lives that brought me joy, living at Wreckers' Cay could also be difficult. My joy at Hannah's birth faded with the reality of the constant loneliness—even more crushing, I realized, after Dorothy left. I had previously missed New Orleans, but, to my surprise, I missed Key West still more, for I had come to regard it as my real home. Sometimes my need for adult conversations threatened to engulf me. The social gatherings, the interaction with Dorothy and Tom and other young families, even the card games and conversation I'd shared with Gran and her elderly friends—all these things I had taken for granted before, and when I thought of them now, I felt a great, indescribable aching in my heart.

THIRTEEN

Wreckers' Cay

September 1839

Four months after Martin's disappearance, September brought a fierce dead heat, with not a puff of wind. Normally, our little island enjoyed a continual play of rippling trade winds, but in late summer and early autumn, the breezes died and we choked on the airless heat that seared our lungs. We wore the lightest of clothing during these doldrums, just enough to protect us from the sizzling rays of the sun. Even my children were happy to lie down during the hottest part of the day to rest until afternoon's end, when we could bathe at the beach. Andrew, too, felt the need to pace himself, resting more and frequently cooling himself off in the ocean.

Martin's absence continued to occupy my thoughts almost every waking moment. Our lives were moving on without him. And I felt sad that he was missing the changes in our family: Timothy seemed to grow every time I looked at him, Hannah was taller, and Martha marked her ninth birthday. There was also my pregnancy, of which he'd had no knowledge when he disappeared.

"Mama, why do people have slaves?" Martha asked me one afternoon. She and Timothy had just been chatting under the mahogany tree with Andrew.

The question embarrassed me. In New Orleans and Key West, owning slaves had been a fact of life—unquestioned. But here on Wreckers' Cay, I realized, my children were growing up without such cultural perceptions. Unlike me, they were not totally desensitized to its horrors.

"To . . . help them with work," I replied.

"Like Andrew does here?"

"Andrew isn't our slave. He's merely someone who helps us."

She frowned. "But we don't pay him. So doesn't that make him a slave?"

"No, it doesn't," I snapped. "We give him room and board. We don't own him. He's free to leave at any time." I hoped my tone made it clear that this was not a subject I wished to pursue.

Martha nodded, and I sensed that, while she saw some inequity in our arrangement, it was overshadowed by the joy she and Timothy found in Andrew's presence.

I was sometimes finding the subject of slavery a difficult one in the classroom. In the days that followed our initial conversation about slave routes, Andrew asked me to read passages of the Bible aloud to him, and while I read from the new one Captain Lee had brought, he followed the text with me in our old Bible, sounding out the words with me. I avoided passages that mentioned slaves, which was difficult, as references to them were liberally sprinkled throughout the Scriptures—a fact I had never even considered previously.

Andrew was beginning to read well, but at sums, he was an ordinary student. Money was not a commodity he could relate to easily, as he'd never earned any. To help him understand, the children and I set up a play store with various grocery items and real money, and we would laugh at arguments that broke out over wrong change. This was also good for my children, who had never experienced the opportunity to shop in a real market.

Science—at least science as it existed around us—also interested Andrew. His questions sent me to Grandpère's encyclopedia on an almost daily basis for the names of star constellations, the discoveries of Galileo and Copernicus, the names of different species of fish and birds. Sometimes this involved a walk along the beach, together with Martha and Timothy, to talk about the night sky. And curiously, in the dark, the differences in the color of our skin dissipated. On these walks, listening to his voice and his breathing beside me, I became more aware of him as a man and less as a Negro. One evening as we walked, the children running ahead, I stumbled and fell; he caught me, and I grabbed his arm instinctively to right myself. Feeling the strength of his hands, I had to admit I found the contact pleasurable—although I continued walking as if nothing had occurred. When we walked back toward the light from the tower, I turned and was almost surprised as his features—so different from Martin's—were caught in its beam.

Andrew was very interested in herbal medicine, an art about which I was completely ignorant, but again with his prodding, we looked up entries in the encyclopedia. "What are all those herbs you have hanging in the playroom?" I asked him one day.

"They're medicine plants," he said. "I learned about them from a Gullah woman who practiced hoodoo."

"You mean voodoo?"

"No, hoodoo. The Gullah lady was a black slave woman who lived near a river in South Carolina. She was sold to my massa, and brought to Georgia. Back where she'd lived, they made the medicines of African slaves from the roots of plants."

"I've never heard of that. And I was around slaves a good part of my life."

He looked at me quizzically. "You had slaves?"

I hesitated. "Well, my husband and I never owned any. But I was raised by one—Eurydice."

"So your parents had slaves."

My parents had owned a few house slaves. I could only remember their dusky faces, careworn or smiling, and seeing them working—always working. But I no longer knew their names; I realized I didn't even know what became of them after my parents died. I'd never thought about it.

I decided not to mention that fact. "My grandfather had slaves to work his plantation," I conceded. "But . . . well, he lost much of his money. Most of it, in fact. He and my grandmother ended up living in a smaller home in New Orleans."

Andrew looked curiously at me, as though he wasn't sure he had heard correctly. "Your granddaddy was a planter?"

"Well . . . yes. That was many years ago. When my sister, Dorothy, was born, my mother died. My baby sister and I moved in with my grandparents. And Eurydice looked after us."

"She was a slave."

"Eurydice?" I felt myself growing embarrassed. I chose my words carefully. "Yes, she was, though we never thought of her as one. She was like family to us. And she still is. She's a quadroon from Guadeloupe."

His voice was mocking. "Oh, a quadroon. A nice light-colored house slave."

I ignored this. "She's the woman who raised me, and I loved her. I still love her."

He stared at me.

I grew flustered. "Eurydice was—is—a wonderful woman. And then she had a sweet little baby, and Dorothy and I just adored her, too. She named her Marie-Francine, after my grandmother. Really, they were like family."

"Well, now," he drawled slowly, a smile playing on his face, "maybe they were family. Have you ever thought of that?"

I sat in shocked silence for a moment as his implication sank in. Then I glared at him, bristling. "How dare you?" I gasped.

He persisted, ignoring my indignation. "Did they keep other slaves in New Orleans?"

I stood up and began to clear the table. "I don't want to discuss this any longer."

"Why not?"

His persistence was exasperating. But I was, of course, withholding some of the truth. The fact was, in his days as a planter, my grandfather had at one time owned as many as a hundred slaves, and would still have that number had Indian raids not destroyed his crops a couple of years running. He still owned the land but no longer went to the estate. He and my grandmother had brought only a handful of faithful slaves when they moved to New Orleans; the remaining ones had been sold off.

When I was growing up, Grandpère enjoyed recalling his planter days, and he often described his sallies into the Algiers slave auctions in New Orleans, and up in Natchez, Mississippi, at the Fork in the Road slave market. He would tell me of his shrewd deals, much like a ranch owner would brag about the purchase of strong, healthy livestock.

Andrew was clearly enjoying my discomfort. I felt myself growing angry, yet at the same time, I scolded myself silently—I had encouraged this familiarity; how could I blame him for his curiosity now?

"Miss Emily," Andrew finally said, "you believe in slavery, don't you?"

I had to think about it. I was tempted to lie again, but under his penetrating gaze, I found I simply could not.

"Andrew," I said in a low voice, "you have to understand that if that's the way you're brought up . . . if your family has slaves, you just accept it. You don't question the grown-ups around you. I was a child of my time and place."

When this was greeted by silence. I added, "But I can truthfully tell you that I married a man with no money and have never owned slaves myself."

"Until now."

I felt color quicken in my cheeks. "Andrew!" I exclaimed angrily. "That's not fair. You know I don't consider you my slave."

"Maybe not your slave. But you do think of me as a slave."

I held my breath. I heard the children running through the garden, and the gentle spray of the ocean. Inside the house, though, the heat had somehow grown heavier over the worktable between me and Andrew.

"Andrew," I said carefully, "you are perfectly free here. You know that. And you may leave here anytime, really."

In actual fact, I was terrified he might indeed quit the island, leaving me alone with the children again. And for him to do so, he would either have to take the supply tender with Captain Lee—which was out of the question—or take one of our vessels, and I could not part with either of my boats.

But he just looked away. "They stole my freedom papers," he said simply.

I let out the breath I didn't even realize I was holding. "Well, then, I guess we'll just continue until we find some way around that. Perhaps, later on, if you decide to leave, I could write you some kind of letter, if I can figure out the correct wording."

He nodded. Then he silently left the house, and I sat alone in the cookhouse for a long time before venturing back outside.

By early November, I was growing quite large with my pregnancy. I was due at the beginning of January, and I no longer could afford to be seen by Captain Lee and Alfie—nor by those other rare visitors, like Mr. and Mrs. Weston, who kept the lighthouse at Garden Key in the Dry Tortugas. I wasn't sure how much longer I could keep up the pretense, so when the supply tender came in mid-November, I took to my bed and told Martha to tell Captain Lee and Alfie that I was resting and had a bad headache. They dropped off the supplies and the mail and left soon after, a little disgruntled at our lack of hospitality, since we offered them no refreshments.

Truthfully, I was feeling so poorly that I welcomed this ruse. The luxury of climbing back to the comfort of my bed in the middle of the day was sheer bliss, for this pregnancy—more than any of the previous ones—often left me exhausted and nauseous.

After the men left, I got up. Andrew emerged from hiding, and the household came alive again. Dusk came earlier now. I quickly began supper preparations so Andrew could get started at the light. As the food was cooking, I tore open a letter written in French from my sister:

Darling sister Emily, I am astonished by what the supply couriers have been telling us! George Lee says he finds you happy and well, and that the light and property are well tended. You may trust that I have mentioned your pregnancy to no one. Sugar, I have a wonderful surprise for you. I plan to book passage with the couriers on their next trip over with your supplies! I know I shall have to stay there for two weeks, until they stop at the island again, but I have plenty of help at home, and I thought it would be enjoyable to get away from Key West society and enjoy some peace and quiet for a couple of weeks. I will see you very soon. Je t'embrasse!

Your loving sister,

Dorothy

I was alarmed. Much as I loved my sister, I did not want her at Wreckers' Cay yet. She was supposed to be coming to help deliver my baby, but that would not be until early January, six weeks from now. And while I knew she would learn about Andrew then, for the moment I was still blissfully keeping my head planted in the sand. But there was no way to get word to her in time and tell her not to come for her unscheduled visit, as she would already be on the next tender. So it was time to face the problem.

I brought up the matter at supper. "My sister is coming from Key West for an unexpected visit on the next tender," I said to Andrew without preamble. "I just received a letter from her." This announcement caught him as he was lifting his fork to his mouth. He stopped and looked at me in surprise. Across the table, Timothy and Martha stopped eating, too.

"How long will she be here?" he asked.

"Two weeks. It sounds like she just wants to get away from Key West for a couple of weeks. She'll be back again in January, when the baby is due." We sat in silence for a few minutes. The children looked at each other, then watched us.

"You can't hide me for two weeks," said Andrew simply. "Either I'll have to leave or she'll have to be told."

"Yes, she will have to be told," I said, ignoring the first option. "I'm afraid . . . well, I suspect you won't like my sister very much."

"Why do you say that?"

"She is a very sweet person, but she's . . . well, she's quite . . ."

"She's a slave owner."

When I didn't answer, I saw the anger creep into his eyes.

"Perhaps I should leave for a while."

Before I could protest, Martha and Timothy both exclaimed, "No!"

Andrew smiled at them. "So what's the answer?" he asked me.

"No," I repeated. "You mustn't leave."

He looked thoughtful. "We could tell her I'm your slave," he said. "I'll work at the light and in the garden, and do my other chores. I just won't eat with you. I'll take my food to the playhouse. I don't think I want to get to know her nohow. Let's tell her I came off a slave ship. It's the truth, ain't it?"

"Oh, Andrew," I retorted with a flash of anger, "please don't start that again. I hardly—"

He broke into a smile, and I realized he was teasing me.

"We'll tell her the truth—that you're a freed slave," I said.

Although I was very excited about seeing my sister again, I was also worried by the problems her visit would create. She wouldn't be able to sleep in the playhouse this time. That meant she'd be sleeping with me in my bed, which would inevitably intrude on my privacy and be difficult for her, for Dorothy was used to a more luxurious life back in Key West. And since she was certainly unaccustomed to doing housework or cooking, I knew she would be standing around, chatting about the social life and gossip of Key West, while I tried to keep up with all the necessary chores around the house.

Even so, I knew I could trust my sister to keep quiet about Andrew, and that was the one bright light in this cloud of anxiety I felt.

On the day Dorothy arrived, we followed our usual supply-day routine. Andrew locked himself in the playhouse, and I again took to my bed with the pretense of a headache.

I watched discreetly from my bedroom window as the captain and Alfie hauled Dorothy's cases onto the dock. She directed them toward the playhouse, where she would normally have stayed, but Martha and Timothy intercepted them, saying that their aunt would be staying in my room because the playhouse was not yet ready. The children took her smaller bags and headed for our main house.

Nonplussed, Dorothy cheerfully dismissed Captain George

and Alfie, who subsequently left, surely now beginning to wonder why they were no longer invited to tea on their visits.

"Just look at you!" she said, after she burst into my room and gave me a lingering hug. "No wonder you're hiding up here. I'm surprised the men haven't guessed. You're as big as a house."

I was overjoyed to see her and held her hands a long time. "You look wonderful, Dorothy. Prettier than ever. You're still the family beauty."

"Pshaw." She laughed dismissively. "Help me unpack! I've brought Christmas gifts and treats for you and the children." Then lowering her voice, she said, "and a few gifts . . . from Gran."

I was pleased, because Gran, I knew, was still angry with me. She'd written to me only sporadically since our move to Wreckers' Cay, despite my frequent notes.

"I'm so sorry we won't be spending Christmas together again this year," Dorothy lamented. "Is there no way you could—"

She stopped in midsentence, staring over my shoulder. The color drained from her face. "Emily . . . there's a Negro man . . . standing behind you!"

I turned and smiled. Andrew was standing at the door of my room, hat in hand.

"Dorothy, this is my new lighthouse assistant, Andrew Dembi Tyler. Andrew, this is my sister," I said.

Andrew bowed politely. "Miss Dorothy."

Dorothy was still recovering. No words escaped her lips.

"I was just wondering, Miss Emily, if we were having schooling today."

I smiled at him. "No, Andrew. Since my sister has just arrived, I'm declaring it a school holiday."

"In that case, I'll go over to the tower and get an early start on the light." Nodding courteously to Dorothy, Andrew then replaced his hat and left as quietly as he had come. My sister looked like someone who had just awakened from a peculiar dream.

"Emily!" she shrieked when she recovered. "What is this about? Who is that Negro? What is he doing here?"

I took her by the hand and led her toward the stairs. "Come, Dorothy, let's go down to the cookhouse for tea. I have much to tell you."

Over tea and slices of caraway-seed cake, I finally explained to Dorothy that I was a terrible fraud. I giggled at this, but Dorothy just looked stupefied. I described how Andrew had been helping tend the light since September, even though I remained the lighthouse keeper of record. And I told her how he was working in exchange for room and board, and for our lessons.

"You're educating him?" She frowned. "Whatever for?"

"Why, because he asked me to. He's very intelligent; he learned how to keep the light straight away. Caught on to it faster than I did."

Dorothy stood. She looked out the window to where Andrew was picking up some gardening tools. "And he doesn't belong to anyone?"

She made him sound like a stray pet, and it surprised me to realize I now found such an assumption offensive. "No. He's a free Negro . . . from somewhere up in Georgia. He was kidnapped and forced onto an illegal slaver heading for the Caribbean—Cuba, I think. He'd been whipped and mistreated, and when he saw his chance in a storm, he escaped and came ashore."

Dorothy continued to watch him from the cookhouse. "That's a rather far-fetched story, Emily."

"Well, I believe him," I said.

That was not what Dorothy wanted to hear. She turned back

to me. "Emily, I'm at a loss, I must confess. I always thought you were mad for coming out here in the first place. And all the more so now that Martin is . . ." Her voice trailed off and she shook her head. "Come back to Key West with me. You and the children will have a much better life there than you ever will here. I worry about you all the time!"

I sat up straighter. Suddenly, it was becoming clear why Dorothy had planned this surprise visit. It was to convince me to leave Wreckers' Cay.

"You want me to just drop everything and move back . . . to what? A settlement where I don't even have a home anymore? With three—no, four!—children to raise? I know you mean well, darlin', but Martin could still be found. And if so, I should be here."

She smiled indulgently. "Poor dear Emily." She sat down again and took my hand. "It's been six months. You must think of yourself and your children."

"The children are fine," I said, trying to keep my temper even. "They work hard on schoolwork and practice their music, and they are very healthy, as you can see."

"They may very well be," she said. "But I don't have to remind you of the Seminole raids on lighthouses. And what if a hurricane hits the island? What would you do out here alone?"

I shrugged.

"Emily, sooner or later, you'll have to come back. Martha will need to marry. And Timothy might want to go away to university. Why not come back now?" Dorothy turned back to watching Andrew. "I'm surprised you're not afraid of this Negro," she murmured.

Outside, Andrew had taken off his shirt in the heat, and his skin was glistening with sweat. Since he'd been here at Wreckers' Cay, his body had taken shape again, and as he headed down to the beach for a swim, I could see his physique was not lost on Dorothy.

"He's young," she said. She paused and looked over at me with a wry smile. "He's quite handsome, actually—for a Negro. Good teeth and an excellent body . . . very muscular; he looks strong and healthy."

"This is not an auction, Dorothy," I said.

She waved this comment away. "I'm sure a man of his age would rather be in a place where he can meet women of his race and have a life of some kind. In Key West, they're always looking for able bodies to crew on fishing and salvaging boats." She frowned. "Where does he sleep?"

"The playroom. Martha and Timothy gave it up for him— they adore him—so that's why you're staying with me upstairs."

"He sleeps in the playroom? Where does he bathe and . . . use the commode?"

"He usually swims down at the beach, but when he wants to bathe, he uses our washhouse," I said, "and I have only one out-house here."

She was stricken by this explanation. "I will be sharing hygienic facilities with—him?"

I had been expecting this reaction. "Believe me," I said, patting her hand, "after the first few days, you won't even be conscious of it. It just takes a little getting used to."

Later, when I cleared away the tea things and busied myself with tidying up my kitchen, Dorothy expressed a need to use the latrine. She looked pained for a moment, and then, taking a deep breath, she headed for our integrated outhouse.

To her credit, Dorothy spoke no more on the subject.

Later, she went with the children to the beach, pulling up her skirts and bathing her feet and legs. Timothy found some crayfish under a rock and put them in a deep covered pail to take back to me for chowder. We ate early, as was our custom, so Andrew could have the light beaming brightly by dusk.

Dorothy offered to set the table. "Does Hannah sit with us?" "Yes," I said. "So set it for the three of us and all three children."

Again, Dorothy looked uncomfortable, as she realized Andrew would be sitting at the table, too. But she merely pursed her lips in disapproval.

When Andrew came in for supper, I could see that in my sister's honor, he had washed and changed into clean clothes. He was quieter than usual, as if he could sense her displeasure. Dorothy was also quiet, and I found myself doing most of the talking. She pointedly ignored Andrew, and barely nibbled at her food.

Martha and Timothy were oblivious to Dorothy's discomfort. They chatted with Andrew, laughing easily, as always. At one point, Hannah knocked over her glass of juice. Andrew immediately stood up and cleaned up the mess with a rag, chatting with Hannah as though nothing had happened. I could not help thinking how different Martin's reaction might have been; most likely, he would have slapped her hands and scolded her.

Through it all, Dorothy just remained silent.

Within a few days, Dorothy was adapting to life on Wreckers' Cay. Her corset was off by the second day, and she sometimes waited until afternoon to get dressed and pin up her hair. By the weekend, she was even going barefoot around the island, or just wearing slippers. I noticed that instead of bothering to do her hair up, she was just tying it back with ribbons.

With each day, she appeared to relax a little more. "Don't misunderstand me, sugar," she said over coffee one morning, "I'd never live out here. But I have to admit it can be pleasant. It's so restful without other people around. And it's wonderful not to have so many mosquitoes!"

She still barely spoke to Andrew, unless it was to order him to carry out some task, but on the fourth morning she heard him singing out in the garden as he hoed. Often his songs were spirituals I had never heard, like "Wade in the Water" or "The Drinking Gourd," but this time he was belting out a religious hymn, "Welcome Thou Victor in the Strife." His voice was deep and velvety, and in fine form that day. Dorothy put her coffee cup down and ran to the window. "That's my favorite hymn," she said, humming along. "It's such a beautiful piece. And how he does sing!"

Then, to my surprise, she began to sing along—softly, but even so, I knew it would carry from the cookhouse out into the garden, where Andrew would hear. They continued this duet for a few minutes, until Andrew stopped, leaned on his hoe, and cocked his ear.

Dorothy's cheeks flushed, and she covered her mouth to suppress a giggle. "I can't believe I was singing with your Negro!"

"Andrew," I reminded her. "His name is Andrew."

Turning back to his work, he had switched to singing "Swing Low, Sweet Chariot," a song well suited to his baritone, but not to Dorothy's lighter voice.

"Why, he is quite entertaining, your Andrew!" she exclaimed. "I wish I had a Negro who could sing like that. You must have him perform for us."

The idea of a little concert seemed like a grand one, for we could celebrate the talents of the entire household—Andrew's voice, Martha's piano playing, and Timothy's facility with the violin. Hannah, no doubt, would love cheering along, as well.

I mentioned it to Andrew at our next tutorial. He agreed, but on his terms. "Tell your sister I'll sing if she'll sing with me," he said. "I heard her. She sings good."

"She sings well," I replied, correcting him, but even as I did, I realized how infrequently I needed to correct his speech now. His language skills had greatly improved.

Wreckers' Cay was truly weaving its magic on my sister, for luckily, Dorothy was receptive to this suggestion. "A concert would be wonderful! Of course I'll sing with him."

She shuffled through my sheet music and found several hymns that I knew were dear to her heart. When she found Schubert's "Ave Maria," she said excitedly, "I'll teach Andrew the Latin words to this, and we'll sing it together." The fact that she'd referred to him as Andrew, rather than "the Negro" or "the slave" was not lost on me. She went off to the parlor, busily humming to herself.

Having Dorothy around to enliven Wreckers' Cay was a breath of fresh air. Martha was happy to be learning new piano pieces, as was Timothy on the violin, and it occurred to me that perhaps my own abilities to instruct their music lessons had become a little stale. Preparations for our musical evening occupied the better part of their time for over a week, after which Dorothy pronounced us ready to perform.

The evening was a splendid success. Dorothy had been singing with the church choir, and her voice had improved since I'd last heard her. Andrew's baritone complemented hers, and when they sang together, the effect was remarkable. I lent my uncertain alto to a few of the less challenging songs, and helped Martha—who sulked in frustration at one point—at the piano. Timothy reveled in his new pieces on the violin. I could see he possessed quite a natural talent, and as I watched my son performing so intently, Dorothy's earlier comments about the limits of his education here on the island sprang to mind. Little Hannah watched it all with rapt attention. How much she could hear, I did not know, but I delighted in how she clapped her hands gleefully and smiled whenever the music began again. Clearly, she was able to intuit some of the musical tones in her own way.

This evening produced another magic effect. The next day,

Dorothy greeted Andrew at breakfast and didn't ask him to pour her drink or remove her plate. "He really is quite remarkable," she confided to me later. And I was pleased that she did not add the qualification "for a Negro" to her praise. She whispered, "Have you noticed his eyes? They're a hazel color. Obviously, he's the product of more than one generation of owners messing around in the slave shack."

"That's entirely possible," I said, pretending I hadn't noticed. But, of course, I had noted all this and more about Andrew. Dorothy was correct: He was quite handsome. His skin was a rich coffee color, and his smile, which revealed his beautiful white teeth, made you want to smile along with him, to catch the joy that glowed from his lips and eyes.

Dorothy began to go to the beach with the children, even when Andrew was there. I stayed back in the cookhouse to rest, for I was growing ever larger, and my size was weighing heavily on me. I could see from the window that they would return to the house, each holding Hannah's hand, swinging her between them, and chatting amiably. In fact, Hannah unwittingly brought them together in other aspects of her play, asking them to help her build a castle on the sandbar, or to hold her up as she tried to swim.

When I was too ill or tired to do the schooling, Dorothy cheerfully took over with the children, and though she did not initially offer to help Andrew, she consented when Martha and Timothy asked her. She would listen to his questions and ideas, just as I had, though he was far less confrontational with her. I often heard them laughing together from my bedroom upstairs, and despite my headaches and aching back, I had to smile.

One afternoon, I awoke from a nap to the sound of loud laughter downstairs in the cookhouse. When I joined them, Andrew and Dorothy were sitting at the table, sharing an old clay pipe of Martin's that they had packed with a sweet-smelling tobacco. "What are you doing?" I asked.

Dorothy had a bemused smile on her face. Looking more relaxed than I had ever seen her, she exclaimed, "Oh, sugar, come sit with us! Andrew has this wonderful plant. You absolutely must try it. You hang it from the rafters till it's dry, and then"—she giggled—"you just crumble it up like tobacco and smoke it!"

Beside her, Andrew also seemed deeply content. His eyes were half-open and he was grinning broadly. He offered me a puff from his pipe, but feeling slightly nauseous, I declined.

"Let me see that tobacco," I said. Andrew showed me a plant he had freshly cut. The leaf was rather large and had seven fronds. I had a vague recollection of seeing it growing at the far end of the island. It seemed to have a tranquilizing effect, and clearly, Dorothy had really taken to it.

She turned to Andrew. "Andrew, darlin', you must give me some to take back to Key West!"

"I'll do better than that," said Andrew. "I'll give you some seeds to plant and you can grow some in your garden."

I had been too busy to think much about the herbs Andrew was finding around the property. A few weeks earlier, I had seen Hannah wearing a small pouch around her neck. When I asked her where she got it, she gestured toward the playhouse.

To me, this smacked of the voodoo dolls used on Louisiana plantations by slaves wishing to hex their masters by sticking them with pins. "What is this all about?" I asked Andrew, although not unkindly. "What is in that little gris-gris bag?"

"Just herbs to help her hear better," he said.

I could not help but smile. It brought back memories of the freed black people back in New Orleans, performing rituals in Congo Square on their Sundays off.

"Oh, you Africans and your voodoo and mojo and juju," I said, laughing. "Do you really think all that black magic works?"

"It's not voodoo. It's hoodoo. Remember? From the Gullah," he protested. "More of a white magic, from Africa, not Haiti. The Gullah use healing herbs to make people feel better, to cure sickness. The herbs I put in her little pouch are to help improve her senses, like sight and hearing."

To me, of course, it was all rubbish and nonsense. But it wasn't doing her any harm. And if it made Andrew feel productive, well . . . I decided it was an innocuous enough amulet, no stranger than the scapular medals Dorothy and I had worn as girls at the convent. Secretly, I even wished I were not so cynical, that I, too, could believe Hannah's problems might be so easily solved. And for Hannah, the small pouch became a thing of veritable wonder. She never went anywhere without her little herb pouch and her rag doll; I even had trouble getting her to remove it at bath time.

As Dorothy prepared for her departure, she asked Andrew to make up little gris-gris bags for her own children to ward off colds or the dreaded yellow fever over the winter.

She had, of course, failed in the purpose of her visit: to convince me to return to Key West. I was sure Gran and Captain Lee had put her up to it. Still, it had been a surprisingly pleasant visit. "I'll be back soon, sugar," she said with a resigned smile. "I just hope that little baby of yours doesn't come early!"

I smiled. "I'm sure it will be fine."

"Do you worry about Indians?"

I shook my head. "Not really, Dorothy. I'm well west of their territories. They're more likely to attack Key West than Wreckers'." But we both knew I was whistling past the graveyard.

Just before the supply tender was due to arrive, Dorothy and

I enjoyed a pot of tea and some lemon pound cake, treasuring our last few moments together. With a giggle, she confided to me that she couldn't wait to get home and have her gardener plant some of Andrew's "marvelously wonderful herb" in her Key West garden.

FOURTEEN

Wreckers' Cay

December 1839

During our morning lessons, Andrew had a new topic of
fascination: Indians. "Why do people keep warning you
about them?" he asked one day. He'd been aware of coalescent
tribes in Georgia but knew little about their history. Of our
unrest in Florida, he knew nothing.

"It's because of the recent Seminole War."

"What're they fighting about?"

"Land. The government has been removing Indians east of
the Mississippi to reservations in the West for some time. About
ten years ago, the Indians in Florida were told to move out and
go to western reservations."

Naturally, Andrew related this to the movement of slaves
over the seas. "Well, nobody can blame them for fighting to
stay!" he said.

As usual, when our discussions turned difficult in this way, I
tried to maintain a neutral attitude. "I couldn't say." I shrugged.
"I know very little about it."

In truth, though, I'd been following stories of Indian raids
in the issues of the *Enquirer* that Captain Lee and Alfie brought

me. The early, native tribes, like the Calusas, were reported to have been savage, piratical salvagers, who often brutally killed off the crews of ships unfortunate enough to wander into their territory. When they died out, the coalescent tribes—mostly Creek Indians—had come together under the Seminole name, and these tribes were far less dangerous. But even so, just being Indian at that time inspired fear. Since the Indian Removal Act of 1830, some eastern tribes had grudgingly accepted their fate and left. But the fierce, intransigent Florida Seminoles stood their ground. The result was a series of bloody encounters that became known as the Seminole Wars.

The incident that frightened everyone most was the massacre of the Cooley family in January 1836 at their New River plantation. The Indians had killed Mrs. Cooley, three of her children, and their tutor. Mr. Cooley had been absent at the time. Later that same year, in July, Indians attacked the lighthouse at Cape Florida—a remote place just like Wreckers' Cay.

Though I abhorred these deeds—and here on the island, I was secretly terrified of being attacked, or, worse, abducted—after the way the government had removed my own family from our land, I could empathize with how the Indians must feel.

As I'd said to Dorothy, the Seminoles' territory tended to be farther north and well east of Wreckers' Cay. Our lighthouse was out of the way for them. But still, I worried.

"I've decided to teach you to shoot guns," I told Andrew one day. "That is, if you'd like to learn."

He seemed intrigued. "You think I need to?"

I related the story of the Cape Florida lighthouse, and his eyes widened in alarm. I worried he might lure me into another discussion about the government's injustice toward the Indians—and by association, slaves—but he just looked intently at me; then a smile broke out on his face. "I reckon I just better learn to shoot!"

We began training twice weekly. Martin's guns had been well cared for, but dust and salt air could affect their efficiency. It was time to remove them again from their locked cabinet to clean them. Timothy, Andrew, and I carefully went over each weapon, taking them apart and cleaning them. Then we set up targets and practiced. Under Martin's tutelage, Timothy had become quite proficient with firearms. Now he assisted me in teaching Andrew, who learned quickly, soon hitting all the targets with great accuracy. He loved shooting from the moment he picked up one of Martin's Springfield rifles, and watching Timothy and Andrew practice for hours, I thought how this skill—so distasteful to me—could be so largely appealing. Was it the noise? The smoke? Or was it that men instinctively enjoyed the power it gave them?

Around that time, I learned I had more to fear than Indians: I'd suddenly stopped feeling life in the baby I was carrying. The charging and kicking of an active child had quieted down to a weak flutter, and one evening, while lying in bed, I prodded my stomach in a panic. I no longer felt anything. To make matters worse, I was experiencing blinding headaches and dizziness. My back was subjected to severe pain, and I heard a constant ringing in my ears. Nothing like this had ever happened to me during pregnancy before.

At dinner the next day, I began to bleed. I excused myself quickly and rushed upstairs, curling up in bed, trying not to scream, for my abdomen was cramped in knots, turning on itself, and I was shaking with chills. Soon I heard Martha knock softly at my door, calling my name, but I was too weak to reply. I could see lightning strikes behind my eyes, as if the lamps from our tower were blazing in my head. I felt I was on fire, like I might perish from thirst. I saw creatures flying through my window, misshapen birds of prey that grew larger as they flew toward me, approaching so closely that I screamed, thinking they would engulf me. Indians crept through my mind in snatches, morphing into black slaves shooting at my grandparents. My dreams brought up visions of Eurydice—once dressed like an Indian—and then Martin, Captain Lee, and Alfie Dillon, circling the island, and my husband calling out for me to get up and look after the children. "Emily, Emily," he called. "They need you. You must get up!"

In this state, one day passed into the next. I do not remember lifting my head. I occasionally heard muffled voices around me, but they seemed far away. I felt firm hands pressing lightly on my abdomen, causing severe pain. I remember sips of water, warm tea, fruit compote, and soup, as well as cool compresses on my forehead. Nights melded into days; nightmares became strange daylight dreams. And through it all, the only constant memory was the light from the tower at night.

Suddenly, it was over. I awoke one morning in a clean, dry bed, wearing a freshly laundered nightgown. A hygienic cloth had been placed between my legs. I probed my quiet, flat abdomen and knew that the baby was gone. Daylight slanted in gloriously through the windows. I thanked God that I was alive, though I lay in bed for a long time, feeling a deep sadness for the child that was gone.

When I sat up, I realized the bed had been turned around, which confused me. A little gris-gris bag pinned onto a cord encircled my neck. I tried to stand but felt so weak, I sank back down onto my bed. I heard Hannah outside, playing fetch with the dog; I could hear birds twittering, and Martha practicing a sad hymn on the piano. My family seemed to have carried on, despite my illness, and for this, too, I was grateful.

There was a timid knock on the door. "Come in," I said. Andrew appeared with a tray of tea and a small bowl of mango preserves.

"You're awake!" he exclaimed. He set the tray down on my blanket box and ran out, shouting the news to Martha and Timothy. They all scurried up to my room, with Hannah bringing up the rear.

"Mama!" called out Martha, and she threw her arms around me. I hugged her and fought back tears of gratitude. Timothy hesitated, but I could see the relief on his face; then he, too, came to my bedside and took my hand. I kissed his cheek and ran my hand through his hair. "We shall have to give you a haircut soon," I said with a smile.

"How are you feeling, Mother?" he asked me anxiously.

"Better," I said weakly. "Much better. But I seem to have trouble getting up and walking."

"You shouldn't be up walking around yet, especially without help," Andrew said. "And you need to eat. Here, drink up this tea. Martha will give you the fruit. I'll go down to the cookhouse and make you a proper breakfast."

"I'm not very hungry," I protested.

"You must eat! You haven't had a proper meal in about ten days."

I looked at him in astonishment. "Ten days?" Had it been that long? Ten days! My eyes fell upon my thin wrists and arms. Ten days of my life had just evaporated away?

"We thought you were going to die," whispered Martha.

"Who has been looking after me?"

The children looked at Andrew.

"Well, we took turns," he said. "We all looked after you." He lowered his voice and added, "Miss Emily, I'm afraid the baby's gone . . . a little girl." I nodded. "She was born dead," Andrew continued. "I pressed your belly to make sure the afterbirth was out after she came."

Again, I was astonished; I blushed to think of Andrew acting as my midwife, seeing those parts of me that only Martin and Dorothy and their helpers had seen. I fingered the gris-gris bag nervously. "How did you . . ."

"I helped with plenty of babies back in Georgia. And I saw one happen like yours did. It'd been dead awhile."

"We buried the baby in the grave the captain and Mr. Dillon dug," Timothy said.

"We wrapped her in a blanket," added Martha, to assure me that all had been done correctly.

I nodded. "Thank you. All of you." I smiled up at Andrew. "You moved my bed and placed this gris-gris bag around my neck?"

It was his turn to look embarrassed. "The bed has to be parallel to the edge of the ocean for the charm to work."

I managed a weak laugh.

It was a few days before I was strong enough to handle stairs easily. I had shed a lot of weight, and my energy disappeared with it. I tried to eat as much as I could, and like a ghost returning from a phantom underworld, I wandered aimlessly from room to room, trying to focus on spaces and shapes.

My children appeared happy and well cared for after my illness. The house had clearly been well tended. Hannah, who had probably been the most upset by my absence, now demanded my full attention. She rushed often into my room, and I spent many hours nuzzling her in my bed as I napped, soothing and reassuring her. I took short walks around the island with her, breathing the fresh salty air in great gulps, luxuriating in the sun's warmth on my skin. I marveled at the wind through my hair, the sand glittering around my feet, and the ospreys, gulls, and pelicans tracing circles above us. The lighthouse still stood guard, piercing the sky, and I could not help but recall its bewitching welcome when we first arrived. I yearned for the strength to climb to the top of its glass enclosure once again. How grand it is just to be alive, I thought, to savor the day and the simple joys around me as I hold the eager hand of my sweet child.

We visited my baby's grave and laid wildflowers over the earth that covered it. Hannah just vaguely understood these gestures, but she was eager to help, picking the flowers and patting the dirt around the grave site. "I'm sorry," I whispered sadly to the baby. "I never even got to see you. . . ."

I'd risen from my bed just in time, for Captain Lee and Alfie arrived soon after. As Brandy's bark announced them, Andrew hastened to the playhouse. Everything was back to normal. To make up for my strange behavior on their previous visits, I made the effort to appear at the dock as soon as they stepped off the tender and secured it. "You're just in time," I said. "I have some homemade biscuits fresh from the oven. Come to the veranda when you're through."

They beamed. "That sounds mighty fine," replied the captain.

He handed me my mail and Alfie began to unload the containers of oil. While the men worked at stowing my supplies, I opened my letters to see if they required immediate attention. There was one from Dorothy, reporting all the latest news from Key West and saying how much she was looking forward to coming over again for the birth. I felt my sister should know of my loss, so she could cancel her plans. Tired as I was, I wrote her a note in French, telling her of my ordeal. Then I sealed the envelope securely and handed it to the captain to deliver.

"You're looking a mite peaked," remarked Lee. I knew I looked terrible: I had circles under my eyes, my hair was thin and limp, and I'd lost a great deal of weight. "I have been a little tired of late," I admitted. "I've been down with some kind of grippe."

He shook his head. "Miss Dorothy said you're working very hard out here."

I had to smile. "Yes, but as you can see, we are still managing."

The captain was staring at my bosom in a peculiar way. "You practicin' magic out here, Miss Emily?" he asked. He had spotted my little gris-gris bag.

I blushed. I'd planned to remove it while he was on the island, despite Andrew's warnings that it had to stay on until the full moon.

"I heard tell you folks from New Orleans are into that . . . voodoo stuff," he ventured cautiously.

Hannah chose that moment to run up to us, and he saw that she, too, was wearing her gris-gris pouch. I could just imagine the gossip he would take back to Key West this time. That mad woman out at the Wreckers' Cay lighthouse, practicing black magic! What would Gran and her friends say?

With absolutely no reasonable explanation prepared to offer him, I simply laughed. "Hardly, Captain. It's just a little project I have been doing with the children. Shall we have some tea and biscuits?"

FIFTEEN

Wreckers' Cay

December 1839

The captain's visits, which I'd once looked forward to during that terrible time after Martin vanished, were now becoming stressful. They interrupted our work on the island, and forced Andrew to remain in the playhouse, often for many hours. Much as I needed the supplies, by mid-December, I found myself dreading their delivery days. After their latest visit, I was feeling particularly high-strung from the hours of forced politeness in the captain's company.

When they had left, I approached Andrew. "Remember when Dorothy was here, the two of you were smoking an unusual plant in one of Martin's old clay pipes?"

He smiled. "You want to try it?"

"Well . . ." I hesitated. Why was I acting so coy? "Yes, perhaps. It might be nice to relax, and I don't much approve of alcohol."

"This is not like alcohol," he said.

"Isn't it just some kind of weed?"

"It is. Quite a powerful weed."

Never having tried a cigar, I had trouble at first with the

technique of inhaling smoke from the plant. I choked on the first few puffs, and thought the experience somewhat vile.

Andrew watched me, amused. "Take a puff and then hold it," he suggested.

After a few more tries, I succeeded in taking in the smoke without coughing, and soon I began to sense a feeling of great calm descend over me. "Well," I said. "That's quite . . ."

He was smiling. "Nice, isn't it?"

I nodded, inhaling again.

"Some of the slaves at the plantation in Georgia showed me how to cut it and dry it out. It grew wild there, too. We were on a tobacco plantation, so nobody noticed. We just dried it along with the regular tobacco. Soon's I saw it growing here, I recognized it and thought it would be a good medicine to have for pain. I gave you some in your tea while you were sick."

"You can make tea from it?"

"Oh yes, it makes a fine tea. You can put it in biscuits, too."

Oddly, this notion struck me as quite funny, and I began to laugh. It occurred to me that I had not laughed like this since before I lost my baby. Then suddenly, I felt serious again. The weed had made me light-headed, and since the children were outside playing, we were in the cookhouse alone. Emboldened by the weed, I placed my hand on his, which was resting on the table. He looked up in surprise. But I felt no shame or surprise of my own. It was the first time I'd ever consciously touched him.

"Andrew, I want to thank you. You saved my life here. We owe you—I owe you—a great deal."

He shook his head. "No, you don't. I'm just glad I could help."

"Well, I'm grateful," I said. I suddenly felt incredibly fatigued, and I fought the urge to nod off. "So grateful to you."

"You're tired," he said. "And I think the herb has made you even drowsier. Let me help you upstairs."

He did, and I quickly fell asleep, waking in time to make the family's supper. I ate a little, but I had an inordinate urge to eat sweets with some tea.

During the night, I awoke several times when I noticed the lamps had been extinguished. They were immediately relit, but I had to wonder why they continued to go out, for there was little or no wind to temper the flame.

"I don't think we got good oil this time," Andrew said to me the next morning. "I got tired of running up the stairs, so I got out a blanket and slept up there. Must have relit the lamps half a dozen times. And the oil was so smoky, I had to keep washing the carbon off the lens and reflectors to keep the light sharp. It was hard breathing up there, too."

"That's terrible," I said. "It's never happened before. They're supposed to test the oil beforehand."

A batch of impure oil would be a terrible problem, since the supply tender would not be back for two weeks, and I had no way of even letting the department know until the captain and Alfie returned.

To my good fortune, this was solved by a surprise visit the next day from Rebecca Flaherty, who, until recently, had tended the light at Sand Key. She had sent her family on to Key West and then had stayed behind to clear out the keeper's house. Before joining her family, she made the rounds to bid farewell to other lighthouse keepers in the area.

Rebecca Flaherty, who was reputed to be something of a scold, was one of a very small sisterhood: widows who had inherited their husbands' light-keeping positions in the Florida Keys. Rebecca had taken over the Sand Key light station from her late first husband. When she remarried, she tended the lighthouse for another three years. Over time, she had been a continual annoyance to the Lighthouse Services, sending her frequent complaints directly to Mrs. Adams, wife of the president at that time.

"I declare, I don't know how you manage it, Miss Emily," she said, looking around. "Lordy, just look at this place; everything is so well kept. You really make the rest of us look inefficient!"

Her praise embarrassed me. I almost felt like admitting the truth to make her feel better. Instead, I explained my problem about the contaminated oil and asked her to take a sample of it back to Key West for testing.

"I'd be more than happy to," she said. "It doesn't surprise me one whit. I'm sure the oil gets a cursory inspection, if any at all." She seized on the opportunity to vent about the superintendent of the Lighthouse Services, Stephen Pendleton, whom she despised. I recalled how he had groped me when he came to inspect the light that first time, and I wondered vaguely if she had also experienced such inappropriate behavior.

She ranted about his delay in the installation of a superior new lens at her lighthouse in Sand Key. A phenomenal new kind of lens that provided a much stronger, steadier light had recently been developed by Augustin-Jean Fresnel in France. "But Pendleton, he's struck deals with Winslow Lewis to keep the old-fashioned ones working. Anything to save money!" she said with vehemence.

"Who will now work the light at Sand Key?" I asked.

"Josiah Peartree. That old pirate! I'm sure he'll be over to introduce himself; you should probably lock up the silver," she added with a wicked smile.

I'd read much about Josiah Peartree in the *Key West Enquirer*. He was a man of some sophistication, a wrecking captain from Rhode Island, who had at one time been arrested by Commodore Porter for his dealings with a notorious privateer, Captain Phillip Halston. The newspaper described how Halston had plied his nefarious trade along the coasts of the Keys as master of an armed Colombian schooner. Peartree had evidently facilitated his work with underhanded dealings that eliminated the need for Halston to have his wrecking cases adjudicated in court. This had done much to taint Peartree's reputation, but nevertheless, when he was released, he moved to Key West and made new friends in high places. Widowed for a second time, he was getting on in years, and was now being given the post of lighthouse keeper at Sand Key.

"Goodness knows what kind of dishonest tricks he will be up to once he gets there," Rebecca said.

I considered this. There were certainly ways a keeper might be corrupted. By dimming or quenching lights at the right time, he could arrange for ships to run up on the reef, to the benefit of salvagers.

"Anyway, he's welcome to the place," she continued bitterly. "I've had quite enough of Sand Key."

Captain Lee and Alfie Dillon arrived just a few days later with a shipment of clean oil. As they were on their way to Havana, they promised to relieve me of the defective oil on their way back, or on their next supply trip.

Andrew noticed the difference immediately. "Much better," he said on the first night after they left. "Lights up right away. No smoke." He placed the jugs containing the inferior-quality oil outside the door of the oil-storage house so it would be easy for Alfie to haul them to the supply tender.

In previous years, Christmas had always been a beautiful time on the island. The weather, while still warm, had cooled down enough to be pleasant, and the soothing breezes of winter had chased away the still, stuffy doldrums of early autumn. It had been a difficult year for me and the children, and facing the holiday without Martin—or the baby I had lost—was a daunting prospect. Yet, I knew that for the sake of the children, I would have to make some effort to celebrate the holiday.

Andrew sensed this. He cut down a small pine tree and we all contributed to its beautification. A box in the storage shed held ornaments that Martin had painstakingly crafted years before—wooden pieces shaped like mermaids, boats, starfish, and anchors. But when I took these out, I could only think of Martin. With tears in my eyes, I put them away, urging the children to make new decorations. This was a good decision, for they busied themselves with crafting and painting, taking their minds off their father's absence. Andrew found seashells and sea glass worn from the pounding of the ocean on the beach, and together we all hung pinecones, painted eggshells, and cutout paper figures; the children threaded red berries from palm trees; and we hung cookies shaped like stars throughout the house.

On Christmas Day, we gathered around the piano. Martha and Timothy played carols, Andrew sang Christmas spirituals, and Hannah, as always, clapped enthusiastically, her eyes shining.

There were the gifts Dorothy had brought earlier: Gran had sent Martha some watercolor paints. Timothy received a spyglass, which he had always wanted. For Hannah, she had purchased a beautiful new doll with eyes that opened and closed. Hannah delightedly showed it to everyone, but I had to laugh later when I found her asleep on the sofa, cuddled with her old rag doll.

Best of all were the gifts we created for each other. Andrew gave me a sweetgrass basket. He made Timothy and Martha gris-gris bags, which they promptly put on. Martha made everyone sweetly scented pomanders from oranges she had studded with cloves and tied with pretty ribbons. Timothy had been busy carving things from wood and had sculpted a wooden figure of a dolphin for me and a duck decoy for Andrew. Hannah had drawn pictures for everyone; they were happy scribbles, reflecting her sweet personality, with the sun shining and stick people smiling in a garden of green-and-red swirls.

Having been ill for so long, I'd been unable to make many gifts myself. But I had managed to crochet some hand puppets for Hannah, which delighted her. When I gave Andrew one of our used geography books, I heard him catch his breath—it was his first book. To the elder children, I gave new sheet music that Dorothy had left me.

We treated ourselves to a couple of stuffed chickens for Christmas dinner, and I served cooked squash and some preserved green beans from our garden. For dessert, I made a Key lime pie, and Andrew served us slices of one of the pineapples from the garden.

"This is the nicest Christmas I ever had," he announced with a broad smile.

I had fully expected our first Christmas without Martin to be unbearably sad. But to my surprise, it was not. The children seemed to have long accepted that their father was gone. It had been seven months, after all, and we were gradually losing hope that he would ever reappear in our lives. We seldom spoke of Martin now. Andrew's presence had made an impact on all of us: Andrew, who appeared out of nowhere at just the right time, almost as if he had been sent by Martin to replace him at the light. Out of habit, we still scanned the beach almost every day with the thought that Martin, or something belonging to him, might wash up onshore. But it did not happen, and we were spared the ordeal of having to deal with a grisly discovery.

SIXTEEN

Wreckers' Cay

January 1840

One evening, just a week into the new year, Hannah—usually so good about bedding down for the night—disrupted the peace of our household by looking for her rag doll. We all launched into a search for it throughout the house and garden. Once darkness descended, we soothed her as best we could and promised to look for it at first light.

The weather was still warm; the seas were calm. Brightness glowed from our steady lighthouse beam. And the moon glowed like a polished pewter plate suspended over the water. My bed was still in front of the window, where Andrew had placed it, and I told myself it was high time to stop this foolishness, especially now that the moon was full; I vowed to move it back in the morning.

After mumbling briefly in a drowsy conversation with Martin, I fell asleep, only to be awakened in the middle of the night by Brandy's frantic barking. Normally, she kept Andrew company at the tower and dozed off and on throughout the night, so this kind of behavior was highly unusual. Alarmed, I sat up in bed and peered out the window. From where my bed was now positioned, I could clearly see that the beam from the lighthouse was picking up a dugout canoe with a small Indian party, heading toward our beach. My hands began to shake uncontrollably. Most accounts of previous attacks reported that Indians traveled in large groups, with sometimes as many as forty braves in several canoes. I scanned the surface of the water between the palms to see if others were close by, but I saw nothing.

My heart pounding, I hurriedly unlocked the gun cupboard, awoke Timothy, and forced myself to load the rifles with him. Calmly, I told Martha to keep an eye on Hannah. Then I heard Andrew's heavy tread on the stairs as he ran up to join us. Thanking God he was there, I handed both him and Timothy a firearm and some additional ammunition.

"It's a small party," whispered Andrew. "I think we can take them pretty easy."

"There's something strange about this," I whispered back. "There are so few of them. They may just be scouts. And why would they come here when the moon is so bright that they can easily be seen?"

Andrew had been unable to coax Brandy into the house, and she continued to bark frantically. We were poised quietly at the windows of my room, which faced south, overlooking the beach. Patiently, we waited until they landed. The braves came ashore, whooping and yelling. This noise itself was enough to rip our hearts from our chests. The first one to land ran directly to the oil-storage house, and seeing the jugs of oil Andrew had set out for Alfie, he shouted to the others. Then he began to shake the oil around the base of the lighthouse, whooping all the while. My entire body was pulsating with fear, and when I looked down at my trembling hands, I wondered if I could even hold on to my rifle.

"They're going to set fire to the lighthouse tower," I said, my gun raised. A second brave leaped out of the canoe and the pair of them worked quickly to spread the oil around the tower walls. But still we held our fire. "Not yet," I cautioned Timothy and Andrew as they began to aim. "I want to see them clustered closely together before we start shooting."

The other braves had pulled the canoe up onto the beach and then began to help those already at the tower, spreading kindling at the base. Our dog's barking became even shriller, lending itself to the general cacophony and confusion. One of the Indians raised his rifle, aiming directly at Brandy. We heard a shot ring out; she gave one last yelp, then landed in a twitching heap by the door of the oil house. As Brandy had been Timothy's dog since he was a baby and she a puppy, he could not contain himself; he immediately screamed.

The men below froze. Then a shot whizzed past, shattering the shutter of my window into splinters. The party continued to set fire to the tower, but now they also shot up in our direction. There was a light but steady breeze that night, and their flames raged to life, quickly drawn up the sides of the brick tower walls in a huge smoking blaze.

I looked at Andrew, whose face was knotted in anger. He took aim, and suddenly the Indian who had killed Brandy collapsed in the sand. A strange kind of calm settled over me as I followed suit and aimed my first shot. After that, I remember only the terrible confusion as we exchanged shots with the Indians on the ground, ducking below the windowsill, then quickly aiming and firing and ducking back.

Then, as suddenly as it had started, the fire around the lighthouse went out and their whooping subsided in disappointment.

"They used the bad oil!" whispered Andrew, and I was amazed to see that he was smiling. Taking advantage of their consternation, he took aim at yet another, who fell over in a heap on a thicket of shrubbery near the tower.

The gunfire resumed, and suddenly Andrew flinched. A

bullet grazed the flesh of his shoulder, only to exit and hit the wall behind him. Ducking down, I crawled over to him, but he waved me away. "I'm fine!" he hissed. "Stay over there!"

I moved back to my post, aimed, and pulled the trigger. The Indian who'd shot Andrew fell to the ground; I summoned more courage and hit another one.

Meanwhile, Timothy, enraged at Brandy's death, had begun to lose control. His shots rang out indiscriminately. "Easy son," I cautioned. "Conserve your bullets. Make every one count!" But he was not listening. Andrew and I were taking our time and aiming carefully, effectively picking them off one by one. They were making their way back toward the beach now, one running and the other limping along behind him, when Andrew again raised his rifle and shot them both. I was stunned at his accuracy, despite his shoulder wound, which was bleeding profusely. Beside me, Timothy continued shooting in a rage, spraying his shots across the beach after the Indians until he ran out of ammunition and fell back, sweating.

Suddenly, the night was wrapped in eerie silence. We had killed them all. I did not know how many—perhaps as many as eight or ten. I couldn't keep track in the dark. Exhausted, I fell back on my bed; the gun fell from my hands onto the floor as I took deep breaths to calm myself.

"Look," whispered Andrew. Alarmed, I sat up, expecting to see more canoes. Instead, an approaching sloop was visible through the trees as it glided along the silvery water and landed at the beach. Andrew raised his rifle. "Reload!" he commanded us hoarsely. Timothy obeyed, and I picked up my firearm and prepared to do battle again.

Timothy had brought his new spyglass into the room and trained it on the beach. In the moonlight, he was able to see the silhouette of a lone figure tying his boat to our dock. "He's alone," announced Timothy. "I don't see anyone else."

The man held aloft a stick with a white flag. He waved it

slowly as he stepped quietly onto the beach. Andrew raised his gun, but I whispered, "Wait. . . ."

Andrew paused.

"I think he just wants to recover their bodies," I said. "Give him a minute."

"Why?" demanded Andrew. Blood continued to ooze from his shoulder, and his face was twisted in pain.

"I don't want to be stuck with their bodies. They would just send another party back to collect them." Andrew did not lower his firearm, but he was considering what I had said.

For the next fifteen minutes or so, keeping the white flag planted in the sand, the lone brave wordlessly dragged the bodies of his cohorts one by one and placed them on the deck of his boat. Then he tied the dugout canoe to the stern, untied his line, and, catching a good breeze, disappeared silently into the night.

Andrew and Timothy were jubilant, laughing and congratulating each other with slaps and jokes. But I was silent, filled with a feeling of dread. It occurred to me that they had deliberately set out to destroy the lighthouse first. Killing us had seemed . . . almost secondary.

We were about to go downstairs to examine our poor Brandy, when Martha burst into the room. She screamed, "Mama, I can't find Hannah!"

I froze. Earlier that night, Hannah had been crying over her missing doll. Could she have possibly gone out to . . . .?

Martha was sobbing. "I thought she was in bed, but she's not!"

Frantically, we all flew down the stairs. I rushed through all the rooms of our first floor, and I heard Andrew crashing through behind me. When I could not find her, I ran outside. Debris was still smoldering at the base of the tower. The acrid smell of the dying embers and gun smoke assailed my nostrils and dimmed my watering eyes.

My baby—Hannah. She was nowhere to be seen. I screamed out her name. "Hannah!" I was out of my mind, running through the garden without shoes, tearing up my feet as I kicked through the plants, searching for her. I rushed toward the tower, and then I saw her.

My little girl lay on the moonlit turtle grass, which glistened with dew. She was bleeding from her chest. The white embroidered nightgown she'd gotten from Dorothy for Christmas was drenched in crimson. When I reached her side, her bright eyes were wide open in surprise and confusion, but she was perfectly still. There was no pulse and no breath.

A few feet away was her little rag doll.

The pain of losing Hannah was almost too much to bear. A cloud of grief settled over me that night, burrowing into my soul. It was an agony so acute, it sucked the air from my lungs and kept me from breathing. Andrew had to lead me back to my room and place me in bed. I could not move; I found I could not even speak.

We all mourned our sweet little Hannah. And none of us would ever know whose gun had delivered the mortal wound.

The next day, I rose after a sleepless night and tended to Andrew's injury. Finally allowing himself to give way to grief, he began to sob. "That poor little girl," he said.

I nodded sadly. "She loved you," I told him.

Hannah had meant the world to Andrew, I knew. For a man who had been whipped and abused and sold, removed from his milieu, imprisoned and kidnapped, the unconditional love of a small child—a little girl who asked for nothing in return—was an inestimable gift.

Later that day, we buried Hannah in the grave where my dead baby already lay. Timothy and Martha gave short eulogies, and we held candles and said a little prayer together; then we sang "Panis Angelicus," led by Andrew. Bread of the angels. So appropriate for our innocent little angel.

I could easily have taken to my bed again after that. The anguish was so piercing. The deep wound in the earth we had readied for my husband was instead filling with his children. Would there be no end to this grief?

I led Martha and Timothy back toward the house as Andrew gently spaded the moist earth over Hannah's body.

A few days later, Martha came to me in the cookhouse with tears rolling down her face. "Was it my fault?" she asked.

"Of course not, darlin'," I said, kissing her forehead as I took her in my arms. "No. Of course not. We thought she was in bed. It was a terrifying night for all of us—except for Hannah. She couldn't hear the commotion, so she had no idea what was happening till she was outside." I could only imagine her last terrible moments when she saw the Indians and the fires.

No sooner had Martha dried her tears than I went past the parlor, where Timothy was supposed to be practicing his violin. The silence drew me into the room, where I saw him sitting on the horsehair sofa, his head bent. I sat next to him and saw anguish etched on his face. "I think I might have killed her," he whispered. "I just blasted away at those Indians without aiming or thinking. It might have been from my gun."

I put my arm around his shoulder and kissed him. My son—who in recent months had normally resisted this kind of affections—leaned into me. "Timothy, you mustn't think that," I said softly. "It could have been fire from my gun, or Andrew's rifle. Or even from the Indians. We were all so . . . involved."

He looked up at me. "You don't think it was me?"

"No, of course not."

But in my heart I did not believe the fatal shot was from an Indian. It had to have come from our venue on the second floor. And more than likely, it had indeed been from Timothy's gun. Andrew and I, being less rash, had been more deliberate in our aim. Timothy was still a child, still immature in many ways, despite his many adult responsibilities on Wreckers' Cay. In retrospect, it had been a mistake to allow him to take up arms. But I took comfort in the fact that we could never truly know one way or the other.

The next day, Andrew helped him dig a special little grave for Brandy. Timothy and Martha both wrote little poems to her, and Andrew marked the grave with a large conch shell.

One evening soon after Hannah's burial, after Andrew lit the lamps, he and I sat together in the parlor, smoking some of his peculiar weed. The night was cool and he lit a fire, a cozy fruit-wood blaze.

"She was the child I thought I would always have," I said after a long silence. "When Martha and Timothy would grow up and move away, I saw myself growing old with Hannah by my side. I knew her opportunities in life would be"—I paused—"limited. I wanted to be there for her—and I always assumed she would be with me."

Andrew stared into the fire, and finally spoke: "Seems like whenever I start to love somebody, they disappear from my life."

He had never spoken to me about his family. I watched the light from the fire play over his handsome features and flicker in his eyes. We were sitting very close to each other, sharing the pipe, and quite suddenly, without thinking, I leaned toward him and kissed him on the cheek. He turned his face toward me and, affected by the weed's calming influence, I kissed him lightly on the mouth. He returned my kiss, first lightly, then eagerly. But then he drew back.

"Come to my room," I whispered.

He tilted his head, looking at me quizzically. After a long moment, he said, "No . . . I don't think so."

I lowered my head in shame. What had I been thinking? Had my grief finally driven me mad?

He brought his hand over to my chin and lifted my head so he could meet my eyes. "You may already know this, Emily, but I do love you very much," he said simply.

It thrilled me just to have him say my name for the first time.

"I have for some time. But no good would come from it. Believe me."

"Why not?" I asked miserably; I was feeling so empty.

He kissed my cheek, and I realized there were tears streaming down my face. "I'll explain everything to you someday. But this isn't the right time." He wiped away my tears with another light kiss on the cheek. Then he rose from the couch. "Good night, Emily," he said kindly, and left for the playhouse without glancing back, leaving me alone in my wretchedness.

"Well, you've certainly made a proper hash of things," Martin chided me when I got into bed. "You foolish woman, have you no pride left at all? Trying to seduce a black slave!"

"Oh, do be quiet, Martin," I snapped. The weed had muddled my thoughts: I was feeling aggrieved . . . aroused . . . and mortified. I had wanted the comfort of another person under my quilt. Instead, I was to be rebuked by a ghost.

"You surprise me, Emily," he continued. "You certainly never tried to seduce me."

The next morning, and for several days afterward, I avoided Andrew's glance. I continued to serve him breakfast; I coolly discussed our chores. And I tutored him, as I always had. But something had changed between us. The good-natured banter was gone. In its place were silence, tension, and pain—above all, pain.

But incredibly, I wanted him all the more. Now in my clear-eyed mornings, even without benefit of the strange weed, I fantasized about what it would be like to lead him to my bed. When he was not looking, I gazed at him like a love-struck schoolgirl. I watched for him when he came out of the shower area near the cistern; I feasted on the curves of his body when he worked in the garden. Clearly, I was losing my mind.

At times, I wondered if I should just give up and move back to Key West or New Orleans. There seemed to be little reason to stay; I wasn't tending the light anyway. I had wanted to remain on the island because I thought it would be safer for my children to be away from the breakouts of diseases that plagued Key West. But I hadn't counted on raids by warring Indians. Dorothy had been right after all.

Perhaps I was developing these feelings for Andrew because he was simply the only man around and I was still a vital young woman. Maybe it had something to do with having lost another child. I didn't know anymore. All I knew was that when I heard him talking to the children, laughing with them, I wanted him to hold me, kiss me, explore my body. . . .

Finally, after almost a week, Andrew returned to the cookhouse after supper when the children were asleep and asked if I would like to smoke with him. My heart leaped in my chest and I nodded.

When I joined him, he had lit a fire in the grate and made room for me on the couch. We sat sharing the pipe, smoking in silence for a few minutes. Outside, I could see night birds fishing over the water, diving and striking, their squeals cutting through the silence between us.

Andrew put the pipe down. "Emily," he said. "Look at me."

I turned, and he kissed me lightly on the lips, igniting a rush of emotion, which I forced myself to hold in check.

"You've been on this island for too long. You've forgotten the rules."

"But it's different here," I protested. "We can make our own rules about"—I gestured at the space between us—"about this."

"That's not true, Emily. If it was, I wouldn't have to go running into the playhouse all the time."

I considered this. He was right about one thing. This island had become a cocoon of sorts, and perhaps this was dangerous. "Tell me," I said, "I want to know more about you."

He turned back toward the fire. "Well, first of all . . . I lied. I'm not free." He stood up and slowly went to poke the fire, then turned to me with pain in his eyes. "I'm still a slave. I didn't lose my manumission papers. . . . I never had any. I still belong to the captain of *Der Nederlander*."

"How did that happen? You told me you were pressed onto a ship in Savannah." This confession was a confirmation of all the suspicions that had played on the edges of my mind since his arrival.

He just shook his head.

"Well," I managed to say, "as far as I'm concerned, you are free."

"No. Legally, I'm not. My massa sold me to the Dutch captain when he made a stop for supplies in Georgia. The crew threw me down onto the slave deck with the Africans who were going to Cuba to be sold. I was slated for the sugar plantations over there when I jumped ship."

He paused, staring into the fire before speaking again. "Emily, the last time I went to a white woman's bed, I got into a big heap of trouble—you've seen those scars on my back."

Settling next to me again on the couch, he continued. We passed the pipe back and forth between us, and I listened to his story: His grandmother had come over from West Africa in chains when she was fifteen. She was raped often by her master, which was how Andrew's mother was born. Then Andrew's mother was sold to another plantation, one owned by a tobacco planter named Thomas Watson. He raped her—and she became pregnant with Andrew.

"He got plenty of slave women pregnant," Andrew said, "so I got relatives up there in Georgia I don't even know about. Lots of white women liked it if their husbands messed with the slave women. Less work for them in the bedroom. Besides," he added wryly, "more slaves that way, and for nothing."

Thomas Watson never acknowledged Andrew as his son, but he did treat him differently. He let Andrew work in the garden and perform chores around the house. When Watson's wife passed away in childbirth, he was left with a passel of daughters. He soon married again, this time to a younger woman named Sarah, who was from Charleston. She was twenty, and very pretty.

"She smiled at me all the time," he said. He shrugged. "I just thought she was being nice. . . ."

"How old were you at this point?"

"Twenty-three? Twenty-five? I'm not sure what my age is. Slaves there weren't allowed to get married, but I had started to keep company with a nice slave girl named Ginny. She got pregnant and I became a father. . . ." He smiled. "A little girl the massa named Cleo."

Meanwhile, Sarah promoted Andrew to work in the house. She bought him good clothes for serving at the table, and even taught him a few songs and hymns. His mama and Ginny kept warning him about Sarah's attention, but he dismissed their concerns.

"She played the piano, like you." He smiled at me.

"This all explains why you speak . . . better than other slaves."

"I reckon so. I wanted Sarah to think well of me. And she liked that. I think she kind of considered me some sort of experiment. She and massa sometimes had me sing for their guests. I would leave off my work to perform . . . and I loved the applause."

Thomas Watson wanted sons, and he soon turned against Sarah after she bore him two daughters. Sarah grew unhappy, and Thomas became abusive. He had Andrew move her things to a bedroom on the other side of the house. Sometimes Andrew found her alone in her room, crying, and bruised.

"Well, one day when nobody was around, I was repairing some shutters, and she called me upstairs. Said she needed me to do something for her."

"Yes?" I said, urging him to continue.

When he got to her room, Sarah seduced him. (I gathered from Andrew's expression now that she must not have had a difficult time of this.) Their relationship went on for quite a while, many months after that—until Sarah became pregnant.

Sarah panicked. She figured if she could get Thomas to take her back to bed, then she could let him think it was his and get through most of her pregnancy, leastwise till she could figure out what to do. They knew her baby wouldn't be white, so she planned to leave Thomas around her eighth month or so and have the baby in Charleston. Using her wiles and a few shots of bourbon one night, she got her husband to take her back.

But the baby came almost a month early. It was a little boy, and he looked just like Andrew. There was no point in lying after that. Thomas ordered his foreman to tie Andrew down in the barn and slash him with a bullwhip. "Almost down to the bone," Andrew said. Then he took care of Sarah himself. He beat her half to death and packed her off to Charleston with her "nigger bastard."

"How horrible," I whispered.

"He asked Sarah if I'd raped her. She said no. If she'd said yes, she might have avoided the beating, and I would have been lynched on the spot. Instead, I was arrested."

"Did you ever see Sarah again?"

"No."

"The baby?"

He shook his head. "No."

"And what about your family? Ginny and Cleo?"

Andrew didn't answer, and I saw tears in his eyes. Finally, he spoke. "He sold them. I don't know where they went."

After that, Andrew sat in jail for a year. There were rumors of an illegal Dutch slaver arriving near Savannah. Then, one night, a few members of the crew took Andrew from the jail, dragged him down to the port, and shoved him onto their boat. He was tossed down into the slave deck with all the African slaves on their way to the Caribbean, and they secured him in irons with another slave. Andrew overheard two English members of the crew laughing and saying how they intended to "splice the main brace" in Havana—a reference to rum drinking. And he realized they were headed to Cuba, where he would be sold again.

Andrew's chance to escape came the night of the bad storm. The crew needed more hands up on deck, so they hauled Andrew up in chains. They unchained him so he could work alongside the sailors, and then they put the chains back on. But before they could return him to the slave deck, the ship was slapped by a rogue wave, and Andrew was left alone while the sailors tried to stabilize the vessel.

"So I jumped," he said. As luck would have it, he came upon a downed tree that was floating and hung on to it. "Then I saw your beam. And the next day, Martha and Timothy found me."

"And then their mother was horrible to you," I said.

He slowly shook his head. "No."

He reached out and touched the tendrils of my hair that had escaped from my hairpins. "Emily, just having me here . . . it's not legal. I'm not a freedman."

"I don't care about that," I said.

"And even if we did what you're suggesting"—he nodded up

toward my bedroom—"what if you get pregnant? I can promise you, Emily, that baby would be dark-skinned. What then? And what would your children think?"

I sighed and rose from the couch.

"Good night, Emily," he said. Then he kissed me gently.

I left him in the parlor and went to bed alone, checking first on my sleeping children and gazing out at the tower and the light beam from my bedroom window. It was many hours before I fell asleep.

PART TWO

Wreckers' Cay

1840–1841

SEVENTEEN

Wreckers' Cay

February 1840

Captain Lee and Alfie Dillon arrived with supplies several weeks after the Indians' attack. The news of the raid came as a shock, but they were even more outraged to hear of Hannah's death. Alfie's face turned ashen as it registered dismay. Lee seethed quietly before he spoke. "Those bastards," he whispered.

Before they left, I asked them for a new dog to replace our Brandy. The children missed her, and I missed the sense of security she gave me. I also needed to have a dog who would bark at the approach of strangers, for it was Andrew's signal to hide. They promised me they would find a dog and bring it on the next trip.

I gave them letters for Dorothy and my grandmother, so they would all know what happened to Hannah. Several days later, I had a visit from the lighthouse keeper at Garden Key, Jeremiah Weston, and his wife, Ruth, who brought us a rich chocolate cake and an adorable female puppy. Having heard our news from Captain Lee and Alfie, they wanted to pay their respects.

"We were so very sad to hear about your child," Ruth said.

She was a big woman in her fifties, with flabby arms and graying hair pinned back in a bun. The enlarged line of her hips and legs formed a comfortable lap for the puppy, who nestled there, not wanting to leave. The dog was a mixed breed, with floppy ears and black-and-white markings; we all loved her immediately. Andrew particularly took to her, and once she adjusted to his routine, she accompanied him to the tower every evening. Since she had clearly adopted him as her master, we persuaded Andrew to give her a name. "Bourbon," he said, eyeing Timothy with a grin. "Just like Brandy."

One afternoon, Bourbon's barking alerted us to the approach of a boat I was not familiar with. I watched curiously as a distinguished gentleman and a much younger woman tied up at the dock. Andrew was caught unawares on the gallery at the tower, where he'd been painting window trims. He stopped quickly and hid inside.

From his boat, the gentleman called out, "Good day, Mrs. Lowry," bowing slightly. "I've been meaning to stop by and pay my respects—and to offer my condolences."

Speaking in a northern accent, he introduced himself as Josiah Peartree, and his daughter as Mary Beth. He was the new lighthouse keeper at Sand Key, replacing Rebecca Flaherty. I studied him. This dapper man was the disreputable old pirate she had grumbled about?

I welcomed them and accepted their gift of a lovely watercolor painting—tropical birds in flight—that Mary Beth had done. She was a young widow in her early twenties.

"It's beautiful," I murmured sincerely, for she had captured the movement and contrast of a white heron in the mangroves. "Thank you."

In spite of the discomfort Andrew had to be feeling in the heat of the tower, I felt constrained to offer them tea, and hoped they would not dally afterward.

From the beach, Peartree's eyes scanned the island with

both envy and admiration. "I'm truly impressed, Mrs. Lowry," he said. "To think you have been keeping the light at this isolated location on your own, and looking after a family! It's truly remarkable." He began walking toward the tower, and I became nervous. "Is that fresh paint I smell?" he asked.

"Yes, we—I—have been touching up paint in the tower. Please, come this way and join me for tea or some lemonade."

Peartree intrigued me. Despite his infamous reputation, I found him rather charming. We chatted for perhaps an hour or two before they took their leave. As he left, Peartree took my hand with a meaningful look. "I hope to see you again soon, Mrs. Lowry," he murmured. "You must come over to Sand Key for a picnic with your children some afternoon."

I thanked him and said we would try.

As the wind filled his sails, Peartree looked back with a lingering smile, and it was clear that he had visited Wreckers' Cay less to take measure of the tower than to take the measure of its recently widowed keeper. I forced a smile in return, but my thoughts were of Andrew, who had been waiting all afternoon up in the overheated tower amid paint fumes.

I ran to the tower and called out, but there was no answer. Thinking he might have succumbed to the heat and fumes, I rushed up the stairs, but, to my relief, the lantern room was empty. I found him sitting under the gumbo-limbo tree near the lagoon, reading his geography book as he sipped lemonade. He had been in the water and now was covered only with a towel. His hair had grown back since he had shaved it initially, and the sun was infusing the black wires of his damp curls with light.

"Thank God you're all right," I said, sitting next to him.

"I needed a break anyway, and I managed to sneak around to the back while y'all were having your fancy tea and cakes. I went for a long swim."

"You can swim with your sore shoulder?"

"It's a lot better now," he said, flexing his arm. "You know we'll always survive, you and I."

"It must be the gris-gris bags," I said drily.

He grinned. We sat there on the beach of the lagoon in comfortable silence, listening to the calls of squealing birds and the constant thrum of insects.

"So what was the old man like?" he asked.

"An old flirt. He seemed to fancy me. Invited me to go to Sand Key for a picnic with the children."

"Am I invited?"

I laughed. "Not likely."

I leaned back, stretching, and when I looked down, I immediately noticed his arousal spring to life. When I heard sounds from the children in the garden, I began to rise. "Maybe you need another cool swim," I said with a mischievous smile as I turned to go. He laughed.

I glanced back over my shoulder. "Can we smoke your plant tonight after the light is ready and the children are in bed?"

He didn't hesitate. "Yes, but only if you promise to behave." I laughed then. "Of course," I said.

EIGHTEEN

Wreckers' Cay

1840

For the next few months, as the year headed into spring, I tried to comport myself with dignity around Andrew. Meanwhile, my children were recovering some of the joys of being children again. Martha had been charmed by the painting Mary Beth Peartree had brought us, and she tried to copy it with the set of watercolors Gran had given her for Christmas. She did a creditable job and she began to try her hand at subjects around her. Mostly, they were birds, but she also painted tree frogs, butterflies, and tropical plants, like the exotic wild orchids that clung tenaciously to our trees. Timothy was practicing his violin of his own accord—unlike Martha, for whom piano practice was often a chore—and in his free time had begun carving more duck decoys and decorating them.

The Westons had left me with old reading material. Along with books and magazines, there were some back copies of the *Key West Enquirer* that I hadn't read. In one issue there was an article about some Key West fishermen who'd gone missing beyond the reef and were presumed drowned. Like Martin, they were young men who sometimes worked on salvage boats.

I searched the article for names, but none was familiar to me. A couple of them were Bahamian, two were from New England, and there were Spanish names that I guessed were Cuban. I knew only too well the heartache that such an unexplained disappearance could bring to a family, and I felt for their wives and sweethearts.

I had pretty well given up hope that Martin was alive, and though I still wondered if his body might wash up on our shore, it seemed he had simply vanished, like these poor men from Key West.

Because of Martha's newfound love of painting, she often said she would like to meet the French artist James Audubon, who had been living in Captain John Geiger's house in Key West. Fearing impending strife in the settlement, he had since left, planning to return once the Seminole Wars were over.

Martha asked if she could meet with Mary Beth Peartree to discuss techniques and learn more about painting, but I felt that was out of the question. However, Peartree began to make frequent visits to Wreckers' Cay. Little Bourbon, an excellent watchdog, would spot his boat and sound the alarm with her barking. Then we'd all scramble to adjust our situation accordingly.

I did not encourage these visits, but offering hospitality to strangers and wickies from other lighthouses was an established tradition. The problem was that it soon became apparent Captain Peartree was courting me. His eyes freely took in my figure as he'd arrive at our dock, and his unmasked appraisal was quite disconcerting. While I found it flattering, I did not know how to put a stop to it.

Peartree was an interesting man, very intelligent, and well educated. But he reminded me a lot of Grandpère: I suspected his charisma and genteel manners masked a tough, control-ling personality.

Unlike George Lee's supply boat, which had a schedule, Peartree arrived at unexpected and inopportune times. And with Mary Beth to light the Sand Key beacon in his absence, he was rarely in a hurry to get back. Understandably, Andrew was annoyed at these surprise visits.

"Perhaps it would be easier if I just told everyone my grand-father sent me a slave from Louisiana," I grumbled one time as I joined him under his favorite tree by the lagoon.

"And how do you think that would look? You out here alone by yourself, living with a black man?"

"But if I said you were my slave?"

"Even worse. Someone could start sniffing around my his-tory. Lee and Dillon might not be smart enough to figure it out, but your Captain Peartree would."

"*My* Captain Peartree?"

He laughed. "Emily, he isn't coming here for your molasses cookies and tea. I looked at Sand Key on the map. There's nothing there. It's a dot in the ocean. This island is plenty big-ger. He probably wants to marry you and take over the light here."

It was a sobering thought. I'd not suspected Peartree of being attracted to me for these reasons. "Well, he's wasting his time. I would never marry him."

We sat in silence for a while. "Are you jealous?" I asked with a smile.

"Jealous? Of Peartree?" He thought about it for a moment. "Well . . . yes, I am," he admitted.

I vowed to set things straight with Peartree, hoping that his disruptive visits might stop. The opportunity came the following week. He arrived on a day when both Andrew and I had managed to finish most of our chores. We'd planned a leisurely afternoon by the water with the children—we so rarely had a day to just eat outdoors, relax, swim, and fish.

Andrew and Timothy had been hard at work crafting a picnic table, which we'd not yet used. I finished preparing our salad and sandwiches. Martha had plans for painting after lunch; Timothy was trying to catch some mangrove snapper or hogfish for our supper. Suddenly, Bourbon's bark warned us of Peartree's approach. Andrew's eyes met mine with alarm, and my heart sank. A column of fire ants could not have been more unwelcome.

Wearily, Andrew headed for the playhouse with a sandwich and a glass of lemonade.

With no one to greet him at the south dock, the captain tied up his vessel and made his way to the lagoon end of the property. His boldness made me feel violated—this was my family's private space. Even Captain Lee and Alfie Dillon were never invited to take tea in this place.

"Mrs. Lowry, good afternoon," he greeted me. "How lovely you look. And how nice to see your charming family."

Timothy and Martha could barely contain their petulance. They sat in silence behind me, glaring. "Good afternoon, Captain," I managed to say. "Won't you sit down? We were just about to have lunch, if you'd care to join us."

"Well, don't mind if I do," he said easily. Sitting in Andrew's place, he tucked in his napkin. "This is indeed a treat. How beautiful it is down here by the lagoon. I had no idea the property extended so far back behind the house. Believe me, we have nothing this elaborate at Sand Key!"

The children managed to eat their food quickly and excused themselves, leaving me alone with Peartree at the table. As they left, he moved to sit next to me. I could not fault his gentility, as every motion he made was graceful and fluid. "This is an excellent salad," he said. "You are indeed a woman of many talents. I understand you keep your own garden here?"

"Yes."

He marveled at this. "The tomatoes are excellent. Very fresh. They're almost sweet." He looked around. "So much property you have here. . . . Do you know how large it is?"

"I believe we have twenty acres," I replied. "My husband planted the garden and many of the fruit trees you see."

Afterward, he sat back in his chair with a Havana cigar and made a production of licking it, tamping it together, snipping it with tiny silver cigar scissors, and puffing it into ignition.

"Mrs. Lowry," he began quietly, "may I call you Emily?"

I nodded curtly.

"Emily, you've been much in my thoughts."

I suppressed a sigh. Andrew was hiding close by in the playhouse; he could probably hear every word through the window.

Peartree moved his hand over to mine, but I moved it away in time. Nonplussed, he continued: "I know you may find this most audacious of me, Emily—considering your husband has not been gone even a year—but I am very attracted to you. You're a beautiful young woman. I'm sure you consider me quite an old man. But I am still a very vital man, and what's more, I have resources of my own, and experience that would complement yours."

He paused. I kept my face impassive, staring down at the table through most of his monologue.

"I'm asking you to marry me, Emily."

I took a minute before answering. "This is . . . very sudden, Captain. We've met but a few times."

He smiled broadly. "Please, call me Josiah," he urged.

"Emily, I feel at my age there is no reason to hold back. I was completely enchanted by you the moment we met. And I'm sure your feelings for me will grow once we're married. We would, of course, live here at Wreckers'. I would give up the Sand Key light, and my daughter would return to Key West, where she would prefer to be in any case."

"I see," I said.

"Yes," he continued eagerly. "This is a lovely island. A veritable paradise. You don't even seem to have mosquitoes or gnats."

"There is . . . the matter of your reputation, Captain," I ventured primly.

A shadow crossed his face and he shook his head sadly. "Ah, I see the gossips have gotten to you, Emily. That wretched Rebecca Flaherty, I should sue her."

"You're not a pirate, of course," I said with a smile.

He sat back in his chair, gathering his thoughts. When I realized a long explanation was coming, I waved my hand. "It's of no matter to me, in any event. I am, of course, honored and flattered that you should have asked me to be your wife." I was prattling now in my most refined southern way, trying to emulate Dorothy's effortless charm. "I'm sure a man such as yourself, with so much experience and so full a social life as you've had in Key West and cities in the North, would know many beautiful women."

I began to clear the dishes as though the matter was settled, and he looked at me in shock. "You're saying no?"

"I will need some time to think about it, Captain Peartree. Perhaps it would be better if we didn't see each other for a while. You mustn't forget that I'm still mourning my husband. I'm really not legally free to marry yet."

After I'd seen a disappointed Peartree off on his boat, Andrew emerged from the playhouse. He struck a feminine pose, using a folded piece of paper as a fan. "You mustn't forget that ah'm still mourning mah husband, Captain Peartree," he said, mimicking my Louisiana accent.

"Stop it!" I said, and we collapsed with laughter. With luck, I thought, Peartree would consider the matter a closed issue and not return.

NINETEEN

Wreckers' Cay

March 1840

During our study time the next day, Andrew asked me why Latin was important. My two eldest children were otherwise occupied. Martha's new interest in painting meant that we had added "art" to our curriculum—not that I could teach it, but because I felt it was enriching for her, I gave her some school time to work on it. She was outside, sitting under a mango tree, trying to paint the tiny green fruit beginning to form on the tree. Timothy was sitting at the picnic table near the lagoon, engrossed in a book Dorothy had sent him.

"Latin?" I was caught off guard by his question. "I don't know. It's just always there—on buildings, inscriptions, in hymns and church books. And we use Roman numerals for clocks, chapters of books, and dates. . . ."

"Do you speak Latin?"

"Heavens no; nobody really speaks it," I said. "I do speak French and Spanish, which are based on Latin. And English has many Latin roots."

"I'd like to learn Latin," he said.

I laughed. "Well, I'm not the one to teach it to you," I said.

"I know only a few words." I wrote two words on a small card. "Here," I said.

He tried to sound out the words.

I corrected him, pronouncing the words carefully: "Carpe diem."

"What does it mean?"

"Seize the day," I said.

"Ah." He smiled. "Embrace the moment?"

"Yes. You mustn't waste opportunities in life."

He sat back and looked at me. Then he reached out and covered my hand with his own. His hand was big and warm and brown, covered with calluses from hard work, and I loved how secure its touch made me feel.

"Well," he said slowly, "perhaps tonight after the light is lit and the children are in bed . . ."

A shiver of excitement went through me. Obviously, Peartree's visit the day before had affected him. I nodded.

"Just remember," he said sternly. "We do nothing that would make you pregnant."

We prepared as for a wedding night. I took a long, languorous bath, letting my hair down, applying scent, and then I put on a loose white nightgown that revealed much of my breasts. Andrew spent more time than usual in the shower, shaving and grooming.

He did not knock. When he drifted silently into the bedroom, I held his gaze in the lamplight as he slowly undressed. I could clearly see the desire in his eyes and in his aroused body. I pulled back the counterpane, and he climbed into my bed. Accustomed to Martin's almost chaste trysts, I rolled up my nightgown halfway. But he wanted it off completely. He began to peel it away, with my cooperation. Then I was in his arms.

His body was curiously hairless and smooth, which excited

me as I drank in the clean smell of his still-damp skin. Gently, I explored the smooth muscles of his neck and carefully fingered the jutelike ropiness below it—the web of firm ridges on his back, permanently embossed by cruel whips. Unbuffered by clothing, our naked skin melded together, and he began by kissing me slowly, on my lips and in the hollow of my neck, as he finally whispered all the things I'd been yearning to hear. He gave due attention to my breasts, arousing sensations I had never realized a man could bring about in my body; certainly Martin had never managed to. He continued kissing me down the concave curve of my belly, my legs, and even to my toes. Then he kissed his way back up, setting me afire, and I parted my legs to allow his deep kiss free access.

"Are you sure, Emily?" he whispered. "We can't go back after this."

"I know," I replied. "Yes, I know."

For once, Martin was silent. In fact, I heard my husband's voice no longer after that night, as if I had nothing more to say to him and his ghost—unable to convince me of my folly—had finally drawn a shade to preserve our privacy.

After that glorious first night, Andrew moved in with me and became, as far as I was concerned, my new husband. As we had anticipated, it was not long before Timothy and Martha understood that the status quo had changed. And they were not happy about it.

"Mother, what are you thinking of?" Martha hissed one morning after she'd seen Andrew emerge from my room to go over to the tower. She usually addressed me as "Mother" only when she was unhappy with me. "When we gave Andrew to you, we didn't know he would start sleeping in your bed."

"I love Andrew," I said simply.

She looked down the stairs, as if worried he might overhear. "Yes, well, we like him, too. But what about Father?"

"What about him?"

"What if he comes back? We don't know if he's dead or not."

What indeed would I do if he literally resurfaced? But the prospect was so unlikely, I did not think that was the real issue. "If he weren't coming back, would you be uncomfortable with the fact I'm sharing my bed with someone? Even if it wasn't Andrew?" I asked.

She thought about it. "Yes. I don't want you to have any more babies. I don't want you to get sick again . . . and maybe die."

I took her in my arms. "Martha, I love you so much. I'm touched that you care about me. But I must have a life, too."

"So you're not going to have a baby?"

"No, darling, of course not," I said.

She was silent for a moment. "Mama, are we going to move back to Key West someday?"

Her question took me by surprise. My children had never raised it before.

"Why? Would you like to?"

"I think about it sometimes. I should like very much to meet Mr. Audubon, if he's back, and perhaps find an art teacher. And it would be nice to make friends with other girls. And visit with Aunt Dorothy and"—she smiled—"perhaps have a beau one day."

I smiled and kissed her cheek. "I can understand that."

My poor daughter, I thought, studying her carefully. I noted her budding breasts; she was now nearly ten years old. I'd been so absorbed in my own feelings that I had not stopped to think of her nascent ones.

Then she continued: "Timothy says if you have a black baby and we go back to Key West, nobody will even speak to us."

My breath caught. From the mouth of babes, I thought.

"Timothy and I think you should marry someone like Captain Peartree, or Captain Lee."

"You don't think they're a little . . . old?"

"Well, yes. But they are more like Father."

"What about Andrew?" I asked.

Martha frowned. She looked at me incredulously. "Mother! He is a Negro slave. You could never marry him."

Later on, I had a similar conversation with Timothy. But in the end, I let it be known to both of them that they would have to accept Andrew's sharing my bed. The children said no more about it, and for the next few months, Andrew and I found joy in each other whatever way we could, keeping our promise to do nothing that might cause a pregnancy. We had to be careful, but that was clearly not a problem for Andrew. He was gentle, sensitive, aggressive, adoring—and endlessly creative.

August arrived, debilitating us all with its oppressive heat and stillness. Hannah had been gone seven months, and Martin had been missing well over a year. It had been almost that long, too, since Andrew entered our lives. My grandfather wrote to tell me that Grandmère had died, which filled me with great sadness. I was still receiving letters from Dorothy, entreating me to return to Key West. To my surprise, the news of Hannah's death had precipitated long, friendly letters from Gran, who wrote to me now every month. And I occasionally received letters from a nun who had taught me at the convent. Her name was Mother Saint Angela, and she had been my favorite teacher.

There had been many changes, yet some things stayed the same. Captain Lee and Alfie Dillon still arrived on the duly appointed days. I kept their visits short, jollying them back onto their boat after they'd had their tea. Storms also worried us in August. Because it was the peak of the hurricane season, I cautioned Andrew that the lighthouse could be affected by sudden strong winds. He now redoubled his efforts to make sure the wicks were well trimmed and the lenses kept clean. Timothy was teaching Andrew how to sail the *Pharos* and our skiff, in case we had to evacuate.

I rose one morning, to see dark anvil-shaped clouds gathering on the horizon of an angry red sky. Pelicans were feeding close to shore, an indication that bad weather was coming. The day was hotter than usual, and deadly still—yet another ominous sign.

To my chagrin, in the early afternoon Bourbon barked to announce the arrival of Captain Peartree. Traveling from a westerly direction, he was alone and looking perturbed as he docked his sloop. The way the day was shaping up, I suspected he might fear getting caught in a storm on his return to Sand Key and need to stay the night on Wreckers' Cay. As I expected, with many apologies for disturbing me, he said, "I wondered if I might take shelter here."

"Do have some lunch with us," I replied, with forced cordiality. "Then we can see which way the weather will go. I'm afraid I don't have very luxurious guest quarters, but there is a small cot in the storage house."

"I'm an old sailor, quite used to cramped conditions," he said, smiling. "However, I insist you allow me to contribute some work. I shall light the lamps for you tonight."

Since we could not have Andrew anywhere in sight while he was about, I agreed. Taking Martha aside, I told her to tell Andrew what was happening, and that he was not to light the lamps.

I busied myself with chores while Captain Peartree strolled around, acting like someone about to buy the property.

"This is such a splendid little island," he said pleasantly as he entered the cookhouse, where I was preparing an early supper. "And it's surprisingly cool here for August."

"I actually find it very warm and humid," I replied irritably.

I did not want to agree with him on anything. "There's no breeze today."

We were silent for a few minutes, until he spoke again. "Emily," he said, "have you given any more thought to my proposal? Respecting your wishes, I've stayed away. But I have truly missed seeing you these past few months. I've thought about you every day."

"I'm afraid I am still mourning my husband," I replied. "I'm not yet ready to make such a commitment."

"But your husband has been gone over a full year now," he persisted. "You really should be thinking about a new life for yourself, my dear. You and I could be very happy together, and—"

I interrupted him, no longer able to contain myself. "Captain Peartree, when I'm ready to remarry, you will be the first to know."

He blinked and his mouth snapped shut.

The wind gradually began to pick up, and we had short, intermittent bouts of rain. After supper, Peartree rose with confidence and announced that it was time for him to go up to the light. I gave him the keys to the tower and sent him on his way, grateful for a few moments of peace.

When I did not see the light shining twenty minutes later, I walked over to the lighthouse and called up to him. There was no answer, though I could see the glow of his lantern farther up the tower, and I rushed up the stairs. Not having worked at the light for so long, I was quickly out of breath, but I carried on until I was almost at the top. There I saw him, looking ashen, in a crumpled heap on the staircase; he was grasping his chest and breathing with difficulty.

Peartree gestured to his pocket; I took out a vial of pills and opened it. He placed one under his tongue, trying to regain his wind and his dignity. Suddenly, it struck me. "It is your daughter who tends the light at Sand Key, isn't it?" I asked, my tone accusing him.

He nodded sheepishly.

We sat there on the steps, puffing, two frauds caught in an entanglement of falsehoods, laboring to catch our breath. Once assured that he was recovering, I brushed past him and lit the lamps, for the sun had just set and it was fast growing dark.

"Come down to the house, and I'll give you some brandy," I said afterward.

He cooperated like a helpless child. Outside, the wind and rain blew stronger as flashes of lightning burst over the water like garish fireworks. As we slowly made our way back to the house, I could see that the wind was stealing his breath again; I called for Timothy to come and help. We managed to get the captain into the parlor, and I brought him brandy, a blanket, and some hot tea. Despite the heat, I lit a fire to dry some of his wet clothing.

I sensed this kind of spell was something he had coped with before. He also seemed quite accustomed to having a young woman wait on him. My frustration finally overcame my patience. "You want to marry me so you can live here at Wreckers' Cay, but you still planned to have me work the light. Is that correct?" I asked.

He looked surprised by my hostility. "Well, you've been doing it all this time," he said amiably. "I thought you'd carry on as before. I want to marry you because I love you, my dear."

"Of course," I said. "And what would your contribution be to our blessed union?"

"Well, I could work some in the garden. A little weeding. And help with various lighter chores."

I repressed the urge to laugh aloud. He had made me very angry. Not only had I been required to light the beacon along with my other chores, but I'd had to nurse a sick old man, and would be deprived of Andrew in my bed to offer me comfort on this stormy night.

Umbrella in hand, I escorted Peartree to the storage shed

and left him with a candle, a chamber pot, a water basin, and some towels for washing. I was tempted to stop at the playhouse to see Andrew afterward, but I resisted, lest the captain's eyes follow me back to the house through the window.

I arrived in my dark bedroom in ill humor, drenched and chilled from the rain. I stripped off all my clothes and began to towel myself dry.

"I've got your bed all nicely warmed up for you, darlin'."

I whirled around. It was Andrew, lazily waiting for me in bed. He smiled in the soft light as he lit the oil lamp on my nightstand. I fairly dove in beside him and cuddled up to get warm. He fingered my wet curls, and slowly he began to make love to me in our usual way. But this time, I stopped him. "No," I whispered. "Not like that. Please, just this once."

He hesitated. "No. I shouldn't."

"Hush," I whispered, tracing my finger over his lips. A shudder of excitement rushed through me, turning my insides to jelly. I took the little gris-gris bag from my bedside table and placed it under my pillow.

He rolled over, so that I was under him. "I'll be really careful," he whispered.

When my menses appeared that month, we were emboldened. Perhaps the amulet did work. We continued making love in our new, free way and by October we had virtually convinced ourselves that my previous difficulties had left me infertile, an assumption that was as precipitous as it was foolish. My next menses did not occur. Despite the fact that I had none of the nausea I usually felt in the early stages of carrying babies, by November I was convinced I was indeed pregnant.

Andrew was alarmed when I told him. "My God, Emily!" he exclaimed as he covered his face with his hands. "What have we done?" I shrugged. He looked at me in anguish. "I knew better. I should never have let you talk me into it."

I tried to match his somber mood—after all, I did understand the gravity of the situation—but it was as though I'd lost my mind. Andrew's love, and this new baby . . . they were intoxicating gifts. I felt joyful and heedless, and with the pregnancy now a fait accompli, I felt I had nothing more to worry about. After all, the worst had happened, and yet the sun still rose and set every day, just as before. We would manage.

Andrew's despair over the pregnancy lasted a full three days. By the third day, I felt it had gone far enough. My pregnancy unleashed a new libertine spirit in me that I'd not known I was capable of. When Andrew went up to the lantern room of the tower, I removed my underdrawers and mounted the stairs. He was seated on the bench with some tools, and his eyes widened when he saw me.

"What're you doing here, darlin'? Shouldn't you be resting?"

I merely smiled. I lifted my clothing and sat on his lap, facing him. In a moment, I was straddling him in a flurry of raised skirts and fumbling of trouser buttons.

"What're you doing?" he cried out. But he made no move to stop me. He was smiling now. "My God, Emily. There's no satisfying you. You're like a drunken massa set loose in a slave compound!"

"Hush," I said. "I'm seizing the day."

Captain Peartree never returned to the island. We had a few minor storms that season, but otherwise we fared well. Life went on peacefully. The children were healthy. Captain Lee and Alfie continued their visits diligently—and on schedule, thankfully. My pregnancy was easy, with none of the other terrible symptoms I'd experienced last time.

Finally, by December, I felt it was time to tell Dorothy. I wrote my letter to her in French, and she replied, also in French, by the next courier:

Ma Chère Emilie,

Tell me your last letter was a joke. Tu plaisantes, n'est-ce pas? *No, knowing you, it is probably true. I knew that lonely island would get the better of you eventually. Dearest, I am very worried! You had so much trouble last time. But even I couldn't have suspected that leaving you alone with* ton beau nègre *could lead to this. What will you do? Perhaps we could find a home for it in New Orleans. I can write to the nuns. Or to Eurydice. I'll tell them it is the orphaned child of a servant.*

In the meantime, stay well. I shall come to you when you think it might be your time. It sounds like it will be May or the beginning of June? You may count on my absolute discretion, even with Tom. I love you.

Your sister,
Dorothy

Christmas that year was our first without Hannah. Whenever I thought of her face lighting up as she beheld previous Christmas trees, I felt the ache of losing her all over again. But in spite of that, the holiday was quietly joyful, for this year had been rich with blessings.

Embarrassed after my earlier reassurances that I would not get pregnant, I hadn't as yet told Martha and Timothy that our family was about to expand. But I could not hide much from Martha. She had not seen my hygienic cloths on the line for a few months and approached me accusingly one day in January.

"Mother, are you going to have another baby?"

I was in the middle of preparing supper in the cookhouse and replied distractedly, without looking at her, "Well, yes. Yes, I suppose I am."

When I turned, her eyes were filled with angry tears. "You promised!" she screamed. "You said you wouldn't! Now we'll

never get off this island, because of you and Andrew and your
nigger baby!"

I had never struck any of my children, but my hand slapped
her full in the face before I could stop myself. It sent her reeling toward the door just as Andrew came in. Martha glared at
him and sped past, out of the cookhouse.

"Whoa! I seem to have stumbled into a hornet's nest," he
said, looking at my stricken face.

"God help me. I lost my temper," I said, tears gathering in
my own eyes.

"I know. I was listening at the door."

"Tell me," I said bitterly. "Say you told me so."

"No, I won't." He stroked my hair. "She had to get it all out.
I know Timothy feels that way, too. I'll talk to them."

I nodded as he wiped away my tears. That evening, I took
Martha in my arms and kissed her cheek. "I'm so sorry, darlin'. I know how you and Timothy feel. I really do. And I'm so
sorry I struck you. Please forgive me?"

She managed a smile as she cuddled up to me.

"Everything will be fine." I reassured her with a hug as I
fingered her silky curls. "We'll figure out a way for you and
Timothy to move off the island soon, I promise."

"Yes, Mama, everything will be fine," she repeated crypti-
cally.

Dorothy did not have a chance to deliver me this time, either. My
baby, a healthy little girl, arrived in the summer of 1841. She
was a couple of weeks early, so again, Andrew was my midwife.
Far from the horrendous delivery of my last pregnancy—almost
my undoing—this baby came easily into the world.

Andrew washed her, then wrapped her in a blanket and
gently put her to my breast. My family watched with awe as I
fed her. The baby's eyes were as blue as my own; as blue as my

grandfather's. And I suddenly realized that Marie-Francine, Eurydice's little blue-eyed daughter, had to be Grandpère's child. Our new baby's skin was light and rosy, but I knew that it would darken over the next few weeks, as had the color of slave babies I'd seen when I was a child.

Andrew's face was illuminated. No complicated feelings seemed to be on his mind; he was totally smitten by this tiny bundle of pink prettiness. He extended his large brown hand, and her little fist seized his index finger. "Isn't she perfect?" was all he could say. "Isn't she beautiful?"

"I'd like to call her Ebony," I said. "Ebony Hannah."

Martha and Timothy approached their new sister with hesitation, peering down at her in silence. But they loved her immediately. Over the next weeks, they observed, fascinated, as her skin transformed into a rich tan color. Martha was charmed, she never needed to be asked to change her sister or sing her to sleep. She and Timothy seemed to have forgotten all their anger. Never had a child been more loved.

TWENTY

Wreckers' Cay

October 1841

The summer passed quietly as Andrew and I settled into a rhythm of family life. He used any excuse to come inside to play with Ebony, or simply to gaze down at her crib and watch her sleep and breathe. "Thank you," he would sometimes whisper to me.

I would awaken at night, sensing Andrew was no longer in bed, and I'd see him in the steady beam of light from the tower, standing over her crib, touching her cheek or her little hand, and making sure she was properly covered. As he had acquired more knowledge and education, Andrew had become less superstitious and bothered less with his spells and charms. Yet now, he was not taking any chances. Ebony had a small sachet of herbs in a gris-gris bag pinned to her little crib.

That summer was idyllic, but even then, deep in my heart I knew such happiness could not last.

I awoke one October morning to a dead, windless calm. Andrew had already risen to extinguish the lamps at dawn. I threw open the window to greet an oppressively hot day brushed with splashes of crimson. The pelicans were close to shore, and the seas were oddly quiet. These were ominous signs. A storm was brewing, perhaps a bad one.

I was changing Ebony's diaper when Andrew came down from the airless tower drenched in sweat. "Look outside," he said.

My eyes searched the horizon distractedly. "I don't see anything."

"Exactly. Look again."

I did. And this time I understood. There *was* nothing. Not a single ship in sight.

"My guess is there's a hurricane in the Caribbean, probably now somewhere in Cuba," he said. "It must be bad to keep the big sailing ships from leaving."

I nodded.

Suddenly, his voice was urgent. "I'm worried about you and the children. I don't think there's any time to lose. Start getting your things together. I want you to take the *Pharos* and get to Key West before the storm hits here."

"But if the storm hits here, it will surely hit Key West, too."

"Yes, but you have a better chance in Key West. And there are people there who can help. Here, you have no chance. A bad hurricane could blow away the tower, the house, boats, everything."

"But what about the animals? Bourbon? Our chickens and rabbits . . . our goats?"

"Take the dog, but we'll have to leave the other animals."

"And you would go with us?"

"No. You know we can't arrive together. You and the children go ahead in the *Pharos*. I'll follow in the skiff. I can sail it well enough. We'll stay in touch through Dorothy once we're all there. But I don't think there's any time to lose. We could get hit in ten to twelve hours. Maybe less."

I didn't argue with him. With two children and an infant to

protect, I wasn't going to take any chances. In a bad hurricane surge, Wreckers' Cay could be completely washed away.

Andrew and I outlined the plan to Martha and Timothy, who listened carefully. Martha and I hurriedly gathered supplies for the journey, while Timothy and Andrew moved both boats from the lagoon to the docks. The wind was picking up, which would help us travel through the currents, but it did not bode well for what was to come; I knew we would all have to hurry. Though it was not yet a storm, the sky was beginning to darken, and ominous anvil-shaped clouds—larger than I had ever seen in my years on Wreckers' Cay—were forming quickly.

I rushed the children down to the dock, carrying cases of our supplies. "Mama, you get in with Bourbon," Martha shouted over the rising wind. "I'll take the baby."

Without questioning, I settled into the stern of the boat with the dog. Andrew and Timothy untied the lines, and Timothy boarded.

And then my world crashed down around me. In one swift gesture, Martha handed Ebony and the case containing her supplies into Andrew's waiting arms from the bow. Then she clambered quickly back into our boat. By the time I understood what was happening, she and Timothy were hoisting the sails, and the *Pharos* had pulled well away from the dock.

"No," I screamed. "Stop!"

I stood up in the boat, causing it to teeter. Martha and Timothy pulled me down, ordering me to sit. I realized they had taken complete command of the situation. Suddenly, I had become like a child, and they like the strict parents.

Standing on the dock, Andrew held my precious bundle as he waved sadly. Then, as if he could bear it no longer, he turned away, placed Ebony into the skiff, and busied himself with his own travel preparations.

I was nearly out of my mind. I tried to jump off, but Martha and Timothy shoved me back down. "Stop it, Mother," Timothy yelled. "You're going to tip the boat and drown us!"

Hysterical and sobbing, I looked out over the sea with my empty arms outstretched, as though Ebony could somehow fly into them. In a very short time, Andrew and Wreckers' Cay receded from view, and we were almost past the reef, heading out to perilous seas.

I knew then that Andrew would not be going to Key West. I turned on Martha and Timothy. "This was all arranged?" I screamed. The wind whipped my hair across my face, stinging my eyes. "How could you do this to me?"

I could see the pain in their faces. Part of me knew they felt the same grief, for they were also leaving their home, their sister—and Andrew. But at that moment, I could only think of myself, and how I had been betrayed so completely.

Fortunately, the children were experienced sailors, for I was no help on the voyage. I sat at the stern, weeping. As we headed to Key West over dark, menacing seas that grew increasingly choppy, I began to feel nausea on top of my anguish.

It was a long voyage. The white-capped waves mounted higher and higher, tossing our boat wildly about. Water poured over the children's faces, tangling their hair and drenching their clothing; their hands bled from handling the sheets, and I could see they were tiring and frightened.

Suddenly, not halfway to Key West, we spotted a light flickering on a ship in the distance. Martha and Timothy clambered up to the roof of the slippery cabin, clutching the mast as they waved for the approaching ship. Soon, the schooner *Foxfire* appeared out of the inky gloom alongside us. It was a merchant ship that had made an early escape out of Havana ahead of the storm.

The mariners helped us board their ship and tied up our sloop to tow her in. The captain was American, and when he learned we were the lightkeeper's family from Wreckers' Cay, he and his crew could not have been kinder.

"So you are the woman at the light!" he exclaimed over the roar of water and wind. "You're well known among us ship captains, Mrs. Lowry. Many's the time you've guided this ship through the straits. Glad to be able to help y'all now."

Encouraged by his kind words, I sought to prevail on his gratitude. "Please," I shouted back, "we've left some people at Wreckers' Cay. We must go back."

We were clinging to the ship's railing as it rocked violently. He looked at me, incredulous. "That'd be mighty risky, ma'am," he said finally. "Who all was left back there?"

I hesitated. "A man. A . . . Negro. And . . . his baby."

His expression relaxed. "Sorry, ma'am, I ain't goin' back there and risking my ship for a couple of niggers."

As he and his first mate turned their attention back to the turbulent seas, reality finally sank in. I glanced up and saw Martha and Timothy looking at me, and their expressions told me everything. The children had understood; I had refused to. I had lost my child and my husband—for that is how I thought of Andrew now—but to the rest of the world, we had simply left behind two worthless Negroes in a storm.

I sat quietly for the rest of the voyage, head down, my stomach churning. Timothy and Martha left me alone until we arrived in Key West.

A carriage at the docks taxied us to Dorothy's house. My sister flew down the stairs when her maid announced our arrival, and she gathered me into her arms. Exhausted from our ordeal, I fell into her embrace and allowed her maid to fuss over us and make us all comfortable. Dorothy made no mention of the absent members of my family, but she knew me well enough to sense my despair.

Tom made us all feel welcome, and my children adjusted to Dorothy's household almost immediately. They helped with preparations for the hurricane—for the entire family and servants were bracing themselves as we arrived—and renewed acquaintance with their cousins and aunt. Dorothy led me upstairs and helped me into bed. There, I cried myself to sleep.

Dorothy came upstairs when it was time to eat. "Emily, come down and have some supper. You haven't eaten all day." She lowered her voice, pulling me into another embrace. "Martha has told me—"

"We never even got to say a proper good-bye," I sobbed.

"I know, I know, darlin'," she said. "It's going to take time, but sugar, you must think of your children. It broke their hearts, too."

"I would never have agreed to this," I said miserably. "Oh Dorothy, if you could only see her. She's so beautiful. Such a lovely, sweet baby. You would love her." I felt my breasts engorge with milk at just the thought of her. "And Andrew! I cannot believe he has done this to me."

"Emily, he just did what he thought was right. They all did."

I leaned back into her shoulder, crying. "My own children! I shall never forgive them."

Later on, Gran arrived. Her servants had readied her own home, battening down the scuttles, and she was going to weather the storm with Dorothy and Tom. Gran was genuinely happy to see me. "Emily, you're back!" she exclaimed as she hugged me. "I was hoping I would see you and the children again before I died."

"Yes," I said flatly. "I think I will be here for a little while." My mind was not yet able to accept that Wreckers' Cay, like a drifting log, was slowly floating beyond my reach forever.

PART THREE

Key West

1841–1883

TWENTY-ONE

Key West

October 1841

The hurricane, it turned out, was of moderate strength, with no deaths reported. But it did cause damage to roofs, shutters, verandas, and windows. Several trees had toppled and crashed onto homes, letting in water that caused flooding. All this took weeks to repair and clean up. Wreckers' Cay had certainly suffered worse; as much as I still hated to admit it, Andrew had probably been right in getting us all to leave.

I yearned to go back to my paradise to see how it had fared. But what I really wanted was to have everything exactly as it had been before, as though none of this had happened. Tom told me that he'd had very preliminary reports from shipowner clients and sea captains, and their reports were not good. He and Dorothy urged me to remain until more specific facts came in.

Though surrounded by family, I felt empty. My breasts ached for want of suckling, and I was sick with worry over Ebony. How was Andrew feeding her? The void left by their absence was almost more than I could bear. And I was still angry with Martha and Timothy.

I had been stoic after Martin's disappearance, and bolstered everyone else when Hannah was killed, but this time I wanted nothing more than to just sit in my room and weep. I knew that to thus indulge myself would be unfair to Dorothy and, worse, it would arouse Gran's suspicions. So I had to act like nothing was amiss.

We decided that I should move into Gran's house, which was far larger, and she owned four slaves. Back to her old self, she welcomed us in her cool, brittle way, and lost no time reminding me that my children had been brought up as heathens. "We must enroll them in Sunday school at once," she said urgently, as though their perdition were imminent. "I shall take them myself to St. Paul's tomorrow and introduce them to the rector's wife. We must also place them in regular school. They've already missed over a month into the year."

My nerves had been wrung raw, and I merely nodded. As long as the children were safe, I was in no position to stand up to her.

Then she turned her attention to me. "For heaven's sake, Emily, get yourself some decent clothes, and a corset. You're spilling out everywhere! And do something with your hair. I've never seen anything so wild. You'll never find another husband, looking the way you are."

"I am more interested in another post of some sort."

"Don't be silly." She laughed. "If you can find a husband, you won't need a post!"

The evening after we'd moved into Gran's, Martha passed a letter under my bedroom door. Recognizing Andrew's handwriting on the envelope, I ripped it open.

6 October, 1841
My darling Emily,
If you are reading this, my prayers have been answered and you and the children have survived. It breaks my heart and I am most sorry about Ebony. I know how

much pain this must be causing you, and if you hate me, I do not blame you at all. But some day, my darling, you may realize it was the only way, and you will forgive me.

I have lost so many people that I've loved, I couldn't bear to lose Ebony, too. She will be happier if I raise her where I can try to keep her free. I could never see her abused as I have been.

Perhaps we will meet again someday, Emily. As you may have guessed, I am not going to Key West. I will be setting my course for New Orleans. I wish you nothing but love, my darling. And I sign this with tears in my eyes.

Andrew

PS. Emily, do not be angry at Martha and Timothy. They understood what you were too blinded by love to accept.

I reread his letter many times.

My first impulse was to book passage on the next ship heading to New Orleans. But had they survived the trip? How could he have fed her? Would they have been able to go directly there without interrupting their journey elsewhere? Which way had the storm blown? If it had headed toward the Gulf states, they could not have survived. But if it had blown up the east coast of Florida, their chances might have been better.

Even if they had managed to reach New Orleans, I knew Andrew would be difficult to find. As a slave without manumission documents, he would be forced to go underground. In any case, I had no money—and I certainly could not leave Martha and Timothy with Gran so soon after I'd arrived. How could I possibly explain myself?

The letter made me rage, then weep. For I could not hate Andrew. In my heart, I knew he had made the right decision.

I had brought virtually no clothing, and I could not afford to acquire any. Dorothy lent me a corset, pantalets, and a few day dresses to wear. When I found some fabric at O'Hara's warehouse, I sewed up clothes for the children and a frock for myself.

My return to civilized society was demanding things of me that I hated. I chafed at having to wear undergarments, proper laced boots, gloves, and a bonnet again.

After a couple of weeks, I started looking for a position, and the first place I headed to was the Key West lighthouse at Whitehead's Point. As I arrived, Barbara Mabrity, the lighthouse keeper, was still cleaning up the grounds after the storm. She was awaiting some tradesmen from the U.S. naval station to repair damage to her roof.

Miss Barbara was delighted to receive me. "Why, Emily Lowry! I'd heard you were back," she exclaimed when she saw me. She propped her rake against a large sabal palm and hugged me warmly.

I had met the Mabritys not long after Martin and I first arrived in Key West, and while they were not close friends, we had enjoyed their company. Yellow fever had taken Michael Mabrity the previous year, and Miss Barbara had assumed his posting. As widowed female lighthouse keepers, we felt an immediate bonding, sharing as we did a most unusual sisterhood.

"So you've had to leave Wreckers' Cay, Miss Emily," she said, leading me into her cozy cookhouse. "Rebecca Flaherty just marveled at how well you managed to tend the light and keep the grounds out there. You were an inspiration to the rest of us wickies."

As I looked at her lean, muscular body, I had the good grace to blush at her praise. Here was a woman who, unlike me, was worthy of the title lighthouse keeper, for she really did perform at the tower. She was older than I by more than twenty years, but she still managed to mount the stairs to tend the lamp at least twice every day and was raising five children. Over tea and fresh pecan tarts, I told her tearfully about the horrendous Indian raid on Wreckers', and we chatted about the common problems we shared as keepers and mothers. We also gossiped about the inner workings of the U.S. Customs Department, the Lighthouse Services, and Superintendent Pendleton.

Finally, I broached the reason for my visit. "Miss Barbara, I wondered if you might need help here at the lighthouse. I need a position. I am"—I played awkwardly with my teacup—"virtually destitute. My family—we have lost everything."

She was sympathetic. "I could certainly use the help, and I'd enjoy your company. But I could not afford to pay you from my salary. I earn only five hundred dollars a year. You, of all people, know how underpaid we wickies are."

Clearly, the department had been giving me isolation pay. She looked thoughtful. "You know, there's a gentleman you should talk to. His name is Pedro Salas. He's a cousin of Juan Salas, you know—that fellow who used to own the whole island before he sold it to John Simonton?"

I nodded.

"Well, anyhow, Pedro, this cousin, is a Spaniard who spent a long time in Havana. He has a cigar factory over there and he's recently started one up in Key West, on Fitzpatrick Street. I understand he's bought a few rooming houses where he puts up some of his workers, leastwise till he can build cottages for them." She paused. "I don't suppose you know any Spanish, do you?"

"Yes, I do. In New Orleans, I spoke both French and Spanish. And I studied it in school."

Her eyes lit up. "Why then, you'd be perfect to run one of the rooming houses for Señor Salas. Can you cook for a bunch of men? Nothing fancy—just good, plain food?"

"Yes, I could do that." I found myself interested. Cooking for cigar workers would be preferable to sitting about my grandmother's house, subjected to her carping and advice. It would place me back in the community, keep me busy, take my mind off worrying about whether Andrew and Ebony had made the trip safely—and more important, it would bring in some money, which I could use toward locating them.

Thus began a very bizarre phase of my life.

The next day, I had two visitors. First, an elegant landau drawn by two fine chestnut geldings arrived at my grandmother's early in the morning. The Cuban driver alighted and delivered a message on behalf of Señor Pedro Carlos Salas. Barbara Mabrity had recommended me, and he requested I join him at the boardinghouse he owned on Caroline Street at ten o'clock the following morning.

The other visitor was the first mate from the schooner *Thomas Jefferson.* He told me Captain William Loxley—one of the sea captains Martin and I had known before we left the settlement—urgently needed to speak to me, as he had something very important to discuss. The mate left Loxley's address and said he would be home until he headed out to sea early the next morning.

Curious, I hurried over to the captain's immediately. The Loxleys lived in a charming two-story whitewashed clapboard house with gingerbread trim and a pretty garden, surrounded by a white picket fence. His wife, Mathilda, graciously received me. "Dear Miss Emily, how lovely to see you again! Welcome back to Key West. You're lucky to catch William in. He's not often home." She ushered me into his study. "All that business out at Wreckers' Cay . . . Would you like a cup of tea or coffee, dear?"

"Coffee, please, if it's not too much trouble," I said as I entered the room. "What business at Wreckers' Cay?"

"With the light down, there's plenty of work to do, as my husband will tell you."

William Loxley's study looked much like that of any busy sea captain, with maps, charts, and papers strewn about. Walls and drapes were infused with the smell of pipe tobacco so common in a male domain. The room was well appointed, with nautical paintings, ships' models, an old ship's wheel, a barometer, and a sextant as decorations on the walls. The furnishings were mostly mahogany, with comfortable seating covered in a floral chintz that reflected Mathilda's influence.

The captain rose from his large Chippendale-style desk when I entered. A tall, trim man in his late forties, he was an imposing figure, with a full head of dark hair streaked with silver. His eyes were dark and piercing when he looked at me from under his graying, bushy eyebrows, and a tight smile appeared briefly under his mustache.

"Miss Emily! So good to see you after all these years," he said in his Bostonian accent. He shook my hand gravely. "You've earned quite a reputation for yourself at Wreckers'."

I returned his smile but said nothing. Like someone long incarcerated, I was feeling awkward in these more formal situations—especially when my reputation was referenced.

He invited me to sit in a large wing chair near his desk. A maid brought in little cakes and coffee, which she served in Sèvres china cups off a gleaming silver tray. I imagined they were booty from wrecked ships, like all the beautiful furnishings around me.

Captain Loxley cleared his throat. "As you may or may not know, Wreckers' Cay sustained considerable damage during the hurricane."

"No, Captain. I suspected as much, but I've received no reports as to how the island fared after my hurried departure."

"Well, much of the lighthouse tower was destroyed, and your home has lost its roof. There was extensive flooding, as the surge washed over the island. The house needs to be completely rebuilt. And most of the outbuildings were blown away. I just came from there yesterday."

I fought back tears, thinking about my daughters' graves on the island, and our animals, our furniture and worldly goods, now blown out to sea. It was becoming clear that I would have to remain in Key West for a long time.

He sighed. "This is quite a disaster for ships in the straits."

"It is indeed a busy channel," I murmured. "At least three thousand ships a year pass through it now. A lighthouse at that juncture in the straits is absolutely necessary."

"Yes. Quite so. Wreckers' Cay had one of the few lighthouses in all of Florida that was intelligently placed by the administration. Most of them aren't where they should be at all. That one, especially since it was well tended, was desperately needed. There've been two wrecks at the reef already, and we can expect many more before the light is working again."

I shook my head. "My husband put up all those outbuildings. And he planted the wonderful fruit trees," I said softly.

"Yes, I understand he made many improvements to the island."

I nodded as my mind began to wander. Since my return, I had created a recurrent daydream to subvert my pain: I was back living at Wreckers' Cay with Martha and Timothy. Up in the glass lantern room to light the candelabra just before dusk, I looked out and saw Andrew and Ebony gliding up to our dock in the skiff. Ebony, a toddler in my dream, was giggling and trying to wrest the oar from his hand so she could control the boat. Andrew—my handsome Andrew—flashed one of his beautiful smiles as he kissed her and easily lifted her from the boat onto the dock.

Suddenly, I realized Captain Loxley had said something, and I sat up. Unable to grasp what it was, I said simply, "I loved it there, Captain Loxley, and I left Wreckers'—and my post—with great reluctance. It will be difficult for me and my children to begin a new life in Key West." As there seemed to be nothing else left to say, I put down my coffee cup and rose from my chair. "Thank you for giving me this account. I do appreciate it."

"But that's not all," he said quietly, his hand motioning me to sit back down as he poured me a second cup of coffee. "As I just mentioned, there is something else I must tell you."

I looked at him curiously, noting that his manner had changed. His face now bore a look of sympathetic concern.

"My first mate found a battered wooden coffee crate that drifted ashore from the reef on the southern side of the island. It had been weighted down, probably by a rock, but the storm savaged the area with such ferocity that it broke loose from its location. It was washed up on the beach by the high winds."

I sat down, intrigued. "What was in the crate?"

"A body. Quite decomposed. I suspect it had been there for some time."

I gasped. "Do you know whose body?" Yet, even as I asked the question, I knew the answer.

"Well, we don't rightly know. It was someone who met a bad end, from the looks of things. There is a large crack in the thighbone, and what looks like a bullet hole at the back of the skull." He reached over to a shelf and produced a box. "The remains are still on my boat and will be sent to the sheriff's office today, but here are some items that we found in the crate with them. We reckoned it was a man, judging from what he was wearing."

I stared inside the box. The clothing had rotted away to ragged shreds and the wooden buttons had largely deteriorated. But I immediately recognized the monogrammed silver belt buckle and pocket watch Martin had inherited from his father. I caught my breath. "Oh, God," I said, unable to keep my voice from quivering. "I think . . . these belonged to my husband."

He nodded. "Yes, that's what we suspected."

"I can't believe this." I shook my head miserably. "I have wondered for the past two long years what happened to him.

All this time, I thought he might even have deserted us, or been injured. Or that his mind had left him and he was wandering somewhere on a distant cay . . . or perhaps eaten by sharks. Killed by Indians . . . pirates." I realized I was rambling.

"I'm sorry, Miss Emily. I have good memories of Martin. We often worked at wrecks together. He was a fine man."

I nodded. Martin had been a decent, hardworking man. Perhaps he had not always been the husband who fulfilled my heart's desire, but he loved me very much, and was a good father to our children. For that, I still felt great affection for him—and now I could finally let myself feel true sadness at his passing.

I looked up at Loxley. The crate had been weighted down by a large rock. Clearly, this had been no accident. My husband had been killed. But by whom? And why?

"There will have to be an investigation. This was obviously a murder."

I nodded numbly, repeating through tears, "Murder. But who could have done such a thing? To me? And to my children?"

"Well, it could have been pirates, as you suggested, or, yes, possibly Indians. Though I think they would have taken his valuables." He paused, then added wryly, "I think it's quite safe to say it wasn't a shark."

My tears were flowing freely now. I said, "I loved Martin dearly and needed him so much—especially living out there on that remote island."

"Perhaps we'll learn more after the investigation. I'm sure the sheriff will be in touch with you soon. I just hope we get to the bottom of this tragedy. Nobody is safe out there with murdering brigands roaming the seas. As you may know, we've had other men disappear in the past year or so. They're still investigating those cases, too."

"But what would they have to gain by killing Martin in his

little skiff? He was simply fishing. He had no money with him. They didn't take his few valuables—not even his boat."

"It doesn't make a lot of sense," he agreed.

Dabbing my eyes and tidying my nose with a handkerchief, I stood up to leave. "Captain, when may I have Martin's remains? My family and I will want to give him a proper burial."

"Of course. I'll tell Sheriff Patterson to have them taken to the funeral parlor just as soon as they are done with their investigation."

I hurried back to Gran's and rushed up to my room, feeling numb. How I wished Andrew were there to comfort me, as he had been during my previous tragic moments. I yearned to sink into his arms, to hear him whisper comforting words, to have him left my chin and dry my eyes. His absence now drove home how empty life was going to be without him.

The next morning, Dorothy appeared at Gran's door at eight o'clock with a new corset, pantalets, several frocks, and bonnets for me to try on before my interview with Señor Salas.

Unfortunately, she also brought the morning's *Key West Enquirer.* The bold headline read MARTIN LOWRY FOUND! INVESTIGATION OF SUSPICIOUS DEATH UNDER WAY. I was aghast. I hadn't yet summoned the courage to talk to Gran and the children about my visit to Captain Loxley's. How could I possibly go to a meeting involving a position today? Dorothy had already heard the news, which had spread like wildfire in the settlement. She'd been very fond of Martin and tearfully took my hand in hers. "Oh, sugar, I'm so terribly sorry! You know how much we all loved Martin. Of course, after all this time, we didn't think he'd still be alive. But none of us thought he had met with a violent end."

Together, we woke the children. Martha was irritated at being awakened, while Timothy simply looked at me sleepily.

When I told them the news, trying to speak honestly but gently, they both snapped wide-awake. Martha wept bitterly, and my heart welled at the sight of her sad little face. All my anger over her part in Andrew's deception melted away in that instant. I folded her into my arms. Timothy's eyes had blinked to alertness and, though I saw his lip quiver, he kept calm and put his arm around my shoulder, helping me comfort his sister. Grieving as I was, I questioned my own sanity in choosing this day to apply for a position.

An hour later, Dorothy pronounced me ready for my foray into the workplace. She had chosen the outfit, for I was incapable of focusing on any kind of decision. To my surprise, she'd selected a rather daring shiny blue taffeta dress, more suited to a social than an interview. Cut low at the bosom, it was fitted around the waist, and made me look a bit like a tart. On my head she placed a pert little hat that matched the fabric, adorned with a fluttering blue plume.

My sister then laced me tightly into a corset in a way that squeezed the breath from me and accentuated my breasts. She did my hair up, holding my curls in place with tortoiseshell combs adorned with pearls. Finally, she applied powder to my face, charcoal on my eyebrows, and bright red rouge to my lips and cheeks.

"Are you sure this is appropriate?"

"Hush, sugar. You want the post, don't you? I don't know Señor Salas personally, but he has quite a reputation. This will impress him."

"Is Señor Salas not married?"

"Apparently, he's been married twice. No children. Both his wives died rather young."

Martha and Timothy had watched my image transform from wild island woman to flamboyant courtesan with confused fascination. "You look nice, Mama," said Martha uncertainly, watching me through eyes that were still red with grief.

Timothy said nothing, but there was a trace of disapproval in his appraisal.

We heard the thumping of Gran's cane on the stairs, earlier than was her custom. Her personal servant, Dinah, usually brought her breakfast, which she ate in bed.

"So, I see everyone is already down here," she observed. Then, eyeing me, she asked suspiciously, "And where are you going all dressed up so early?"

"I'm going to inquire about a position as cook," I said, bracing myself for her reaction.

"Cook?" shrieked Gran. "A cook? First a lighthouse keeper, and now you want to be a cook? Is there no end to what you will do to embarrass this family?"

With my sister's cheerful encouragement, I brushed past Gran and headed for the door. "Leave Gran to me," Dorothy whispered, her arm around my shoulder. Then she said aloud, "Good luck, sugar!"

Señor Salas's landau arrived to take me to the interview, then juddered over the rutted streets as it carried me from Gran's genteel neighborhood toward the seaport and warehouse district. As we passed the grog shops frequented by grubby seaman and wreckers, I was reminded of my early days in Key West with Martin. Even at that early hour, a few sailors were already staggering around under the influence of grog and ale.

The driver pulled up in front of the boardinghouse on Caroline Street and helped me to alight. It was yet another weathered house badly in need of whitewash. Located close to the pond, it was almost within sight of the busy harbor. The man led me through a foul-smelling corridor to the room Señor Salas kept as his office on the property.

I knocked tentatively; a male voice called out *"¡Adelante!"*

Opening the door, I found myself in a cluttered office. A

man in shirtsleeves was seated at a battered old pine desk, his feet up, reading the front page of the *Key West Enquirer.* Señor Salas was a man in his mid-fifties, with a face that might at one time have been very handsome but was now following the inevitable course of gravity. He still had his hair, although it showed signs of thinning. His face was deeply tanned and featured a grand waxed black mustache tilted up at the ends in the Spanish style, which did not match his graying goatee. He greeted me lazily from his chair, without bothering to rise. Salas was staring at me with the kind of bold, lascivious appraisal of men in attendance at slave markets in New Orleans assessing the value of black women stripped to the waist on the auction block.

I remained standing. He had not invited me to sit, and I wasn't sure I wanted to stay. "Señor Salas? I am Emily Lowry."

He smiled, flashing beautiful white teeth. "Yes, yes. Pedro Salas," he said, extending his hand as his mischievous brown eyes settled boldly on my cleavage. He gestured for me to sit, then, leaning back in his chair, continued to assess me audaciously. *"¿Tu hablas español, Chica?"* he asked.

I bristled and my eyes narrowed. He was addressing me in the familiar *tu* instead of the polite form of *usted.* Among well-bred people in New Orleans, the *tu* form of address was reserved for relatives and close friends, animals, and very small children. It was also used for slaves and prostitutes. This lack of respect on his part, accentuated by the diminutive word *chica,* was surely calculated to show his disdain for me, and I would not stand for that.

"I would appreciate your addressing me as *usted* and calling me Señora Lowry," I shot back in Spanish.

He raised an eyebrow. *"¿Usted?"* he asked. "Well, excuse me. I guess I just feel I know you so well, after reading about you in the paper this morning, that I thought I could use the *tu.*"

Disregarding my protest, he had continued on in the familiar form.

I stood. "Good day, Señor Salas," I shouted angrily in English, and, turning on my heel, I hurried out the door.

He was after me like a shot. "Wait," he called out, this time using the respectful form. "Wait, señora. I'm sorry. I'm sorry. Come back."

But his words fell on my departing back as I began walking back to Gran's. Soon his carriage, obviously on Señor Salas's orders, pulled up beside me. Since my boots were pinching, I got in, and the driver headed in the direction of my grandmother's house. I wept silently all the way home.

Gran was seated in the front parlor when I arrived. She, too, was reading the paper as she sat sipping her second cup of coffee. She looked up, surprised, when I rushed through the door. "Well, that was quick," she said. Seeing that I was upset, she beckoned me. "Come here, child. Come here and talk to me." Her voice sounded kind for a change, and I could see a measure of affection in her eyes. I sat next to her on the Louis XVI settee and put my face to her shoulder. She said nothing, just put her arm around me and let me cry.

"Did he do anything to you?" she asked finally.

I shook my head. "No. He was just insulting."

"I see." Her eyes appraised my outfit with disapproval. "You know, I thought Dorothy was wrong to rig you out the way she did, especially now that everyone knows Martin has passed away. He just figured you were a merry widow. You should have worn one of my frocks, not hers. I have a black one that I last wore to your grandfather's funeral; it would have been much more appropriate for your meeting with that Salas man. The bodice has a high neckline, and it has long, plain sleeves. "I wouldn't have done up your hair like that, either. And all that makeup she put on you! She made you look like a whore.

No wonder he was so disrespectful. I had it out with Dorothy afterward. She and I don't agree on things any more than you and I ever did."

Gran was just getting started. "In any case, Emily, you know I don't approve of your applying for this post—a woman of your breeding! It is very déclassé. And it's totally unnecessary. I have enough money to help you financially. And you're welcome to stay with me as long as you need to—or until you find a husband. . . ."

In her ignorance of their existence, she could never guess to what lengths I would go for money to reunite my family. She smiled as though the matter were closed, and I smiled back through my tears—which she took for aquiescence.

"Now go upstairs and take off all that frippery and face powder and those ridiculous shoes. We'll have a cup of coffee and chat about this business in the paper."

Sheriff Patterson did eventually come and speak to me of Martin's death, promising to do all he could to solve the murder. He also mentioned that the discovery of Martin's body caused much consternation among the relatives of those other men who had disappeared. Until Martin was found, they'd all accepted that their loved ones had been involved in some kind of accident. Now they wondered if their remains would soon wash up as my husband's had. Was it possible their men also met a sinister end?

The next morning, Señor Salas's carriage arrived with a small parcel for me. The driver stood outside after he delivered it, indicating he'd been instructed to await my reply. Curious, I went inside to open it and I saw that it contained a weighty gold chain. With it was a note written in a strong masculine hand in Spanish, using the formal, polite *usted* address throughout:

My dear Señora Lowry,

I am writing to beg your forgiveness for my rudeness yesterday. Please accept this small gift as a gesture. I was so captivated by your charms, I'm afraid I forgot the true purpose of your visit. Could we start over again? Tomorrow at the same time? My driver will come by for you at ten o'clock.

Yours very sincerely,

Pedro Carlos Salas

I rewrapped the chain and replied:

Señor Salas. I am returning the gift, for I cannot accept it. If you still need a cook at the boardinghouse, I might be interested in the position. I will be at your office tomorrow at the appointed time so we can discuss the terms.

Yours truly,

Emily Lowry

It was a chastened Señor Salas, wearing his jacket, who opened the door of his office to me with a respectful bow the next day. Grandly, he reached for my hand and lightly brushed his lips over it. As he took in my outfit, his face registered disappointment. I had taken my cue from Gran and, wearing her plain black mourning dress, now looked like a dowdy matron. I wore no cosmetics, and I'd pulled my hair back in a tight bun. I'm sure I had added about ten years to my actual age.

He immediately invited me to sit down, offered me coffee, and acted very businesslike. A man with a fine education, he spoke in the pure Castilian Spanish I had learned at the convent.

I was seeing him standing for the first time. He was my height, rather heavyset, doubtless the result of a good life of rich food and good wine. His gaze still fell occasionally on my well-covered bosom, but on this occasion he was courteous and discreet. Then he switched to English, which he spoke correctly and with only a slight Spanish accent.

"Last year, I started up the first cigar factory here in Key West," he began. "I bring in workers and tobacco from my plantation in Cuba. The humid Key West climate is just like Cuba's and it keeps the leaves nice and moist. We hand-roll the cigars here. Then we send them all over, mostly to New York, where many of them are shipped somewhere else. They're the best in the whole world. I have no competition yet, so the business is doing very well." He sat back after this explanation, a broad smile on his face, his fingers enmeshed over his chest.

"Where is your factory?" I asked.

"On Greene Street, at the corner of Fitzpatrick. That's where my office is, if you ever need to talk to me. This is just a little space I use to administer this rooming house."

He went on to explain the responsibilities of the position. Salas's plan was to map out a little village within Key West just for his cigar makers, erecting little shacks for them to live in. "I'll call it Salasville," he said, flashing another self-satisfied smile.

In the meantime, the workers were housed around Key West, and he needed a cook to serve them breakfast—just Cuban bread and strong coffee with jam. They would need to be at the factory by seven o'clock, and would eat a small meal at midday on the job, so I would pack their lunches, too. Then there was dinner, served in the evening.

"Nothing fancy, señora. Usually some paella, *picadillo, ropa vieja*, or some fish. . . ." He paused. "I have about fifty workers in all. About sixteen of them are housed here. Some of them are freed blacks. You might not like having to serve Negroes, but they are among my best workers, and—"

"I have no problem serving Negroes," I replied stiffly.

"Good," he said. "Fine, then it's settled. Come, I'll show you around the house."

As I expected, the house was filthy. It had the sour stench of dirty, rumpled sheets, sweat, urine, and tobacco. The four spacious bedrooms were furnished with sagging cots. Work conditions, I suspected, would be appalling.

"How much does the position pay?" I asked boldly.

"How much do you want?" he countered.

I was not expecting that question. "I think . . . thirty dollars a week," I replied. It was an outrageous amount—$1,560 a year, $610 more than I had been earning at Wreckers'.

"That's fine," he said, immediately. He smiled broadly. "In fact, I'll give you . . . thirty-five dollars a week. Come, I'll show you the cookhouse."

The figure danced in my head. Thirty-five dollars a week! I was glad I had refused Gran's offer the day before to support me and my children beyond our temporary arrangement. With this kind of income, I could start repaying the debt Martin and I had incurred with her years before; I could also save toward the children's education. And, if I could earn some time off, I might be able to afford a trip to New Orleans to search for Andrew and Ebony. This possibility made me eager to start.

We shook hands to seal the bargain. As I was on my way out, Señor Salas stayed my exit with his hand on my shoulder. "Señora," he said softly. "A woman should never reject the gift of a gold chain from a gentleman."

"I did not feel it was appropriate," I replied.

He took the chain from his pocket, dangling it in front of me. The faint light through the dingy window caught its glittering links. Among these decrepit surroundings, it sparkled like a chest spilling with valuable treasure.

"Such a chain is like currency. A lady may remove links whenever she requires money. Let me see how it looks on you," he said. Leading me to the large dirty mirror in the foyer, he carefully placed the chain around my neck like a clerk in a shop, taking great care not to touch any part of me untowardly. Against the black lace trim of Gran's frock, it glowed like sunlight, making the dreary outfit look chic and expensive in the mirror's grimy reflection.

I smiled in spite of my reluctance.

"Please," he said. "Accept it. It's a token of my gratitude for your taking the post."

"Do you reward all future employees with such gifts, Señor Salas?" I inquired. In reply, he simply smiled and bowed.

When Gran saw me return with the chain around my neck, she looked at me in disapproval. "Humph," she grunted. "Amazing what a little trinket will do to change a woman's mind."

I did not wish to dignify her remark, so I continued walking silently and headed to my room, a secret smile on my face.

TWENTY-TWO

Key West

December 1841

I detested my new position. The work was monotonous and tiring. I labored in the cookhouse from dawn—or even earlier, for I tried to get things done before the heat of the day held me in its debilitating grip—until dusk: cooking, washing, making sandwiches, and packing lunches. I managed to simplify the process by having Key West's small Cuban grocery store deliver whatever they had the most of in supply.

I had little time for my family now, and none for myself. By day's end, I was stiff and aching all over, and I would return to Gran's house, trying to smile as I greeted my children. But I often just headed to my room to collapse. Señor Salas owned two other rooming houses besides the one on Caroline Street, where I worked, and as my reputation as a cook grew, there was now a waiting list for roomers from the other houses who wanted to be moved to mine, at least for meals.

I made sure that my dealings with Señor Salas were kept impersonal and professional, yet he was attentive to any suggestions or complaints from me. At my insistence, he hired a woman to clean the house daily, and also sent over help at serving times. I suspected that most cooks in my position would not be given such extra consideration.

Most of the cigar workers were well behaved; a few of them were free Negroes, who put me in mind of Andrew. One of them in particular had hazel eyes like his, and a ready smile that revealed beautiful teeth. Distracted, I would sometimes add a little more to his plate than the usual portion.

Some of the other men would occasionally grow rowdy and flirtatious, especially if they had been drinking. Señor Salas continually warned them, but a few still managed, usually after a visit to a grog shop, to brush their hands across my bosom when reaching for food, or "accidentally" touch my backside. Many were family men, frustrated to be away from their wives and children in Cuba or the Bahamas, so I did not report these incidents; I just brushed them aside. I was learning to bend with the wind.

Because I understood Spanish, I was privy to many bits of gossip. "Funny. He never used to come by here," I heard one mutter. "But now he's here all the time."

It was true. Salas dropped in every day, sometimes alone, but often with a woman on his arm—a different face each time, always heavily made up. These women studied me pityingly, sniffing at my plain black dresses. Señor Salas did not seem to notice what I was wearing, though I still felt his stares at my back.

"Aren't you bored with that terrible post yet?" asked Gran one night, after I'd been working down on Caroline Street for a few weeks.

"Bored to tears," I replied truthfully.

"I know you don't care what I think," she said. "But I still feel you should be looking for a husband instead of working. Look how rough your hands are, child; they're ruined. You're still young and beautiful, Emily. There are rich men who would treat you like a queen. Don't squander this time of your life. Lord knows, it will go by fast enough."

"Who?" I asked, amused. "Where are these crowds of rich men here in Key West?"

She sighed. "Well, there's your friend, Captain George Lee. He's a widower. And he attends church when he's not at sea. He thinks very highly of you."

I laughed. "George Lee! Please, Gran."

She sniffed. "Well, maybe not. But you need to get out to more socials. You'll meet acceptable men that way, just like Dorothy did. You can't do that while you're cooking for a bunch of cigar makers."

"Yes, Gran."

"A woman needs a good man to protect her from the predators in this society," she continued.

"Yes, Gran."

"Dinah says she hears people gossip about you when she goes to the stores."

"Yes, Gran." Then I realized what she had said. I looked up. "What are they saying?"

"Idle gossip. *Una mujer buen notada.* Seems you're becoming 'a woman of interest.'"

I sighed, too weary to be angry.

Gran handed me a letter. "Here's a note that came while you were at work. It's from the supervisor of Lighthouse Services, Stephen Pendleton." She paused before leaving the parlor. "Now there's another widower with a fine position! He lost his wife in childbirth last year."

Remembering Pendleton's inspections on Wreckers' Cay, and his groping, I could only smile, shaking my head. I opened the note, written on his official stationery, asking me to stop by his office at the Custom House the next day at eleven o'clock. After my previous summons to Captain Loxley's home, I was apprehensive. But I managed to be there at the appointed time.

When Pendleton arrived, he fussed over me, offering me tea or lemonade. Profuse in his sympathy about Hannah, he decried the Indian attack, and the present state of affairs at my home on Wreckers' Cay.

I thanked him, but before he could turn his attention to the news of Martin, I said, "Mr. Pendleton, I'm afraid I must get back soon to my present work. Was there anything further you wished to discuss?"

"Yes. Yes, there is. Due to the importance of its location, we have crews working overtime to rebuild at Wreckers'. Barring another hurricane, it could be ready by the summer. Would you accept an offer to return to your post when the island is again functional? We think it's safe to offer you the position, say next July . . . or perhaps August."

I was taken aback. Much as I hated my present work, I had come to think of my days at the lighthouse as a beautiful time in the past—a time that was now over. When I pictured the light, Andrew's face sprang into my thoughts, especially the image of him on the dock that day, holding Ebony to his chest. . . . I closed my eyes; that heartbreak was just beginning to heal.

Yet, the prospect intrigued me, and I thought it wise to keep my options open. I was growing weary of Gran's constant meddlesome carping.

As he droned on, I was briefly visited by my familiar daydream: I saw myself up in the lighthouse tower at Wreckers' looking out on the water, seeing Andrew and Ebony gliding back toward the island in the skiff. Far from fading, I continued to expand and embellish this beautiful scenario, seeing myself emerge from the lighthouse tower and Ebony running to meet me as Hannah used to. This time, they'd been fishing together, and Andrew gave Martha their catch to carry to the kitchen, while I swung Ebony in the air.

"Mrs. Lowry?" Pendleton had been speaking.

I found myself saying: "I . . . shall have to give it some thought."

"I do hope you will," he replied. "We would . . . even be willing to give you a raise. Perhaps to nine hundred dollars a year?"

Clearly, his back was up against it. For the parsimonious Stephen Pendleton to offer me more money, I was sure he was under pressure from his superiors to rehire the legendary woman who'd kept the light so well. But of course, this time— without Andrew—I couldn't possibly live up to my mythical reputation.

"I shall have an answer for you soon," I said graciously as I rose from my chair.

The next morning, the *Key West Enquirer's* headline was PENDLE-TON: LIGHTHOUSE KEEPER AT WRECKERS' CAY STILL EMILY DINSMORE LOWRY. The lead story quoted Sheriff Patterson as saying he was still investigating Martin's death, but it focused on me as his replacement.

I slammed the paper down when I saw it, startling Gran and Dinah. I had never asked for attention or notoriety. I'd been away from Key West for five years, two of them serving as the official light keeper. Now, I was doing demeaning but honest work, worthy of no attention; yet still, here I was in the paper again. *Una mujer buen notada.*

The headline was bound to come to Señor Salas's attention, I realized. Indeed, he arrived at the boardinghouse that morning looking very concerned. "Señora Lowry, I can't believe what I am reading," he said.

I assured him I had made no such commitment to Pendleton.

"Are you not happy?" he asked.

"I'm managing very well; don't concern yourself," I said simply, and returned to the cookhouse.

Dorothy knew how unhappy I really was. "I declare, I don't know how you stand it, darlin'," she said, shuddering. "All those awful cigar makers."

I had always missed Dorothy at Wreckers' Cay, so it was wonderful to be seeing her again. My children had started school and went to bed early, so I tried to spend some time with them, and if I had free time afterward, I'd head to Dorothy's. Sometimes we would smoke Andrew's weed, for Dorothy had planted it in her garden.

"It's quite wonderful," she said delightedly, showing me the plants. "It grows so easily!"

When we smoked, sitting lazily in her garden, my thoughts always turned to Andrew and Ebony. "She'd be six months old now," I said to Dorothy one night. "How I wish I knew what happened after they left Wreckers'. . . . Did they reach New Orleans? . . . Did he manage to feed her properly? . . . If they arrived there, are they faring well? I worry so much about them, Dorothy. It's not knowing that is so terrible."

"Yes," said Dorothy, looking back at the house to make sure no one was listening. "But you must try not to think of them now, sugar. You have another life here."

"Oh Dorothy, I think of them every single day!" She was silent, and when I turned to her, she was stifling a yawn.

Christmas came. Stephen Pendleton had not pressed me for an answer about going back to Wreckers' Cay, but I knew he soon would.

For the holiday, Señor Salas allowed some of his workers from Cuba time off to return home to visit their families. For those who remained, he hosted a pig roast on Christmas Eve—*la noche buena*—rubbing the pig with olive oil, salt, garlic, and fresh

pepper. He personally supervised the roasting while his workers took turns manning the spit and basting the meat with a
mojo marinade. Their wives brought platters of black beans and
yellow rice, scented with cumin and saffron. Plates of warm
molletes and small bowls of *picadillo* were passed around as appe-
tizers. They brought platters of grouper, dolphin fish, conch,
snapper, crayfish tails, and stone crabs—all fresh from the dock
that day—and flan, guava bread puddings, and Key lime pies.
Children frolicked and played games; guitarists sang Spanish
carols. A visiting padre blessed the workers and officiated at a
midnight Mass.

I was missing Andrew and Ebony acutely, and thinking of
our lovely Christmas together at Wreckers'. At Señor Salas's
insistence, I invited Dorothy and Tom, with their family, and
Martha and Timothy, all of whom were delighted with the fes-
tivities. I also invited Gran, who, predictably, was stiff-necked
about the whole business.

"I've never understood why you Latin people make such a
fuss over Christmas Eve," she said rudely to Señor Salas later,
when we were eating. "Christmas Day is the proper time to
celebrate the Lord's birth."

Salas just smiled broadly, "Ah, well. Evening entertaining
seems to suit our temperament," he replied.

"Hmmmph," Gran muttered.

Later, he whispered to me, "Señora, would you come into
my office, please?"

I hesitated, looking around for Dorothy to join me, for Salas
had drunk a fair bit of rum over the course of the day. But she
was nowhere to be seen at that moment. I followed him warily.

In his office, he extracted a little box from his desk. "These
are for you, Señora Lowry," he said, showing me two exquisite
emerald ear bobs in a velvet-lined box. "*Feliz Navidad*, señora."

I tried to protest, but Salas insisted, begging permission to
place them on my ears. I looked at myself in the foyer mirror,

which now shone from recent polishing. The ear bobs were dazzling, with gold filigree and large emeralds surrounded by small cut diamonds. I saw him smiling behind me in the mirror; his white teeth looked brilliant in the dim room.

Again, I protested, but he silenced me with a gesture.

I finally acquiesced. "But I've nothing to give you, Señor Salas."

"Ah, señora, just grace me with one of your beautiful smiles. That is gift enough."

"Thank you so much," I said.

Here was a man, I realized, who in some ways reminded me of Martin. They could both be rude and single-minded, but at heart, they were gentlemen. Impulsively, I planted a light kiss on his cheek. Then I quickly turned to go, lest he misinterpret my gratitude.

TWENTY-THREE

Key West

January 1842

Over the holidays, my duties were lightened as many of the men were away. After Christmas, I left work early one evening and saw a shiny new cabriolet, hitched to a fine horse, under the lamplight outside the boardinghouse. The driver was none other than our old friend and supply courier, Captain George Lee, looking handsome in a new suit and a tall silk hat. How different we both appeared from that first time I'd seen him so disheveled and badly dressed at Madame de Saumur's home in New Orleans. Now it was I who looked poor and shabby.

"Ahoy there, Miss Emily," he called out. His greeting brought back the memory of his arrivals at Wreckers'—always a welcome sight. "Heard you were workin' here and thought I'd stop by to wish ye a Happy New Year."

"Why, Captain Lee," I called out, smiling. "I've not seen you for ages." In fact, I had seen nothing of him since my escape from Wreckers', but I had never forgotten his past kindness.

"Wanted to offer my condolences," he said as he tipped his hat. "Heard they found Martin's remains."

I nodded sadly. "Thank you, Captain. Have you recently been to Wreckers' Cay?"

"Yes, ma'am. I bin mighty busy out there," he replied.

No doubt, I thought, with all those wrecks on the reef now that the lighthouse is not functional.

"Well, it's very nice indeed to see you," I said warmly.

"I was hopin' to catch you. Was wondering if you'd like to join me, along with your grandmother, for supper at my home this evening?"

I was tired and would have appreciated an early night. But I owed the captain so much; I did not want to be rude. I certainly owed him a friendly dinner, especially after the way I had treated him once Andrew came into my life.

"I would love to," I said. "But I shall have to go home and change, and tell Gran."

"No need," he called out. "You look wonderful as you are, Miss Emily. And I already took the liberty of inviting your Gran. She's probably already waiting for us."

Ah, so this had all been planned out. I was warming to the idea. "Well, we musn't keep Miss Hester waiting." I smiled.

"Indeed!" He extended his hand to help me mount the carriage steps. "Hop up."

Captain Lee's home was well lit and inviting as we entered the foyer, and we were greeted by the delightful scent of rosemary and garlic, lamb, and roasting vegetables that wafted in from the cookhouse. I expected to see my grandmother in the front parlor, but she had not yet arrived.

"My housekeeper's just left," he said. "But I had her make a nice dinner, and it seemed a shame to set out such a grand feast without sharin' it with good friends."

"It smells wonderful!"

I looked around his home. Like Captain Loxley's, it was built in the New England Greek Revival style. And like the Loxleys', it was beautifully decorated with objets d'art from disabled ships. He led me through the well-appointed dining room to the cozy conservatory, where we chatted while waiting for Gran. Because the evening was cool, the captain lit a fire. I relaxed in its cozy warmth as I watched the flames licking the air and little Roman candles of sparks swooping up the chimney.

"I understand they are nearing completion of the new lighthouse," I said.

"It's comin' along," he agreed, but without enthusiasm. For a successful wrecker, replacing the lighthouse was bad for business.

After nearly an hour of inconsequential chatting, I stole a glance at the clock—a gesture not lost on him. "Well, now," he said, "your grandmother seems to have been delayed. We should eat while everything's still hot. I'm sure she'd want us to start."

He rose from his chair and led me to the dining room, where the glowing mahogany table had been set for three people. His late wife's sterling silverware and Waterford crystal goblets softly reflected light from the candles.

I had to smile at the situation: It wasn't like Gran to dine at this hour. But I knew she liked the captain, and had previously encouraged a romance between us. Her tardiness now was surely a ruse to give us time alone together. How predictable, and even oddly charming.

The captain served the meal and decanted some fine wine with uncharacteristic sophistication. "This Bordeaux came off the *Dumfries*," he announced grandly as he swirled it around in his glass. He sniffed it, held it up to the light, and took an appreciative sip. I stifled a laugh; these affectations were quite transparent, but he was trying hard to impress me, and I did enjoy the meal. It was a pleasure to be eating a dinner I hadn't cooked, not one grabbed in a few spare minutes in the cookhouse—or one eaten while seated at Gran's table, listening to her correct my children's table manners.

After a delicious Key lime pie, he made us coffee, then offered brandy, which I declined. He poured himself several generous shots, and soon I made ready to excuse myself and head back to Gran's.

"There's somethin' I want to talk to you about, Miss Emily," he said. "I read in the *Key West Enquirer* that you might return to Wreckers' to run the light again. Now that you're back here and your children are in school, well, it don't make much sense to go back out there." I remained silent. He was clearly working up to a bigger question. "What I'm sayin' is . . . well, would you consider marrying me?"

His question didn't take me completely by surprise. I let him continue, and he rambled on somewhat nervously.

"You can see what a nice house I got here. It's right next to your sister's and not far from your granny's. I'd love to have your children around. And you wouldn't have to work for the Spaniard no more. I bin thinkin' about it for a long time, Miss Emily, for I've always fancied you. Broke my heart back in New Orleans that Martin wooed you first."

This declaration now saddened me. It had been a pleasant evening, but as I had no such romantic inclination for him, I felt awkward. After being happy with Andrew for so long, the idea of marriage now . . . well, it was unthinkable.

"Dear Captain George," I said, placing my hand over his, "I had no idea you had such feelings. I care for you very much as a friend. I don't know what I would have done without you and Alfie after Martin disappeared. But"—I lowered my eyes—"I'm not ready to marry again."

"Well . . . when d'ye think you might be ready?"

I smiled. "Perhaps never."

He sat up. "Never? You won't think it over?"

I shook my head slowly. "No, Captain George. I am greatly honored that you have asked me, but I'm sorry. I do hope we'll stay such dear friends."

He looked petulant for a moment. The brandy was clearly affecting him. "I don't want you as a friend," he said evenly.

I sucked in my breath, suddenly very uncomfortable at his abrupt change of attitude. It really was time for me to leave. I rose from my chair.

"I must go, Captain. I rise very early to make breakfast at the boardinghouse. Thank you so much for this lovely evening," I said, extending my hand. "I'll see myself back to my grandmother's."

"Wait. Don't go just yet," he said, his voice softening. Taking me gently by the elbow, he led me into the parlor. "I want to show you some of the things I've acquired recently from the wrecks."

I feigned polite interest for several minutes, murmuring appropriate compliments, and then again announced it was time for me to take my leave.

Suddenly, he spun me around and pushed me gruffly into the large cranberry velvet couch behind me.

"Captain!"

I was horrified to see that he was fumbling with the buttons of his trousers. "My dear Miss Emily," he said, his face red, "the evening is still young."

"Captain!" I screamed. "That is quite enough!"

He tried to kiss me, the smell of brandy heavy on his breath. Though a strong man, he was also quite intoxicated. I shoved him away and was back on my feet in a moment. Then I kneed him hard to get free of his grasp. He did not expect it, and doubled over for a moment, which gave me a chance to run toward the foyer, leaving my reticule behind. The door yielded easily, and I was on the porch, when I felt him grab my arm and spin me around. He was glaring at me.

"Well, now, ain't you Miss High-and-Mighty. What's the matter? A wreckin' captain ain't good enough for you? All's you are now is just a scullery maid. Or do you offer the Cubans more than just their meals? Lots of talk about you in Key West, Emily. You're lucky I'm offerin' you a good life for all of that, especially since I could have some interestin' things to tell Superintendent Pendleton. And your Señor Salas."

He had my attention, and because I was already outside, I felt safe enough to stop. "What interesting things?"

"I can tell them how you practiced black magic out there, with those little sacks you put around your children's necks. And your retarded daughter . . . did you sacrifice her in one of your voodoo rituals? I know you bin practicin' witchcraft, Emily. Don't deny it. We used to hang witches, y' know, and not that long ago, neither."

"Enough," I said. I turned to go.

"And what about the nigger?"

I froze.

"Peartree told me. He got up around midnight for a piss when he stayed in your storage house. He saw the light was waverin', so he started off to go up and trim the wicks. But then he saw a nigger there, headin' up the stairs of the tower."

I turned to face him. "Your friend Peartree is senile, and he was drunk and blind from too much brandy, as I recall. Just as you are now."

He tightened his hand around my arm so hard that I winced in pain, trying to pull farther away from him.

"Funny, Emily. Said he looked for the nigger next day but couldn't find 'im anywheres around. I told him"—he stumbled a bit and caught his breath, spitting—"I told him he should've looked in your bed."

Lee roared with laughter, but suddenly his smile disappeared, and, keeping pressure on his grip, he said, "What kind of fool d'ye take me for, Emily? Didja really expect me to believe you put up that fence at Wreckers' by yerself, with just the boy? Drilled through coral rock? I knew ye had help. How did you come by a nigger, Emily?" he persisted. "Did he drop off a slaver? That's my guess. An African? Did you like it with him?"

I did not dignify his accusations with a reply.

Abruptly, he changed his tone: "Let's talk business, Emily. You've got something of mine."

I stopped in my tracks, confused. "What?"

"The money!" he replied harshly.

"What money?"

"Don't pretend ye don't know what I'm talking about. Where's my damn money?"

I was bewildered. He thought I had money? It was almost laughable. Clearly, he was more intoxicated than I thought.

I'd had enough. I finally managed to pull my arm free, flew down the steps, and fled home. Thank heavens nobody had been around on the street to overhear our conversation. When I returned to Gran's, the household was asleep. I rushed up to my room, locked the door, and sat on my bed, shaking.

I felt angry and violated. And what on earth had he meant? Martin had no money! I would have known. We had kept no secrets from each other.

Initially, I spoke to no one about the captain's assault. I went over it in my mind, asking what I'd done to encourage him. I was a fool to have trusted him. Had I been too friendly with him in the past? Too flamboyant in my dress out on the island? And Andrew! I had thought Peartree was sound asleep in the storage shed when Andrew got up to trim the wicks. And now this reference to money the captain thought I had. That had certainly come out of nowhere. Finally, as I went about my daily chores and helped the children with their homework, I decided to dismiss it as drunken babbling.

George Lee's carriage arrived the next day with my reticule, Alfie at the reins. The captain had sent along a note.

Dear sweet Emily,

I'm sorry. I did not behave like a gentleman. It must have been the brandy. I still want to marry you. Let's meet in the next few days so we can discuss the date, as well as the business about the money. Alfie will wait for your reply.

All my love,

George Lee

The money again! I tore the note into pieces and pressed them into Alfie's hand without explanation. "Take that back to him," I said. Poor Alfie just looked confused.

The captain's grip had produced a large bruise on my arm, which was not lost on Señor Salas. I had rolled up my sleeves to wash dishes a couple of days later, and he come into the cookhouse. He waved away the woman he was with and examined my arm.

"What happened, señora?"

I shrugged, avoiding his gaze: "I . . . I fell."

But Salas was not easily fooled. "Who?" he asked. "Who did this thing?"

For a second, the terrible scene with Lee flashed before me and I just lowered my eyes. This intensified his interest.

"Who?" he persisted. He was angry now. "Was it one of my men?"

"No, no . . . it was a neighbor of my sister's. I thought . . . I thought I knew him well. He used to bring our supplies when I tended the lighthouse at Wreckers' Cay. He was even a good friend of my late husband."

"Do I know this man?" he demanded.

I shrugged. "I don't know."

"His name? Give me his name."

"Captain George Lee."

He shook his head and frowned as he tried to make a connection. "A Bahamian?"

"No. American. A New Englander. You may be hearing from him. He said he had things to tell you."

He looked at me quizzically. "What could he say that would interest me?"

"He said he would tell you a pack of lies about me, that I was a . . . a witch, and that I'd murdered my daughter and kept a Negro slave at the lighthouse on Wreckers' Cay. Foolish things."

"Why would he do that?"

"He had asked me to marry him, and when I said no, he became angry. He . . . he tried to attack me and . . . he wanted to extort money from me."

He raised his eyebrows in surprise.

"Señor Salas, I have no money . . . other than what you pay me. I cannot explain his behavior."

He rubbed his chin, looking steadily at me. "If I thought you needed money, señora, I would be pleased to lend you some. But not for an extortionist."

"No, of course not. And I would never accept your help in such a situation! I must get back to my work."

"Leave this with me, señora. Please. Tell me if you hear from him again. And don't worry any more about it."

Telling him had left me feeling liberated, like when I was a child and whispered my sins to the priest in the confessional. I suddenly felt protected and at peace; I had to admit that there were some situations where the commanding presence of a man was essential for a woman on her own.

The sheriff's office released Martin's remains in January and we had his funeral on a cool, drizzly day. After the requiem service, we laid him to rest in a grave on Gran's plot, next to her vault. My sorrow was intensified by the sight of Martha and Timothy, who stood at the graveside, looking disconsolate. My mind flew back to the humble service years ago, when we laid their sister Hannah to rest, and Andrew had been there to console us all.

Señor Salas attended the service with some of my Cuban boarders. Barbara Mabrity and her two youngest daughters, Stephen Pendleton, Rebecca Flaherty, Ellen Mallory, the Watlingtons, the Hackleys, and the Marvins all came. John Whitehead and Pardon Greene also went to the church, as did many of the men Martin had fished and crewed with on salvaging expeditions. Alfie Dillon stopped by and offered his personal condolences to our family; nothing was said of Captain Lee, who, thankfully, stayed away.

Sheriff Patterson was there to pay his respects. He assured me that he and his deputies were still doing their best to find out who was responsible for the murder. "If it was Indians . . . or pirates . . . I'm not sure what we can find out, especially after all this time, but we won't stop trying," he told me.

The discovery of Martin's remains was sad but also anticlimactic. He had, after all, been missing for quite some time, and the children and I had eventually, each in our own way, accepted that he was not coming back. But the funeral at least gave us a greater sense of closure. It meant, finally, that I was now officially a widow.

When I arrived back at Gran's, there was a note slipped under the door. As I read it, I felt my breath catch. "Emily, where is my money? If you don't want all of Key West to know about your nigger lover, you'll hand it over. I'll be aboard the *Outlander* at the docks all weekend. Bring it there. George Lee."

The next day, as I had promised, I took the letter to Señor Salas. I could see the muscles around his jaw quiver as he read it.

"Do nothing. Leave it to me," he said. "I think it's time I talked to this man."

The following Sunday, the *Key West Enquirer*'s headline read TWO KEY WESTERS BADLY BEATEN. With growing horror, I read that the victims were Captain George Lee and Alfie Dillon. The article described how the pair had been viciously beaten as they'd staggered out of the Gem, a grog shop near the wharf, in the early hours of the morning on Friday. A witness who saw the assailants from afar said that there had been five or six of them. The beatings had been brutal: Captain Lee was in the navy military hospital with a fractured jaw, a broken arm, and numerous internal injuries. There was also the possibility of a paralyzing spinal injury. Dillon, too, was at the navy hospital, suffering from severe internal injuries and lacerations. The motive for the assault was attributed to robbery, as their money and pocket watches had been stolen.

As I read the story, a lump formed in my throat. It would be a lie to say I was sorry about Lee's injuries, but I was shocked to hear that Alfie Dillon was also severely hurt, for he had always been a kind and gentle man.

Suspicion gnawed at me. Remembering his anger, I was convinced Señor Salas had something to do with the attack on the men. When I dropped into his office to present him with bills from the grocer's, I showed him the *Enquirer*. "Did you see the paper this morning?"

He was sitting at his desk with his Cuban coffee and a pastry, and he barely gave the paper a glance.

"No, I have not."

I placed the paper in front of him and pointed at the article. "Do you know anything about this?"

He took a quick look at the headline.

"Me? No. Why would I? I don't know these people," he said dismissively.

"That's the New England captain I spoke to you about. And his mate."

He picked up the pastry and chewed thoughtfully, then looked at me and said, "Sounds like a man who makes a lot of enemies." Then he turned the page over to glance at the previous night's cockfight results, as though the matter was closed.

After I left his office, I let out my breath, standing frozen in the hallway outside his office. What had I done?

For my next birthday, Gran received a few friends for dinner, and Captain John Geiger was among the invited guests. He brought along John James Audubon, who had become somewhat famous as a naturalist artist, especially for painting birds and other wildlife in watercolor. He was an attractive man in his early forties, with clean-shaven features and long chestnut hair sprinkled with just a hint of gray, giving him an artistic persona. As soon as I met him, I realized that we had previously met one evening at the de Saumurs' home in New Orleans many years ago when he arrived in America. As the son of a French officer and a native Creole in Sante Domingue, he had grown up in France, and later had left to escape being conscripted into Napoléon's army. Even after many years in America, he still spoke with a distinctly French accent.

Audubon was now back again, living in Geiger's home on Whitehead Street. Meeting him was a moment of great excitement for Martha, for she had been wanting to for a long time. Her birthday gift to me was a sketch she had done, a small portrait of Andrew and Ebony. She handed it to me in the secrecy of my bedroom before Gran's dinner.

"Happy birthday, Mama."

My heart leapt when I saw it. She had captured them in a loving moment, with Andrew smiling tenderly down at our

baby and her tiny face tilted up toward him, her blue eyes looking intently into his. I hugged Martha gently to me.

"Darlin', thank you. Thank you so much."

"It's very, very good," said Audubon sincerely when I showed
him the portrait—at Martha's urging. He discussed composi-
tion and technique with her, then asked, "Whom do you use as
models?"

I held my breath, but Martha simply shrugged. "Just people
I see."

I doubted that she'd painted it from memory. Andrew had
to have posed for her. I suddenly remembered her secretive
forays down to the lagoon with her pens and paints, and I shot
her a complicit smile, which she returned with a wink.

A short time after Martin's funeral, I decided that I had managed
to save enough for a trip to New Orleans. I desperately needed to
see if there was any possibility of finding out if Andrew and
Ebony had managed to survive and reach Andrew's proposed
destination. The alternative was not anything I wanted to contemplate, but I had to know. By living at Gran's and saving fru-
gally, I'd put by enough for my own return passage and their
voyage back with me—assuming they could be found. If I didn't
find them, the trip would not be in vain, as I would be able to
visit with my aging Grandpère, and see Eurydice and Marie-
Francine.

One evening, I confided this to Dorothy.

"Sugar," Dorothy said softly, "you know that would be foolish.
You don't even know if they survived the trip from Wreckers'.
That would have been such a long, perilous voyage . . . especially
with a small baby. I know you don't want to consider the possibility, but . . . even babies that are properly cared for and well-
fed often don't live."

I was disheartened by her remark but by no means crushed.

"Besides, all that time you'd be away . . . and your other children need you here. . . . Señor Salas would be left with no help. And it would be expensive."

"I've saved the money, Dorothy."

"Since you don't know if they survived, you'd have no idea where to look for them," she countered. "Why can't you just try to make a life here without them?"

I bristled at this. "But they are my family, Dorothy!"

"Yes, dear, I know. But they are . . . well, they're family that you have different obligations to. Think of Martha and Timothy. It would be very unsettling for them if you were to disappear and leave them with Gran right now. You've been back only a few months. They're still just getting used to living in Key West again."

Perhaps she was right, but still I fretted.

Dorothy looked thoughtful for a moment. "Listen, sugar. I have an idea. Tom recently took on a new client who lives in New Orleans, and he's going to be going there for business reasons fairly often in the future. In fact, he's planning to go in a couple of weeks. What if I went with him and looked for them?"

"Oh, Dorothy! You would do that for me?"

"Of course!"

I scooped her into my arms. Dorothy laughed and hugged me back. "Believe me, it will be my pleasure, darlin'. I'm very fond of Andrew, don't forget. And I haven't been back to New Orleans since before I got married. I'd love to go, if you think I could help."

TWENTY-FOUR

Key West

March 1842

True to her word, Dorothy did accompany Tom a couple of weeks later. The day before their departure, I went over to the Farrell home with a list of ideas, suggesting names they might look up and places where they might go to search for Andrew. Dorothy was out, so instead I gave the list to Tom, who was in his study.

Dorothy had always respected the silence I'd imposed on her and never mentioned Andrew or our baby to her husband. But she'd had to tell Tom now to elicit his help in New Orleans.

Tom was usually a jovial, friendly man, and he and I had always enjoyed an excellent relationship. But when I entered his study, I immediately sensed something was wrong. "Morning, Emily." He gave me a cool look, scowling. Then he closed the door to his study. He indicated a chair for me. "Dorothy told me. Emily, I just can't believe you had a . . . black baby."

I was nonplussed. "Yes, an adorable little girl. We named her Ebony."

Tom was reacting with more alarm than I'd expected. "And

a black lover. . . ." He began to pace the room, running his hand nervously through his hair: "Emily, I can't understand the purpose of all this business, getting Dorothy to go searching New Orleans for . . . some slave."

"Andrew isn't just 'some slave,' Tom!"

He held up his hand, not wanting to hear painful details. "All right . . . all right . . . let's just assume we find this . . . Andrew. What then?"

I smiled broadly. "Why then, I'll go to New Orleans and bring them to Key West."

"Emily, what are you thinking?" He was almost shouting. "What about our family? Gran?"

I stiffened.

Tom sat down then. He had decided to take a more lawyerly approach: "Emily, just think about it. If he is a slave—and it sounds like he does still belong to someone—it would be illegal to bring him here. Assuming he's alive to begin with—and we don't even know if he is—we should be returning him to his owners. You should know better. Bringing him to Key West . . . it would be like stealing someone's property."

"And what about my child?" I challenged. "What about Ebony? She has a white mother."

He shook his head. His tone was gentle. "Emily, you know the rules. Your baby is a slave. She belongs to Andrew's owner, too. I'm sorry . . . but that's the way it is. It's the law."

Dorothy chose that moment to arrive home and entered the study. Seeing me in tears, she put her arms around my shoulders and chided Tom. "And what kind of mean things are you saying to my poor sugar?"

"I'm just trying to get Emily to face facts."

"Well, you just stop that now, darlin'. I've told Emily I'd do my best to find Andrew and Ebony if they're alive. And I will, even if I have to search every slave shack in New Orleans!"

They exchanged meaningful looks, which silenced Tom.

After hugging Dorothy and wishing her a good trip, I went home, feeling considerably deflated—but no less determined.

They were gone for three weeks, during which time my moods fluctuated from excitement to joy to misery as I thought of each possible report she might bring home. Most important to me was to know if they were alive. I would go from there.

I fretted. At work, I was distracted, sometimes miscalculating measurements or portion sizes. People were having to repeat things to me a couple of times before what they said registered. Even Gran, who often got sidetracked herself, noticed. "I declare, Emily, you're getting more absentminded than some of my eighty-year-old friends!"

The Farrell children stayed with their nanny, but just as often they chose to spend their time with my children at Gran's, so I had plenty to do at home. In my leisure moments, I created another daydream: Dorothy and Tom arriving with Andrew at the docks. In this scenario, the reverse of our last scene at Wreckers' Cay, Andrew would be holding Ebony, the infant Ebony, in a blanket. Martha would take Ebony from him to cradle her. Then I would throw my arms around Andrew—bystanders be damned.

After perusing boat schedules, I made ready to leave quickly for New Orleans if Dorothy's news was good. I had even thought up a story about an illness for Grandpère to tell Señor Salas, so he would give me time off. In the meantime, I was on tenterhooks.

On the day their ship was due, I took the Farrell children down to the docks to greet Dorothy and Tom. I could barely contain my excitement as the gangplank was lowered.

My niece Maureen flew into her mother's arms, followed by the younger two. Dorothy gave each of her children kisses and hugs, then looked over their heads at me. She shook her head sadly, and I felt myself quietly disintegrate. "We tried very hard, Emily," she said, as the children ran ahead to the carriage. "Please believe me. Tom even hired an investigator. We checked out the orphanage at the convent; we enlisted the help of Eurydice and Marie-Francine, who made inquiries of slaves they knew; we checked the jail, and looked for bills of sale for slaves at the registry office; we asked around at Congo Square. "And then finally"—and here she took my hand and looked sadly at me—"we heard through Eurydice . . . I'm so sorry, sugar . . . we heard that Ebony did not survive the trip to New Orleans."

"Oh, Dorothy!"

She paused to let one disaster sink in before she gave me the second part of her bad news: "And Andrew . . . Andrew did manage to reach the port, but he was caught by the slave patrol soon afterward. He had no manumission papers, so they sold him somewhere, probably out of state, since there were no records in New Orleans. He could be anywhere—Mississippi, Alabama, back in Georgia with his original owner, or even Arkansas—really, anywhere."

She put her arm around my shoulder and said gently, "I'm so sorry, sugar. I know you didn't think Tom and I were on your side in this, but really we worked very hard to find them both. Tom was wonderful. He used all his connections."

I stumbled onto the bench in the waiting area by the dock to catch my breath. A part of me had ceased to exist at that moment, departing the core of my body almost visibly, like a phantom shadow.

Dorothy sat next to me and held me: "There now . . ." she said. "There now. I know, I know. The news could not be worse. I just wish I weren't the one to have to tell you. . . ."

A slave! Andrew? The wonderful man who had saved my life, and was the gentlest of lovers? The man who had sung as he worked and cared for my children as his own? Andrew, who had gloried in his freedom at Wreckers' Cay? Yes, he knew the truth about his freedom—he had been much wiser and more realistic than I.

And I had suffered the loss of yet another one of my daughters. My beautiful baby. What had she been given in her short life? Just a few months with people who loved her. Then what? Starvation? Fever? Drowning? Only Andrew knew. And where was he? How could I even start to look for him in the large area she had described?

I don't remember how I made it home to Gran's. I went to my room feigning a grippe, and I spent the next couple of weeks a virtual recluse.

Though life was moving on for me, I frequently thought of Captain Lee and Alfie Dillon, who continued to languish in the naval hospital. I still suspected Pedro Salas was responsible, and though Lee's nasty threats kept me from wasting much pity on him, I felt terrible about Alfie. On several occasions, I went to the hospital to see if I could visit him, but he was allowed no visitors. Poor Alfie. He had probably just tried to help Lee and been drawn into the melee.

One of the local ladies, Señora Ximenez, was a nurse at the hospital, and whenever I saw her, I would ask about their condition. "If they are friends of yours, you should pray for them," she would say.

So I struggled with my remorse, but Señor Salas harbored no conflicted feelings. He carried on as before, still visiting me in the cookhouse at inopportune times, still parading his string of women past me, and still staring at me when he did not think I was paying attention.

Perhaps it was Gran's constant carping, or perhaps it was my hands growing rawer with each passing day, but gradually my heart began to harden, and I began to question my own motives. What am I doing here? I wondered. Is it really for the money? Or is it to get away from Gran? She was right about one thing: I was wasting my youth in a steamy cookhouse. I was working at a soul-destroying job I hated, and depriving my children of the time I should be devoting to them. It made no sense.

I needed money, but on a far grander scale than I was capable of earning it in this position. With more funds, I could send my children away to school when it was time. I could have a home away from my grandmother, and—though material things had become less important to me over the years—perhaps it could be a beautiful home, and I might have nice clothes and jewels.

Once, I thought I had married for love, but it was an illusion. When love truly found me—I squeezed my eyes, trying to push the memory of Andrew away—it brought me only heartache in the end. Now all I had was a post with no status. George Lee had called me a scullery maid. I'd dismissed his cruel jeer, but it had hurt, because it was close to the truth.

It was the most innocuous event that finally changed my thinking: I was scrubbing dishes in the cookhouse, for the maid was nowhere to be found that day, and one stubborn pot would not release its dried rice. I scrubbed harder, and realized the sweat on my brow had turned to tears. I stopped, I sat down at the worktable, and sobbed into a clean rag. This, I decided through clenched teeth, is going to change.

It was in this fresh frame of mind that I turned to Señor Salas one day and remarked, "I understand you have a beautiful home, Señor Salas."

My comment startled him. I had until now kept our exchanges brief and impersonal. We no longer even referred to Captain Lee and Alfie. But on that day, I wore the emerald ear bobs he had given me at Christmas. I had also taken extra care with my hair and dabbed a little powder on my nose.

"Yes. Yes," he agreed. "I've built a splendid house on White-head Street. It's in a Spanish style, with beautiful tropical gardens. You must come and see it, señora."

I responded warmly. "I would love to," I said. "Perhaps my sister and I could drop by one day when you are not occupied with other, more important matters."

"When?" he asked immediately. "Today? Tomorrow? Anytime you like!"

"Tomorrow. Perhaps we could join you in taking tea. Around three o'clock? I shall have to be back at four-thirty to begin supper for the workers."

He was visibly excited. "Of course! Yes, yes, Señora Lowry. Tomorrow would be perfect. I don't usually drink tea myself, but I will have my housekeeper, Juanita, prepare it for you. And some good Cuban coffee for me."

"You know," I said demurely, "I think we know each other well enough now for you to call me Emily."

He smiled broadly, revealing his beautiful white teeth. "Emily," he repeated. "Yes. Of course. And you must call me Pedro."

It was almost too easy.

He sent his carriage for Dorothy and me the next day, and we went over to look at his home, which was indeed beautiful, although not built or decorated to my taste. A Cuban servant opened the massive wrought-iron gates, and the carriage clattered along the brick courtyard until it came to a halt before a porte cochère to the left of the house. We were then ushered up the steps and along the vast veranda to the elaborate front door.

Greeting us in the grand foyer was Juanita, a surly Cuban woman in her mid-forties. She was thin and reasonably attractive, with graying hair pinned up in a severe bun. Eyeing us suspiciously, she served tea and Cuban pastries with barely a word, despite my attempts to make conversation in Spanish.

Unlike the clapboard New England–style homes that surrounded it, Pedro Salas's house was an enormous Spanish Colonial structure, covered in white stucco, with a tile roof and decorative grillwork. He had filled it with massive antiques and paintings. Lacy wrought-iron chandeliers hung from the high ceilings, heavy velvet drapery enhanced the many windows and kept the interior cool, and the floors were decorated with Oriental rugs he'd imported from Spain. A cool white Italian marble stairway, decorated with graceful gold leaf filigree, swept up grandly past an indoor fountain to the open second story, where it enclosed a gallery overlooking the foyer.

It was excessively lavish. Yet, even as I appraised his home's extravagance, I was imagining myself as its chatelaine—though I'll confess, in this dream I saw Andrew by my side, rather than Pedro, and my Ebony and little Hannah still alive and playing in the garden. Away from Gran's scowls and disapproval, I could see Martha happily teaching them to skip rope on the patio to a tune she'd learned at school, and Timothy delighting them with booming sounds as he blew into a big conch shell. Since Dorothy's terrible news, I was trying to focus more on my children and less on the unrealistic hope of my whole family united again. But for me, it was difficult. My daydreams were still frequent— just different.

Salas took pride in guiding us through the rooms, pointing out each important item and explaining how he had come by it. Many of his furnishings and most of his artwork had been inherited. And like everyone else in town, he regularly attended auctions and had bought many artifacts from wrecked ships.

Beyond the courtyard was a luxuriant garden with an Italian fountain and ornate cages containing exotic South American parrots. Behind a cluster of thatch palms, a separate cottage housed the maids, and the coach house had living accommodations above it for his driver.

When we left, he kissed Dorothy's hand first and then mine, holding it longer than necessary as he helped me to mount the steps of the landau. I'd discreetly pulled my skirt up, showing as much of my leg as possible as I stepped into the carriage. My shameless coquetry was not lost on him: As he said good-bye, he invited me to dinner, and I agreed—so long, I added, as Dorothy could join us. After my disastrous experience with Captain Lee, I was quite happy to insist on Dorothy's inclusion. And for her part, she was delighted at how things were progressing.

"This could turn out well for you," she said excitedly on our way home. "He's obviously very rich, and it's clear that he adores you."

"Yes, he seems to," I said. "I don't love him, of course."

"No, of course not," she agreed. "Not that it matters." She thought for a moment and added, "Frankly, I think both Gran and I would have preferred Captain Lee—"

I cut her off. "I do not love Captain Lee, either," I said coolly. "In fact, I don't even like him."

Dorothy was taken aback by this. We rode along in silence for a few minutes. Finally, I said, "I've decided that I shall marry Señor Salas."

"Oh, Emily. How wonderful! When did he ask you?"

I shook my head. "He hasn't yet, but he will."

And indeed, several weeks and dinners later, he invited me into his office and proposed.

"Oh, I know that I am much older, and that you don't love me yet," he said, "but I will do everything I can to make you happy. And maybe," he added with a smile, "just maybe, you will learn to love me . . . a little." He held his thumb and index finger up hopefully to indicate the very small measure of love he expected.

I smiled and nodded. Being courted by yet another older man put me in mind of Peartree's proposal, but I knew this would be quite different. This marriage would free me from menial work, not chain me to it.

"Yes, I would be honored to marry you, Pedro," I said, adding, "and I have become very fond of you in the past few months."

Excitedly, he drew out a dark green velvet box and produced an antique gold ring with an emerald large enough to weigh down my hand. The stone had to be about four karats, with baguette diamonds on either side. It beautifully matched the ear bobs he had given me at Christmas. "It was my *abuela's*. She told me to place her ring only on the finger of a woman I truly adored."

"Oh Pedro, it's beautiful!" I exclaimed, admiring it on my finger. I marveled at myself—I had never lusted after fine jewelry. When did I transform into the sort of woman who exclaims excitedly over elaborate rings? I wondered.

"It is you who are truly beautiful," he said. "I cannot wait to place the second ring on your finger."

I smiled, but inside I was screaming questions at myself. What have I just agreed to do? What about Andrew? But—no. There can be no future with him if he can't be found. And Ebony is dead.

Can I trust Pedro? I wondered. The beatings had shown me that he was a complex and unpredictable man. And I did not love him. But I realized how much I respected him nonetheless. Better to be married to a wealthy man, I told myself, a kind and loving man who can protect my family, than to remain alone.

TWENTY-FIVE

Key West

June 1842

When the Huguenot prince, Henri of Navarre, ascended the French throne as Henri IV, he accepted the condition that he convert to Catholicism, shrugging as he declared: "Paris is worth a Mass."

Pedro put no such conditions on me. But in return for the status he would be conferring on me as the wife of Key West's wealthiest businessman, I was willing to switch back to my former faith. It was all in the interest of presenting ourselves as an integrated family. And since my belief in God was more pantheistic than Christian, it made no difference whatsoever to me. I could have gone to any church, or none.

Gran, who was a devout Anglican, was so disgruntled, she almost did not attend my wedding. But though Pedro would never have been Gran's choice of a husband for me, she was pleased that I had finally "come to my senses" and would now be living in luxury, something that she could take pride in. I suspect that she was also happy to have her home to herself again, for although she loved my children, I knew they tired her. And she could not abide our Bourbon, who chased her cats and the neighborhood chickens, causing a noisy fracas of flying fur and feathers, which upset Gran's peace.

Our June wedding was an elaborate affair. The ceremony took place in Pedro's tropical garden and was performed by a priest from the cathedral in Havana, invited over to officiate. Our friends, boarders, and factory workers all attended. Martha was lovely as my bridesmaid; Dorothy was the matron of honor. Tom Farrell and Timothy joined in giving me away. When I looked into the adoring eyes of my groom, I could not help but wish it were Andrew by my side. And in my mind's eye, I could see Ebony as our little flower girl.

Even Gran shed a tear during the service. I wore Dorothy's wedding gown, which was a little short and tight. "Something borrowed," she chirped happily. But by the time my sister and Gran's servant Dinah tightened my corset—with no small effort—the gown suited me nicely, though I could hardly breathe.

Juanita had arranged for bowers of tropical flowers to decorate a small gazebo in the garden. She and Pedro's other servants made all the food, including a huge decorated fruitcake infused with Cuban rum and lavishly covered in mounds of white almond icing.

From the start, Pedro adored my children. Although not particularly devout, he enjoyed attending church services on Sunday. As the Catholic church was not yet built, we attended St. Paul's, which somewhat pacified Gran.

In a flourish of diamonds, gold, and ruffled shirts, Pedro would beam with pride as we walked down the aisle to one of the front pews with Timothy and Martha. He was delighted when visitors assumed they were his own children, since he had not produced any with either of his two previous wives.

My children were not unhappy with our marriage. They loved their new home and were relieved to get away from Gran. They viewed Pedro as a kindly grandfather, and he was, from the beginning, generous to a fault. He bought them sweets and toys, and listened intently as Timothy played his violin and as Martha practiced on the piano.

"You'll spoil them," I would say if I saw him slipping them pocket money for the penny-candy store, but he just shrugged. "Let me spoil them, *querida*. It's the first time I have ever had children around."

I had discussed boarding school with him, and he had no quarrel with spending the money, only—as I did—with seeing them leave home.

So on the surface, our life together was an ideal one. But our intimate life together was not nearly as perfect. In fact, from my point of view, it quickly accelerated into a nightmare. After our chaste courtship, he was now champing at the bit like a frisky young stallion.

We were unable to consummate our marriage right away, because Pedro scheduled our honeymoon along with a business trip to Cuba in early June, right after our wedding and just before hurricane season. He was intent on taking me to Havana to show me off to his cousins and friends there. I dreaded the journey, as I knew it would make me seasick, and indeed almost from the moment I boarded the schooner bound for Havana, I found myself deathly ill. The seas of the Florida Straits were very rough that particular week, and as the vessel rolled back and forth with the heaving waves, my stomach seized up and I took to my cabin for the voyage, while Pedro spent most of his time on deck, chatting with the crew and passing out cigars. Mercifully, it was a short trip, just ninety miles.

I did not know what to expect of Havana—or "La Habana," as the Cubans called it. Key Westers looked upon Cuba's capital as an elegant, exotic place that was a pleasure to visit. Ladies with money would go there frequently to buy fashionable hats and gowns. And they would stock up on coffee, sweetmeats, molasses, rum, and sugar, Men were drawn there for its many bars and other, more risqué entertainment.

Cuba was the jewel of Spain's colonial possessions. As the biggest island in the Caribbean, it had for centuries been the portal that ships bearing rich treasures plundered from South America sailed through on their return to Spain.

A large port city, Havana reminded me a lot of New Orleans. From a distance, El Morro loomed into view, its ominous brooding tower and prison fortress guarding the harbor. As our vessel approached the dock, I was shocked to see a slave ship unloading its miserable cargo directly across from us. I could hear cries of despair as the slaves were pushed onto the dock. Some of them were so ill, they could barely walk, and the ship's crew members were brutally whipping them. Even from where I stood, I could see blood glistening on fresh lash marks across their backs.

I gasped, thinking of Andrew, remembering the feel of the scars across his back. It was just such a ship, I reflected, with the same destination, that brought him to Wreckers' Cay. Pedro noticed me cringe, but when he asked if anything was wrong, I said I was still queasy from the boat.

I averted my eyes, but the cries continued to reach my ears. I remained silent throughout most of the drive along El Malecón, the shore road that bordered the seawall. Pedro, invigorated by his return to Havana, enthusiastically pointed out various monuments and scenes to me, explaining their historical background.

At that time, the city had a population of about 180,000. Pedro told me that over the years, at least 400,000 Negro slaves had been brought in from Africa to work the cane fields. The country also had many Chinese indentured servants, who were just slaves with a different name. That meant the slaves here no doubt outnumbered the Spanish elite—a situation I was familiar with from my time in Louisiana.

Havana had, like many medieval European cities, been contained by a wall in the sixteenth century. As the city grew around it, the wall came to define Vieja Habana, its older section, a beautiful area with broad plazas fed by arteries of charming cobbled streets.

"They built walls to keep the pirates and other undesirables out," explained Pedro. "But Havana has continued to grow well beyond the gates."

"Do they still worry about pirates?"

"Pirates wouldn't dare come into Havana! They know they would end up in El Morro and nobody would ever see them again." With that, he grinned and drew a finger across his throat.

With its wide paved boulevards, Havana had European grace and style. Vieja Habana was an especially rich architectural kaleidoscope of Spanish Colonial structures. "It's very beautiful," I remarked, looking around.

"Yes, it's nice. A lot like the cities in Spain."

The underlying power of the Church became evident as we traveled through the city, and I noted many priests and nuns in the streets near the Italian baroque cathedral on the Plaza de Armas—a reminder of the New Orleans I'd known as a child.

The carriage came to a stop at an elegant villa just outside the gates of the old walled city. "Who owns this lovely home?" I asked Pedro as we alighted from the carriage.

"I do."

I should not have been surprised, for it was a smaller version of the mansion he had built in Key West.

"Tomorrow, you will see my estate on the tobacco plantation in Vuelta Abajo," he said. "And my cigar factory."

I had always thought of Pedro as an émigré from Cuba who had come to settle in the United States, but during this carriage ride, I came to see him in a different light: He was really a Spaniard, who had gone to Cuba to capitalize on the rich profits of colonialism, and then to Key West to expand those profits.

Pedro led me into a large bedroom furnished with Spanish

antiques and summoned a servant to draw water for bathing.
Then he went down to the cookhouse to order us lunch and
talk with his housekeeper. It was a hot, sultry afternoon, and a
cool bath in the spacious copper tub was exactly what I needed.

Now on dry land, I was gradually feeling human again. I still
experienced the strange sensation that the room was listing,
and I was haunted by the terrible scene on the slave ship at the
dock. But at least I was becoming used to my surroundings.

Pedro was feeling expansive and relaxed after our lunch of
gazpacho and red snapper, followed by fresh mango. I had eaten
carefully, but he relished his food, washing it down with French
wine from his cellar.

"So, *querida,* what do you think?" he asked.

"This is all quite overwhelming," I said. "I had no idea that
you maintained a home here, or that you had an estate in the
country."

"Yes, my tobacco plantation."

"Do you have slaves working for you at the tobacco farm?"

He raised his hand in protest. "No, *querida,* I do not. When I
came to Cuba from Spain, there were many little farms in the
country where peasants—we call them *'guajiros'*—grew tobacco.
They were barely making a living, growing it and rolling the
cigars themselves, usually a family operation. Then they would
sell them in Havana. What I did was to hire them for my fields
and at the factory. We sell some cigars locally in Cuba, but
mostly they are sent all over the world from here. The *guajiros*
make a good living; I make a lot of money, and everybody is
happy."

I nodded, happy to know that I had not married a slave
owner. "But . . . it sounds to me like you are competing with
yourself by having set up a factory in Key West."

He laughed. "Yes, *querida,* I am. For now. I like to 'hedge my
bets,' as you Americans say."

When he talked about business, Pedro became animated and focused. But finally, he broached the inevitable. "Now," he said, with a twinkle in his eye, "you are about to learn more about me. No more talk of business. This is our wedding trip!" Leaning toward me, he took my hand and brought it to his lips. "Come, *querida*, it is time for our siesta."

It was that siesta that introduced me to Pedro's version of intimacy. And its account is quickly told. First, he removed all my clothing while administering wet kisses to my lips and face, murmuring terms of endearment in Spanish. Then he led me to the bed and hurriedly stripped off his own clothes. Pedro's idea of lovemaking was to cup my breasts with both hands, rotate them a few times, and then ram his body unceremoniously into mine. The heat of the day caused him to sweat profusely as he puffed, groaned, and panted, urgently taking his pleasure. Mercifully, it was all over in just a few minutes.

"That was fantastic," he roared delightedly as he rolled over, spent from the exertion. "Wasn't that wonderful? You enjoyed it, too, eh, *querida*?"

"Fantastic," I agreed. "Just . . . fantastic."

"You were wonderful," he said, planting a gentle kiss on my cheek. "I'm so lucky. We're going to have a good life together."

His praise surprised me, since I had done virtually nothing except lie there. In fairness to Pedro, I tried to suppress memories of how different it had been with Andrew. Yet these thoughts continued to surface. I could still feel how Andrew had once touched me, gently probing the sensitive corners of my body with astonishing accuracy—places no one had reached before. Unlike Pedro and his offensive fumbling, Andrew had fondled and kissed my breasts until I grew aroused. He had come to know my body's every fold and crevice, and explored each with certitude, as if he could read my mind; afterward, we would lie in delighted silence, hands joined, listening to each other's breathing until sleep overtook us. These were the thoughts that wound through my mind as I lay there beside my new husband, watching him fall quickly asleep, snoring.

When Pedro awoke, refreshed from his nap an hour or so later, he pounced on me again. To my consternation, he was again ready to perform that evening. And so it went, day after day.

At thirty-one, I believed, erroneously, that men in their fifties had left off thinking about such things. But Pedro and I quickly settled into a routine that was more like two or three times a day. While I had married Pedro for his companionship and protection, money had been a strong motivator. But obviously, I had vastly miscalculated just how often I would be required to earn it. I had not yet asked him how his two previous wives died. But my guess was that they had probably expired from fatigue.

In Havana, we found ourselves caught up in a flurry of social gatherings, received by many of Pedro's cousins and friends. Pedro also had acquaintances in the Cuban government, and we were invited to a formal reception at the Governor's Palace. There, I was presented to Governor Jerónimo Valdés, former viceroy of Navarre. He was governing Cuba in the name of Queen Isabella II of Spain, who had succeeded to the throne as a three-year-old child, and her regent mother, Maria Christina. The governor—who, as it turned out, was a good friend of Pedro—was a patrician-looking man of military bearing, with bushy arched eyebrows, thin lips, and a penetrating gaze under his hooded eyelids. His cheeks were hollow and his hair was remarkably thick and dark for a man of his age—which, I guessed, was about sixty.

"Congratulations, Don Pedro," he said after he kissed my hand and exchanged a few pleasantries. "You have found yourself a very charming woman. And I am very impressed to hear an American woman speak such proper Spanish."

"You flatter me, Your Excellency," I murmured.

"And what do you think of Cuba so far?" he inquired.

"It's magnificent! So very beautiful, and so big. I am used to living in a small village."

"It is very beautiful, *muy hermosa*," he agreed, smiling proudly. "We have tried hard to create in La Habana a city to rival the most elegant in Spain."

He was about to move on to another group of people, when I thoughtlessly added, "The only thing I find disturbing is the number of slaves I see here."

Pedro stirred nervously, shooting me a quick look.

Valdés frowned. But he said pleasantly, "Ah, the slaves. Yes. They are an important part of our economy. Of course, slaves should be no novelty to you, since you are from the Deep South of the United States. It is my understanding, in fact, that there are slaves throughout your country."

I took this as the rebuke it was meant to be. "Yes," I admitted. "The concept troubles me there, as well."

Far from letting the matter drop, Governor Valdés seemed to be enjoying my discomfort, and he added, "It is also my understanding that in some of your southern states, there are even farms where slaves are bred to create more slaves."

I felt myself blushing. I began to realize how stupid and discourteous I had been to criticize a country where I was a guest. I should have backed down, but something—perhaps my thoughts of Ebony and Andrew—kept me from doing so. "I have heard nothing about breeding farms, Your Excellency," I replied. "But I personally do not favor the practice of slavery in any country, and do not find it humane in any of its forms."

His eyes flashed angrily, but he remained cordial. "An interesting viewpoint, my dear, but not very practical. This beautiful city you admire was built with slave labor, as were many of the cities throughout the Americas, including those in the Caribbean and in the United States. We need African slaves, our fine, strong *bozales,* for the sugar fields. No one else could do that kind of work in the heat. They are used to it. They even have resistance to the fever. As for breeding . . . well, we believe in just letting nature take its course." He flashed me a brittle smile and bowed his head courteously. "Now, if you will excuse me . . ." And with that, he moved on.

Pedro cleared his throat. "*Querida,*" he said softly. "I know the scene you saw at the dock—those slaves being pushed and whipped—disgusted you. But . . . it's just business. And—ah, here is my cousin Juan," he said, happy to change the subject. "Come, I'll introduce you."

I had heard much about Juan Salas. When I first arrived in Key West, Martin had explained to me how Salas had sold the island a few years earlier to Alabama businessman John Simonton when the two men met in a grog shop in Havana.

Juan was a good-looking man, somewhat younger and taller than Pedro, but there was a family resemblance. Juan kissed my hand courteously. Throughout our conversation, a cloud of heavy smoke from his cigar encircled him, so that he was visible only through a bluish veil.

"So you live in Key West," he said. "I used to wonder how anyone could ever live in that mosquito-infested swamp."

Though I had at one time been critical of Key West myself, I found myself once again feeling like I was on the defensive that evening. "Still," he said thoughtfully, flicking a gray rope of ash, "I may have made a mistake selling the island so quickly."

"Why? Do you think you sold it for too little?"

"In retrospect, yes. Perhaps. I wanted to be rid of it because the Americans had acquired the Florida Territory." He shrugged. "But ah . . . an island, it can never grow. In the end, a property like that can only become more valuable. A jewel in the middle of the sea." He stabbed the air with his cigar for emphasis and smiled. "You would do well to remember that, Señora Emily."

I nodded politely—but some years later, I would indeed remember these words of wisdom.

Contrary to what I'd hoped, our activity in the bedroom did not abate when we returned home. Back in Key West, Pedro wanted me every night. And sometimes, he came home for a midday siesta! Because I could not repel his advances outright, I began to make plans to be away from the house during the day, running errands, visiting friends, and having lunch with my grandmother or Dorothy. When I was home, I could sometimes distract him, innocently raising questions about the business, since I knew he would quickly shift his focus to the factory. This started as simply a tactic to withstand his advances, but I began to learn a lot about how he ran his cigar business. And I must confess that I found the idea of administering a manufacturing company fascinating. His factory was a source of employment for many, and as such, it was an important business in Key West.

Pedro's open admiration of my body was unwavering, and he continually showered me with gifts. When we arrived in Key West after our honeymoon in Cuba, a shiny new cabriolet and a fine young mare stood waiting for me next to his landau in the courtyard. He never passed an auction at O'Hara's or Browne's warehouses without bringing me home pretty clothes or objets d'art. And hardly a week passed when he would not surprise me with a new piece of jewelry, which he always gave me before leading me to bed.

I gradually learned to mask my distaste for the physical side of our marriage. After all, I told myself, I had a good life. I had gone from being the poorest woman in Key West to being the richest—or at least married to the richest man.

Was I a *mujer buen notada*? Perhaps. But the gossips could talk all they wanted. I was the wife of Pedro Salas, and in Key West, that meant something.

TWENTY-SIX

Key West

November 1842

O ne warm day in late November, about five months after we'd been married, I told Pedro I would be going to Gran's for lunch. When I got there, I found her in bed, ill with a cold, so I headed home.

As my carriage pulled up in the courtyard, I noticed that Pedro's was still there, and I hoped he was asleep. Juanita met me at the door. "Señora, come rest in the shade on the terrace at the side garden, and let me serve you some nice cold lemonade."

I was surprised at this unusual offer. I had tried for months to engage Juanita kindly, but she usually sniffed indifferently at me. "Why, thank you, Juanita," I replied warmly. "That's very nice of you."

"Make yourself comfortable; I'll bring it to you, and I'll bring some *molletes*," she said before hurrying to the cookhouse.

"Perfect. Just put them out. I'll be right down. I'm going upstairs to change."

She looked confused. "But you'll wake up Don Pedro," she protested. "Why not eat now, then change after you eat?"

I smiled. The last thing I wanted was to awaken the sleeping tiger.

"I won't wake him up," I promised, my voice dropping to a mock whisper. "I'll be very quiet."

And I was quiet. I crept silently up the stairs and turned the bedroom doorknob slowly—so slowly that when I opened the door, the two people inside did not notice me right away. My husband was seated on the bed, naked, and an equally nude young woman was kneeling in front of him. Her clothes were strewn around the room. One bedpost was festooned with her undergarments. A dress lay in a heap next to a chair, and a mound of collapsed petticoats was on the pillows of the bed. I could just imagine how she had pranced around, coyly removing one item at a time—with my husband chasing her, trying to tear them off.

"What is this?" I shrieked.

They both jumped up.

"*¡Bastardo!*" I screamed at Pedro. "What I do for you day after day is not enough? You bring a whore into our home? Into our marriage bed?"

Her whalebone corset was next to me on the floor. I picked it up and started beating them both with it, screaming every Spanish obscenity I had ever heard from the men at the boarding-house. I'll confess that I was less upset at the betrayal than by all Pedro's endless thrusting I'd had to endure—and why, when he was also carrying on with whores at the same time?

Carmen—for that was her name—was a woman I recognized as one of those tarts Pedro used to parade through the boarding-house before our marriage. Quickly gathering her clothing, she fled the room. Finally, I threw the tattered corset at Pedro. I saw now that Juanita's offer before had not been a gesture of friendship. It was only meant to draw me to the other side of the house, so I would not see Pedro and Carmen escape in his carriage.

"Juanita," I screamed from the top of the stairs. I knew she would not be far.

"Yes, señora?" Slowly, she began to make her way up the stairs.

"No more games, Juanita. I want you to make up the bed in the guest room at the far end of the hall, and then transfer all my clothing there. Move everything: my jewels, my bonnets, my shoes. Everything."

"Yes, señora," she said. I could see she was resisting the urge to peek into the master bedroom, and I pushed past her, stomping down the glowing marble tiles of the hallway to the guest bedroom. Fuming, I sat down on a large wing chair to remove my shoes. My hands were shaking. I heard Pedro's carriage outside as it rattled over the brick courtyard. And while most of my fury was spent, I was still seething when Juanita came in with the clean bed linen.

While Juanita quietly set to work, I could see that her defiance had returned. As she slipped a case over a pillow held under her chin, she looked boldly at me. "Did you really think you would be enough for such a man?"

"What do you mean, 'such a man'?" I asked scornfully, but even as I said it, it occurred to me that Juanita knew far more about my own husband than I did.

"A man like that never has enough with one woman," she said. "For him, sex is like rum. Or opium. Or gambling. It's his nature."

"Well, Juanita, in case you haven't noticed, he has been quite obsessed with me for the past five months."

"He loves you," she agreed. "But I am not talking about love. I am talking about sex."

Resisting the urge to snap back at her, I thought instead about what she was saying. "You seem to know a lot about my husband. What happened to his first two wives?"

"The first one . . . I did not know her. It was back in Spain.

But his cousin Luis in Havana told me about it. Doña Isabella was only sixteen when Don Pedro married her. She was from an aristocratic family in Madrid. A very frail girl. Don Pedro was probably even more demanding with her, because he was much younger then. Eventually, she went a little . . ." She tapped the side of her head. "She lost her mind. They put her in an institution. She later died of tuberculosis there."

"Was he terribly upset?"

"I think he was. Luis said he loved her."

I glanced down at my emerald engagement ring and vaguely wondered if it had once graced young Isabella's hand. "And his second wife?" I asked.

She hesitated. I could see she was weighing her loyalty to Pedro against my anger. I glared at her. "Juanita?"

"You will not tell Don Pedro I told you?"

"No," I said, sighing.

She stopped fussing with the linens. "This wife, I did know. I was working for them. She was born in Cuba of Spanish parents. She looked a lot like you, though she was younger, maybe nineteen. They had only been married a year or so. She grew melancholy for months, and then"—Juanita crossed herself—"she cut her wrists. I found her in the bathtub. It was terrible. Blood . . . everywhere . . . you should have seen it. *Madre de Dios*"—she crossed herself again—"that was terrible."

There was something else I wanted to know. "And you, Juanita?" She began to smoothe out the sheets and didn't answer. "Have you been to bed with my husband, too?"

She sighed, and looked down. "Not since he has been your husband," she said quietly.

I nodded. "When?"

"It meant nothing. It was just something I did for him, like the cooking and the laundry. It was what he needed until he married you, and I supplied it. Often." She rolled her eyes. "Too often. I was very happy when you got married."

She looked up at me; she had finished making the bed. "Are you going to stay in this room for good?"

"Why? Are you worried you will have to perform for him again?"

She glared at me. Even in my anger, I realized how rude this comment was. "If you deny him," she said, ignoring my question, "he will just go to that *burdel*, like he used to."

These revelations stung me. I now wished to be alone. "I'll stay in this room for as long as I need to," I said. "Now, please bring me that lemonade. And the *molletes*."

She stared in disbelief. "You still want to eat?"

"Yes, Juanita. I'm not a fragile little girl; I am not going to lose my mind or slash my wrists."

After she left, I slumped back in my chair, taking deep breaths to calm myself. My hands were still quivering.

In a few minutes, I went back into the master bedroom, and from a hidden drawer in my armoire, I pulled out a pipe and a small snuff box containing some of Andrew's weed that Dorothy had given me. Back in the guest bedroom, I closed the door, opened the window, and began to smoke until I felt calm. Gradually, a relaxed smile crept over my face. The whole incident seemed so farcical now, and the memory began to amuse me. Alone in the room, the more I thought about it, the funnier it seemed. I only wished I could have shared the story with Andrew. And I could not stop laughing.

The French word boudoir is from the verb bouder, which means "to pout"—the boudoir being a room to which a lady could retire and sulk as she pleased.

I felt I had every right to pout. The day after I moved into the guest room, I hired a locksmith from the chandlery to install a lock on my door. I remained in the guest room for the next three weeks. It was not that I really cared about Pedro's philandering; I didn't love him the way I had loved Andrew, after all. But I was deeply offended—and what if the children had come home early from school that day?

In any case, I had earned a rest from my wifely duties. It was almost like a holiday, and I made plans to enjoy it. I did not eat with Pedro, I did not sleep with him, and I did not speak to him. I felt like a newly manumitted slave. I went out whenever I wanted. I visited people like Ellen Mallory, went to see Barbara Mabrity at the lighthouse, and played whist or euchre with Gran and her cronies. Occasionally, I stopped for tea with Dorothy and her friends. Pedro had not cut off my allowance, so I often joined them at the warehouse auctions. There we would compete with men from Charleston, Mobile, or New York to snap up pretty things.

After these outings, I returned home to my cozy boudoir, feeling exhilarated. The children always knew where to find me and came in after supper to ask for help with homework, or just to tell me about their day. They sometimes asked me when I was going back down to eat with the family, for, like an invalid, I had asked Juanita to bring up my dinner on a tray each evening. Breakfast, I ate on the veranda after everyone left in the morning.

Pedro slipped notes under the door—which I immediately pushed back out. When necessary, I left messages for him with Juanita.

Our housekeeper was angry with me, both for my hauteur and the nuisance of having to serve me upstairs. In the beginning, she approached me when we were alone at breakfast and upbraided me as tactfully as she could, pointing out the many jewels and presents Pedro had brought me. But as time wore on, she dropped any pretense.

"You are disrupting this household," she snarled at me one day, slamming down my dinner tray. "Do you not care about anyone but yourself? It is hard on everyone, especially your children."

I pretended I had not heard her, for I was long past trying to earn her affection.

The children knew I was angry with their beloved Don Pedro, but they had no idea why. A week before Christmas, Martha came in to show me some sketches she had done. Her eyes were shining. "Mama, Don Pedro thinks some of my art is good enough to use on his cigar labels at the factory!"

I looked at her designs. Pedro had come up with a series of names that evoked the sweet, mild taste of his cigar brands: Amor de Cuba, La Dulce Habanera, and others. Martha's labels featured illustrations of exotic smiling women and tropical flowers. She encircled some with stylized tobacco leaves, and I could see what Pedro had already discerned: She was beginning to show a good deal of aptitude. My heart swelled with pride, and I felt a rush of gratitude toward Pedro for making my daughter so happy.

"They're beautiful, darlin'!" I exclaimed.

"He's going to use some of them on his spring shipments," she went on excitedly. "He thinks I should try to get into an art school up north."

I smiled at my pretty daughter as we chatted about that idea for a while. How much longer would I have her? I ran my fingers through her thick blond curls and kissed her. Soon she would have to leave me.

"Mama, I know you're angry at Don Pedro," she said. "But I wish you could make up. We are all so fond of him. And he loves you."

"I know," I said. "I know he does."

"If you stay angry, it will ruin our whole Christmas."

And at that moment, I knew that my vacation from Pedro was over.

◦ℓ◦

The next morning, while I was having coffee in the side garden, Tom Farrell appeared on my terrace.

"Hello, Emily. Any coffee left?"

"I'm sure we can find some," I said with a smile, and I rang for Juanita to bring a fresh pot along with some of her Cuban pastries. I was curious, for Tom did not customarily drop in for a social call by himself during the day. We chatted for a few minutes before his coffee arrived; then he came to the point.

"I was just on my way home to pick up some documents for court this afternoon. I thought I'd stop by and let you know that Pedro came to my office last week to have me draw up a new will."

"Really?"

"Yes. I didn't bring a copy. But except for a few token gifts to his staff and cousins in Havana, he has left his estate entirely to you and the children. He wanted me to let you know that. And, Emily, I don't mean to be indiscreet, but I must tell you that he is much wealthier than you might have thought."

Amounts did not interest me. "As long as there is enough to see to the children's education. That's all I care about."

"Believe me, there will be plenty for that!"

When Tom left, I told Juanita I would be having lunch with my husband that day. She looked relieved; I daresay she almost smiled.

Pedro's eyes came to life with relief when he entered the dining room and saw me. "Hello, Pedro," I said.

He said nothing, but he knelt down, reached for my hand, and kissed it fervently. Then, reluctant to let it go, he held it for a full minute against his cheek. When he looked up at me, there were tears in his eyes. Later, after we made love and he was leaving for work again, he slipped a beautiful diamond bracelet on my wrist.

ஃ

The children were thrilled that everything was back to normal.
We spent Christmas Eve at our house, and Dorothy hosted us
on Christmas Day.

On New Year's Day, I organized an open-house social for all
our friends. Ellen Mallory came with her son Stephen, now the
collector of customs. To my delight, she brought me some of
her famous conch fritters, along with her special sauce, made
from Key lime juice, homemade mayonnaise, and hot mustard.

In true southern tradition, Dorothy had made us a New
Year's casserole of hoppin' John, a dish of black-eyed peas and
rice. "For luck," she said brightly. "I have a feeling this will be
a lucky year for you."

"Luck would be to find out where Andrew is," I said, lowering my voice. "It's not knowing his whereabouts that torments
me. That, and thinking of Ebony's last days. Just imagine,
Dorothy: If she had lived, my poor darling Ebony would be
walking now—no, running probably—and beginning to talk.
She'd be nineteen months old!"

Dorothy sighed. "Don't torture yourself like this, Emily.
You should be enjoying the children you do have."

Pedro was his usual ebullient self over the holidays, delighted that all was back on an even keel. One cool night in
January, he cuddled up to me in bed and whispered, "*Querida,* I
have something to show you. My cousin Diego in Madrid found
this book in Paris and sent it to me for Christmas. It's all written in French; you will have to translate it for me. But I think
it can make a big difference in our lives."

I groaned inwardly, for he had that familiar twinkle in his
eye. I picked up the book and read the French title out loud:
Sexual Positions of the Kama Sutra and the Ancient World. I flipped through
it quickly, glancing at some of the illustrations. Those in the
first half were of Hindu statues, carved in stone, featuring

people with oversized genitalia in various sexual poses. Along-side each artifact was an illustration of two nude human be-ings in that same position. The second half of the book dealt with pictures of paintings taken from the walls of brothels in ancient Greece and Rome and from the Lupanar in Pompeii. The whole body of work was a depiction of twisted, tangled limbs. It all seemed terribly uncomfortable.

"You would have to be a contortionist to follow this" was my only comment as I handed the manual back.

"Well, perhaps. But I was thinking, *querida*. What if we tried doing it less often and concentrated more on these interesting ways?"

I liked the sound of "less often."

"We could start with page one and do a different position each night," he suggested.

I thumbed through the pages again. There were sixty-six positions in the Kama Sutra section alone, and almost as many in the section devoted to the ancient world. By the time we got through the book, I would have tried every sexual trick in the history of mankind. I looked at Pedro and shrugged. "Well, if you really want to, I suppose we can try. We'll just skip the complicated ones."

And so I began to read the French, translating as I went along, feeling like one of the *lectore* readers that Pedro hired to read to his workers in the tobacco factory. Pedro listened in-tently, and although he did not complain, I was sure I saw him many mornings thereafter trying to soothe an aching leg or shoulder. We advanced through the book night after night, and soon I wished myself back in my boudoir.

TWENTY-SEVEN

Key West

1843

A short time after the holidays, I stopped off at Dorothy's to return a shawl I had borrowed. She was not at home, but Tom greeted me enthusiastically. "Emily! It's good to see you. This is a coincidence; I was going over to see you this afternoon. Let's go into my study. I have some wonderful news."

I was certainly ready for good news. In his study, he closed the door behind us. "Remember how we launched that suit against the U.S. government for the land Commodore Archer expropriated from you and Martin in order to expand the navy base?"

"Of course," I said. "But I think we agreed that we would never see that money in our lifetime."

"Yes, we did." He smiled. "But it turns out we were wrong! The government appointed someone to assess values in Key West, so restitution can be made for every piece of land the commodore expropriated in the navy's name. You're to receive a bank draft from the Committee for Naval Affairs. They want to compensate you at full current market value of the land, plus the estimated value of the pineapple crop that year, and full replacement value of the house. There were fourteen acres, at seven thousand dollars per acre, plus buildings and crops. It comes out to one hundred and ten thousand dollars."

"What?" I shrieked in disbelief. "We paid only a thousand!"

"Quite a good return," he observed with a smile.

I was dumbfounded. I had money! My own money—a small fortune—and now, in the present, not Pedro's bequest sometime in the future. This money meant that if Pedro ever left me—or if I chose to leave him—I could afford my children's education without assistance; I could even afford to buy a beautiful house of my own choice. I made a decision in Tom's office before I left. "Tom, I must beg your discretion. Pedro . . . Pedro is not to know about this yet. Can we agree on that?" Tom nodded.

As I rose to leave, I felt light-headed and happy, as though I could dance out of his study and along the hallway. At the back of my mind, I continued to dream of a miracle that would bring Andrew back into my life. I did not know his whereabouts, but he certainly knew mine. If he ever managed to obtain freedom, or run away, he might well find me. And if he did, the money could change things considerably.

TWENTY-EIGHT

Key West

1843

Tom's Louisiana business contacts meant a positive change in the Farrells' financial situation. In the spring, Dorothy decided to enjoy their new affluence with a major renovation of their home. Most of the tradesmen and decorators were brought in from Cuba, and they slept anywhere they could in the house. It was to become a hive of activity, with people coming and going and workmen toting ladders and spreading drop cloths everywhere. It would fall to her servants to do all the cleaning up.

"We don't want to live in the mess," she said. I've timed the work to coincide with a trip: I'll be going with Tom to New Orleans again. Could you possibly keep the children at your house?"

"Of course. We'd love to have them."

"Funny," she said with her silvery laugh, "I hadn't been back there for all those years. But now that Tom is going so often, I find I want to go with him. Especially since the children are getting older."

Pedro was delighted to host their children. Sand Key was

only nine miles out on the reef, and following a tradition for Key Westers to go there on weekends for picnics, Pedro would pack them and my children into a hired boat and go sailing and fishing. I was still not a good sailor, so I would remain at home to read or visit with Gran. They would all return tan and happy, and talking about the kindly Captain Peartree, who made them welcome at the lighthouse.

This time, Dorothy had more bad news when she returned.

After we had all settled into the carriages at the docks, she took my hand and said softly, "Grandpère is dead, Emily, He'd had a massive stroke a couple of weeks ago and died while I was there. He looked terrible when I saw him. I'm not sure if he knew who I was; he might even have thought I was you. But he seemed pleased to see me. We buried him in the family plot at the old cemetery. A lot of people, old friends like the Beaubiens and the de Saumurs, came to the funeral, and even some former slaves. I wish you'd been there, sugar."

"Oh, Dorothy . . . I'm sorry now that I didn't go with you."

Dorothy nodded sadly. "Yes. Everyone was asking for you."

"I wonder if he ever forgave me for marrying Martin and moving to Key West?"

"Oh, I'm sure he did, sugar. He was angry at me when I got married, too. Remember? I was just supposed to be in Key West for a short visit, and then I met Tom. But he got over that."

"We must have been a big disappointment to him."

"No, I wouldn't worry about any of that, sugar. He knew he had raised a couple of headstrong girls. But he did want us to be happy. Eurydice said that he was very proud of us and was always mentioning us to his friends."

"I just wish he'd gotten to see his grandchildren."

"Yes. I do, too. Apparently, before he became ill he was talking about coming to see us all here in Key West so he could meet them. He certainly could have afforded to come. I don't know why he didn't."

At this, Tom, who had been listening, chimed in: "Yes, he most certainly could have afforded to. We settled his finances before we left. One of my former classmates at law school who lives in New Orleans helped us to accelerate the process while we were there."

I was hardly listening, as I was still contemplating what my grandfather's last days would have been like.

Tom smiled at me. "Aren't you curious about his wealth?"

"I suppose," I replied dully. As I was no longer desperate for money, numbers now meant little.

"There will be some medical bills to pay, and some charities . . . and taxes. He manumitted all his slaves, and left a house and a pension for Eurydice and Marie-Francine. But even after all that, once the properties are sold, there should be about five hundred thousand dollars. You will each get about two hundred and fifty thousand dollars."

Stunned, I turned to him. "So much?"

"At least that much," he said. "Perhaps more."

"He always told us he was poor!" I exclaimed.

"Yes. And he gave us such small dowries," Dorothy added, laughing. "But he had a great deal of property in New Orleans, and over the years it seems that its value has grown considerably."

We were all silent for a moment. The fact that I was gradually becoming quite a wealthy woman was beginning to take hold in my consciousness. All this money could shift the power in my marriage. And the thought of being so free made me light-headed. When Tom suggested I stop at the house for a glass of champagne to celebrate their safe arrival and our new-found financial security, I readily agreed.

We stopped to pick up Gran on the way, and we all marveled at Dorothy's new renovation as we walked into the Farrell home, although Gran found fault with some of the color choices, since she had not been consulted. When we told her about Grand-père, she just said tartly, "So that ornery old Frenchman finally kicked the bucket!"

When she learned of our inheritance, Gran turned to me. "So what are you going to do with all that money? You're not going to stay with the Spaniard, are you?"

Gran's question lingered in my mind.

A couple of weeks after Dorothy's return, Pedro and I finally completed his cousin's manual. It had taken three months. I thought we were done with such foolishness. But he closed the book and asked, "Shall we start over from page one?" I rolled my eyes.

After weekends, Pedro was usually well rested, but one Monday he came home from the factory in the evening looking exhausted and haggard. Over dinner, he leaned toward me and whispered, "Let's go to bed early tonight, *querida*. I'm feeling very tired."

"But it's only seven-thirty," I protested. We normally did not retire until around ten o'clock—late for Key West, where fishermen and wreckers rose early—but it had been Pedro's custom from his early childhood in Spain.

Upstairs in our room, he even dispensed with the tiresome manual. "We'll just do it the old way," he said.

I sighed. We prepared for bed, I extinguished the bedside oil lamp, and he assumed his regular position. But suddenly, I heard a strange sound in his throat. Clutching his chest, he abruptly rolled off me, and with his face turned away, he was sick over the side of the bed. I quickly relit the lamp, and when I looked at him, he was turning blue. I had seen that look before; it was a more severe form of the heart seizure Josiah Peartree had had in the lighthouse tower years ago.

"Pedro, are you all right?" I cried.

"Padre . . ." he said faintly.

I was not thinking clearly. "Padre? Your father?"

"A . . . priest."

I raced downstairs, shouting for Juanita. Because it was so early, she was in her sitting room, sewing.

"Juanita, hurry! Go fetch a priest and Dr. Fogarty. Don Pedro has had a heart attack. Get the doctor over here first. Then the priest. Hurry!"

Dr. Fogarty arrived in about ten minutes, just as Pedro's life was ebbing away. Close behind him was the local Catholic priest. Father Lopez had just enough time to give Pedro the last rites. A few minutes later, Dr. Fogarty closed Pedro's eyes and pronounced him dead. It had all happened so fast, I was numb with disbelief.

Juanita remained standing outside the door, weeping. The other servants stood at the bottom of the stairs, muttering among themselves and reciting the rosary.

Martha and Timothy, who had been doing their homework by lamplight in their rooms before all this started, had wandered out to the hall. I saw their stoic faces peering into our room, and I allowed them to come in to say good-bye, hugging both of them close to me.

Later, Dr. Fogarty took me aside. "I'm sorry, Miss Emily. There was nothing to be done."

I just stood there, dry-eyed. I did not know what to say.

"I tried to tell him he was overdoing it," he continued.

"He had consulted you?"

"Yes, he's been having pains in his chest off and on over the past two years, and he had all the classic signs of a bad heart: shortness of breath, dizzy spells, palpitations. . . . I advised him to bring his will up-to-date and to sort out his business affairs. He knew he was not going to live very long."

"He knew? This was before we married?"

"That's right. I also told him to slow down. He worked too hard. And taking a young wife was risky for a man in his condition."

I nodded sadly. At least, I reassured myself, I had brought some measure of happiness to his last days.

And with that, another door in my life had closed: the end of my days as a wife. I vowed that unless it could be Andrew, no man would ever share my bed again.

Pedro's funeral was a large one for Key West. We placed his coffin in an elaborate vault only steps from where Martin was interred. I had now buried two husbands. Two gravesites would mark the years of my life.

To my amazement, Gran insisted we have a reception at her house for "dear Señor Pedro." Many of the town's citizens and workers from Pedro's factory came to comfort my family, all of them offering kind words in my husband's memory. My children went to Dorothy's afterward, and I went home to a largely empty house, except for the servants. Juanita emerged from the kitchen to greet me. She had been helpful throughout the funeral and surprised me by gently taking my hand when I arrived.

"Are you hungry, señora? I can make you something light. An omelette, perhaps? A little salad . . . or some soup?"

I found my eyes welling up. I realized that she had been crying, too. Both of us were mourning the kinder side of Pedro that we had known.

"Don't trouble yourself, Juanita. I'm just tired. I'd like to lie down for a while."

"Of course, señora."

"Juanita," I said. She turned back. "I want you to stay on working here. And for now at least, all the other servants, as well."

She smiled. "They will be glad to know that, señora."

I suddenly felt a surge of affection for this woman who had fought my presence in the house for so long. I added, "Juanita, from now on, please call me Miss Emily."

"Yes, señora . . . Miss Emily."

I lay down and noticed that Pedro had left the dreaded manual on his nightstand. I blushed, wondering if the priest had seen it the night Pedro died. There was a bookmark stuck in page sixteen, our next tryst. Glancing through the pages, I noticed that he had made annotations on his favorite pages about what was good and what wasn't, what hurt his back the next day, which positions I seemed to respond to best and which ones repulsed me. I shook my head. He had been a strange man. But in spite of everything, we'd had an interesting, if brief, life together.

I dozed off, and when I awoke, it was already dark. Juanita fussed over me and insisted that I eat. She handed me an envelope. "Señora Ximenez brought this while you were asleep," she said.

It was a note from Alfie Dillon, offering me his condolences and inviting me—if I was able—to visit him at the hospital the next morning.

I was shocked when I saw Alfie. A nurse wheeled him out to the back garden for some fresh air, cautioning me not to stay long. He looked very ill and bloated: his legs and feet were swollen, and bruises covered his body. I barely recognized him, and I knew immediately that I was looking at a dying man. On his lap was a cigar box.

"Alfie, how are you feeling?" I asked brightly.

He just smiled. "I bin wantin' to talk to you for a while, Mrs. Lowry," he said, using my former name. "I heard you tried to come see me."

"Yes, but you were not well enough to have visitors. I'm glad to see that you're doing better."

"I ain't," he replied wanly. "I'm afraid I'm on my way out, ma'am. The beatin' ruined my left kidney, and th' other one don't seem to be workin' too well, neither."

My heart sank as I collapsed in the nurse's chair beside him. I took his hand in mine and whispered, "Oh, Alfie, I'm sorry. So very sorry."

"But I wanted to see you, 'cause there's something I have to give you, and there ain't much time."

"What is that, Alfie?"

"First, I want to tell you. You mustn't blame Martin. It was for you and the children he done it."

"What are you talking about, Alfie?"

"The beatin' I got, Mrs. Lowry—that was the Lord's way of punishing me on this earth for what I done. I deserved what I got. Y'see, ma'am . . . the captain, he tried to make a deal with Martin—Mr. Lowry."

"Yes?"

"Your husband was concerned about money and he done told the captain that. He was worried about you, and about educatin' the children and all. The captain said that if he could turn off the light once in a while, when you wasn't aware of it, we could get a few wrecks goin' out there."

My jaw dropped. Martin *had* let the lights go out sometimes; in fact, we'd had three wrecks on his watch. But at the time, I thought he'd simply dozed off and it had happened by accident.

"And Martin," I prodded softly, "he . . . went along with it?"

Alfie nodded. "He did, yes, for a share of the cargo proceeds, ma'am. But don't hold that against 'im. The captain was mighty persuasive."

I felt dizzy. "Alfie, do you know what happened to my husband?"

He nodded. "I wrote it all down here," he said, opening the cigar box. He handed me a letter he had written to the sheriff.

As I read, a heavy gauze was lifted from my eyes. Suddenly, it was all clear. The reason Martin hadn't taken Timothy with him the day he disappeared was because he was going out to meet with Captain Lee and Alfie on the *Outlander.* He had gone out to tell them he could no longer allow himself to cause more wrecks. No wonder he seemed so happy that day, I thought. He was probably enormously relieved.

"Mr. Lowry told the captain he wasn't goin' to turn the light off no more. The captain, he got really fussed about that," explained Alfie. "They argued. Then they came to blows. Captain Lee picked up an iron gaffin' pole and hit Mr. Lowry so hard across the thigh that I heard a crack. He howled with pain and rolled around in the boat. I knew his leg was busted. He tried to crawl back to his own skiff, yellin' out to Lee that he was goin' to tell Pendleton the truth, and damn the consequences. Then Lee, he . . . he . . ."

I was leaning forward. "Yes? Alfie, tell me, please."

"He shot 'im in the head. I couldn't stop it, God help me, Mrs. Lowry. I'm sorry. He was like a madman."

I sat in shocked silence.

"We knowed we was in big trouble if yer husband's body washed up on the island, so I helped the captain dump a crate of coffee into the sea, one you'd ordered and we'd picked up in Cuba. Then he crammed Mr. Lowry into it. He attached one of our ballast rocks to a rope, and we sailed our boat out a little past the reef and dropped the crate into the deep. Only a hurricane could've found it."

"Yes," I managed to say. "That's what happened."

"I reckon now we should've gone out farther, because it sounds like it might've caught somehow on the coral. It's all written down here, Mrs. Lowry. I wrote it up so's you wouldn't wonder who killed your husband no more."

I breathed in deeply. "What else should I know?"

"Well, you was doin' such a good job, the captain, he got worried we wouldn't get no more wrecks, so he tried to get you out o'there. He kind of hoped all them presents he brung you would make you like him and y'd want to marry him and go back to Key West, but you didn't show no interest.

"We did some arguin' over your supplies one time. He thought if he skipped a delivery of food, you'd git worried 'bout yer family. But I wouldn't go along with that. I'd not see your children go hungry. He gave in after a week and we brought you the food."

I remembered that well. They'd been late with supplies one month because the captain was ill—or so he'd said. How I had blessed Martin for the bin of food he reserved in the storage shed. A new surge of rage welled up inside of me.

But Alfie was not yet through. "Then he tried to sabotage your oil. Mrs. Mabrity had sent back a batch of bad fuel that was delivered to the Key West lighthouse, and he brung that out to you instead o'the clean oil you was supposed to git. He was fig-urin' it would take a long time t'git that straightened out, but Rebecca Flaherty, she seen to it right away, and Pendleton made sure we brung you out some good oil a couple days later."

"You're saying that the contaminated oil was brought out to me deliberately?"

"Yes, ma'am. And when that didn't work, the captain, he got really fussed, so tha's when he sent in those fake Indians."

I felt my breath coming faster. "Alfie, are you saying . . . those braves who savaged the tower . . . they weren't Indians at all?"

"The lads was just some young fishermen he met in a grog shop in Key West. Talked them into puttin' on war paint and feathers and goin' out there howlin' and yelpin' in a dugout canoe to set a fire at the lighthouse. They thought it was a lark. He was goin' to give 'em each ten dollars to do it."

Abruptly, like lightning shattering a dark sky, another ques-tion hit me. "Those men. Were they the eight fishermen who went missing from Key West?"

"Aye. They was supposed to bust into the tower and burn the wooden staircase to cripple the light. But they got it wrong. . . . Anyhow, they wasn't plannin' to kill nobody, jes' wanted to wreck the light. And the captain never expected you to start shootin' at 'em. But you managed to pick 'em all off. Lordy, wasn't he some angry at you over that!" And he managed a weak smile as he slowly shook his head.

"What happened to their remains?" The memory of the lone figure waving a white flag in the moonlight as he collected the braves' bodies flashed into my mind. He'd been dressed as an Indian, but of course it had to have been George Lee.

"He didn't want nobody to know 'bout the mischief he done. He picked up the lads and he buried 'em all far out to sea so's nobody'd find out that you wasn't attacked by real Indians. And he told me . . . well, he said later . . . you wasn't that good a shot because"—here he lowered his voice—"well, a few of 'em was still alive." At this, I gasped. To what lengths would he have gone to cover up his crimes?

"We never brung you newspapers around that time 'cuz he was afraid you'd make the connection between the missin' Key Westers and the fake Indians at Wreckers'."

"I might have. But I never would have thought the captain was responsible. I trusted him . . . trusted both of you."

He hung his head. "I know you did, ma'am. That's why I'm feelin' so guilty. And when we heard yer little girl . . . Hannah . . ." he stopped—he was sobbing like a baby. "I thought about her all the time. Couldn't eat or sleep for awhile after that. But the captain, he said she was retarded, so it didn't much matter."

I had to take a deep breath. My anger was so overwhelming now, it was attacking my chest like a knife.

"That's why I think this beatin' was needed," he continued, oblivious to my rage. "Y'know, he even tried to cause a wreck that night we was bein' so helpful after he killed yer husband.

D'you remember how we stayed overnight in our boat and the captain kept letting the light go out?"

I nodded. So what I had taken for incompetence was actually an act of sabotage. "Is there anything more?" I managed to whisper. My head was reeling.

"Well, then he tried t'git you interested in Captain Peartree. Talked Peartree into wooing you out there, but that didn't work, neither. You turned him down."

"That was the captain's doing?"

He nodded. "Well, Peartree was fond of you, but he would never have pursued you without the captain pushing him. So . . . yes. Then we had that hurricane, and you come back to Key West. Storm was a blessin' because it busted the light. But when he heard that Pendleton was plannin' to send you out there again after it got fixed, he got really fussed. Tha's when he tried to git you to marry 'im." Here he lowered his voice, even though there was no one around to hear. "Well, he told me later what happened, and I'm real sorry he was so disrespectful to a fine lady like y'self. I reckon you was just too good a lighthouse keeper, Mrs. Lowry. With you out there, we didn't have much chance of no good wrecks. He knew you'd never go along with lettin' the light go out."

I slumped back into my seat. So, it had all been about the light. It had never been about me, or my charm, or even—I smiled bitterly—my cleavage. And poor Alfie was merely his dim-witted pawn.

Seeing that Alfie was tired and, by now, a little confused, I made ready to leave. "I should let you get some rest," I said, patting his shoulder. I took the letter addressed to the sheriff and prepared to leave.

"I should've spoke up before, God knows. But I was scared of the captain. He said he'd kill me if I ever told anybody about any of this."

"Well, he certainly can't do that now," I assured him. I felt drained and raw and was not sure I could listen to any more. But I knew in my heart that Alfie would not be around much longer, so I pressed on.

"Is that everything?"

"Yes, ma'am. 'Cept for the money."

"What money?"

"Martin's share. It was about seventy-five thousand dollars. He never really trusted the captain, so he gave it to me for safekeepin'. I was supposed to open an account for you at the bank, but I never got around to it. I would've given it to you after the captain killed 'im, but I didn't know how to splain it all to you . . . so when nobody was lookin', I . . . I put it into a sugar sack and stuck it into the grave we dug."

I stared at him. So that was the money the captain was after! Buried in the ground. Only a simple man like Alfie would have hidden it there—and in a sack that would deteriorate. In my mind's eye, I saw the money rising from its grave in a hurricane and, like a swarm of bees, swirling away into the air on the wings of blustering gusts, bound for destinations of its own resolve.

"I sure ain't proud o'what I done." He leaned forward and looked at me beseechingly. "Please tell me you forgive me, Mrs. Lowry," he whispered.

"Yes, of course I forgive you." Much as I felt like lashing out at him, I wanted to let him die in peace. "Good-bye, Alfie, and thank you," I said, reaching out and taking his bloated hand in mine. A half smile spread across his face, but his features were almost unrecognizable. "Godspeed," I whispered.

I left Alfie in the care of a nurse and hurriedly made my way through the dreary halls of the hospital, heading toward the exit, where my carriage awaited. I wanted nothing more than to breathe some fresh air outside. But when I happened upon a door with the name George Lee on it, I stopped. There was a sign below his name that said NO VISITORS. There was nobody around. After a moment's hesitation, I quietly opened the door and slipped in.

A stench of sweat and stale urine permeated the hot, airless little room. The captain lay dozing by the window on a sagging navy cot, immobile, looking thin and ashen. Gone was the tan color of his years in the sun. His leathery face was sallow, etched with crevices; his oily hair hung limply past his shoulders; his beard, too, had grown long and straggly, and he was glistening with perspiration. A metal brace seemed to be holding his broken jaw together. His breathing was labored, and clearly he, too, was in a bad way, but I could summon no pity for him.

I conjured up a vision of Martin and Hannah. "You monster!" I whispered. "They are preparing a special place in hell for you."

His eyes fluttered open and registered shock as they focused on me. Then they became defiant. He opened his mouth to speak, but, lacking control of his muscles, he could only drool. The words gurgled in his throat.

Disgusted, I turned to go, but then I saw a smug look steal over his features. A muffled sound escaped from the bed. I realized he was actually laughing at me. He closed his eyes again, as though savoring a memory.

With renewed fury, I taunted him. "Did you think it was a random beating?"

His eyes flew open.

"It wasn't," I whispered. "It was my husband, Pedro. Pedro's men, acting on his orders."

As he absorbed this, I could see his eyes flash with anger. Rage replaced his amusement, and his face reddened.

"Oh, and by the way, Captain. I found out where your

money is. Alfie buried it in a sugar sack at the grave site out at Wreckers'. At this moment, it is probably still in flight across the seven seas!"

Furious, he tried to talk again, but this only brought on a violent coughing spell. I gave him one final look of loathing. And then I left.

TWENTY-NINE

Key West

June 1843

A week later, the *Key West Enquirer*'s headline was ASSAULT VICTIM CAPTAIN GEORGE LEE SUCCUMBS TO INJURIES. Alfie was to outlive him by just a couple of weeks. By that time, his letter to the sheriff had been published, and the shocked townspeople did little to mourn either of them.

Tom Farrell came over a few weeks after Pedro's funeral to read his will. "Pedro left you property in Madrid, a hacienda in Castile, and another in the Canary Islands," Tom told me. "He left you the house in which you spent your honeymoon in Havana, the tobacco plantation and factory at Vuelta Abajo in Cuba, and the house in Key West, along with three boarding-houses, some empty lots, several cigar makers' cottages, the cigar factory here, and . . ." Here, Tom paused.

I was gazing at him, trying to absorb it all. "And?"

"Well, he didn't want you to know this, but he also owned a huge sugar plantation and factory in Cuba. He knew you'd disapprove because of the slaves. You now own over three hundred slaves, Emily."

I slumped in my chair. So, Pedro had lied to me. I wondered vaguely if any of those poor devils we saw abused near our ship in Havana were destined for his plantation . . . *my* plantation.

Aside from all the property, Tom began to rattle off numbers that bewildered me. Pedro had never told me how wealthy he was. There were cash accounts in New York, Havana, and Madrid, and he had other investments, as well. As Tom talked, I glanced over Pedro's bankbooks and noticed a recent cash withdrawal of $100,000.

"Do you know anything about this?" I asked. He suddenly looked uncomfortable. "What was that, Tom? Where did the money go?"

He cleared his throat. "Emily, remember that one hundred and ten thousand dollars the government paid you in compensation for your land?"

"What about it?"

"The government settled for only ten thousand dollars, Emily. That's not bad; it's still ten times what you and Martin paid for the land. I happened to mention it to Pedro the day I received the letter, and he got this idea—"

"What idea?"

"I told him at the time it was foolish. I said you might find out."

"What? Tell me, for heaven's sake."

"Well, Pedro knew you married him for his money, but he adored you. Really, Emily, I've never seen a man love his wife as much as he loved you."

"And . . ."

"Well, call it a whim. But he wanted to see if you loved him enough to stay with him if you had your own money. So he added one hundred thousand dollars to what the government gave you."

I felt my jaw slacken. "That was all Pedro's money?"

He nodded. "I'm sorry, Emily. I shouldn't have deceived you. But he was adamant, so I . . ." He held up his hands helplessly. "He was my client. I went ahead and looked after it."

I stared at him. "You lied to me?"

He nodded. "I felt I had to," he said. "I'm sorry."

I got up and asked Juanita to bring us coffee as I mulled over this latest development. And then, as we sipped, I turned my attention back to our work, for Pedro's estate was now mine to manage; there was no time for sulking.

"Are there any more secrets that you and Pedro kept from me?"

Tom shook his head. "No. Really, there are not, Emily. And I'd be happy to help you, if I can regain your trust."

"Good. But I want an honest relationship with you. No more secrets, Tom."

"I promise, Emily."

I nodded. "Very well, then. Here's what needs to be done: I want the sugar plantation and factory over in Cuba sold at once."

"That won't be difficult," Tom said brightly as he flicked through some recent statements. "They're very profitable."

As he began writing on a notepad, I continued: "Perhaps they won't be, Tom. I want all those slaves set free. The new owner will have to pay them if he wishes to keep them on."

"But Emily," he protested, "those slaves, they'd be worth"—he scribbled some calculations—"maybe four hundred thousand dollars! And all that free labor . . ."

I just glared at him. He gave me no further argument.

By the time Tom was through selling off the properties in Cuba and Spain, I was awash with cash. Pedro's American holdings, including the Key West cigar factory, were all that I retained. I had well over two million dollars, plus some choice properties on the island, which I intended to keep.

Thinking about what Juan Salas had told me in Havana, I set out not to sell land, but to buy as much of it as I could in Key West. I purchased properties beyond William Whitehead's delineated plots, acquiring undeveloped oceanfront land at the south end of the island. Much of it was still just wooded forest or salt ponds tucked among mangroves inhabited by birds and mosquitoes.

Tom thought I was foolish. "Swamp . . . no fresh water? What are you thinking, Emily?" But then he said no more about it. He reckoned I had so much money that if I did make a few mistakes, it wouldn't matter.

I hired a new manager for Pedro's Key West factory. The next thing I did was to hire more women, a move that shocked most Key Westers. Pedro had employed a few women as low-paid packers, but not as cigar makers. I made it known that if they could roll cigars, they could work as rollers, and I paid them the going rate for men—twenty-five dollars per week. I knew the men would resent this, but I didn't care. I was going to run the company my way, with the best employees I could.

I did make a few mistakes along the way. My first was the cigar box fiasco. Because it usually took so long for the boxes made in New York to arrive, I started a small factory to manufacture them in Key West. But half the time the cedar wood did not arrive from South America when it was supposed to, and I was left with idle employees at the box plant, packers at the cigar factory with no boxes to fill, and a mountain of cigars piling up. I soon closed the box plant.

Selling off the tobacco plantation in Cuba had not been wise, because it made me vulnerable to the vicissitudes of suppliers over there. I had perhaps been a little hasty in my decision, but it was not a disaster—just an inconvenience.

There was much stress, I was to learn, in running a business. Distribution of the cigars was my biggest problem. I usually had to wait for a ship loaded with cotton from the Gulf states to head north and pick up our shipments. This meant that sometimes our cigars languished for a week or so before I could get them shipped off. And again, our production would get backed up.

Once the cigars were picked up and loaded onto ships heading for places like Baltimore or New York City, they were at the mercy of sudden storms. So I had to pay large insurance premiums to protect my seabound assets.

But overall, the next few years were an exciting challenge for me, and a valuable learning experience. I had been a working woman for a good part of my adult life, but always in a minor, menial role. Now, for the first time, I was in charge, managing my own business, and I enjoyed the power that came with that status. It was also good for me, as it occupied a lot of my time. Since I could not be with Andrew, I had to focus on something that could consume my interest. And managing a business helped fill the void in my life.

"*You just amaze me,* sugar," Dorothy said over tea on one of the rare days when my sister and I could spend free time together. She looked thoughtful. "Do you think you'll ever marry again?"

"No. Absolutely not."

She smiled. "Remember how Gran and I were always after you to set your cap for George Lee? Thank goodness you paid us no mind. What a terrible man he turned out to be!"

I finally told her about Lee's attempted assault, and Dorothy looked at me in astonishment. She took my hand. "Oh, Emily. I wish you'd told me at the time."

For a long moment we sat quietly. Dorothy opened her mouth to speak, then stopped herself. After a pause, she said in a small voice, "It happened to me, too. I was attacked, in fact, it was much worse. But at least I had Eurydice."

I almost dropped my teacup.

"You're surprised?" She smiled bitterly. "Yes, sugar, your little sister managed to get herself into a whole mess of trouble with all her flirting. I . . . wasn't the chaste little virgin bride you thought I was."

She described what had happened years ago, at the home of Maurice de Belisle in the French Quarter, just before she came to Key West for Timothy's christening. She'd been madly in love with de Belisle's handsome nephew, Claude, an officer in the army. At a large social, Eurydice had been keeping a watchful eye on Dorothy, but there was a slight chill in the air and Grandmère sent her back home in the carriage to fetch her wrap. As soon as Eurydice left, Claude steered Dorothy into the study.

Dorothy blushed. "I was led willingly enough," she admitted. "It felt naughty. I'd been sipping punch and I just wanted to enjoy myself. We were kissing and touching, and it was very exciting. But then . . ." Her voice trailed off.

"Then?"

She was silent again. It was still difficult for her to talk about it.

"I couldn't get him to stop," she said, lowering her head. When she looked back up at me, her eyes had filled with sadness and pain. "It's as simple as that. He attacked me. I struggled and tried to push him away. When I tried to scream, nobody could hear me above the music. Besides, he kept putting his hand over my mouth. And he just . . ."

As her voice trailed off again, I stared at her. I could not help but recall how she had confided in me years ago about her delight in surrendering herself to Tom.

"That isn't the worst of it," she continued. "A few weeks later, I missed my menses. And I just knew I was pregnant. I tried to get in touch with Claude, but he ignored my notes. Then his unit shipped out. I never heard from him again."

"What happened to the baby?" I asked. But suddenly, I already knew the answer.

My sister was now crying quietly. "I've been wanting to tell you all these years," she said. "I was pregnant when I married Tom."

"Does he know?"

She shook her head vigorously. "No. No! And you mustn't tell him. Ever! Maureen is his favorite. No. He must never know. Nor should Maureen. She adores her father. And it's just lucky her appearance favors mine."

"Why are you telling me this now?" I asked.

"Because I always felt I owed you an explanation for my hasty wedding, and for making the plans with Gran instead of you. I know you were hurt, but you would have wanted me to take my time and have a longer betrothal—which would have been the sensible thing to do. But I couldn't wait. I needed a husband quickly."

I gathered her into my arms. Dorothy continued to cry. "He mustn't ever, ever know. Promise even if I die first, you'll never tell him."

I held her tightly as I soothed her. "Of course not, darlin'. Of course not."

I thought I'd really known my sister well, but her ability to harbor secrets continued to astonish me. What else lay hidden inside her pretty head? I hugged her to my chest and rocked with her until a calm settled over her.

THIRTY

Key West

1846

Time flew by. I was busy with the factory, with my children and Dorothy's family, and looking out for Gran. There was little time for socializing; I just did not have enough hours in my day. And with no man in my life, I was becoming as chaste as a nun.

When I had moments to myself, I still recalled those happy and amorous moments with Andrew: Quite suddenly, yet another daydream would surface and drift me toward Wreckers' like a bird in the wind. With a smile, I found myself caught up in thoughts of my mischievous seduction of him up in the lighthouse tower—his astonishment at how I reveled in my boldness. In my mind, I sometimes relived pressing against him in my bed on cool nights, the light from the tower stretching, caressing his features as he slept. And my dreams still included Ebony—the moments when I cuddled and nursed her, even though when I opened my eyes, I knew the terrible truth.

Martha and Timothy had been getting restless in Key West and wanted to go to school in New York City. I wasn't sure why they chose New York instead of New Orleans or Baltimore, which were closer, but I felt if that was what they wanted, I should not deprive them of it.

Martha, now sixteen, had found out about an art program in New York run by nuns; Timothy, now fifteen, was hoping to be accepted in a preparatory school which would eventually lead to studying architecture at King's College in New York. I wasn't sure I could bear the idea of both of them leaving home at once, but I wanted them to be happy, and, I told myself, at least they would have each other there. In the early spring of 1846, I sent out applications to the schools, secretly hoping that one winter in the cold Northeast would be enough for them.

I also decided that no matter how ill the journey made me, I would accompany them to New York to get them settled. I had the entire summer to prepare.

Around that time, Tom Farrell told me about a friend of one of his clients who was interested in buying a Key West business. There had been inquiries made about my cigar factory, and they wondered if I would be interested in selling. Tom and Dorothy brought him around one evening for dinner, and Juanita served us one of her splendid paellas.

Jonathon Levy was about my own age—thirty-five or so. A New Yorker, he was, much like Tom—smart, educated, and very handsome. I quite enjoyed his company.

"I'm very impressed with your cigar operation here, Mrs. Salas," he said finally, over Juanita's orange-flavored flan. "Is there any chance that you might like to sell it?"

Even though I was prepared for the question, I still hesitated. I had been running the business since Pedro died, and I enjoyed doing it, but my enthusiasm was beginning to wane.

"I don't know," I said. "It was my husband's favorite enterprise. And I've found managing it an interesting challenge."

"I would offer you two hundred thousand dollars for the business, including the building," he said.

That was twice the book value. I immediately countered with $300,000, without even thinking the matter through.

"Would you take two hundred and fifty thousand dollars?" he asked.

I looked at him for a long moment. "Done," I said, and with that, I had sold the last of Pedro's businesses. After dinner, I felt an incredible weight lift from my shoulders. I directed Tom to draw up the papers before Mr. Levy changed his mind.

When I told Jonathon Levy that I would be going up to New York with my children for six weeks in the fall, he urged me to stay with his sister, Abigail Dreyfus. A liberal bluestocking who was popular in literary circles, Abigail was well known for the salons she hosted for New York's literati in her beautiful town house on Washington Square. The home he described was filled with books, antiques, and splendid art.

When he wrote to his sister about me, she readily agreed.

"You may find my sister unusual, Emily," he warned me. "She has quite . . . outlandish ideas about many things. I just hope she doesn't shock you."

I smiled. "I'm not easily shocked, Jonathon."

Of my miserable voyage on rough seas up to New York City in late August, I will speak little. We were traveling at the height of the stormy season, so the weather was unpredictable and the seas choppy. But the children, both good sailors, were in great spirits. They listed with each pitch of the ship and slept like babies, unlike their mother. I practically kissed the ground when we arrived in New York.

Abigail Dreyfus sent her brougham to meet us at the ship.

At her stately town house, we were welcomed by her servants with dinner and comfortable rooms. The children would stay with me for a couple of days, and then, with her brougham at our disposal, I would take them to their respective schools. I knew it would be many months before I would see them again after this trip, and during the next few days I had to restrain myself from hugging them tightly at many random moments.

I finally met Abigail the day after we arrived. She was a pretty auburn-haired woman in her mid-thirties, with a pert nose dusted lightly with freckles. She had wide blue eyes and perfect teeth set in a full sensuous mouth. Her hospitality was overwhelming and she seemed genuinely happy to receive us. Abigail's husband, Anton, an art dealer, was in Paris. I would not meet him for a few weeks.

I discovered that I loved New York. After Key West, which now numbered about seven hundred inhabitants, it was exciting just to walk the busy streets of a big city again, absorbing the sights and smells of strange foods. And I found hearing diverse music and accents very stimulating. New York was a port, like Key West, but there the similarity ended: It was a huge and infinitely more dynamic place. There were endless streets to explore, carriage traffic to watch for, tall buildings, and crowds of people—many of them speaking in foreign languages.

I cried when Timothy and Martha finally had to leave me.

"We'll write to you every month," Timothy promised.

"And we'll visit each other on our days off, and explore the city together while you're still here," Martha assured me.

But I could only hug them tighter, dreading the time I would return to my empty house in Key West.

When Abigail saw I was on my own, she invited me to join her many activities. "Now that you've settled the children, you must live your life to the fullest," she announced cheerily. "We can go to the theater, the new opera, and go shopping!"

Jonathon had been right about his sister: Abigail was an intellectual who loved to receive clever and famous people for dinner parties and salons. Yet she was very involved in social issues, and like a busy cricket, she hopped from one meeting to another.

"There is a group of us who support voting rights for women," she told me. "I've been attending meetings lately to see how I can help. Wouldn't it be wonderful if we could achieve that equality?"

I could barely imagine a world where I would actually have a right to vote and have any say in government. But it was an exciting idea, and I greeted it with enthusiasm.

Abigail abhorred the concept of slavery. "I'm working with some Quakers and Mennonites who are abolitionists," she said another time, lowering her voice. "I've been helping people involved with the Underground Railroad."

"Why, that's wonderful," I said, and urged her to tell me about the inner workings of the movement—for it was one that reached deeply into my soul. There had been talk of such clandestine groups who assisted slaves, and I wished that Andrew had known about them in New Orleans, for they might have offered him help. It was heartening to hear that there were good people like them risking their own safety to abolish the evils of slavery so others—like Andrew—could live freely.

Around Abigail, I began to feel like I was just waking up after a long sleep. I had been leading a very insular life on a tiny island detached from the world, while people like her were involved in solving social problems. Her ideas made me dizzy; it would take a long time for them to filter down to a backwater like Key West. But they were heady views indeed.

During Abigail's dinner parties and salons that autumn, I met a number of creative people—writers like Alexis de Tocqueville,

Walt Whitman, and Edgar Allan Poe; artists like John William Casilear and DeWitt Clinton Boutelle of the Hudson River School, whose works Abigail and Anton collected.

But it was the French poet Charles Baudelaire who was of particular interest to me. I'd heard much of Baudelaire and his dissolute lifestyle before actually meeting him. His writings, while brilliant, were mostly about decadence and eroticism. He had, it was said, a fondness for opium and hashish—and for spending inordinate amounts of money, having squandered a fairly large inheritance. He was now on a stringent allowance from his family, who recognized his dark side and tried to rein in his profligate ways.

Abigail told me that debts, loneliness, and a lack of prospects had weighed heavily on him the previous summer and he had attempted suicide by stabbing himself. Fortunately, his resolve had not been as strong as his need for attention, and the knife wound had been merely painful, not life-threatening.

But the incident had created an aura of sensual sadness and melancholy around him that was strangely charismatic. Dressed entirely in black, Baudelaire cut a bizarre figure. He was an attractive, delicate-looking young man of about twenty-five, with fine, thinning hair. On his arm was his beautiful mistress.

"Madame Salas," he said, kissing my hand when Abigail introduced us. "May I present the woman who brings love and inspiration to my life, Jeanne Duval."

She was a lovely young woman of about twenty, with a glowing complexion and curly raven hair. Her lips were full and sensuous; she wore a fitted gown of brilliant scarlet, which accentuated the charm of her smoldering dark eyes. I guessed that she might be from French Polynesia rather than the Caribbean. And her skin was as dark as Andrew's.

Baudelaire adored Mademoiselle Duval. Clearly, she had

given him a reason to go on living. He held her close all evening, proudly introducing her to everyone. At one of the salons, he read a poem about her tresses, *La Chevelure*, just one of
many verses she had inspired him to write. Here was a pale
young white man with a dark-skinned lover—he called her "my
Black Venus"—and nobody there seemed to care.

One evening, I begged Abigail to seat me next to Charles at
dinner so that I could learn more about him and his mistress.
I had to find out how they flouted their love so openly, without
fear of recrimination or arrest. For I still had not given up on
the possibility, however remote, that Andrew might one day be
free and come looking for me in Key West.

"Everyone wants to sit next to Charles." Abigail laughed. "But
you're a special guest, and your French is good. Yes, of course."

And with a shuffle of her place cards, I found myself sitting
next to France's most notorious Romantic poet. I was delighted
to be speaking French again, the language of my childhood,
and bursting with curiosity.

When Jeanne Duval was out of earshot, I took a direct approach: "Tell me, monsieur, is your mistress well received when
you take her to social gatherings in France?"

He thought about it for a moment. "In Paris, she is regarded
as something of an oddity, perhaps. But we French welcome
people who are a little . . . different."

"And she is never made to feel . . . inferior?"

He cocked his head and looked perplexed. Then he laughed.
"I would not tolerate such an attitude! If she is not welcome, I
am not, either. She is my muse."

"Are there black slaves in your country?"

"No. Slavery has been abolished."

After much hesitation, I decided to confide in Baudelaire
about Andrew and my poor little Ebony. He nodded sympathetically as I told him what had happened, and appeared shocked

only when I explained why, even if I were to find Andrew, we could not be together openly in the South.

"If he ever comes back into your life, take him to Paris!" he said grandly. "There, nobody will care. It isn't perfect, of course—after all, France wrote the brutal Code Noir for its colonies. But that is all in the past. The consequences you describe would never happen in Paris now, I assure you."

Before he left for his hotel, Baudelaire gave me the address of the apartment he shared with Jeanne Duval on Ile Saint-Louis, in the heart of Paris. "If you ever find this man you love so much, write to me," he said. "Perhaps I can help you."

Flushed with gratitude, I reached out and pressed his hand. "Thank you," I whispered.

THIRTY-ONE

New York and Key West

October 1846

The day before I was to leave New York, Abigail's husband, Anton, arrived home at midday on his way back from the customs office, where he'd been tracking a shipment of artwork.

"I hate to be the bearer of bad news, Emily," he said gravely. "There's been a terrible hurricane out of the Caribbean, and Key West has taken a direct hit. My understanding is that there were about fifty deaths in Key West alone, Cuba's death toll was in the hundreds."

I stood looking at him in shock. "When did this happen?"

"About a week ago. On October eleventh."

"Are the ships sailing?" I asked.

"Yes, they've just resumed after almost a week. There's been a great deal of devastation there, according to what I've been hearing, and a growing number of fatalities resulting from it."

It was to a very different Key West to which I returned.

The Great Havana Hurricane of October 11, 1846, would go down in Key West history as the most destructive storm to hit the settlement in the nineteenth century. I was stunned when I saw the damage ashore from the deck of our ship as we approached the port. Even though almost a month had passed, about a dozen large, damaged vessels were still stranded on the reefs near Key West. Wreckers were hard at work trying to unload cargo and salvage ships, while trying to fix their own homes, as well.

I looked around at the altered shoreline and the debris that had washed up. I could see Tom waiting for me at the recently rebuilt docks. As ill as I was from the trip, I was in a hurry to disembark and find out if my family was all right.

In contrast to the sight of the spirited, lively crowd that Martin and I had watched onshore that first day we arrived in Key West, the scene that awaited me was somber and grave. People trudging along the dock looked confused. What had been a vital, bustling port was now a jumble of fallen trees, disabled vessels, buildings without roofs, and inhabitants stricken with grief. Even the church was gone.

Tom's face was grim. He supervised the loading of my baggage into his landau and helped me up. "I have some bad news, Emily," he said when we were settled in the carriage. "Gran had a heart attack during the storm, and . . . we lost her. I'm sorry."

In spite of our past differences, I dearly loved Gran, and now I buried my head in Tom's shoulder, weeping. We were trying to make our way along a rutted, still-mucky road partly blocked by fallen trees, which befuddled his driver and the horses.

In the absence of the usual landmarks, I felt disoriented. "I don't see the lighthouse," I said as I looked over the vacant, wasted landscape toward Whitehead Point.

"No. It was washed away."

"Oh no. Not . . . Barbara Mabrity!"

"No. Miss Barbara herself survived. But her five children were drowned."

This was almost more than I could bear. Gran's death . . .

the image of Barbara's children . . . . it was beyond belief. Tom offered me his handkerchief, put his arms around me, and let me cry. I felt a deep sense of shame. While this calamity had struck my home, and my family had all been suffering, I'd been enjoying New York, with not a thought of Key West. "And what of Wreckers' Cay?" I asked.

"It's gone, too. The lighthouse keepers both lost their lives. The island just washed away, along with all the buildings on it. I'm sorry, Emily. I know your heart was out there."

I nodded. After a moment I said, "My heart is still out there."

Pedro's opulent house had been unroofed and virtually destroyed from flooding. I mourned the loss of my belongings and my memories there, for many of them had been good. To my amazement, Juanita had met a widower from Havana over the summer and had returned to Cuba to be married. Our driver had lost his life in the storm while trying—in vain, as it turned out—to save our horses and tropical birds. A couple of the other members of the staff had taken jobs with families desperate for help. Another servant had drowned, and our cook had died of asthma because of the stress. I heard each of these accounts with profound sadness.

But despite these horrors, and my sorrow at losing Gran, I was home at last. I moved into Gran's beautiful Greek Revival mansion on Caroline, which had fared well in spite of some water damage. The elegant structure had remained intact, a tribute to the craftsmanship of Key West's shipwrights. Her slaves, who were living in the servants' cottage, were bewildered. Clearly, Gran's estate needed to be sorted out as soon as possible.

In her will, Gran had left me her house, and Dorothy her investments. But with Gran's house came her slaves: Dinah, Bess, Hagar, and her gardener, Cato, who was also her driver.

"But I don't want slaves," I protested crossly.

"Well, you could give them to me," said Dorothy. "But of course, then they'd still be slaves."

I sighed impatiently. "I'll talk to them," I said.

This, as it turned out, produced mixed results, largely determined by their ages. Cato, who was the eldest at sixty-eight, said he wanted to stay on as a slave. Dinah, who had worked as a lady's maid for my grandmother, was in her late thirties and gratefully accepted my offer of manumission and a cash gift to see her back to Charleston, where she had been taken from her family years ago. Bess was forty-five. She said she'd be quite pleased to continue to work for me for a salary, her keep, and manumission papers, but she said she might move on to New Orleans later on. She had a sister there who was free, and a daughter who was still a slave.

That left Hagar, who was still only in her twenties. Gran had bought her in Key West from a widower who was returning to Kentucky and wanted to travel unencumbered. Hagar wanted manumission and a cash gift. She would find other living quarters in Key West, and we agreed that she would continue to clean the house for a salary.

With that settled, my days back home became a flurry of activity. I began to help with hurricane relief for the villagers who had lost everything—ladling soup, sorting through piles of donated clothing, and working as a volunteer at the hospital. It would be a long time before Key West recovered.

THIRTY-TWO

Key West

December 1846

A couple of weeks before Christmas, Dorothy and Tom decided to take a trip to Havana on a private boat with some friends for a few days.

"Tom is using the trip to meet with some shipowner clients over there hit by the hurricane. And I just have to get away from Key West after all we've been through," said Dorothy. Then her eyes kindled with glee: "It will give me a chance to freshen up my wardrobe, and to buy Christmas gifts. If you want anything over there, sugar, just make me a list."

During their parents' trips, the Farrell children now preferred to stay with me rather than remaining in their own home with Dorothy's nanny. With my own children away, I missed the lively presence of young people in my nest and welcomed their company. Maureen was now thirteen years old, Alexander twelve, and Mary Elizabeth nine.

On the second day, the weather turned chilly and breezy. Noting that Maureen had brought no warm clothing, I volunteered to go to Dorothy's and pack a few things. With a brisk northerly wind, Alexander wanted his kite, and I offered to fetch that, too.

I was admitted by the housemaid, who told me to take whatever I needed, then left for the slave quarters. The Farrell house was deadly quiet. I set about completing my errand, startled at every rattle of the windowpanes and time's creaky settling of floors and walls: the eerie sounds of emptiness in someone else's home.

I hurriedly completed my chore and headed for the front door. As I did, I passed Dorothy's desk in the hallway. The paddle wheeler *Isabelle* had just docked the day before with its twice-monthly delivery of the townsfolk's mail via Charleston. As she usually did, the Farrells' housekeeper, Delilah, had gone down to the boat to collect it, placing the mail in a neat stack on the top of the desk. But with it being close to Christmas, there had been a lot of it, and the pile of letters and cards had collapsed. A few of them had tumbled to the floor, and I reached down to pick them up.

Putting the children's things on a chair, I divided the mail into two piles to fix the problem, but by cutting the stack like a deck of cards, one letter buried in the pile surfaced to the top. It was postmarked New Orleans and was addressed to Dorothy. There was no return address, but there was something very familiar about the handwriting.

I stared at it for a full minute, examining the envelope. Suddenly, I felt something brush against my ankles, and I had to cover my mouth to muffle a scream. It was Myrtle, the family's loudly purring cat, who had chosen that moment to display her affection. "Did you scatter the mail, you naughty cat?" I asked her, pushing her aside with my foot. "Shoo!"

Although her visitation had been unnerving, it had not deterred me. I reexamined the envelope, cheeks flushed and short of breath. I recognized that handwriting. . . . It was Andrew's!

Was he living in New Orleans? I was about to rip it open

immediately, justifying my indiscretion by telling myself that Dorothy would most certainly have shared whatever the letter contained if she had been home. Wouldn't she? It had to be about locating me. Had Andrew run away? Earned his freedom? I had to know.

I could barely contain my excitement. My heart was racing as I tried to flip down the front panel of the desk to find Dorothy's letter opener, and discovered it was locked.

Only my single-minded obsession with Andrew could have overridden the qualms I might have felt about invading my sister's privacy. And a nagging question began to form in my head: Had he ever written to her before?

Remembering that Tom kept a set of keys on a hook near his desk, I ran into his study. When I found the correct key, the front panel flipped down, and my search ended. There was the opener, and next to it a large envelope propped against the pigeonholes. It had a single name written on it: Andrew.

My hands shaking, I threw both the new letter and the big envelope into my reticule, quickly relocked the desk, and then replaced the keys. Picking up the children's things, I headed for the front door, arriving just in time for the children's nanny to pad into the hall from the front parlor.

"Did y'all find what you was lookin' for, Miz Emily?"

"Yes, Lizzie," I replied. "Yes, I have everything."

Stepping over Myrtle, who tried to trip me on my way out, I quickly left for home. I could not remember ever having been so excited.

Feigning a headache, I took to my room after instructing Bess to give the children their supper. Only then did I open my reticule and spill the contents of the envelope onto the bed.

And thus did I begin to read an epistolary chronicle of the past five or so years. Dorothy, in her organized fashion, had tied the letters together in order of date, so it was easy for me to follow their sequence. Some were from Andrew, a few from Mother Saint Angela at the convent, from Eurydice's daughter Marie-Francine, and from someone I did not know named Gladys Rathbone. To my further shock, a couple of recent ones were addressed not to Dorothy but to me!

They were all from New Orleans, except the first one, an undated note from Andrew.

Dear Miss Dorothy,

I got the letter you sent me through Martha. Please don't worry. I will remember what we talked about when you were here and what you wrote in your recent letter.

We are all hoping for a quiet hurricane season. I'm glad we both agree about the wisdom of me taking Ebony with me if Wreckers' is hit with a bad storm.

I'll be ready if and when the time comes. I understand your feelings perfectly. The children and I will make sure it all works out.

Thank you for the names you gave me in New Orleans. They may come in handy.

Sincerely, your friend, Andrew

There had been no date on that one, but it had to have been included with a letter from Martha to Dorothy while we were still at Wreckers' Cay.

The next one was also from Andrew. It was longer, and described the terrible voyage to New Orleans with Ebony.

Dear Miss Dorothy,

I'm sorry I could not write to you before this.

Leaving Emily, Martha, and Timothy was the hardest thing I've ever done. I loved them all so much. I hope that one day Emily can find it in her heart to forgive me. The trip from Wreckers' was a nightmare, especially with worrying about Ebony. The seas were rough, though I stayed as close to shore as possible.

The biggest problem I had was feeding her and giving her water. She got sick a couple of times, and I thought I'd lost her. We stopped in an Indian village, where they welcomed us for a couple of weeks. The Indians were very kind. One of the women had just lost a baby, and she was happy to feed Ebony. They had a gifted medicine man there, and he gave her something made from tree bark, which lowered her fever. Later, we moved on to another village, where there were many runaway slaves. A woman there was able to feed her, and even wanted to keep her.

As you suggested, when we got to New Orleans, I went to see your former nanny, Eurydice. Her daughter Marie-Francine knew a woman who could care for the baby. Then, I went to the convent to see that nun you told me about. She was kind and helpful, and they gave me a job. A couple of months later, Ebony was old enough for them to keep in their orphanage, so now I can get to see her often.

Your friend, Andrew

My eyes widened in amazement as I reread the last paragraph. Ebony *had* survived the trip? Was she still alive?

I could not scan the letters fast enough. The nun in question was Mother Saint Angela, who had taught Dorothy and me at the Ursuline convent. She had written:

Dearest Dorothy,

I received your letter asking me to help Andrew Tyler, your sister's former slave, and his child. This I have willingly done in Christ's name. Your check was not necessary, but it can go toward the keep of his daughter. We have employed Andrew as our handyman, and he works diligently and contributes to her keep. While he is not a Catholic, he is able to assist Père Beaubien, our chaplain, at the altar. He knows Latin prayers and verses of the Mass. Mother Saint Cecilia adores his voice, especially when he sings "Ave Maria" and "Panis Angelicus."

Yours in Christ, Mother Saint Angela

Ebony was alive! There were sporadic letters with positive progress reports from both Andrew and Mother Saint Angela for a couple of years. But then things took a turn. The slave patrol had been cracking down and Andrew had been arrested for lack of manumission papers. The nun wrote an urgent plea, asking Dorothy to find Ebony's and Andrew's documents and send them. Otherwise, Andrew would be sold to pay for his keep in jail. Ebony, though a small child, was also officially a slave. Since such papers did not exist, Dorothy had done nothing about this. There were further letters from Mother Saint Angela. And then nothing. Finally, there was one from Andrew.

Miss Dorothy,

I got the letter you sent to Marie-Francine and Eurydice for me. Yes, I am now back in servitude. Thank you for getting your family's friends to buy me. At least I've been able to remain in New Orleans, where Ebony is. They have been kind enough so far. I work as their gardener and serve at table. But I am still a slave, and will probably be one the rest of my life. It is terrible being separated from Ebony. I desperately miss being back at Wreckers' with Emily and the children. I think of her all the time.

Your friend, Andrew

So Andrew's owners lived in New Orleans? The next one from Andrew was addressed to me, in care of Dorothy, and had been opened. It was dated around the time I had married Pedro. Evidently, Dorothy had told him I had met a wonderful man and was madly in love. In his letter, he wished me nothing but happiness. He assured me he had told Ebony all about me and what a wonderful mother I had been to her. And he was happy to hear that I now understood his motives for leaving Wreckers' with our baby.

Dorothy's secret envelope was a virtual Pandora's box for me, and as I sat there reading, I had felt myself tense up—in apprehension, love, joy, and, finally, rage.

I dropped his letter to me into my lap. Oh, Dorothy, I thought, seething. How could you? *How could you?*

There followed a couple of letters from Mother Saint Angela.

Money had not been important to her in the beginning, but she hinted that the mother superior now felt inclined to be rid of Ebony. She was not old enough to do much work, and there was the matter of her keep. Andrew had been helping before, but he was no longer earning money. Dorothy did not appear to have answered these.

The next letter was to Dorothy from a Gladys Rathbone. Apparently, she was a girlhood friend, though I did not remember her. She seemed to have been one of her regular correspondents in New Orleans. The first part of her letter was of little interest. Then:

About the child you spoke of to me in your letter, I did go to the convent and asked them if they wanted to rid themselves of her. I gave them a donation of twenty dollars, and took her home. You hadn't told me her age; she's not even quite six, and a bit useless. It's not even legal to buy children so young. But she might be of some help to Antoinette in the kitchen. We've named her Penelope.

Yours, Gladys

A regretful letter from Mother Saint Angela followed. As Dorothy had not answered, the nun assumed my sister had lost interest. Yes, Gladys Rathbone—they knew her as Gladys Matthews—said she would take her. The nun hoped she would be well treated there. The family lived in a lovely home in the Garden District. Mr. Rathbone was a bank president.

By this time, I was frantically making notes.

There were two more letters to Dorothy from Andrew, including the one that arrived the day before.

In a letter dated a month ago, he told her he had seen Ebony carrying very heavy baskets at the market, and he reported that she had bruises on her face. It was a desperate plea, begging Dorothy to try to buy Ebony from the Rathbones. This one was still sealed. Clearly, Dorothy had indeed lost interest. She had not even bothered to open it!

The most recent, which Dorothy wasn't aware had arrived, was more urgent, and as I read it, I realized I was bathed in my tears. Andrew had managed to speak to Ebony at the market and she'd told him Mrs. Rathbone had been beating her. Another one to me from Andrew begged me to help. In it, he admitted that he had made many mistakes. He had tried to keep our little girl free and safe, but he had failed. This letter was also unopened.

I stood, flung open my closet doors, pulled out my suitcase, and began to pack.

When Dorothy arrived the next morning, she threw her arms around me and began to tell me about their trip. "Havana was hit much worse than we were by the storm! It was hard to find anything in the stores. But I did manage to get you something nice," she bubbled. She handed me a beaded evening bag.

"I have something for you, too," I said. I handed her the envelope.

Dorothy paled. "You . . . you invaded my home? Went into my locked desk?"

"You were hiding this from me all these years. So many lies! Dorothy! How . . . ." I was so frustrated, I was losing my breath.

Dorothy sat down, visibly shaken. "Well, I thought I had to. You were so blinded, sugar. . . . I was just trying to help. Andrew understood. I wanted what was best for you."

I stood over her, resisting the urge to grab a handful of her curls and shake her. "How could you presume to know what was best for me? Listen to yourself. You're still lying. You were doing what you thought was best for *you!*"

She was in tears. "What would Gran have thought if you'd had your way and brought them here?"

"Don't bring Gran into this. You were just thinking of

yourself." I picked up the envelope and shook it in her face. "Thanks to your meddling, Andrew and Ebony are slaves."

Tom moved over to Dorothy and stood behind her, placing his hands on her shoulders.

I exploded with anger. "I read *all* the letters, Dorothy! You told me my baby was *dead*. And to think—I believed you. All those years wasted! Poor little Ebony, abused—and you didn't lift a finger to help her."

"I didn't know Gladys would be so hard on her. . . . She was always a nice enough person."

"To you, maybe. But obviously not to her help. Did you ever try to find out? Did you even drop by when you were in New Orleans?"

"No," she said softly. "I didn't." Her hands were resting in her lap, and she began twisting and curling her fingers around a handkerchief.

I'd been pacing the room and brought myself up to face her. "You even stopped opening your own mail!"

"Well, I . . . Sugar, I had done all I could."

"But it didn't stop you from opening *my* letters from Andrew!"

Dorothy blushed and hung her head. Tom tried to get involved at this point, and I turned on him, my hands on my hips. "As for you . . . , my 'attorney'! What happened to all that honesty you pledged to me? I should have known better than to believe you. You'd lied to me before."

Tom turned his head and stared out the window to where their children were playing outside.

Finally, our shouting subsided and an exhausted calm descended on us. I sank into a chair. Dorothy sniffled, but I said nothing. A plan was taking shape in my mind.

Dorothy rose and took my hand. "I can't bear to have you angry at me, Emily. Is there anything I can do to make up for what I've done? Anything at all?"

I was quiet for a few moments. "Yes," I replied calmly. "Yes, there is."

By the time I boarded the *Santa Trinidad* a couple of days later, I had lists of names and addresses, my checkbook, access to my New Orleans bank account, which contained my share of Grandpère's legacy, and two precious forged documents.

When the ship arrived at the port of New Orleans, I took a carriage directly to the home of Eurydice, who offered me lodging. I poured out my heart to her and Marie-Francine, telling them the whole story. Eurydice's eyes widened at my revelations. Knowing Dorothy so well, she understood, and could only shake her head. *"Elle a toujours été fouinarde, ta soeur!"* she said. ("Your sister was always meddlesome.") They pledged to do everything they could to help. I subsequently hired a carriage driven by a free black friend of Marie-Francine's.

The French Quarter address Dorothy gave me for Andrew looked familiar, and as the carriage approached it, I realized why. It was the home of my grandparents' friends Madeleine and Jean-Philippe de Saumur, where I had met Martin all those years ago. At the front gate, I was flooded with memories of the scent of jasmine that had wafted from their terrace that night.

The de Saumurs, now in their sixties, were delighted to see me. They welcomed me warmly and ordered a servant to bring some champagne to the smaller parlor. After a couple of glasses, I produced the fake document of ownership that Tom had drawn up and validated with his official embossed stamp.

"It pains me to tell you this," I said politely, "but you have one of my slaves working here for you."

They greeted this with disbelief. Monsieur de Saumur put on his glasses and read through the document. "Andrew Tyler?" He showed it to his wife and together they nodded and discussed it in French.

"It must be our Napoléon you are referring to, Emily. You say he ran away from you?"

"Yes, it has taken me some time to find him."

Monsieur de Saumur was furious. "A runaway! This is a serious crime he has committed. You realize we paid sixteen hundred dollars for him at auction? He was in irons. The city was selling him. They said he didn't belong to anyone. Your sister told us about him."

"Yes, I knew you'd bought him." I took out my checkbook. "My sister misunderstood about me wanting him back. But I am prepared to offer you full compensation." This changed things considerably and his bonhomie returned. As I handed him the check, he ordered "Napoléon" to appear in the parlor.

A few minutes later, Andrew entered the room.

It was much like the first time he came to me in the darkness of my bedroom at Wreckers'. I'd been waiting for him to come up from his shower for what seemed like an eternity. I even fretted that he might not come. And finally, there he was, removing his clothing as the light from the tower stretched over him, playing on the glossy curves of his muscles.

Now, as he came into the parlor, I had to take a long, slow breath as our eyes locked. I had never seen him look so handsome and distinguished. He was dressed in formal livery for serving at dinner, complete with a white dress shirt, white silk gloves, and a cravat. He was still as slim as I remembered; his hair had begun to be salted with gray, which made him look mature and dashing. My heart fairly leaped from my chest; even after all these years, my feelings had not changed, and I wanted nothing more than to run into his arms.

He gasped when he saw me.

I fought to look back at him coolly, without emotion: "Yes, that's him."

Monsieur de Saumur jumped to his feet. "So, you are surprised to see her, eh?" he shouted at him. *"Maudit salaud!"* Bringing his hand back, he hit Andrew hard across the face, and I felt as though he had punched me in the stomach. I waved frantically for him to stop, but he misunderstood. To me, he said, "We'll be happy to have him whipped for you. Or I could have his ears cut off." He lowered his voice: "La Code Noir . . . We're not really supposed to do it anymore, but . . ."

"No!" I shouted. He looked startled.

I recovered my normal voice. "No. I will deal with him when I get back to Key West. Just put him in chains and give me the key. My driver will help me."

The de Saumurs ordered "Napoléon" to remove their fine livery for his successor. Five minutes later, he emerged, chained and wearing Martin's ragged clothing; he was once again the beloved Andrew I remembered from Wreckers' Cay.

In the carriage, I closed the curtain between us and the driver. "Let's get these off!" I whispered, quickly unlocking Andrew's chains.

As his shackles tumbled away, he held out his arms. "Hello, Emily," he said at last in his velvety baritone. "Thanks for coming by."

"Hello, Andrew," I said with a wide grin as I fell into them.

I couldn't believe I had pulled it off! I was barely able to touch him without shaking. The toll of Andrew's recent hardships were marked indelibly on his face. But he was still a very handsome picture. He kissed me gently as he ran his fingers through my hair. "God, Emily, is it really you?"

So many years away from each other, I thought. Yet, it was as though we'd never been apart. I clung to him tenaciously, fearing he might disappear through my fingers like sand. Briefly, he held me away from him.

"Let me look at you. You're more beautiful than ever, darlin'."

"Do you still care about me?"

"What a question, Emily! What a question." He kissed me then, a long, ardent kiss, like the ones locked in my memory that had sustained me all those years. I could barely speak.

It was time to find Ebony. I left Andrew with Marie-Francine and Eurydice, and had the same carriage taxi me to the Garden District address Dorothy had given me. I presented my card to the servant who opened the door: "Please tell Mrs. Rathbone I am Dorothy Farrell's sister from Key West."

Moments later, I was ushered into a vast parlor, where I was soon joined by a small, slight woman in her early thirties with thin, limp brown hair, a weak chin, and rodentlike eyes set too close together. I vaguely remembered her from school; she was just Dorothy's age.

"How very lovely to see you, Miss Emily," she said, greeting me enthusiastically. "Dorothy mentions you often in her letters. May I offer you some tea? Or coffee?"

"No, thank you, Miss Gladys. I can't stay. I just wanted to drop by and pay my respects. Dorothy sends her regards."

We continued in this friendly vein for a few minutes before I said, "I'm also here to discuss a business proposition with you." She raised her eyebrows. Without more preamble, I drew out my fake document of ownership authored by Tom and asked her permission to remove my slave, Ebony.

She examined it for a few minutes before handing it back to me. "No, I'm afraid not. This document might mean something in Florida, but I doubt it would stand up here. You're talking about the girl I call Penelope. I bought her from the nuns for several hundred dollars."

I sighed. Were there no honest people left? Her letter had said twenty dollars. I wanted to remind her that buying a child under the age of eleven without a parent was against the law in Louisiana. But I was not about to argue.

I took out my checkbook and offered her one thousand dollars for "Penelope," a price that would normally have bought a full-grown healthy woman at any auction in the South. The usual price for children Ebony's age sold with a parent was about $450, or less.

She peered at me for a long moment; I began to feel sweat trickling down my back. Finally, she shook her head. "No, Miss Emily, I'm sorry. I couldn't possibly! She's a terrible servant now, but I feel that with the right discipline, she could become a halfway decent worker. After all, we've been putting up with her now for several months. If I thrash her enough, she'll eventually learn to stop dropping my pretty china."

I was so angry, I wanted to strike her. But I had already devised a backup plan, so instead, I put away my checkbook, smiled sweetly, and rose to leave. "Good day, Mrs. Rathbone." I resisted the urge to slam the door on my way out.

By the time I settled back into the carriage, the alternative idea had taken shape in my ungovernable mind. Money does talk. I was convinced of it. I had just not directed its honeyed tongue in the right direction. I gave the driver yet another address from Dorothy's list.

As we arrived at the First Delta Savings Bank, I stepped down from the carriage and told my driver to wait. With directions from a bank employee standing outside, I walked purposefully up the marble stairs, petticoats swishing, heels echoing my determination, and barged into Mr. Rathbone's office. He was in the middle of conferring with a subordinate and looked up quizzically. I stood there for a moment, saying nothing. Then I found my voice. "Mr. Rathbone, may I have a word?"

He was a rather homely man of about forty, with pale, spotty skin and thick spectacles. "Leave us," he said to the younger gentleman, who quickly rose and left. Rathbone stood, smiling as he reached his hand out in greeting, and I noted how large his teeth were, climbing over one another, far too big for his mouth.

"I don't usually see people without an appointment. Is this something important?"

"Mr. Rathbone . . . I'm Emily Salas, Dorothy Farrell's sister. Our grandfather was Jean-Jacques Lacordaire."

"Ah, yes, of course. Mr. Lacordaire. Well known in the community. Sorry to hear of his passing." He had suddenly became cordial. "May I offer you some tea? Lemonade?"

"No, thank you. I'm here to discuss a proposition with you, Mr. Rath—"

"Herbert," he said, interrupting me. He indicated the seat across from him. Then sitting down, he laced his hands together.

"I won't take up much of your time." Carefully, I weighed what I had rehearsed in the carriage: "My grandfather has left me a considerable legacy. And I've come to see if you would welcome my account . . . here. At your bank."

His eyes lit up. My question unleashed a flurry of obsequious and extravagant compliments. "Why, that would be wonderful, Miss Emily! I'd be most honored to have you transfer your accounts to us. Believe me, we would provide you with excellent personal service. Are you sure I can't get you anything?" He was smiling so widely now, his lips had peeled back beyond the equine teeth, showing a broad expanse of gum.

I shook my head. "No, thank you." I paused. "There is a condition, however."

"A condition?"

"Yes." Now I reverted to being a sweet and demure southern lady. "I would ask a huge favor of you, sir." I smiled.

"Yes, yes. Anything . . ." he replied, leaning toward me.

"The child . . . the young slave you and your wife bought from the nuns . . . Penelope? She is actually my property, as I own her father."

I showed him my document.

He examined it closely. "Penelope?" He seemed to be trying to remember which of his servants she was. Then a look of recognition settled on his face. "Oh, Penelope. Of course. The child who breaks things!" He seemed relieved and laughed. "You want *her*? We had no idea she belonged to anyone."

"Yes. I would like to have her back."

He looked incredulous, but didn't argue. "Why, then, if she's yours, of course, She must be returned to you. In any case, I'm sure my wife will be more than happy to be rid of her."

I simply smiled. "Why, then, that makes it of benefit to all of us! Could you please send for her?"

"Today?"

I nodded. "Yes. Now. Then I will make the arrangements to change over my account. I want to take her back to Key West with me tomorrow morning."

It was as easy as that. Within the half hour it took to draw up, sign, and witness the papers to change banks, my daughter was dropped off at the front door with a paper bag containing her things by the slave who'd admitted me to their home. As she had been instructed, the woman helped her into my waiting taxi. To my surprise, she leaned down and kissed Ebony on the forehead, whispered something to her, and then disappeared into the busy street.

When I left the office, I felt as if my heels never touched the marble of the bank's lobby. Ebony looked bewildered as I climbed in next to her in the carriage. She was a beautiful little child, as I knew she would be, with skin the color of *café con leche* and bright blue eyes, enhanced by long, sooty lashes.

"Oh, Ebony, how grown up you are!" I held her little hands in mine, taking her in as I fought to keep from crying. "You've become a proper young lady."

Ebony giggled shyly. She was dressed in a threadbare frock and her tiny toes peaked out from holes in her worn shoes, but she was neat and clean, and her hair had been nicely braided— probably by the slave who treated her kindly. But I was dismayed to see some welts on her legs from a switch.

"Ebony, honey, I'm taking you to be with your daddy. Would you like that?"

Although she did not appear to be surprised, her eyes brightened, and she nodded. I kissed her soft cheek and she cuddled up to me. I wanted so much to blurt out "I'm your mama." But it was too soon. Besides, I wanted Andrew to be there, so we could tell her together. I put my arm around her and experienced that splendid maternal rush I'd always felt when I held my children. In that, at least, nothing had changed. We drove the rest of the way in silent contentment.

Back at the small, neat home of Eurydice and Marie-Francine, we celebrated our joyful reunion. Andrew had been correct at Wreckers' when he hinted that they were family. Eurydice told me Grandpère had been her paramour for many years. Marie-Francine, now eighteen, was indeed his daughter: my half aunt.

It was touching to see Andrew and Ebony together. He hugged her and swung her around, making her laugh. He playfully planted a kiss on each of her cheeks and they rubbed noses—as little Hannah had taught him to do at Wreckers' Cay. And then he officially introduced us. Squatting down, he held her hands. "Ebony, darlin', remember your beautiful white mama I always told you about . . . and how she still loved you?"

She smiled up at me and nodded.

"I never forgot about you," I assured her as I applied some balm Francine gave me for the welts. "And tomorrow, you and your daddy are coming with me on a big boat to my house in Key West."

Ebony immediately loved Eurydice, who made us a wonderful jambalaya and corn bread for supper. And she delighted in Marie-Francine, who played chasing games with her in the garden. Poor Ebony had not had much time to learn about play.

We spent the evening getting to know one another. When it came time for bed, Eurydice, with a discreet smile, insisted Andrew and I take their big bedroom.

"*Il est beau, ton mari. Et ta petite aussi!*" she whispered to me. ("Your husband is good-looking. And so is your daughter!")

Yes, he is my husband, I reflected. Back by my side.

I brought the lamp into the bedchamber and placed it on the nightstand. Then our eyes met in its flickering glow and I hurriedly made to rip off my clothes. But he stopped me with a gentle motion of his hands. "Whoa, whoa. Not so fast. What's your hurry, darlin'? We have lots of time."

Slowly, he began to ease off my clothing, kissing me with utmost gentleness, one part of my body at a time. He nuzzled my neck while he removed my frock, pressed his cheeks to my breasts as he unlaced and took off my bustier. Then he removed my pantalets, caressing my navel, and skillfully worked his way down. Gently picking me up, he placed me down on the bed, leaving me to tingle with anticipation as he removed his own clothes.

He was lying next to me in just a few moments. As he'd showered while I was out, the fragrance of soap lingered on his smooth, silky skin, further exciting me. He moved down and parted my legs, kissing and caressing until, quite suddenly, he was inside me. I caught my breath, and arched my back to drive him deeper. By this time, I was whimpering—no, begging. I had waited five years for this moment.

Afterward, our passion spent—at least temporarily—we lay in each other's arms, breathing and touching each other tenderly as we whispered endearments. And I reflected how the French writer Stendhal described the transformation of a lover's ordinary characteristics into sparkling perfection—a mental metamorphosis he called "crystallization." There had certainly been plenty of sex with Pedro. But I could only marvel at how dissimilar it was. Because I loved Andrew, I viewed him through the perfect beauty of a glittering crystal. It was quite extraordinary, really, loving someone like that. It made all the difference in the world.

The next morning, I handed him a peace offering Dorothy had sent him. When he opened the little package, he burst out laughing: It was a clay pipe and a snuff box containing weed from her garden.

I finally felt whole again; I had my family back. I could embrace life as before. Andrew and I talked and planned all the way back to Key West, and we did not stop after we arrived. We knew we could not live openly as husband and wife. But we could live together. I would just have to tell everyone that he was a slave I had bought on my recent trip to New Orleans.

"I would like to tell the whole world that you're my husband—and that she's my daughter."

He shook his head. "You know it's not possible."

Yes, I knew. I would have to be happy with what we had. At least we were as one again. Back in Key West, we walked together out the French doors to the garden, standing in the shadows, watching our daughter play. She looked so happy, and pretty in the new clothing I'd bought her in New Orleans. I leaned back into Andrew and I felt his arms pull me gently. We stood there in silence, and for a few moments, I let myself believe we were standing again at our bedroom window, watching the light caress the island at Wreckers' Cay.

THIRTY-THREE

Key West

1883

The years have sped by and I have grown old.

About a month after Andrew arrived, we lost Cato when he suffered a stroke picking up my mail at the dock. Soon after, I again offered Bess the money to move to New Orleans, and this time she accepted.

Without servants to disturb our privacy and with only Hagar as day help, Andrew became my husband once again. Ostensibly, he was employed as my handyman. Nobody in Key West knew that he slept in my room instead of in the servants' cottage. Ebony's expression when she viewed us together was inscrutable. So as not to confuse her, we were careful not to indulge in any displays of affection when she was around.

Ebony got to know Martha and Timothy when they were home for vacations. Though my children were delighted—and amazed—to see her again, they understood that they had to maintain discretion.

The following spring, I wrote to Charles Baudelaire to ask

if he would help me rent an apartment in Paris and a country villa where we could all spend time together, away from prying eyes in Key West.

Baudelaire wrote back immediately. He and Jeanne Duval found us lodgings on the Left Bank in Paris. And to my delight, an artist friend of theirs owned a rambling country villa near Nice and was willing to offer it to us for part of the summer. Our entire family spent a glorious few months in France, living in quiet anonymity. It brought us so much pleasure being together this way that we braved the annual ocean voyage to return to France most summers. For me, it was worth the seasickness I suffered each time.

Timothy was enthralled with French architecture; Martha loved to paint in the olive groves at the villa. Over time, they, and Ebony, became quite fluent in French. Ebony adored Martha, who gave her paints and paper and often took her on short treks in fields and gardens to draw and paint. But while Martha painted nature, Ebony was more inspired by what fashionable French ladies wore, and she liked to sketch their hats and pretty gowns.

If Ebony found any of our life strange, she did not show it. My guess was that being returned to Mrs. Rathbone was her ultimate fear, and if discretion was the price she had to pay, she willingly kept silent. I educated her at home, as I had my other children when we were on Wreckers' Cay. She was a very clever child and learned fast. And, like her father, she loved music and had a beautiful voice.

My other children finished their schooling in New York. Martha married a southerner and lived for a time in Charleston, until her husband joined the Confederate army and was killed at Antietam. She then moved back to Key West with her five children. And Timothy? He became an architect and lives in New

York. He has never married. Recently, he confided to me that he has a gentleman companion. It is not a relationship that I easily understand, but I have told him that he and his friend will always be welcome in my home.

Ebony was happy to stay in Key West. Her interest in fashion when she was a child in France inspired her to open a millinery shop. I was in awe of her talent, as she created beautiful confections of soft voile, plumes, and brightly colored flowers and birds, and her hats delighted the ladies in the village. When she was twenty, Ebony, who had been singing in the choir of the new black Baptist church in Key West, caught the eye of the Reverend Everett Sawyer, its handsome young minister. And she fell deeply in love with him. Andrew and I gave her a beautiful wedding, and I financed the building of a home for them on one of my properties. She, in turn, rewarded us with two lively grandsons.

I harbored anger against Dorothy and Tom for a short while, but Andrew would not allow me to let it fester. He insisted I forgive Dorothy, as he had. And Tom remained my attorney. Dorothy did everything she could to befriend Ebony, and my daughter—who knew nothing of the early treachery—came to love her. Eventually, we all became civil again. She was my only sister, after all. But I have to say, I never could trust her as I had before.

Sadly, Dorothy did not live past her fortieth birthday. Like so many other Key Westers, she died of yellow fever. In spite of our differences, her death was a terrible blow to me, and I miss her still.

With Tom's assistance, I had drawn up documents of manumission to free both Andrew and Ebony soon after they'd arrived in Key West. Thus, when my beloved Andrew left this world, succumbing to a lingering lung disease, he did so as a proud freedman. When he passed away, it was as if a part of me had also died; I was thankful for every day we'd been back together—and rued each day we'd been apart. But we agreed when we found each other again that bitterness was an indulgence. In a world where disease could suddenly end your life, you learned to enjoy every crumb of the cake as if it were your last.

Those precious years had gone, never to be recovered. Yet, in a strange way, our separation had made our reunion and our remaining days together all the sweeter. And, of course, I still had my darling Ebony. She and I grew very close; Key Westers thought she was my companion. And she was, in a way. A wonderful companion. And a great consolation to me after Andrew passed.

My thoughts ramble now. Happy memories of my younger days threaten to be replaced by the sight of coffins sliding into crypts under gray morning skies. And the names of my departed friends and family can be recited like beads on a rosary. I have become a tiresome old lady, talking about the past. I repeat myself to the point where my listeners no longer hear me, and they hide behind masked yawns. I am Gran reincarnated, and it amuses me when I catch myself tartly complaining of boisterous children and disruptive dogs, or wondering aloud what the world is coming to.

Increasingly, my thoughts shift to Pedro—poor, excessive Pedro, and his bizarre appetites. I look with revulsion at my thinned, shifting skin, my winglike arms, the deep creases of my face, my gnarled hands, and my once-beautiful legs, now so cruelly marred. And I marvel at how anyone could ever have lusted after this body as he did.

With difficulty, I climb the stairs to my widow's walk to view the Key West harbor, listening to towering masts on proud tall ships chime gently in the breath of trade winds. Before she passed on, Barbara Mabrity, my dear old friend, often joined me there, for she missed the view of Key West from the lighthouse.

When she turned eighty-two, the department discharged Miss Barbara—not for incompetence, for she was still conscientious and nimble on the stairs, but for her pro-Confederate remarks. Florida, a state since 1845, was the third state to secede from the Union and remained a slave state. But early in the Civil War hostilities, a Union army detachment under the command of Captain James Brannan seized Key West in order to intercept supplies heading from the Gulf states to the southeast coast. And because he forbade the Confederate flag from flying in the settlement, Barbara Mabrity openly rebuked him.

For years before she died, we would explore the ever-changing streets of Key West. By that time, I had ceased to be of interest to anyone, and the gossips no longer murmured about me as I passed. Instead, people greeted us deferentially: "Howd'ye do, Miss Barbara, Miss Emily." We were just two sweet old ladies taking our constitutional, aging matrons of another era. We would talk about the houses we saw along the way, the people who had once lived in them, and the socials we'd once attended. And because we were old and forgetful and forgiving of repetition, we went over such details with a frequency that would have driven anyone else quite mad.

Clusters of cigar makers' cottages now dot every district. The factory owners, like Jonathon Levy, have plotted out entire neighborhoods, establishing little fiefdoms, which include a factory at the center, with tiny shacks for the workers, and sundry stores close by. These cigar moguls have bought much of my land, earning me yet another fortune. But remembering Juan Salas's advice, I have still kept the choice properties on the island for my own family.

As I bring this memoir to a close, there are now around two

hundred cigar-making factories in Key West, and I'm told their six thousand or so workers produce almost two million cigars a year.

The wrecking and salvaging industry has also grown more than I ever thought possible—for I had never believed Martin. Key West now has a population of almost 25,000 people. It is the largest and wealthiest city in all of Florida; some even say it's the wealthiest per capita in all of the United States.

Pedro had predicted it. He always told me that a lot of people would leave Cuba if there was unrest there. And the Cuban revolution for independence from Spain in 1868 sent many cigar workers and wreckers scurrying to our island.

And always, of course, my thoughts return to Andrew. For every elderly person, there is a place in the mind that can be revisited to re-create the happy, fleeting moments of youth. For me, that place will always be my time at Wreckers' Cay, when Hannah was alive and Andrew and I and the children were all together and free. For such happiness comes but once, and then only if we are very lucky.

EPILOGUE

Key West

1883

Y ou know, you shouldn't be sitting here in this heat. It's
   not good for you."

It is Charles. His sudden presence by my side in the cemetery startles me. He looks concerned as he proffers his firm
dark hand. And this time, because I am tired, I willingly take
it and he pulls me up from the bench.

"Are you all right, Grandma?"

Yes, Charles is my grandson, Ebony's eldest. I have proudly
acknowledged my handsome brown grandsons, you see. And
for me, this has been very liberating. Of course, it also means
I have become a pariah. Imagine. In the twilight of my life, I
am again a woman of interest. Do I care what people are saying? Not a whit! I'm too rich, and I am too old.

As Charles leads me along the path toward the victoria, we
approach a grave that is familiar to me near the entrance. It
has long been neglected, and the gnarled, braided roots of a
geiger tree have aggressively tunneled below the marker, heaving it to one side so that the name George Lee is askew and
barely recognizable. A small gray ratsnake slithers out from an

opening behind it and positions itself into a coil, watching us as we pass.

At the carriage, Charles clears away the books he has been studying while waiting for me. And he helps me up to the driver's seat next to him, where I always insist on sitting.

"So, how was your visit with the old bones?" he asks. He knows I will tolerate his impertinence without reproof because of his resemblance to his grandfather.

"It was an excellent visit," I reply with a wry smile. "We had a very good chat." I'm silent for a moment and then I add, "They keep asking me when I shall come to stay. . . ."

His smile fades as my meaning sinks in. We are sitting together in the carriage now, and he puts his arm around my shoulder. "Grandma, you tell them they're going to have to wait," he says softly as he kisses me on the cheek. "We're not going to let you go for a long time yet!" Charles flashes his smile at me again. Then, with a determined flick of the reins, he urges the horse to move forward at a lively canter.

AUTHOR'S NOTE

Without the help of Dan Lazar, my gifted literary agent at Writers House, this book would not have seen light of day. With his hard work, talent, savvy, and support, he made this book happen, and I am very grateful. Thanks also to Julie Trelstad, Digital Rights Director at Writers House, who helped me to bring the present version to fruition.

My editor, Charles Spicer at St. Martin's Press, deserves my profound gratitude for his astute and constructive suggestions for improving *The Woman at the Light*. Thanks to his input, it is a much better book. Thanks also to Elena Karoumpali for her lovely cover.

In Key West, I wish to thank the Anne McKee Artists Fund of the Florida Keys, Inc. and the Florida Keys Council of the Arts for their encouragement and financial support while the book was being written.

Thanks go to many of my friends in Key West who read the original manuscript, especially Florida historian John Viele. To my family, who were always there to encourage me, a special thank you. Thanks also to the many readers who enjoyed the book when it was first published by McMillan in 2012, and posted such kind comments and reviews.

Readers will not find Wreckers' Cay on any map of the Florida Keys; it exists only in a happy compartment of Emily's mind. But I have tried to keep early Key West landmarks authentic and have, I hope, described historical events of the times with accuracy.

Juan Salas did indeed exist, and once owned the island of Key West. His cousin Pedro Salas is fictitious. Jerónimo Valdés was the governor of Cuba at the time Emily would have been there. Commodore Porter was a real presence in Key West history; Archer was not. Ellen Mallory was real, and did own a boardinghouse in the settlement. Her son Stephen Mallory became a well-known Florida politician. George Lee and Alfie were figments of my imagination. The French poet Charles Baudelaire was, of course, real, as was the French nature artist John James Audubon who did live in Key West at that time. The Levys of New York are all fictitious, as are Stephen Pendleton and Captain Peartree.

Lastly, light keeper Barbara Mabrity was very much a real person, as was Rebecca Flaherty. They, along with Mary Carroll and Mary Bethel, courageously tended lighthouses for many years in the Florida Keys and inspired me to write this book.

Key West, 2016.